Gillian White is a journalist and lives in Devon. She has four children.

Critical acclaim for Gillian White:

'A novelist of the highest quality . . . an intense and vividly-written novel which takes you by the throat and won't let go' *Sunday Independent*

'Bitingly brilliant . . . complex, witty and sinister' *Daily Mirror*

'A wonderful mix of storytelling and hilarious entertainment' *Annabel*

'A gripping read' *Today*

'A rich and wonderful tale of conspiracy and domestic infamy' Fay Weldon

'Creepy and insightful' *Ms London*

'This is clever, clever writing, to mix tragedy and comedy and present it as easy reading . . . it is a Martin Amis with heart' *Glasgow Herald*

Also by Gillian White

The Plague Stone
The Crow Biddy
Nasty Habits
Rich Deceiver
Mothertime
Dogboy

Grandfather's Footsteps

GILLIAN WHITE

PHŒNIX

A PHOENIX PAPERBACK

First published in Great Britain by Orion in 1994
This paperback edition published in 1995 by Phoenix,
a division of Orion Books Ltd,
Orion House, 5 Upper St Martin's Lane,
London WC2H 9EA

A CIP catalogue record for this book
is available from the British Library.

ISBN: 1 85799 337 3

Typeset by Deltatype Limited, Ellesmere Port, Cheshire.

Printed and bound in Great Britain by Clays Ltd, St Ives plc.

For Lord Longford who once took an approved schoolgirl to tea at the House of Lords because she wrote to tell him that she was unhappy.

Chapter one

Who would I most like to be? In the whole wide world, I mean. Who would I most like to be. . . ?

Thus muses Brenda Hodges, sitting, bored and thin at her desk at the very worst time of the week – nine-thirty on a Monday morning. She's wearing her black New Look skirt – already wrinkled round the bum – and her Dorothy Perkins blouse with the nylon ruffs round the cuffs, which has a tea-stain circular as a penny stamped like a badge underneath her left breast. How did the tea-stain get there? With that perky little overhang of hers, how on earth did it manage to get up under there?

Brenda doesn't know.

Brenda knows nothing.

But a wispy, gossamer *Monday-morning* feeling tells her that she'd quite like to be Jessica Holden, her boss, who doesn't arrive till ten o'clock and who's never been seen with a tea-stain – or any other stain, for that matter – anywhere on her person. And Jessica is even allowed to bring in her dog.

Clack clack clack goes Brenda, fingering her way across the keys, feeling as green as the screen of her state-of-the-art computer.

Brenda's gran says that some people are born with silver spoons in their mouths. Brenda doubts whether any of the spoons in the drawer at home, even the ones from Jersey, the Isle of Wight, or Majorca, are made out of real silver.

Well, they never get tarnished, you see, and they are certainly never polished.

Jessica's dog has tits like toggles. She is long and lean, a sleek brown sausage with nails that need clipping because she never gets to walk the correct sort of distance on pavements. That is what the vet says. She is a dog for homes and gardens – and you cannot travel far on a patio. *Clack clack clack* on her tinfoil feet goes Jessica Holden's dog, peering up through cherubic eyelashes at poor, bored Brenda, who glares back jealously through her stiff, mascara-black ones.

When it is winter, Jessica's dog wears a neat tartan jacket, with straps under her belly that regularly get pissed on.

Clack clack clack on her sharp Gucci heels goes Jessica.

Brenda wouldn't be seen dead with a dog like that. If she had a dog it would be a proper one – male, with a studded collar, and preferably a black Alsatian.

'Good morning, Brenda. Any calls? Just give me a minute, will you, and then come through.'

'Good morning, Jessica.'

Oh yes, she's allowed to call her boss Jessica. Everyone goes by first-name terms in the office of Jackson Willow & Sons, Est. 1862, Auctioneers and Valuers by Royal Appointment.

Jessica Holden (she swings, with her hair and her bracelets) doesn't ask herself who she'd like to be – she hasn't the time, for goodness' sake! – but if she did, she'd agree that one of the people she'd *least* like to be would be Brenda. She doesn't take much notice of her secretary, but if she did she would see chips-and-vinegar skin under bright orange No 7 make-up which stops abruptly at the ring round the neck like a necklace, colourless eyes, greasy hair, and the inevitable stoop, almost a hump, of a low-quality person.

How did the slovenly Brenda get this job in these prestigious city offices in the first place?

She got the job because her shorthand is an incredible 150 words per minute and, so desperate was she for a job, so eager to get herself out of the house, that she allowed herself to go cheap, for almost half that shorthand speed in money.

Wherever you look these days, standards are slipping.

Jessica's dog turns round and round and nests in her office basket. Jessica's dog costs two pounds a day to keep, and that is without the vet's bills. 'Mr Special' is the only brand of food she will touch. She would starve to death if left in a room with only a bowlful of Chappie.

And that is, almost to the nearest penny, what Brenda spends on her twenty Silk Cut.

'It is all a matter of priorities,' Jessica confided to her hairdresser, Bryan, when she went to get her highlights touched up last Thursday. It is irritating to have to keep reading about the poor. And depressing. After all, what can one do? She peered forward approvingly into the rose-tinted mirror, searching for the blemishes that were not there in the way that she searches the park grass with her hand encased in a plastic bag for pieces of the dachshund's solid waste. 'Some people just don't bother to shop around for bargains. It's expensive frozen food, or packets all the time, and grumble, grumble, grumble, while I, well, *I* take the trouble to pop into *Doughnuts* after work and pick up all sorts of cheap cakes and buns. And you can make some delicious vegetable dishes by shaking about a few green bits and pieces. Herbs and wine thrown in, of course, to bring out the natural flavour.'

Her legs whisper as she crosses them. She settles behind her desk, she wriggles her bottom into shape and then she presses her buzzer with her beautifully painted nail. 'Coffee I think, please, Brenda,' she says in her cool, cultured voice.

Jessica's not a snob, is she?

I think she probably is.

Her expertise lies in Oriental Art – watercolours of purple mountains, ivory and jade. Jade suits Jessica. It matches her eyes. She will spend the morning preparing a catalogue for the auction next month, and setting up the necessary photographic sessions.

Now, Brenda's gran lives next door to Jessica Holden . . . but Jessica doesn't know this.

Holden says the sign beneath her bell in smart italics, but only a milkman's note stuffed in an ill-washed bottle identifies the neighbour next door. Jessica would hardly recognise Brenda if she met her outside the office, for she's never seen her in her outdoor clothes, so why should she know Brenda's gran, shuffling to the post box in hairnet, overall and slippers?

Uneasily, she only knows she lives next door to a rather distasteful person who refuses to make any concessions to aesthetic sensibilities of any kind. But of course, Jessica does not tell it that way, not when people ask her.

'She's a real old character,' she says, but her laugh is hollow. 'Her name is Vera Evans. She's lived in that house for years. Quite an eccentric.'

Jessica is politically sound. So is the virile Rudi, the man with the ponytail and earring, with whom she lives.

The person next door is, frankly, disgusting, not eccentric – a word all too often lightheartedly misused. 'Eccentric' here means dirty, rude, difficult, obnoxious, and smelly. Mrs Evans is old. She will soon die – or the landlord will shift her. And then, Jessica thinks happily, the house will be bought by people of a similar outlook to her own.

Lately, Jessica's house has lost a quarter of its value, but this doesn't bother Brenda's gran. She rents hers, always has. It is expensive to run, though, and far too big for one person. Brenda's gran rattles around inside it with her feather duster like a pea in a pod, achieving nothing. It's a tip.

Number 6, Lippington Road, Pimlico. That's where Gran brought up Brenda's mum, Rita, in the fifties, in the days when they didn't have bathrooms. In the days when the kids used to play in the street and Jack, her coalman husband, used to park his horse outside with a nosebag while he stopped in for his dinner. The house went suddenly cleaner after Jack died. Then Rita moved up the social ladder when she married Derek, and now lives in a pebble-dash house with a garden on the Pennystone Estate – a bus-ride away in Vauxhall, a 70p return.

On a quiet night you can just hear the chimes of Big Ben.

What *is* the matter with Brenda the typist? She feels slightly sick this morning.

She draws a deep breath.

A little bile comes into her mouth as, carrying the coffee through to Jessica's sumptuous office, Brenda wishes she was back in bed, snuggled up warm round her own smell with her eyes closed and her tea going skinny on the bedside table next to her, like Derek, her dad, does, these days.

'Well, lass, I'm off to bring home the bacon,' he used to say in the faraway days when he had a job and was up at six and brought her a drink before he left for work as a driver for Tesco.

Now, sometimes, he's still in bed when Brenda gets home from work. 'It's the women in this family that keep it going,' Rita says bitterly, after a day in Woollies, rolling down her stockings with her massive freckled arms and blowing on her aching corns. How could such a rough, shaggy woman, built like her father's cart-horse, give birth to a skimpy tadpole of a thing like Brenda?

All Rita's kids turned out tiny.

'It was just the same in Mum's day. It was her who worked in the end, never mind that she'd had seven kids and was worn down to nothing. It was Dad who stayed home rolling his fags and cooking the dinner during the times when his back went. Sampson Shag in the sausages. Sampson Shag in the custard.' She sat back and gawped, spreading her reddened, hammer-shaped toes. 'Look at that one! It's hard like one of those gobstoppers you used to buy. D'you remember, Derek, you used to choose the colour you wanted, out of those big jars. Ye gods, it throbs.'

Dad got down beside Mum's feet. 'That's not a corn, Rita, that's a bunion.'

'That's a bugger, that's what it is. D'you think it'd change colour if you sucked it?'

Brenda lit a fag. 'Put your slippers on, Mum, it's too disgusting to look at.'

'You wait, my girl . . .'

'But she's not on her feet all day like you are.'

'No.' Brenda ponders. 'I spend all my time on my arse. So I'll only get piles.'

'And no one'll want to suck those. If you don't smarten yourself up, Brenda – look at yourself, lazy filthy sod, go and wash your hair – all you'll get is the sack.'

'What's for tea?'

'I can't be bothered to cook tonight. Listen out for the chippy van, love, and ask how many want it, Brenda. There's a ten-pound note in my purse.'

Last night's chip paper in its pall of vinegar still overflows from the kitchen bin.

The picture above the fireplace shows a Chinese maiden with long black hair. An Oriental picture. You could not imagine Jessica Holden with a corn, bunions or piles. You could not really imagine she even *had* a fanny – she was too ornamental for that. China dolls don't have fannies, nor do jade figurines. But she must have a fanny because she sleeps with a man. Rudi. Huh! What a name. Sounds more like a bum-boy to Brenda.

The four-bedroomed council house is full. Even the walls feel as if they're bulging, not with damp, like in Gran's tall, thin, draughty house in Lippington Road, but with people. Most of the kids have left home, failed, and come back to stay.

As far as they could see, there was nothing much better on offer anywhere else.

'Useless, sodding lot.' Mum, wearing her most dangerous look, says she doesn't know how she keeps going and they might as well not have bothered at all, but she's forever grumbling on like that and nobody really knows what she means.

At her desk, Jessica shapes her hand round the flanks of a cool, green Buddha. Last night Rudi, with his dark hair flying, rode her like a horse till the brass bed shook and slammed against the bedroom wall.

Before she reached orgasm the old witch next door started banging again.

Life, eh?

'Pleasant weekend, Brenda?'

Brenda's eyes are dull as dust. 'Nothing much. Just boring as usual.' The bile rises again. The typist controls a sickly burp. 'Where d'you want it?' Only just seventeen, this is Brenda's first job so it's hard not to call Jessica 'Miss' like at school.

'Just put it there please, dear, and you can take away the sugar.'

How the coffee arrives each morning is a bit too much of a

lottery for Jessica. Brenda's nails are never too clean. Jessica lifts her eyes and gazes at Brenda – whatever is the matter with the girl? – and suddenly remembers how she read somewhere, was it in *The Color Purple*, about someone who felt helpless, spitting into coffee to make themselves feel better.

Now what is it about this particular Monday – no different on the surface from any other – that makes Jessica aware that Brenda might actually want to do that? But Brenda should not feel jealous of Jessica, or consider her more privileged than she, for Jessica, like the rest of us, has her fair share of sorrows to bear.

Chapter two

Yes, another boring uncomfortable weekend, same as the last one, same as the next one, sitting round at The Bull with Ginger and Ginger's mates, sipping rum and Cokes and watching him play pool.

What is the matter with Brenda these days?

Why is she so guarded and grumpy?

There's nothing wrong at work, is there?

She hasn't finished with Ginge?

'What time will you be getting in tonight, Brenda?'

Even Shane, who is twenty-five, a father of two, and has been married, is asked this same question by Rita his mother.

'I'll be in when I've straightened my hair and put on my knickers, as soon as I've finished with Ginge round the back of the garages.' But oh no, Brenda does not say this.

What does Rita imagine her seventeen-year-old daughter gets up to with Ginge after the pubs have closed, after the pool match is over?

Perhaps it would be more reasonable were Rita to invite her daughter's boyfriend into her home, out of the cold and wet, maybe allow them to go upstairs and 'listen to records' in Brenda's little back bedroom.

Rita would go spare if any one of her five kids came out openly and declared that they were making love with a member of the opposite sex. A clean-living woman with her mother's values, she expects them to say goodbye to each other at the door.

*

Has she honestly forgotten how it was?
Is she jealous of their youth and freedom?
Or is she afraid they might get into trouble like she did, get hurt?

They called her 'Big Rita'.

She was born in the image of the coalman, identical to her six older brothers,

In 1955 her father stumbled like an old horse under a sack of coal, and died of a heart attack there on his knees down on the London cobbles.

Like most of the people of that generation, the sixties passed Rita by.

Oh, don't take any notice of the chattering classes.

Or perhaps it was her grieving mother's shadow that somehow cut off the light.

You can live through an era and not be touched by it; you can live through life and not feel part of it . . . part of the party that's going on at somebody else's house. But is it really? It certainly wasn't going on at Rita's house in Lippington Road – or anywhere else down the road for that matter.

The most exciting thing that happened between 1960 and 1970 was that Dominic Bassett, an actor from the television, bought Number 18 when Gwenny died.

Dominic Bassett bought Number 18, and for almost two years his suspicious neighbours watched the interesting skip in the road outside.

The sixties and Rita Evans eyed each other from the sidelines. Her brothers were gone and she was the only child left at home. Mary Quant was as far from Rita as the Cavern Club, as flower power, as California, as the pill. She never had any money to spend down Carnaby Street because as soon as she left school and started working in the stores at Moffat's the builders, she had to give all but five bob to her widowed mum.

'Not Moffat's, Mum, please! Why can't I try for hairdressing, like Patsy?'

'Because I know Mr Moffat and he'll do well by you,' said Vera, 'and it's only round the corner so you won't have to waste money on bus rides, or lunches like Patsy, that flibbertigibbet. You're near enough to come home at one. It's a fair wage, Rita, and you ought to be grateful. Do stop your complaining!'

I won't stay, thought Rita. I'll earn some money and then I'll go. Get a flat somewhere, with a friend.

Ah, such stuff are dreams made of.

Poor Rita came home every night with brickdust in her hair.

'Honest dirt,' said her mother proudly, just as she used to talk about coal as she scrubbed at the rim round the old tin tub.

At Number 18, Dominic Bassett installed two bathrooms. Everyone watched as the burnished copper pipes were carried inside. Everyone marvelled as his old garden privy was turned into a shed.

Awkward, just as she'd been at childhood parties, Rita did not want to join in this teenage game. So much tougher than most of the boys in the street, now she was acned and overweight, and she knew she could not win it. Rita, a sad adolescent, read about the sixties in *Blue Jeans*, she saw it happen on *Juke Box Jury*. The sixties came to Rita softly and secretly at night in her bedroom, yearningly restlessly, on sad strands of *Carolina Moon* and *Don't*, ballads of love and moonlight. She listened to Radio Luxemburg under her covers at night, never dreaming that there really was such a place.

She dreamed half-formed dreams that were easily broken. Where was the girl in the fairy tale, the princess that used to be her?

She wept into the darkness.

But perhaps she understood, deep down, that Derek the teddy boy was as close to the sixties and the prince of her dreams as Rita Evans, the coalman's daughter, was ever likely to get.

A large ungainly girl, on Saturday nights she went to the flicks with her mates where she flirted in the darkness, available to anyone who wanted a grope, until the lights went up. She lost her virginity that way – for how could she leave it to God and Providence? She lost it to a stranger's finger under a pall of blue cigarette smoke, while Elvis the Pelvis wriggled his hips temptingly on the screen before her. He was gone by the time the ices came round. Sometimes, frightened and angry, she went dancing, but was rarely asked to take the floor.

She watched in panic and despair as her friends paired off one by one. Rita covered her shame with a brazen face and much brassy laughter. She was popular among the men down at Moffat's yard – all married, unfortunately, but Moffat's men knew how to have their fun. In those days you could buy a lot for ten bob. Those friends who were left went out without her. Unpopularity might be catching.

She could now afford to drink cappuccino.

She had money in her pocket at last. First she wore flares and then she wore mini-skirts and her hair was so permanently backcombed, peroxided and lacquered solid that it was years after the style went out of fashion that it finally recovered. Derek's ring was firm on her finger long before her hair was supple enough to wind around a curler. The shameless creature had tricked him to the altar.

Derek Hodges was a fifties man himself.

He had never been able to relinquish that era. With his quiff, sideboards, winklepickers and drainpipes – a combination which made him look taller than his five foot four – Derek went down big as he stood on street corners and combed his hair and whistled boldly to the girls as they swaggered by.

Any girl. Shape and size didn't matter to Derek. He didn't take it that seriously. He got a shock one Sunday morning when Rita Evans smiled back.

'Fancy a drink?' He adjusted his tie.

'Why not?' said ruthless, big Rita Evans.

They married and moved onto the Pennystone Estate two months before Shane was born.

'You ought to move in with me,' said her mother, Vera, a knotted scarf tied round her head of stiffly curled waves. 'There's plenty of room and I wouldn't charge you much rent.'

'It's okay, Mum. Derek and I have been offered a place by the council.'

'I've done it! I've done it!' she wanted to scream with a frantic desire to escape her mother. 'Against all the odds and without your help, I've bloody well done it! It's my life, my man, my baby, my home.'

Rita nearly burst out crying when she first saw her new and beautiful house. She couldn't wait to get inside, light her own fire, pad around on the wall-to-wall carpets – no more lino for her! – and lock the door on her precious treasure.

'I love you,' she said to the mesmerised Derek, cushion-plump under flesh-coloured satin.

'And I love you too,' he whispered, so much smaller, almost shrivelled without his clothes on.

When Shane was born she walked down the road with the poshest pram on the whole estate. Then came Eddie, then came Roy, then came Doreen and then came Brenda and the pram got shabbier and shabbier. Money was short without her working. She used to spend more time round at Vera's in those days – well, the kids loved playing in that rambling house of stairs and corridors and it was only a brisk walk away. It was always interesting to see what the new owners had done with the houses.

Still . . . she'd got herself a man, hadn't she?

But that was then; and now is now, and anyone can see that standards are slipping.

Rita, forgetting all about Moffat's yard, presents a moral face to the world, and to her children. And oh yes, Rita, big and powerful as ever, believes in maintaining firm care and control over every one of her five, no matter how old they are.

Her two daughters are not going to end up on their backs for any old bugger to poke when he fancies. Her daughters aren't huge and spotty like she was, and they bring home their own pay packets. They've already got careers . . . and now Brenda has started at Jackson Willow & Sons. No, Brenda and Doreen will never have to put up with this endless round of feeding and clothing and scrubbing and sweating, none of the stuff that she has had to endure.

Rita's had a hard life, one way and the other.

Brenda and Doreen will marry up and then, perhaps, they'll look after her. Well, Doreen is already going steady with that nice-mannered Nigel from the Post Office. The lad has brains, spends more time at his house than here, and Brenda is a baby yet, she'll soon grow out of Ginge.

Chez nous.

In the last thirty years, the status of Lippington Road has gone up, while that of the Pennystone Estate has dropped like a stone. Whoever would have thought that the upwardly mobile would start buying up those old slums in Pimlico?

Vera's house must be worth a small fortune by now. Pity she doesn't own it. Pity they haven't enough money between them to raise a small deposit.

You don't know your neighbours any more.

Other people on the Pennystone Estate might not know how to behave, others might treat the place no better than a lavatory with their litter and their broken cars, might bring their kids up any old how, but not so the Hodges. If she has a spare moment Rita looks out with tightened lips, affronted. This is not how this hopeful, brand-new estate had started. But now look – neglect, vandalism, boarded-up houses. Men in prison. Kids on drugs. Women wasting their money on booze. The words 'shame' and 'disgrace' don't seem to mean anything to anyone any more. Rita has standards. Rita puts her litter in a bin bag and does not deposit it outside, to be got at by dogs until the day for the dustbins. Rita keeps her windows clean and her nets are as white as driven snow.

Of a summer evening Derek cuts the patch of grass outside, wearing boots because of the dog shit – he has long ago given up his chrysanths because the kids just come and cut off their heads – and tinkers with his motorbike. But he never fails to put down pages of the *Sun* to stop the oil from marking the concrete.

He has time to read the paper from cover to cover these days since he lost his job at Tesco. While Rita is out, breaking her back stacking shelves, Derek is either asleep upstairs, snoring wetly with his teeth in the glass, or sitting in front of that damn telly with Shane, fugging the air with their farts. And they say it's doubtful that men of his age will ever work again. Rita will never, ever, have her precious house to herself again. There is absolutely no time when there will be nobody in it. As if to remind her of this fact, when Rita gets home Derek calls out, 'There's a cup of tea in the pot.'

Cold tea. The colour of settled mud.

Hell, couldn't he get off his sodding arse and start peeling the spuds for supper?

Rita looks at her daughter closely. If only she'd buck herself up. Wash her hair. Make up her face and buy some decent clothes.

She is always in black these days, and subdued, like a widow. Perhaps leaving school has upset her.

What *is* the matter with sulky Brenda? She hasn't gone and done anything stupid, has she?

Chapter three

Well – and did Jessica Holden have a good weekend? The way she asks Brenda about hers suggests that her own weekends are always successful. Not dull and boring. Nothing like poor Brenda's.

In Jessica's expensive Covent Garden diary, which has a shiny great page for every day – not a scruffy little pocket diary with a map of the London tube on the back like Brenda's – the bold handwriting suggests that something exciting is planned for every day of Jessica's life, right up until the end of August. She uses dashing green ink. Green for go.

If there weren't such things as dental appointments and family birthdays, Brenda's simple little diary would lose its point entirely. Once she was given a five-year diary by her brother Shane for Christmas. It had a key, but she lost it. She started filling it in every night but the whole page gave too much room for feelings. It soon became too personal, too dangerous. 'Have you been reading my diary, Mum?'

'Don't be so sodding stupid. Why would I want to do that?'

But the day before, Brenda had cunningly stuck a hair across her bedside drawer; it wasn't there when she came home from school. She was too afraid that Rita had read her diary so she stopped keeping it and put it away forever.

Brenda's current diary suggests a rather restricted lifestyle, but of course she does not fill in her dates with Ginge or Uncle Bill's fiftieth party or her recent day out at the Zoo, because these are the highlights one tends to remember. Strictly, one does not need to write them down. But Brenda does draw a star at the top of the page whenever she starts or finishes her period – *. She really doesn't know why. It is just a habit she fell into.

Unfortunately for Brenda the last star sits on the first Saturday in February . . . and it is now 8 March.

No wonder Brenda feels queasy.

But it is early days yet. Brenda keeps her fingers crossed; pity she'd not done the same with her legs. But Brenda cannot be certain.

It is easy to make your life appear exciting on paper – look at how people tart up their CVs. It is merely a matter of manipulation, of stating the positive and totally ignoring the negative.

Dishonest? Not really.

Jessica's diary has marks in it, too. Secret marks. Monthly marks, like a graph of some kind. A dotted trail of stars which follows the risings and wanings of the moon.

Yes, thinks Jessica, as she matches the items of jade with their various clever descriptions, as she tentatively tastes the dark brown coffee that Brenda has made, she did have a good weekend. A predictable one, but a good one. On the whole Rudi was nice to her and they avoided their usual catastrophic rows. Jessica is a beautiful, intelligent woman, and yet her life revolves, far more than Brenda's, around one man.

If Jessica passed Brenda's Ginge in the street she would not see him.

If Brenda passed Rudi she would turn around and stare.

Strangers do tend to stare at the striking Rudi and every time they do so it upsets Jessica terribly. She is so insanely jealous that the poor thing cannot help it. So imagine how painfully she endures an even closer approach . . . at a dinner party, or at the races, during evenings with friends at the opera or the theatre.

The whole thing's a nightmare, it really is.

Rudi does not see it this way. He finds Jessica's reaction silly and boring; it annoys him. 'Just because I'm talking to a female friend does not mean I want to leap into bed with her. Just because I am sitting next to Gloria, does not mean I am dreaming of sucking her tits, or that I prefer her to you.'

Well, obviously not. How silly Jessica makes herself sound. But the women themselves firmly believe he is suggesting just that. Rudi has come-to-bed eyes and an I-want-to-fuck-you voice. And his body language is as sensual as a snake's.

So what does this Adonis look like? But that's the trouble – it's not so much his looks as his swagger. It is not so much that everyone wants to love him, it has more to do with the way he so obviously loves himself, like the Chippendales. And yet Rudi's claims to fame are no more than a few successful appearances in advertisements for male deodorants . . . a St Michael brand of men's underpants and once, just once, a Porsche.

But one day, one of these days, Rudi is going to make it.

And will he stay with Jessica, once he gets that longed-for television part?

He looks like an advertisement. Even in bed, he sleeps like an advertisement, with one muscled hip curled beneath the duvet; he wakes like an advertisement and he drinks his morning coffee, pads across the floor in his dressing gown and makes love in an advertisement way.

But his slight Italian accent – you can hardly detect it, but it's there all right – narrows his chance of a speaking part.

Perhaps he stays with me for my voice, thinks Jessica sadly to herself, because she has the perfect English accent, nicely modulated, delicately refined, a voice that takes her anywhere. Jessica could step in tomorrow and introduce *Woman's Hour*. And the right-sounding voice is almost more important than appearance these days, especially for men. Men don't have to be beautiful in order to make the big time, to read the news, present programmes, star in soaps. The requirement is that they speak well, have money and look craggy and interesting.

And, just like that trace of an accent, just like those sultry brown eyes, just like that suggestion of a tan, Rudi's natural inclination is directed towards family and children.

He wants to be a papa. But for that you need a mama.

Life is not fair. Life is a series of temperature-taking, filling in charts, attending clinics where Jessica is crudely and painfully mauled and Rudi jerks himself off in a jar, but in spite of these gallant, laborious efforts, nothing seems to be working.

Jessica appears to be sterile. Barren. Infertile. And there are more hurtful definitions than that. Lacking in imagination or vitality. Not stimulating. *Dry*.

Lifeless and cold as a lump of jade.

So every sighting of a newly born baby, every laugh of a little child, every tiny hand stretched out in greeting, every chortle and every gurgle is another stab of pain for poor Jessica.

A child of his own and Rudi, besotted, would be hers for life. He might stray, but he'd always come back to Junior.

'We could adopt.'

'It would not be the same.'

No. Brenda need not be jealous of Jessica.

Inside that scrawny little tummy Brenda might well be incubating the very thing which the queenly Jessica so desperately craves.

Back to the diaries. I know, let's have a peep inside Jessica's.

Friday: Jasper and Sophie, 8 p.m.

On Friday night they had guests – Rudi's 'on-the-fringe-of-television' friends, so what Jessica produced was terribly important. After work she flew in a panic to Fortnum's and before nine o'clock had knocked up a mussel soufflé, two young pigeons in red wine, and *poires belles Dijonnaises*, decorated with two crystallised violets.

This they ate off pure white plates at a glass table where the only colour, apart from that provided by the food, was one rather beautiful sprig of blossom sticking out from a slender vase of jade.

Jessica wore a skimpy little black dress in the style of Suzie Wong, and Rudi, nicely stubbled, a black polo-neck and slim black jeans. The question was . . . who was the more beautiful? Impossible to say: the two complemented each other so well.

The fact that Jessica ended up in the kitchen, loading the dishwasher and cleaning up with Jasper, despite her protests that she would far rather tackle it in the morning as she couldn't bear to face the washing-up straight away, was Jasper's fault, the damn fool, for absolutely insisting. Meanwhile, the silly simpering Sophie lay back on the sofa, blinked her coy blue eyes and allowed Rudi to make love to her with everything except his cock.

Brenda. *Friday: Stayed in. Washed hair. Did washing. Watched* Casualty. *Watched Doreen perm her hair. Fish cakes and chips for tea.*

Only she didn't bother to write it down.

Saturday: Rudi to Garden Centre opening – 11 a.m. Lunch with Sue at Marti's. Meet Avery Brown, Heathrow, 4.30. Drive Rudi to Douggie's party 9.30 on . . .

Rudi could not, or would not drive, so this entailed complicated juggling of the hours in Jessica's day, making sure that her lover was delivered and picked up on time. A minor celebrity in his own right, owing to his advertisements, Rudi was often invited to open local events or give out prizes.

Avery Brown was an American client of Jessica's, and fetching him from the airport and installing him comfortably at Claridge's was a pretty normal weekend duty which, in the course of her work, she was expected to perform. But it still precipitated some grumbling from Rudi. 'Damn it, I wish you'd tell me these things. I kept this afternoon free. I thought we could go and have a look at Daphne's private showing. No, don't worry, you drop me off. I'll go on my own.'

Oh God.

And then there was the party at Douggie's in the evening. Jessica would far rather not attend. Once he'd had a few drinks, Rudi lost all sense of time and as Jessica was driving, she could hardly let herself go and join in the fun.

'I'm tired, Rudi. I've had a hard week. Please let's leave before one.'

'Sure, no problem. I shan't want to stay. Ghastly lot of people, bound to be.'

But he always said this. It never worked that way, though. Jessia found herself sober, sitting in the kitchen surrounded by the stumbling, the lost and the bleary-eyed, so certain they were uttering the wisest words of their lives as they stabbed at the air in front of her, driving their demented points home.

Rudi, of course, was dancing with a woman whose dress was so tight it revealed not only her thrusting nipples, but the mound above her long legs as well. Was it part of the dance?

Was it necessary for Rudi's knee to slip between her legs so often? Was the music really so loud that he had to whisper directly into her ear?

God God God.

They got home at half-past three. Jessica was cold and silent and Rudi was sleeping.

Brenda. *Saturday: The Bull with Ginge. He played pool. Game of darts with Sandra and Judy. Bought chips on the way home. Ginge got pissed. Home across the park. Stopped by garages and he fucked me but I was dry and didn't really want it. Painful. Got spunk all over skirt.*

Only she didn't bother to write it down.

What is Jessica doing with Rudi? He is quite obviously nothing but a pain in the arse, and her friends tell her so quite frankly. So why doesn't she chuck him in and find somebody else?

A kept man, a failed actor, he does not even contribute enough to cover his keep – so what is he doing with the Armani jacket? Well, Jessica gave it to him for Christmas.

She cannot chuck him in, because she loves him. Jessica believes she would disappear if she didn't have Rudi. She would disappear and the world would end.

What is Brenda doing with Ginge? He is quite obviously using her and her friends tell her so quite frankly. So why doesn't she chuck him in and find somebody else?

She buys her own drinks. She buys her own chips. And, if they go further afield, she pays her own fare.

She cannot chuck him in because she might not find somebody else. And then she would be the only one in her group without a regular boyfriend. Brenda doesn't believe it is possible that anyone other than Ginge would want her. And she might need Ginge, if the stars in her diary don't reappear pretty damn quick.

Sunday: Breakfast with Avery Brown, 9.30 a.m. Rudi to the rowing club, 11. Lunch there. Meet Jayne and Tyrone Gordon at 6, Martin's Gate, 4 p.m.

Avery Brown was easy, a lovely, grey-haired old man who

adored being in London, capable of getting himself about museums and exhibitions on his stick, taking pleasure in the sights. Jessica, given the opportunity, might well have enjoyed spending more time with this cultured man, a collector of Oriental art.

But no. At ten-thirty on the dot she apologised – 'Oh, don't worry, dear thing, I shall be as happy as a sandboy wandering round on my own,' said sweet Avery Brown – and was off, for Rudi must not be late. After his ambitious but tenuous career, his rowing meant more to him than . . . she did? No, that was neurotic. But Rudi needs to keep his alluring body in trim and rowing is, for him, like a morning at the beautician's for Jessica . . . a sauna, full wax, full facial, full massage, full manicure and make-up.

Rudi is fit. Rudi is virile. Rowing is a healthy, manly sport out on the river in all weathers, Ratty and Mole, boys together, although some women do it too.

What sort of women?

Fertile women, probably, with strong, childbearing hips. From all that puffing and bending. White knuckles pulling on oars, pulling on the bedstead, grinding, pounding, pushing that baby out. An orgasm of freedom and power . . .

Jayne and Tyrone Gordon are pregnant. Jessica and Rudi went there for tea, to congratulate them and admire their new house with its nursery. Everyone, all her friends, is getting pregnant. It seems to be the craze at round about thirty.

Brenda. *Sunday: Up late. Watched football with Dad and Shane. Doreen gave me her blue dress. Mum's foot still bad. Tried to sponge spunk off skirt but gone all crispy. Sharon came round, played records upstairs but I didn't tell her. Daren't tell anyone. Still don't believe it could happen to me.*

It sounded more like her five-year diary. She could hardly fit so much in.

Only she didn't bother to write it down.

Chapter four

Blue Moon of Kentucky. This is Brenda's dad's party piece. He does it, with a kind of soft-shoe shuffle, to entertain on special occasions like Uncle Bill's fiftieth, weddings and anniversaries. Derek the grey-haired teddy boy mimics the King with a gleam in his eye that gives away his secret, for while his performance lasts he *is* The King. He glowers like The King, he wiggles his hips like The King.

One day, when his ship comes in, Derek has promised Rita that he will take her to Gracelands.

And strangely it is this image of her father, that certain look on his face, which burns itself into her brain and breaks Brenda's heart as she retches into the avocado lavatory reserved for executives and labelled REST ROOM, unable to reach the humbler, white bowls with the hard Bronco paper provided for the staff further along the corridor.

Labelled TOILET.

She dare not risk going that far; there was no time to make it. She doesn't feel human. Brenda feels like a sick animal, gone all quiet with her pain.

She retches, but nothing comes. She wipes her mouth with pale pink Delsey. The taste of bile burns at the back of Brenda's throat like acid.

On those special occasions, Derek looks so happy he might be staring into the face of God and the wild applause he always receives is not so much to do with his actual performance (he brings tears to some people's eyes) but a recognition of a flaming passion, a deep and tortured need for expression – something which pierces every heart.

Brenda is her father's favourite, probably because she's a girl and the youngest and she doesn't cheek him back, like

Doreen. Brenda was never like Doreen, with breasts that shake and wobble, an arse that sticks out and bandy legs in those red high heels. Brenda is bony, more like a boy, and right up until the day she left school she wore her hair in bunches.

Dad has lost so much more than his job in these past few years. Never a big man, he seems to have shrunk even further while her mother gets bigger as she suffers, and Brenda, his princess, the joy of his life, is about to break his heart.

Of her mother Brenda dares not think, for she knows that Rita will kill her.

'You little whore! And me not knowing anything about it! What d'you expect me to do, keep a pair of eyes in my arse? Haven't you seen enough big bellies waddling round this sodding estate? Haven't you seen the heartbreak it brings . . . walking around with a string of bastards and pushing their shopping and what sort of life is that, with the neighbours laughing and sniggering behind our backs!'

'Sod the neighbours,' Brenda would shout.

'You fool! You bloody fool! Who've you been with? Who is it? Come on, it's that Ginge, isn't it? I'd have thought you'd have more sodding sense. Common as muck, no more than a slut, you are – a bitch on heat same as all the rest.'

Cold and shivery all over, Brenda wonders how she should tell them.

Together – or separately? Or maybe she ought to tell Doreen and, like a coward, ask her to break the news.

She rehearses the moment in her head as she peers fretfully into her knickers in search of that precious stain. Oh God, if You will remove this cup I will never take time off from work when the painters are in, no I won't, not ever again.

Sod You, God! Can You hear me? She shoved her finger as deeply as she could, thrust it right up her fanny till it hurt. She brought it out. She pulled a face. It didn't even smell faintly of blood. She wrote SHIT on the pearly pink wall with the slime.

An abortion?

After all, she can't be more than six weeks gone. Again and again she counts the days.

But what if the doctor tells Mum? Rita Hodges is always round at the surgery with her nerves. Dad says it's her second home. Mum is chummy with the doctor; she knows him well, and his family, as she used to clean his house.

Gin and hot baths? Knitting needles?

A private abortion, then? At a clinic? Perhaps Ginge will lend her the money, but he's always complaining that he is broke. Or maybe Ginge will marry her. She hangs above the bowl once more, feeling sicker than ever and sees herself in the mirror, clinging on greyly with her lanky hair in a tangle over her face, like an old woman needing support.

What about Gran? Maybe Brenda could ask Gran for help. Oh, oh, cries Brenda, who will give me sanctuary? Where shall I go and what shall I do?

She knows the very night it happened, the time they did it without a johnny. Drunk like that, he was often bloody-minded and aggressive, and on this particular night Ginge's nose was actually strawberry red and his breath smelt like a brewery. 'No, Ginge,' she said as he thrust his thick cock towards her, jabbing his hands at her breasts and her thighs, like a tin-opener trying to grip before he could wind himself in.

And the next thing she knew she was holding his cold, spiky balls in her hand.

He rammed and banged his way into her and she stood there with her skirt pushed up and her legs forced apart and her back against the drainpipe, grinding and screwing like a road drill, pumping like a pneumatic machine and twisting her tits till she cried out in pain.

And this was love.

He looked so sad from above, toiling and sweating like that.

She stood there, docile and stupid, completely separated mind from body.

He carried on, needful and ruthless, sobbing with every breath while Brenda closed her eyes.

She could have screamed for help, she supposed, but who would have come? And they often had it away by the garages – it was their territory, wasn't it. Why should she protest this time? He shuddered and fastened his trousers. He picked up the fag he'd left burning on the wall and Brenda suddenly felt cold; she felt freezing as something hot trickled out of her and down her legs.

He told her he preferred it that way. He said that you couldn't expect a man to wear a johnny every time; it interferes with his enjoyment. 'Just so long as you're near the start, or near the end, not in the middle, it's safe,' said Ginge. 'It's how the Catholics do it, didn't you even know that?'

'But Ginge, what about Aids?'

'Jesus, what d'you take me for? People like us don't get Aids.'

No. Brenda decides that the last thing in the world she wants is to marry Ginger Taylor. She does not want to marry anyone. Nobody knows what an effort it took her to reach that elusive goal . . . 150 words a minute.

God, what a slog.

'You could work for *Hansard* one day, Brenda, with a little bit of polish,' said Joan Groves, presenting her with her Pitman's Certificate. 'We rarely see these sorts of speeds at night school, not these days. You have applied yourself very well and have every reason to feel proud.'

Brenda flushed with joy. This was the first exam she had passed in her life. Mum would be over the moon.

In an instant, ambition was born. Now Brenda's got her eye fixed on personal advancement: a few years at Jackson Willow & Sons, an excellent reference from Jessica, and she's on her way to Westminster!

Getting married would put paid to all that.

Standards are slipping.

Goodness, there's a typist in the executive loo. It is hard for Jessica not to recoil. She very nearly wrinkles her nose.

Gracious, a client might come in here at any moment!

But wait, there is something wrong. Jessica peers hard at the spindly little body across the yawning chasm of marble between them.

'Whatever's the matter, Brenda? You look absolutely terrible!' Oh dear, has Jessica boobed? Perhaps the wretched girl always looks like this, a bad colour, all puffy and white, in this starker lavatory light . . .

Brenda, caught in the act, stares back stubbornly but says nothing. If they find out she is pregnant she will probably get the sack.

'Why are you here? There must be a reason.'

Brenda hangs her head and says, 'Sorry, Miss. I was just leaving.'

'Miss?' Jessica is quite horrified. Ms, yes . . . but 'Miss' is horrid.

'Sorry, Jessica,' moans the shivering Brenda.

Never, not in her wildest moments, did Brenda consider confiding in Jessica, so hard and ironed. And her clothes are so . . . so . . . beautiful. How does she make her hair shine like that – and look at all the colours in it.

Jessica has more to do than be burdened by a minion's personal distress. Theirs is a special level of language in which nothing intimate passes their lips. Brenda calls it level two . . . level one is reserved for bus drivers and ticket collectors; it's a kind of friendly banter or a short, sharp demand:

'Return to Tottenham Court Road, please.'

'All right?'

'Yep.'

Level two is for Jessica and exchanges between next-door neighbours. It is modified for Jessica: Brenda leaves out the swearing:

'Sodding freezing.'

'God, when is this frigging bus going to come?'

'I hear your mum is in hospital.'

Level three is for people like Ginge, Mum and Dad and most of her numerous relations:

'Where've you been then?'

'I don't like this brown tomato sauce. Why can't we have Heinz?'

'If I don't wash my hair tonight it's going to slip off my bleeding head.'

Level four is more special, and reserved for a valued few,

like her sister, Doreen, her friend Sandra and sometimes even Shane:

'What would you really like to do? If you had all the money in the world, where would you go tonight?'

'D'you think if I had my hair like this . . .'

'Sometimes I start thinking about getting old and dying and I can't sleep, can't stop imagining graves and graveyards and earth and maggots. People turn into soup, you know. Sloppy, like soup. I wonder what it was like for Mum, when Grandad died. D'you think she went to look at him?'

Brenda wishes she had someone to speak to on level five. This she reserves for her own self, under the covers at night, in whispers. If she met someone with whom she could use level five – then would be the time to get married.

She'd leap at the chance.

You really would think the executive loos would be soundproof.

Brenda takes a wet-wipe from the packet beside the dressing table mirror and cools her throbbing forehead. There are little wrapped mints in the bowl beside it.

Weak and dizzy in the lavatory, she listens to the trickle of Jessica's piss, a delicate tinkle, and then to the shuffle of skirts and knickers.

But the cultured Jessica probably doesn't wear knickers, certainly not till the elastic wears loose and they go a kind of bluey-grey.

'They'll do,' says Rita bleakly, dragging them out of the drier. 'Get 'em on. Nobody's going to see you unless you fall down under a bus.'

And Mum is right. Ginge wouldn't notice. Ginger has never bothered to look.

Jessica probably wears those pink silk Reger panties, the ones without a proper crutch. Brenda has fingered them in the shops and Brenda has wondered about that. Surely that seam would cut you in half, or are you supposed to let them dangle?

Jessica probably has an orgasm every time she does it, whereas Brenda wouldn't know there was such a thing if she didn't read magazines.

Well, what should she say to Ginge?

At what point would she inform him?

She'd read all the advice, shocked when she realised that these were Rita's magazines and that Rita must have read it, too. *'Guide him, tell him where his touch will give you most pleasure. Examine yourself in the mirror, explore your genitals, discover your own clitoris. Touch it. Experiment. How can you expect your man to know when you don't know yourself? His needs are no greater than yours.'*

It was like a pig's ear . . . raw and red, something unspeakable you see in the butcher's. She fondled breasts that had never been looked at . . . ashamed and puzzled by the secrets of her own puny body.

Jessica's breasts are large and firm . . . about the same size as Doreen's but not so wobbly, more a part of her general appearance than Doreen's which seem to be separate, striding along in front of her, leading the way and proclaiming her arrival like a shout or a bell.

Brenda imagines that Jessica makes love like they do it on films and in books, like you see on the telly – and how right she is. There is no shame involved between the lovely Rudi and the sensual Jessica; they do not need to read books or Sunday supplements to know where they would rather be touched – or not.

Loud are the demands made upon Rudi by Jessica, and loud are the demands her Italian lover shouts back. Jessica would never allow herself to be backed against the wall, rammed against a painful drainpipe in the rain. It is silk sheets, smoked salmon, porn, music and wine for Rudi and Jessica, whose bedroom proclaims her sexuality in colours and textures both subtle and bold.

But what is the point of it all?

The old woman's bang is sharp on the wall and the neighbour's knock seems to sum it all up. *Rap rap rap*. What *is* going on?

It is the ceremonial passing of seed from one hole to another.

At the end of the day that is what all this frantic banging is about.

And for that, a drainpipe in the rain seems about as good as anywhere else.

Chapter five

There have never been such extraordinary scenes in the rest room of Jackson Willow & Sons since their establishment by Algernon Fermoy Jackson 130 years ago.

Well, look – Brenda the typist is weeping copiously within the capable arms of the Director of Oriental Art, confessing her sins, whispering her secrets while her eyes get redder and her nose gets stickier and Jessica reaches out dexterously again and again for the wet-wipes and endeavours to protect the jacket of her expensive cherry-red suit.

Dismayed, she sees the lapel has already been marked by Brenda's tomato-soup-coloured No 7.

'My dear, it is far too soon to tell,' comforts Jessica. 'You are only getting yourself worked up.'

Sniff sniff. Gasp gasp. 'But I just know it, I just know. I've got this terrible feeling . . .'

'Only six weeks! And it isn't the end of the world. Surely, Brenda, you can get an abortion?'

'I don't want an abortion.'

'But you don't want a baby, either. Not at your age. And single. And still living at home. There's no stigma attached to abortion, you know, not these days, Brenda, my dear.'

Brenda's eyes are awash with tears. They focus sharply like a rat's. 'It isn't that.'

'Then what is it? Tell me, Brenda . . .'

'A girl at school called Linda Bracewell went to have an abortion and they did something wrong inside and it ended up so she couldn't have babies, not ever again. Imagine,' cries Brenda, lifting her puffed-up face towards Jessica and leering horribly through her tears. 'Just imagine that!' she finishes dismally.

Jessica pats Brenda's narrow expanse of nylon back,

surprised to feel how frail she is, and says nothing at all. She is so much larger than Brenda, and stronger in every way. Even the fabrics she wears are tougher. And look at Brenda's poor red hands. It looks as though she does a cleaning job, with her hands in water all day long, not a secretarial job, dry and warm in the carefully monitored temperature of the Jackson Willow offices.

Some kind of pale and speckled ivy has been trained to trail round the powder-room mirror.

'And one day I want to have a baby of my own, and love it,' sniffs Brenda pathetically. Quite without control, she has leapt towards level five in her conversation with Jessica, and all her defences are down. If the doctors mess up Brenda's organs she knows she will feel angry and resentful for ever, blaming Ginge for scraping away her soft insides as though he had done it himself with a trowel, with his carrot-coloured hair and his big red cock.

What else can Jessica say, save that, 'Your friend Linda must have been terribly unlucky. It is very unusual, you know, for anything to go wrong with such a simple and straightforward procedure.'

This is too cruel. Dear God and isn't life unfair. Talk about the Devil's own herd and his steaming, satanic cowpats.

'Come on, Brenda, let's sit down.'

Each of them sits on the edge of a tasselled cushion in a gilt-flecked Lloyd Loom chair.

'Now, Brenda. What we must do is calm down and consider your present position.'

'Oh no,' Brenda bursts out, verging on hysteria. 'Not my job!'

'No, no, I don't mean your job. I am talking about your situation in general – the possibilities, the practicalities, if your worst fears are confirmed. And I think that that is probably the very first thing we should do.'

'What?' squeaks Brenda, so relieved to be sharing her burden with one so sensible and strong.

'I want you to wash your face, dry your eyes, comb your hair, and go to the nearest chemist. Buy yourself a home pregnancy testing kit and bring it back here to the office.'

Perhaps Jessica is reflecting on her own past neglect and unkindness. Normally, she uses Brenda like a machine, and most of the time she isn't even aware of her sniffling presence.

'But it's only ten o'clock!'

'What has the hour got to do with it?'

'I mustn't stop till eleven.' Brenda is her mother's daughter and has never been afraid of hard work.

'Nonsense – this is an emergency. I am not very busy this morning anyway. Come on, buck yourself up. You might find you have messed up the dates, it's easily done, or you might discover that you are perfectly all right and that this was merely a false alarm.'

Jessica's dog, Hiame, is annoyed and surprised to be left for so long. She gets up and turns round in her basket, scratching her cushion with her over-sharp, over-long claws in an effort to make a nest.

Jessica pats her before she settles down again. Brenda has gone, thank God.

Jessica is involved, but would far rather not be. She resents this unwarranted moral responsibility. She has a lunch appointment at one.

What a pity there is no Personnel Department at Jackson Willow & Sons, to which the inadequate Brenda could now be directed, but they are just not that sort of firm. They do not expect their staff to need help. There's a first-aid box somewhere in the basement.

Standards are slipping.

Girls like Brenda, well, really, Jessica shouldn't be having these thoughts, they are terrible thoughts, but don't you think they ought to be sterilised? Compulsorily, in exchange for a CD or something? For their own good, and that of society? Just until they are either married, or earning sufficient to pay for a decent au pair, or a proper nursery place. After all, society cannot afford to keep picking up the pieces for every little scrubber who gets herself in the family way. Look at the problems it causes . . . delinquency, broken homes, drug addiction, crime . . .

Look at the costs.
And all because the uneducated are unable or unwilling to cope with the simple concept of contraception.
After all, Hiame has been spayed, and she has a pedigree as long as your arm. The vet suggested it might be kinder to allow the bitch to have one litter of puppies. 'And then she would settle down,' he said.
But why should Jessica's dog be granted that comfort when her mistress cannot?
Rudi would agree with Jessica's theories on the inadequate. It is quite surprising the number of Jessica's friends and colleagues who would probably, in the privacy of their own homes, agree. If Jessica were Brenda's mother she would march her down to the clinic and get her seen to this very afternoon.
But Brenda's mother does not know.
Nobody knows except Jessica. Damn it.

The test proves Positive.
Brenda gets on with her work but Jessica cannot concentrate on hers. She keeps casting her eyes in the direction of that dratted sample, waiting for her secretary's yellow urine to turn purple.
How many times, alone in the night, has Jessica watched for that wonderful colour of purple?
The colour of Japanese mountain tops.
She is going to have to break the news to Brenda very gently.

'Would you like to go home, dear, take the rest of the day off? Shall I ring for a taxi – on the company, of course?'
Brenda shakes her head.
'What about your boyfriend? He'll want to know about this. He should to told.'
'I don't want him to know. I don't want anyone to know.'
'But Brenda, my dear, I just don't see how that is going to be possible. You can't hide a thing like this forever.'
'I can. And I will.'
She is reacting just like a child – and who can blame her? This

is Jessica's fault, she asked for this. Jessica regrets the way she homed in in the image of Mother, a natural-enough reaction in the circumstances, but still . . . There is a degree of intimacy here that she finds distasteful and Jessica is also concerned about Brenda's mental ability to deal with her problem. She should not have provided a shoulder to lean on because once you have offered that shoulder it is enormously difficult to remove it.

'Well, Brenda, is there anyone you can tell? A friend, perhaps?'

'No,' is the simple answer to that. Damn. Damn. Damn.

'Well, I really don't know what to suggest.' It is already a quarter to one. Jessica is going to be late for her lunch.

'It doesn't matter,' sulks Brenda, sensing Jessica's agitation.

'Well, of course it matters,' snaps Jessica.

'To who does it matter? Who cares?'

'Well, *I* care,' says Jessica foolishly, regretting the words the minute they are uttered but for God's sake, how else can one respond? 'Your mother cares, I'm sure.'

'My mother will kick me out of the house.'

'Brenda! We are not living in the last century. No one gets kicked out of their houses these days.'

'Where I live they do and you don't know my mother.'

'People are different when they are actually faced with a problem like yours. People are always saying things they don't really mean. I expect your mother's firm attitude was her way of giving you a warning, telling you how much she does care . . .'

'You don't know her.'

'No, no. You are quite right, I suppose. I don't.'

Jessica's gone. Jessica will be back by three-thirty. Brenda sits at her flashing screen and writes up Jessica's letters.

If she hadn't done the pregnancy test at least she would still have hope but now there's no point in checking her knickers any more.

She is trapped and does not know which way to turn.

Brenda should not be having these thoughts, they are terrible thoughts but she cannot help thinking what a shame it is that she will give her baby up for adoption and have nothing in return but a bleeding space in her heart, when she has read of mothers in the Third World selling their babies for large sums of money. It sounds so mercenary and hard, but when you think about it, babies are in great demand so why should the desperate and the poor, acting on the morals of others, be forced to give their babies for free?

Where's the good in that?

If she sold her baby she could afford to move away from home, get a flat and make a new start.

She wipes a sweaty hand on her blouse. And now that Jessica knows her secret and is being so sympathetic towards her – why had she always considered her cold? – the fear of losing her job has gone and Brenda feels much less vulnerable. She isn't alone any more.

Is selling your baby against the law? Is it allowed in America?

Would they send you to prison if they caught you?

Jessica will know. Jessica, sophisticated, worldy, successful, wise . . . Jessica has all the answers.

The afternoon sun shines weakly. The booze makes her nod in the taxi and Jessica's dog sits snootily and contemptuously beside her. As if the bitch can read her mistress' thoughts.

In that twilit boozy world of shadows, you can get the strangest notions.

Here she is with an unwanted baby on her hands, and all she can suggest is that Brenda kills it.

Dear God. Jessica wants a baby.

Rudi wants a baby. But Rudi wants a child of his own – genes and all that. His own son or daughter. Not a hand-me-down of somebody else's.

She wonders . . . they have discussed many things but not this one. Would Rudi consider a surrogate mother? If somebody said they were willing to do it, a sister of hers, for example, would Rudi consent to impregnate her?

But Jessica has no sister. No brothers, either.

How about a friend of the family, then?

Or merely an acquaintance?

Brenda is only six weeks pregnant. Nobody could possibly tell. She is going to be one of those tiny women who carry their babies like marbles.

Surely it is not unlawful. Surely nobody needs to be told.

And Rudi would never know. He would always believe the child was his own and it might be, mightn't it?

No.

What a cruel trick to play on her lover.

Cruel to be kind?

If something doesn't happen soon Rudi is going to leave her, but Jessica sails close to dangerous waters. Her thoughts chase over her face as she drowses.

Of all the women in the whole wide world of whom Jessica could never be jealous, Brenda is certainly one. Well, look at her . . . the reasons are obvious. She imagines her lying in bed with her legs apart and Rudi probing and delving inside her. Jessica does not even flinch. Rudi's a stud, but could he bring himself to do that – to make love to a dowdy stranger?

It would be simpler than using a test tube, going up Brenda with a hypodermic or whatever one has to do in such crude circumstances . . .

No more tests. No more awful humiliations.

Could Brenda be persuaded to keep that sort of secret, in exchange for . . . in exchange for what? Money, perhaps? A better job? Everyone has their price and some come a damn sight cheaper than others. But to agree to be fucked by a total stranger . . . oh, for God's sake, Brenda's no angel, so why not?

After all, it's not unnatural. Not so unnatural as tossing off in a test tube.

'Hey lady, wake up!'

Jessica jerks awake, struggles out and pays for the cab with temples throbbing.

Isn't it stupid where your thoughts sometimes take you when you have had a glass of Piesporter too many, especially at lunch-time.

'There's some letters for signing, Jessica.'

'Oh bring them in, Brenda. And a cup of tea. Bring one for

yourself, why don't you? It is high time that you and I had a little talk.'

Chapter six

I know – while we are waiting for the outcome of these sensitive negotiations between Jessica and the grateful Brenda, why don't we take the opportunity to visit Jessica's house while she's out and have a poke around? We won't take any notice of Number 6. We'll skirt around Brenda's gran's house, the one with the boarded-up windows, the messy dustbin and the milk going sour on the step.

There is even a piece of old curtain, striped like deckchair material, hanging across the front door. I suppose, when it is hot, Brenda's gran opens the door and pulls the curtain across to keep out the flies.

Or to keep in the cats?

But let us see what Jessica's got in her understairs cupboard, in her bathroom cabinet, in her bedside drawer. You can tell an awful lot about people by the contents of their bedside drawers.

This is a tall house in a curved Georgian terrace, on three storeys, with a kitchen in the basement. Five steps lead up to the impressive black front door and the minute we step into the hall we think: Goodness, how bright, how spacious, how airy! Because the ground floor has all but been knocked into one.

Black and white tiles lead to a miniature *Gone With The Wind* type of staircase. There are even a couple of tasteful columns decorated with cherubs and ivy. But this is Number 8, Lippington Road, not Tara. Just three rooms lead off from the hall – the dining room, the drawing room and the downstairs cloakroom.

What message do we receive from Jessica's hall?

It is an impressive place in which to greet visitors. There is ample room for people to swing about as they take off their hats and coats. No clutter, but a sturdy sense of permanence. No carpet, just a Persian rug. No silly little ornaments, only a couple of monstrous vases filled with fresh flowers standing on the floor – the steamy scents of a greenhouse at Kew.

There is no understairs cupboard, smelling of mildew and mouse, in Jessica's hall.

Doris from The Hanging Basket comes to arrange the flowers each week.

Humphrey from The Georgian Gallery changes the pictures every month. 'Well, why waste money buying your own? You cannot possess art,' says Rudi rather haughtily. 'That is one thing money can't buy.'

But how would he know?

With a little bit of imagination and some serious investment, houses in Lippington Road can be made to resemble those in Cadogan Square. And these days they are almost as expensive. Years ago, during the war, there were eight families to every house, privies which overflowed in the rain, and washing strung out all over the backs.

So we can tell by one cursory glance at her hall that Jessica Holden, a woman in her early thirties, is certainly not short of a bob or two. She has done jolly well for herself, for a woman of her years.

But that is not the whole story. Jessica's salary is impressive, true, and there are numerous perks that go with the job at Jackson Willow & Sons, but she would not be able to afford this kind of luxurious lifestyle were it not for the benevolence of her father, James Galbraith Holden, late lamented, the widely respected Egyptologist known as the 'Pyramid Man'. With the mournful but honest face of a camel; and a complexion the colour of desert sand, he built up a fortune in a profitable racket, using his own little fleet of ships to move pieces of crumbling Antiquity, wrapped in linen, all over the Western world.

But that's too complicated to go into now.

We don't want to be diverted by that. He is dead, anyway, thank goodness. The man was a pirate and Jessica hardly knew him.

*

Oh, look at this enchanting garden – paradise among the grey London streets. Sniff it! We can reach it by stepping through the drawing-room windows. You would never dream you were standing in the middle of London. And here's the most marvellous patio overhung by a rampantly tendrilled pergola . . . a vine, clematis, a 'Nelly Moser', a 'Mrs Cholmondeley'.

'Yes,' says Jessica, when envious friends admire, 'we are very lucky indeed to have Mr Legg, funny old-fashioned thing. He still uses arsenic you know, for the weeds, out of dented old tins. God knows where he gets it.'

In the summer they mostly eat out here.

In June this garden is going to be glorious. Flowers will weep fire from the ornate urns. Raffia beige umbrellas will rustle in the breeze and a fountain will play onto the lilies in the water, rippling the fish – and smell those roses. . . !

Hang on a minute, I think there might be somebody else in the house!

If we go through the door at the rear and take the stairs to the basement, we come upon a whole separate unit, not just a kitchen but a cheery bedsit with a little fenced-in yard of its own at the back.

This is the domain of Rosita Rodriguez, who cleans, guards against burglars when everyone's out, studies sugar decorations on Monday and Wednesday afternoons, and does the washing-up.

Aha . . . if Jessica wants a surrogate, should she not have chosen the sultry, dark-eyed Rosita – an alien in a foreign land and a servant in her household?

Not strictly a servant. Rosita, wizened in the sun and drained of her juices like a little old mummy, only does what she wants to do. Rosita is a legacy inherited from James Galbraith just as his shrewd portfolio of investments was a legacy, and his collection of antique gold jewellery. The moustached, sixty-nine-year-old Rosita, half-blind, although no spur-of-the-moment affair, was a woman to be bedded, not married. She was a codicil in the will of the Pyramid Man and cannot be impregnated at her age, neither can she be abandoned.

The only food that Rosita ever agrees to cook is a proper *paella*, and even then it takes weeks of persuasion.

Oh Rosita, in vain you stare through your basement bars and dream of sunnier times, of camel rides and the marble floors, the waxy smells of Eastern hotels, the spicy markets of snakes and dates and the hot, crumpled beds and the sinewy limbs of James Galbraith, whom you loved more than life itself.

Ah, you followed him far from your native land only to end up in this shit-hole, this filthy and abysmal city where the only real beauty lies in the multi-coloured sugar strands that you weave and bend to your delicate dreams on a Monday and a Wednesday . . .

'She watches,' Rudi complains. 'She makes me feel uneasy, with her crow eyes.'

'I don't know what you mean,' says Jessica, knowing full well what he means but unable to do anything about it. 'Rosita is a lonely, unhappy old woman and the least we can do is obey my father's last wish and give her a home for ten years.'

'I just wish she would stay below ground. Can't you employ a cleaner?'

'I think you are making a fuss about nothing. Rosita is quite harmless. She doesn't mean to stare.'

'She swears at me in Spanish. She thinks I am a gigolo.'

'Well, behave like one then! Hush-a-your mouth and bed me, Rudi!'

But Jessica thinks, I wish he was kinder. Rudi is a spoilt man, with hardly a good word to say about anyone. It is always scathing, nasty remarks after they've said their farewells to friends . . . even the woman he's spent half the evening slobbering over. He will get into Jessica's car and say spitefully, 'Christ, what a bitch!' as if his sexual arousal can be eased by turning it into resentment. He delivers the same vitriolic blows about the pizza boy, the dustbin men, the meter man, Uncle Tom Cobbleigh – all Jessica's friends and most of his own.

Jessica often wonders why she loves him.

She sometimes worries that, as a woman of means, she

ought to have found a more respectable man, and married him by now. Someone safe with a house in the country, who would be nice to her, and look after her.

Rudi is nothing but a worry. Theirs is not a peaceful love.

And can those be cotton buds in Jessica's bedside drawer?

Cotton buds, which you must never push all the way down inside your ear because the drum is extremely delicate and could easily be perforated. But it is far too tempting to defy the manufacturer's advice, and delve, and it's always nice to see what comes out . . .

There are cotton buds and preservatives of various shapes and forms, and most of them, I am sorry to say, apart from the Oil of Primrose, apart from the Royal Jelly, contain essence of human foetus.

In olden days, to keep themselves young, the rich used monkeys' balls.

Standards are slipping.

Thermometer, chart, a dilapidated copy of *The Story of O*, 'Softwax' eardrops (could there be something wrong with Jessica's ears?), nail-file, tissues, cystitis sachets, a twist of cocaine, two champagne corks, a bright red lipstick . . . surely too red for a face, a razor and a black suspender belt – oh, the hussy!

On this king-size bed of crisp white cotton and lace, all sixty-nine positions are possible; upside down, back-to-back, sitting, standing, riding, pedalling, leaping, bouncing, rearing . . . and all with admirable balance on Rudi's part, as a result of the rowing.

It is possibly all this ferocious activity which causes Jessica's painful and frequent bouts of cystitis.

'We should move the bedroom to the spare across the landing. It's the same size, and then we wouldn't have to put up with that old crone from next door knocking on the wall every time someone turns over.'

'And how can we disturb her if she doesn't use the upstairs rooms? The old hag must be deliberately listening, dirty old thing.'

But although they discuss this perfectly sensible option,

Jessica and Rudi do not move. Some problems are worrying, others are not, especially when you don't give a toss for the opinion of the complainant. Perhaps the neighbour's interference adds a certain frisson of titillation . . . makes them feel naughty . . . groping and smoking in the bike-sheds.

And everyone knows that Mullins Holdings are using every trick in the book to get Vera Evans out of that house, and it isn't as if she hasn't been offered alternative accommodation – on the sixteenth floor of Hooper's Tower, south-facing and far more suitable for a single, unpleasant old woman. Vera probably considers the banging of Jessica's bedstead to be yet another crude ruse initiated by Mullins' men.

It is an urgent business. The next time the lease runs out, at the end of this year, the sitting tenant here has a right to buy. It is a jolly good thing that this old party hasn't two halfpennies to rub together. Even so, the situation is worrying for Mullins Holdings.

So don't they care, Jessica and Rudi, these two politically-sound young people, about the plight of the poor, threatened old woman next door?

They make television programmes about people like her.

Well, the truth is that 6, Lippington Road and Vera Evans are mismatched. Everyone knows that the old lady cannot cope in that mausoleum on her own, living in one room, cooking on an open fire . . . which is against the rules in a smoke-free zone. She might have lived there since time began, but Vera Evans is a danger both to herself and to others, with her unhygienic ways, her bonfires and those half-starved cats.

She cannot have a family, surely, or they would be doing something about her.

'She is mad,' says Jessica, 'poor old thing. Ideally, she wants looking after.'

For once in his life, Rudi is not nasty. In Rudi's country they do not treat old women like that, smashing their windows, cutting off their electric, insensitive to their needs as if they were played-out old donkeys. In England they treat their donkeys better than their elderly . . . there are sanctuaries for them, pastures and trees, while the elderly are positioned on the outer edges of the land, like Bournemouth or Brighton, or pointed prematurely towards the sky.

But Rudi does not protest too much. It is distasteful to see people old and ageing. It reminds one of one's own mortality and Rudi is in his prime.

'*Nearer my God to Thee,*' sings Vera Evans, tunelessly, from the deep insides of her dying house.

But Jessica, think about this for a minute . . . What on earth would become of poor Vera up there in Hooper's Tower, just a mystified face in the clouds with the lights of the world spread out below her, a teller of the time by aeroplane trails, trapped by permanently vandalised lifts?

Rapunzel, Rapunzel, let down your golden hair.

She would have to take the clips out first.

What a good thing it is that new brides, by tradition, do not have to hang out their freshly-stained sheets from the windows of Hooper's Tower. From below, all that their concerned family and friends would be able to make out would be a handkerchief-sized piece of cotton whirling off across the sky, a rag with a bride on the end, whisked away by the notorious turbulence that rocks the building from side to side, at safely calculated angles.

A sorry sight.

But at least in Hooper's Tower Vera could afford the heating, and not have to sleep in that hideous old chair, under that pile of old coats and blankets smothered in cat hair.

So what's up there on the second floor of Jessica's house? Let's go and have a look.

Well, it is a self-contained flat which Jessica allows her friends to use when they come up from the shires to London, shopping, lunching, meeting. It is so much more convenient, and preferable, for guests to be independent. Otherwise, they soon outstay their welcome and become boring.

And Jessica would far rather her female friends remained tucked away at the top of the house instead of flitting round, half-naked, to the bathroom and back, attracting Rudi's excited eye.

So you see how sad it is, and how far this jealousy business has gone. Jessica does not trust her friends. They, being mostly attractive and nice, unmarried or divorced, are the very last people she trusts and besides, most of the women she knows have been betrayed, at the end of the day, by their friends.

The whores.

And that is a fact that really pisses Jessica off.

So she hides them away at the top of the house, like secrets in an attic.

So what have we learned from this visit?

We have learned that the flat would make an ideal nursery and Jessica could entertain her friends safely on the ground floor, if her own bambino was securely installed on the second.

Chapter seven

In fide vade.

Walk in faith.

So, where is Jessica's sense of morality? She, who has been educated as a good Christian woman, who spent her formative years at Ardley Ladies' College, high on a hill, where the old headmistress, Miss Balchin, tapped out to her girls three times on a Sunday and five times a week at morning prayers the importance of taking a moral lead in the turbulent world outside the leafy grounds.

'One day, you gels will be the champions of women, just as Emmeline and Christabel Pankhurst heralded the battle in their day.

'THAT WAR IS NOT OVER.

'The values and vision which inspired our school founders have to be reborn and remoulded by each successive generation here if we are ever to win.

'You privileged few, you happy few will take your places, not only in the professions, as leaders of industry, pathfinders in the sciences, priestesses in the church, but your voices will resound in the corridors of power at Westminster and Brussels as well.' (This last was a re-hash of a war-time speech Miss Balchin found in a cupboard, exhorting the girls to get out of mufti and get out there, drive ambulances, wind bandages, knit squares, and the sporty sorts could take leading roles in the Wrens and the WAAFS.)

Just five years later that same speech was adapted yet again, encouraging the Seniors to wave a gentler flag for God and Queen and play a supportive role this time. Flower arranging. Home-making. Baby rearing. Blue-ing the whites. Sewing and mending. Dust was the new enemy which had to be conquered.

Miss Balchin cast her fierce blue eyes towards the back of the hallowed hall, and rolled the words off her tongue in a rotund Churchillian fashion. 'Those with a good education, in the widest sense, must lead by example, and therefore never forget the words from our inspirational school hymn: *Christ Is Made The Sure Foundation*.

'But even now it is important that we look outward and feel part of the wider community around us, and with this in mind we join with other schools whenever we can in debates, concerts, dances and conferences . . .'

But naturally not schools like Brenda's.

As a boarding-school girl, Jessica is accustomed to hardship; the traumas of cross-country runs in the frost, and plunging into unheated swimming pools are the standards by which all hardships are judged thereafter.

Jessica would probably enjoy a trek across the Sahara, being tough and resilient, or a raft-trip down the Amazon. But would she survive for a single month the sheer futility of life on the Pennystone Estate?

It is money, pure and simple, which stands between the Ardley ladies and their concept of reality.

The phrase, 'your betters,' has no meaning.

The gels from Ardley Ladies' College would blanch and possibly even faint, were they ever to be addressed by the cynical, unpleasantly scurvied Mouldy Waters, headmaster of Battersby Comp, the school where Brenda went.

Where has all that integrity gone? Why has Jessica abandoned that comfortable high moral ground?

In fide vade.

Oh Jessica, just because you must keep your man, does that mean that all that expensive, hard-won moral superiority must go down the pan?

Yes, I'm afraid it does.

*

Brenda sits there stunned and silent with her thin knees wobbling. Her mouth is open – sucking in hope?

'And so, Brenda, as you see, what I am getting at is a kind of innocent bluff which would help you on the one hand, and Rudi and me on the other. I leave the decision entirely in your hands. I do not intend to influence you either way. You can accept my idea, keep your mouth shut and pocket fifteen thousand pounds in eight months from now, or you go home, face the consequences, and either keep your baby and battle on like one of those single parents on Income Support, or go through the agony of having the child adopted with no cushion to fall back on.'

Fifteen thousand! Oh yes, Jessica has decided to be generous. Guilt? Not really. She can afford to be big-hearted.

Give her her due, she tries to be fair. 'But of course, as you know, there is still the abortion option. You don't need to take any notice of anything I have said.'

'There is just one question I would like to ask.' Now that the shock is over, Brenda's skin is still the colour of an uncooked chicken but at least she has stopped weeping for the moment. Her eyes are fuddled as she struggles hard to come to terms with her fate.

'Of course.'

She goes on rather nervously, 'If I did try to . . . battle on . . . as you put it, would I lose my job?'

Jessica draws a deep breath. 'You are employed here on a contract basis, are you not, Brenda?'

'Yes, I am.'

'Well, all I can tell you is that your contract would not be renewed three months from hence, once it was apparent to the other directors that you were pregnant. It would be out of my hands then, Brenda. There would be absolutely nothing I could do to help you.'

Is this the Piesporter talking? For Jessica's sake we must sincerely hope not, because she has laid all her cards on the table.

Brenda was a fool to confide in Jessica so utterly. Communication on level five must be reserved for those you trust with your life. And even then it is dodgy.

*

Jessica's dog gets up quietly and drags its arse across the office carpet. You really cannot blame hotels for refusing to take pets. The habits of a species are inbred, even in the most sophisticated specimens of the breed. Brenda stares, but Jessica ignores it. Hiame has picked up something in the park and will have to be wormed again.

Jessica, a sophisticated specimen of the human kind, who belongs to the world of the lady, not the servant, knows very well that she is being manipulative, using Brenda's fear of her mother, her horror of confessing to her father, her dread of losing her job, her terror of poverty. Poor little sod. After all, everyone with the slightest intelligence knows that the worst imagined situations are normally less harrowing once they have actually happened. Brenda's brutish mother would probably forgive her in time. Her teddy boy father would gather her into his arms. But she would lose her job at Jackson Willow & Sons because Jessica would make damn sure that she did.

Jessica has put herself at some peril by taking Brenda Hodges into her confidence, particularly as, at this point in time, she cannot be sure that the lovely Rudi will agree.

He is choosy with his precious prick and these days, can you blame him?

This is all extremely sensitive stuff.

But Jessica is safer than Brenda, for if Brenda went to a higher authority with her hysterical tales, Jessica would deny all knowledge and nobody would believe the typist. In her hapless predicament there is little for Brenda to gain by telling such tales, inside the office, or out of it.

'And all I would have to do would be to . . .' Brenda drops her eyes, unsure of which words she ought to use for the sexual act, with Jessica.

'Go to bed, yes, all you would have to do would be to go to bed with Rudi. Just once. Or maybe twice. Depending.'

'Or maybe, it might be better if you could give me five thousand pounds, on approval, kind of thing?'

Oh, the cunning of Brenda and her class, with all their tasteless haggling at the wrong times and in the wrong places.

Jessica's thoughts are awful, she should not think this way, but she believes that it is because of people like Brenda that public lavatories are forced to display the sign: *'Please do not flush your sanitary towels down the toilet.'*

It is because of people like Brenda that the notices above the basins shout: *'Wash your hands.'*

It is because of people like Brenda that weary doctors won't visit at night, empty buses clog up the roads, you cannot go into chemists and demand penicillin, or a speedy cure for cystitis. It is also the reason why honest, intelligent people are told to keep off the grass, that game-shows were invented, that crafts have turned into plastic souvenirs, that you have to travel first-class on trains and cannot eat British Rail sandwiches any more . . . They have:

No initiative.

No common sense.

Jessica could go on.

She looks at Brenda as if she is a thorn and Jessica a haemophiliac. And this young woman sitting before her is to fornicate with her lover, taint him with her private parts. *Rudi will have knowledge of her*. 'Oh, no! I am not acting as a pimp, you know, Brenda. That would not be prudent at all. You would receive the money when your baby was born. The first thing to be done after intercourse with Rudi would be to have your pregnancy properly confirmed, by a doctor of our choosing, and you would inform the doctor that your last period happened at the beginning of March, not February, as you told me. Do you understand?'

Jessica is no fool. She is not about to give Brenda some positive ammunition, a cheque for God's sake, that she might hold against her.

Brenda swallows, devouring Jessica's every word. 'And what would I tell my mother? Where would I live?'

'You would say nothing to anyone until your pregnancy was officially confirmed. It would be more convenient for you to remain at home until your condition became too obvious, and then, for the last two or three months I will find you somewhere to go. It's too early yet, Brenda, to tie up all the loose ends. Much of this will have to be worked out on the hoof, at it were. We will just have to muddle along.'

Brenda and her ilk . . . they expect to be given a manual with simple instructions to follow, so that everything in life is reduced to a flat-pack wardrobe from B & Q, or a book of paintings by numbers.

And how is Jessica planning to introduce the idea to Rudi, that sensual, proud, aristocratic Italian with his deep love of opera and anything even faintly artistic . . . his openly declared adoration of beautiful women?

He is quite likely to insist that he pick his own partner.

But Jessica knows only too well what sort of partner her lover would choose.

'There are plenty of struggling women about who could carry a baby for money; there is no need for us to use an ill-educated girl from the lower orders. Graduate men are chosen to provide semen for women . . . genes are all-important, Jessica, we have to remember that. After all, what sort of child could possibly be begotten from those lanky loins?

'And anyway, compared to you, the girl is all but flat-chested.'

'You are not supposed to notice her tits. Do be practical, Rudi,' Jessica would urge him in her modulated voice which is never strident. 'Where are all these obliging women offering not just their cunts but their wombs for money? And how are you going to approach them? Brenda did manage a hundred and fifty words a minute shorthand, Rudi, and that is a quite astronomical speed. She's a bright girl who has been poorly educated, and after all, they use any old cows to pass on the genes of a bull,' Jessica would remind him. 'They don't even care if the cow dies afterwards. We are talking about a vessel here, and that is all.'

In this particular instance Jessica does not want the best for Rudi.

But what if Rudi is horrified by the very idea, insulted and humiliated, and refuses to discuss it at all?

*

Brisk and sensible, Jessica signs the letters which Brenda has typed and says, 'Now Brenda, you go home and give the matter some thought. Spend the evening considering your options as calmly as you can and come and tell me your decision first thing in the morning. If we decide to go ahead then we have to act quickly . . . in a matter of a few days, I'm afraid. Any child can be born a month early, but much longer than that and it starts to look rather odd.'

'But what if he doesn't like me? When he sees me, I mean.'

'This is really not a question of preference.'

Brenda looks at Jessica and marvels. How she envies her; how she would love to change places with her. Brenda admires her boss very much and that is quite right and proper. Jessica *is* an admirable person. 'But I might, you know – I might put him off.'

Jessica blinks. Has the girl been reading her thoughts? She is a mess. If she would only do something interesting with her hair, and choose a make-up that toned in. 'There is nothing wrong with you, Brenda. Why on earth would you put him off?'

Brenda looks down at herself, at her tea-stain. After a struggle she says, 'I dunno.'

Perhaps Brenda's youth will attract him. 'Well, we could freshen you up, tidy you up a bit, couldn't we?' Oh God . . . the word 'sacrifice' springs immediately to mind. 'I mean to say, if that's what you are worrying about, we could soon change that.'

Brenda suddenly brightens. 'I can look nice you know, Miss, much nicer than this, especially on a Saturday night. It's just that my hair gets greasy again by Monday.'

And is Jessica going to lead Brenda in like the high priestess in some primitive ritual, guiding her secretary towards the bridal-white bed by the hand and chanting, 'Please put the cigarette out now because Rudi does not like the smell. Did you have a bath like I told you? It is time to take off your knickers now, Brenda.'

Rudi is going to have to take Brenda stiffly, on her back. No hanky panky. No cystitis.

Might she sulk and moan at the last minute and threaten to run away?

And what about the etiquette? Will Jessica have to provide something to eat afterwards, as a gesture . . . as for carol singers?

These thoughts are too awful to contemplate. Jessica shudders. Could it be that the happy effects of the fatal glass of Piesporter are finally wearing off?

Oh Jessica, walk in faith.

Chapter eight

Brenda's mum, Big Rita, toils around Woolworths stacking the shelves in DIY, sticking the prices on the handles of the hammers and cursing the easy life of Derek, her man, who sits at home with his slippers on waiting for his spuds to be peeled.

An interested mother, directly involved with the welfare and morals of her five adult children, is Rita a wicked daughter, leaving her poor old mother, Vera, to rot away like a discarded carpet in her room in the house in Lippington Road?

Certainly not.

Not a week goes by when Rita does not pop in to see her, bringing hard-earned offerings of eggs, bread, potatoes, or fish off the market. She lets herself into Number 6 with her own key and calls, 'Ma! It's me! How are you doing?'

'Just middling as usual.'

'Have you bagged up your laundry?'

More often than not, Ma is nodding in her chair so Rita pokes up the fire and swivels the kettle over to boil. Before it is properly boiled she fills the washing-up bowl which rests on an upturned orange box ready to sort the dirty pots. She turns round with a smile. 'Everywhere's lovely and clean, Ma. And you yourself, you are looking good.' They have managed to get her hair washed at last but already she is struggling to replace that old headscarf.

'The social's been again,' says Vera. 'They brought me a new fridge, look.'

'They know you can't use a fridge, not without your electric . . .'

'It's on. Listen, you can hear it humming. The social have got it turned on again.'

'That's a sodding miracle if ever I saw one.'

'I think there's squatters in up the top.'

'No, Ma. We have been all through this before . . .' Rita swishes a dirty cup around in the tepid water.

'There's certainly somebody up the top, 'cos I heard the chain pull this morning.'

'You're hearing things. I'll go and have a look before I leave, but you're always hearing noises, Ma, and we haven't found anyone so far. Anyway, if there were squatters, and I'm not saying there are, they wouldn't be interested in hurting you.'

'Terrible things happen to old women living alone.'

'Terrible things happen to everyone, Ma, but mostly it's burglars, and I'm buggered if I know what they'd find here that they'd want.'

'There's the fridge now, Rita. It's a good one – Frigidair. None of the plastic bits have broken and the light still works.'

'I shouldn't think burglars have much of a market for second-hand fridges.'

'How do you know?'

'Well, I don't. I wouldn't know anything, would I?'

'No, Rita, you wouldn't. I'm the only one in this family who's ever had any sense. Anyway, I've put a bit of knuckle end in the fridge ready to boil up for tonight.'

For work, Rita wears a pink and white nylon overall, with a badge on her breast that says *R Hodges*.

To visit her mother she wears her headscarf, a coat of dove blue and a pair of widely cut black trousers with turn-ups. Her hair, cut short in a sensible style, is as thick, straight and brown as it ever was, and her face is large with correspondingly hefty features. Since she married Derek no man has made a move towards her. How could this frail little woman who sits there scrawnily in her rotting chair, how could she ever have given birth to a monstrous woman like Rita?

Rita is her father's daughter just as his sons were the coalman's sons and profited from their inheritance by selling their muscled backs and tattooed arms to the Services, the builders, the smelterers of iron and steel in the shipyards. All her six brothers have done well . . . until just lately of course, what with so many of the heavier industries closing down and shutting up shop.

'A son is a son till he takes a wife . . .'

From their newtown homes the brothers' wives write to their mother-in-law occasionally, and send her Christmas and birthday presents – bright tea cosies, calendars and tea towels of cats, something from Marks which could be exchanged, a pair of slippers, Yardleys' Lily of the Valley – presents chosen for their suitability to travel through the post. Nothing delicate. Nothing breakable. Every now and then they used to bring the grandchildren over to see her, but it's not very nice, is it, be fair, with her living like she does. Vera Evans is not the sort of gran you get in the story books. She is more like one of the witches.

Those children are off their hands now, with families of their own.

There are even more cards at Christmas, with names she finds it hard to place – Jonty, Beth, Suzie, Cara – and more calendars and tea towels to go in the drawer with the brown paper, candles and string.

So you can't really blame the brothers' wives for visiting only once in a blue moon.

Rita moves to the Jiffy mops, hobbling on her sore feet.

Perhaps Rita should have done as her mother suggested and moved into Lippington Road with her baby and her man. Instead of that she went off selfishly and settled herself in on the Pennystone Estate.

If Rita had done as her mother wished, she might have prevented her descent into squalor.

But it happened so slowly it was barely noticeable. The retreat from one room into another, the final closing of another door, the abandoning of a landing, the birth of another litter of kittens and the way the house always felt so cold.

Vera's fear of the squatters is all Rita's doing. Nine cats was more than enough. If Rita suspected another litter she made it her business to search the house.

'What are you doing, Rita? Where are you going?' called Vera. 'There's tea down here getting cold.'

'I am just checking for squatters, Ma. You never know . . .'

'Squatters?'

Rita's voice echoed down through the hollow house. 'They get in everywhere. It's best to make certain.'

Rita would trap the kitties in the boxroom at the top of the house and get Derek to come round the next day and drown them in the water tank. Then he would bag the bodies up and chuck them on the council tip.

They gritted their teeth but they had to do it. It was doing the creatures a kindness, it really was. Their eyes were never open. And the thought of any more cat crap to clear up, lying hard and curled as walnut whirls, reeking around the empty landings and bedrooms of Lippington Road was enough to make Rita puke.

Rita Hodges gave up persuading her mother to move ages ago. It was a waste of bloody breath. Horrified to see her own mother living like this, nevertheless she understands her need to preserve her independence at all costs and remain in the house she has always loved, and Vera's conditions do not dismay the old woman in the way they dismay the hygiene people and the social services. As Vera says, with perfect honesty, she brought seven kids up in far worse conditions than these, and nobody worried about that then. 'And we were none the worse for it,' she says. 'Immune we were to dirt, all through the war with rats and rubble, not like people today with their ten different chopping boards and not allowed to have tiles any more in kitchens, because of the grouting. I ask you.'

'You spent your life cleaning and scrubbing . . .'

'I did. I did 'Twas the coal dust, Rita, it was getting rid of the dust, and then there was all the phlegm.'

'Well, I had no coal dust . . .'

'Then you had no need to clean and scrub.'

'So why do I do it?'

Vera shakes her mottled head. 'Just houseproud, I suppose, Rita. You must've caught that off me. It was the way we were, in those days.'

'Can't stand a muddle,' says Rita.

'Neither could I, but now, oh bugger it, what does a little muddle matter?'

*

A little muddle?

Cats and paraffin.

The room is a tip. The violently red patterned carpet which Rita remembers from her childhood is spattered now with old food, has gone a hard shiny rust. The coalman's chair, which used to be kept so polished and ebony shiny, has been taken over by the cats, as has the broken old sofa in front of the window. The table, with its oil-cloth surface, is covered with burns and saucepan rings, and the windows were boarded up long ago because the Mullins' men came in the night to break the glass. The law said it was kids, but that's all they know.

How come the kids didn't throw their stones at anyone else's house?

A yellow paraffin light breaks the eternal darkness. Everything in here has yellowed to the colour of smoke and it is the paper, not the plaster, that is holding up much of the chimney wall.

This is a room where the sun never gets to shine.

Vera is terrified of going out, lest Mullins' men come while she's gone and change the locks. She makes sure she is never away for longer than five minutes and every journey entails much complex spying out of the land, from every window, from every angle.

Any odd loiterer, any delivery man not instantly recognised is put down as a Mullins' man and Vera will not put her nose outside that door until he has gone.

How can the poor victimised old lady live with such terrible persecution?

Vera revels in it. She thoroughly enjoys it. She says it gives her a purpose for living: thwarting Mullins and his men has become the focal point of her existence.

'They won't get their bleeding hands on this house till I am six foot under.'

'I dunno how you stay sane, Ma. You must be so frightened, here all alone when it's dark.'

'Nonsense, Rita my girl. We used to shelter under the table when the Germans dropped their bombs on London . . . fire and explosions ripping round every corner, devastating every street. And your Dad'd go out with his big coat on and his gas mask and his pump, poor sod . . . And those doodlebugs which went quiet before they fell, that silence, Rita, that eerie silence, well, you wouldn't remember any of it because you weren't born until just before the war ended. Bugger me, Rita, and you're asking me if I'm frightened by such wankers as the Mullins' men!'

'But in the war you were all in it together, with a sense of sharing. It's different now . . .'

'No, dear, not really.'

'But Ma, don't you see? This time you can't bloody well win!'

'Oh, can't I?' And all her spirit was there, in that gleamingly vindictive eye.

If it's bad inside, it is even worse out.

In Lippington Road there is a Neighbourhood Watch scheme, but no neighbourhood any longer. If there was there'd be no need for this Neighbourhood Watch.

From the moment Dominic Bassett from the telly moved into Number 18 in the early sixties, the neighbourhood went into decline. They didn't want to know you, you see, these new people with their media jobs.

They took down their nets and by night you could see all the way through their pine-clad houses . . . right through to the backs. They didn't bother with curtains. They all had dressers in those days, long refectory tables, and brightly coloured Agas. They filled their kitchens with leafy plants, with rugs across the stripped pine floors, and low-hanging lights dangled from moulded ceilings.

They let you look in, but they didn't want to know you.

You could walk by in a morning and they wouldn't pass the time of day. Too busy leaping into their cars and driving off with their music blaring and their toast still stuck in their teeth. All jackets and polo-neck sweaters.

And then, at a quarter to nine, the wives would come out, shiny-haired women with haircuts like children and sandals like children, with freshly scrubbed faces, leading the kids by the hand and taking them off to their posh schools, neat-haired kids, all dolled up and smart in green uniforms.

The neighbours who live on either side of Vera don't want to know, but Rita can hardly blame them. Well, they've got busy lives, same as she has. They have their own problems, same as everyone else.

God knows who they are, or what they call themselves. When you are passing by on the pavement you are not close enough to read those illuminated nameplates but the cars show what kind of people they are . . . all those BMWs, the Jeeps, the Range Rovers and the Porsches.

Number 6, which used to look the same as the others, now stands out like a turd on the tablecloth. The house stares blindly out at the street through its boarded-up windows, and the ones upstairs with no curtains look as vulnerable as men on parade with no clothes on.

If it wasn't for the chink of yellow that peeps through the boarded-up parts at night, you would think Number 6 was deserted.

The gleaming paintwork of the owner-occupied ones contrasts vividly with the sun-blistered, post-war green of her mother's house but what can you do? To decorate a place like this would cost a fortune . . . and for what? To put money in the pockets of Mullins and his men?

Rita stacks the shelves. Her feet ache and she worries. She has too much on her plate, that's her trouble. What with Vera and Derek, now all the kids are back on her hands, crammed up together in that little house which was once the answer to all her dreams.

So much for dreams.

The trouble with dreams is they sometimes come true – and then what? She ought to have made her dream bigger, that's what she ought to have done, and that is what she would do now, if she was Brenda's age with all her future in front of her.

And what is going on with Brenda? The girl has not been herself for days. Perhaps she is sickening for something, but would Derek notice, if she didn't mention it? Would he sodding well notice? Just as long as his belly is full and he gets his end away on a Saturday night, and just as long as there's darts on telly he doesn't give a bugger.

No, Rita is the only one of her family to notice any of these things, and the only one who's not too frigging lazy to get up off her arse and do something about it!

Chapter nine

The humble Brenda droops before the mirror in her little back bedroom.

Once upon a time, where her dusty pink candlewicked-divan now stands, pressed hard against the wall and with useful drawers underneath, there were bunks in this tiny room, and for fifteen years she and Doreen lived here, together. Brenda's posters, mostly of Shetland ponies with flowers in their hair, were stuck with Blu-Tack on the right-hand wall, Doreen's sweaty pop stars covered the candy-striped wallpaper on the left. But Brenda failed to impress herself upon it. Open the door and it stank of Doreen – hair-spray, deodorant and sometimes, old brown blood gone dry.

Doreen insisted on sleeping with the window closed.

And the floor was littered with muddled-up copies of *Photo-Love*.

'You two buggers are a pain in the arse,' scolded Rita. 'Look at the state of this bleeding room! And it's true what they say about girls. The boys manage to keep their rooms clean, so why not you? Forever in bed . . . that's what you think life is, isn't it? One long sodding holiday! You'll learn.'

But Brenda smiled because she knew that Mum didn't really want them to learn. Mum wanted their lives to be different and she was often telling them so. 'Look at me!' she used to say, pummelling her outsized chest with her fist. 'Look at me!'

It was Brenda who always ended by clearing it up. Cleaning Doreen's mess – all that sticky make-up, dog-ends, bubble-gum, and pink blobs of used cotton wool.

She keeps it really nice now, now that Doreen's been given a room of her own, and Shane and Eddie are in the third bedroom and Roy on a put-u-up downstairs. Every item on the kidney-shaped dressing table is neatly arranged. All her china ornaments, and her Smurfs, are wiped at least once a week.

Doreen moved out three years ago, after Shane and Eddie left. Shane got married and went to live with Fay's mum down Bethnal Green, and Eddie moved into his girlfriend's flat. Roy is always coming and going . . . it's one girl after another. He disappears for days on end and some nights he sleeps in his van.

For a while back then the house felt quite empty. You could get into the bathroom whenever you wanted, and could mostly grab a good chair downstairs, although, of course, it was never empty with Dad at home all day, and Shane always visiting with a six-pack to keep him company. But Shane stayed with Fay for three years and had two kids and Mum was so proud of being a granny. She wore a hat with a spotted veil at the christenings, the only times Brenda ever saw Rita wearing a hat.

Brenda wouldn't like to be granny, not ever. Even the word is old and wrinkled, with skin gone rucked like the ripples on a river.

Just like Gran's arms.

Well. Eventually, Shane wandered home one day and just sort of stayed.

'Where's Fay? Where are the kids?'

'We're having a rest from each other,' said Shane.

'A rest my arse! You can't just bugger off! What if your dad had behaved like that? Where would we be today if your dad had behaved like that? Get back over there and behave like what you are – a married, family man with responsibilities for God's sake, or I'll beat the living daylights out of you, big as you are, so there!' Mum shouted.

'Fay's Mum's been stirring the shit.'

Mum bristled. 'What?'

'Fay's Mum's been going on . . .'

Mum lowered her head and went into the scrum with her massive shoulders braced, every bit as big and as solid as Shane. 'You've been up to your old tricks again, more likely! You can't stir shit unless there's something to stir. There's nothing the matter with Fay's mum. Shane, what've you been up to?'

'Give it a rest, Mum.' And Shane grinned nervously, trying to defuse her.

'Give it a rest? Give it a rest my arse!' roared Mum, white with rage. 'And how about me? How about somebody round here giving me a rest for a change? You lot . . . sitting around on your sodding arses all day while I'm out there lifting and heaving my guts out. Just don't think you can come back here cute as you like, cramming into this poky house. Maybe we should've gone to Mum's, Derek and me.'

'I can pay my way.' Shane fumbled in his jeans pockets and drew out a crumpled packet of fags. He offered one to Mum who took it, sitting down heavily and easing off her shoes. 'Come on, Mum,' said Shane. 'You just sit down and I'll get you a cup of tea.'

'Poor little kiddies,' said Mum. But the argument seemed to just die inside her with the first lungful of smoke.

So Shane moved back and for Mum's sake he went on a job-training scheme.

And no more than a month later Eddie moved back, kicked out by his girlfriend, Marge.

When you are little you don't think your mother is different from anyone else's, not until somebody points it out.

And they invariably do.

Mum never missed a school play, or a football match, or a concert, or a parents' evening, or a fête. She'd arrive early, one of the first, 'to get a good seat. There's no point in us coming if we can't see,' dragging Dad along morosely behind her because Derek hated anything like that. Dad wasn't good at looking smart. 'He hasn't the happy knack,' Mum used to say while pressing his good suit from Burtons.

Not many other fathers made that sort of effort and wore a suit for an open day at Battersby Comp.

Mouldy Waters was tall and thin and spoke to the parents with his hands behind his back and his eyes fixed firmly on the distance, like the Duke of Edinburgh. But Mum was every inch his equal – so why did she put on her telephone voice and use her photograph smile? Why did she take her silly black handbag whenever she went to meet him? Mum was diminished by impending authority before she even passed through the gates.

'But Mr Waters, I should like to know why you haven't put Brenda down for any of these GCSEs?'

It sounded as though she'd rehearsed it first, standing in front of a mirror. Her lips pursed together and made a squirming, slimy smile.

'Brenda is not academically inclined, Mrs Hodges,' said Mouldy Waters, with his eyes half-closed. 'Brenda would do better to concentrate on what we call the skills . . .'

'But Brenda says she has difficulty in hearing most of the lessons, Mr Waters, because of the disruption that is so often going on, caused by the same few pupils who everyone knows but nobody seems to want to name.'

Mouldy Waters raised a pair of pale red eyebrows, the colour of his spectacle frames. 'Mrs Hodges, I hope you are not casting a slur upon the competence of my teaching staff. We have our fair share of the disruptive element at Battersby, as do most inner-city schools, but we also have an increased staffing ratio and specialised teachers to absorb the ever-present problem.'

'But Mr Waters, Brenda says that sometimes she can't even hear what homework she ought to be doing.'

'I'm afraid Brenda has been making excuses for not paying sufficient attention,' said Mouldy Waters, edging drily away. 'I think you will find, in her report, a criticism of this tendency of hers to daydream. All children, unfortunately, cannot be expected to attain university grade, Mrs Hodges. And every examination taken costs the school money. Funds are scarce. We have to choose our GCSE candidates with great care or we'd soon be accused of wasting precious resources.'

And he did not add, but could easily have done, 'By people like you.'

Mum followed Mouldy Waters, refusing to be outdone, but by now she was left talking to his dandruffy back. 'But what sort of future can Brenda expect without any exams to her name?'

'May I suggest a course at night-school – a secretarial course, perhaps, or hairdressing, or communication skills, or computer studies. There are many other roads one can travel, Mrs . . . er . . .'

'Hodges,' said Mum, giving up, turning away, and rounding furiously on Brenda.

And even earlier than that.

'Your Mum's big, isn't she? Much bigger than your poor little dad,' Sophie Barker giggled. 'She walks like a man. Perhaps she *is* a man. Dressed up.'

This was the first time Brenda had ever felt that sort of hurt, quite different from a scraped knee or a slapped leg or earache. A hurt in a place which you couldn't reach. A hurt which you couldn't take home. One which you had to keep secret to save passing the ache of it onto anyone else.

'You don't have to come, Mum. I haven't got a speaking part. Lots of mothers aren't coming. You and Dad will probably be the only ones there!'

'Don't talk so daft – of course I'm coming. What time did you tell me it started?'

Brenda flushed, and had to admit it was six-thirty.

Brenda stood silent for half an hour behind the crib dressed as an angel wearing the ugly wings Mum had made. 'There! You'll be the prettiest angel God ever saw.' Mum was tired as usual. She had cleared the sitting-room table and made the wings after work.

She enjoyed making the wings, you could see she did. But that old sheet was no good. No one could have made wings with that.

'But they won't stay stiff. They keep drooping, look.'

'They will if you stick some sodding sellotape here at the back.'

From the stage the audience looked like a navy-blue blanket, all except Mum, who sat head and shoulders above the rest. Her laugh was the loudest of anyone there and she clapped long after the others had stopped. No one but Brenda appeared to notice.

'What size shoes does your mum wear?' asked Sophie Barker, a few days later.

'I dunno. Who knows what size shoes their mother takes? Why should I know?'

'Does she buy them in the shops, like ordinary people?'

'Suppose so.'

'What if you grew to be as big as her? What if you were taller than anyone else, even the boys? I wouldn't want to go round with you if you turned out like that.'

'And I wouldn't want to go round with you, neither.'

But Brenda knew she wouldn't grow up like her mother; she was small-boned, like her dad, that's what Mum kept saying. 'Little' was beautiful in Mum's vocabulary; it went before every description of anything pleasant. 'What a lovely little top.' 'What a dear little dog.' 'What a sweet little cottage.'

Whereas: 'Look at that hideous great big arse on her.' 'What an ugly great brute he is.' 'Where has that horrible big stain gone?'

'Look at your pretty little hands,' she would say to Brenda, stroking them lovingly with her own meaty finger. 'Like a doll's hands they are. You should look after those hands, Brenda. Try not to bite your nails and spoil them.'

Mum is strong. Mum is built like a Biblical ass. Mum can carry burdens on her back. Because she is so big people tend to pile them on, not noticing how the weight of the years has affected her feet with all the carrying.

'D'you know what I'd sodding well do if I had the money, Derek?'

'What, Rita?'

'I'd go and spend the whole sodding day at the best chiropodist in the whole of London and then I'd go and be fitted out with a decent bleeding pair of shoes. They'd be the first ones that fitted me properly in the whole of my life.'

'One day, Rite,' says Dad, turning up the boxing.

'I'm pregnant, Mum.'

How can Brenda possibly do that?

*

'This clever little certificate is going to take you places, my girl,' said Mum, when Brenda presented it proudly one teatime. 'All you'll have to do is play your cards right, and you'll meet some ambitious executive . . .'

'Miss Groves said that one day I might be able to work hard for *Hansard*.'

'Well, there you are, and what did I tell you? Hard work, Brenda, it always pays off in the end. If Doreen had spent more time at school and less hanging around the arcade with those louts like a bitch on heat she might have brought home this same sort of achievement and be mixing with the doctors by now.'

'Ah Mum, that's not fair,' objected Doreen. 'I've always worked, sod it. I've never been without a job, not since I left school. Not like the boys.'

'But there's no *future* in what you are doing, Doreen, that's the difference. There's no ladder you can climb, unless you start taking life more seriously and try to get into nursing proper. An auxiliary, after all, is only a souped-up word for a cleaner.'

'Nigel's earning good money . . .'

'Oh yes, of course he is. Nigel's a bright lad but he's not a *doctor*, Brenda, is he? He is not a professional man. You must find a professional man, Brenda, someone who will take care of you properly. Doreen, don't do what I did. Look at him! Derek? Derek! Shut your gob – you're snoring! And you're more of a fool than I took you for, Doreen, if you go and do what I did and marry a slob.'

Get on and marry well.

Mum does not understand.

It isn't like she imagines it.

Brenda doesn't have the clothes, or the manners, to go with her job. You can't kit yourself out well on thirty quid a week, and that is what she is left with after she has given her rent and her keep to Mum. I mean, she has to keep a tenner free for a Saturday night. You can't sit all night at The Bull and drink lemonade. You'd go barmy.

And she loves to get chips on the way home; they're a comfort after her fuck with Ginge.

She is paying three pounds fifty a week into the Club for last winter's boots, and already they've got a hole in the sole; even when new it was thinner than cardboard.

And then there's birthdays and stuff like the poll tax . . . and she might go with Sandra to see a film in the week. After all, you can't stay in and watch telly every night.

Fifteen thousand!

Bloody hell. What Brenda could do with fifteen thousand. All that money just to rent her body for nine months . . . no, seven. And she is pregnant anyway.

Brenda strips off her clothes and looks in the mirror in her little back bedroom, sideways on. She bends backwards, making her stomach stick out, but it is outclassed by her ribs. Someone has put a price on her body and this pale strip is no longer worthless, something to be jabbed at once a week by a man who stinks of fags and lager.

And Brenda has never liked ginger hair.

'Are you there, baby? Are you there?'

Mum has only ever wanted the best for Brenda. She thinks she has succeeded . . . she tried her hardest, but she couldn't give it.

But Brenda's child?

If Brenda's child could be Jessica's daughter, she would have everything a child could want, every single thing in the whole wide world.

It would never feel ashamed of its mother. It would learn about *style*.

There is nothing for Brenda to consider.

A burden has been lifted. The decision is easy: she will put herself and her child entirely in Jessica's capable hands.

But oh God. Oh God. If she can only do this thing without Mum finding out . . .

Chapter ten

'Rosita! I'm home!' And Jessica bustles downstairs with her bags of buyings.

'I know you are home, Miss Jessica, I heard the car.'

'And I'll be using the kitchen for the next twenty minutes or so. Rudi and I are in tonight and I want to prepare the salad.'

Yes, Rudi and Jessica are in and alone, giving her the ideal opportunity to test the surrogate idea. Jessica is nervous this evening. She thinks she has probably gone too far without Rudi's permission.

This is always annoying, the way she feels she has to ask Rosita before she can use her own cheese-grater, before she can squeeze her own juice. It is even more maddening when Rosita decides to sit in the chair beside the Aga and watch with her bold, black eyes, occasionally changing that curtain of knitting from under one arm to the other. What does Rosita ever make? She never seems to wear anything which slightly resembles that dry grey wool she's forever carting around like an extra limb. Damn it. Is it another endless shawl? It never seems to grow, or get any shorter . . .

How is Rudi going to react?

'What a rush,' exclaims Jessica, puffing away her silken hair, rolling up her sleeves, slipping on her pinny.

Rosita wouldn't know.

She'll tell him that Brenda is pretty.

Jessica remembers that it is a Monday. 'You've been out this afternoon, Rosita. Did it go well?'

'Very well, thank you, Miss Jessica,' and Rosita crosses one darkly stockinged leg over the other. Her slippers are pretty, though, made out of brocade, and silver.

Soon, when the weather gets warmer, Rosita will move her

chair outside and sit, not at the top of the steps, nor below the porch, which would be bad enough, but out there on the pavement. On a certain date, known only to herself, caused by the temperature, the moon, the returning of the birds or a built-in need to do so, she will abandon the warmth of the Aga and go with her knitting and her slippers and sit outside for the world to see, muttering and watching with her mass of black hair stuffed into a glittering snood on her head.

'Tell her she can't,' said Rudi, bored, when Jessica first came home and discovered her at it. 'She's got her own bit of garden, hasn't she?'

'That seems rather unkind. And I did mention it to her just now, but she said she couldn't see out from there.'

'Well, don't worry about it then.'

'But it just looks so odd.'

Several neighbours mentioned it, concerned, they said, about her safety. 'Well, the poor old thing can't see very well, can she, and sometimes when the dustcarts come along, or the road cleaners, it's worrying. What if she doesn't see them? She might come to some harm.'

Jessica wouldn't care very much if Rosita did come to some harm. It isn't the present that concerns her, but the future. What if Rosita lives beyond ten years which are covered by the codicil? Then she won't be so spry, and these little eccentricities of hers will become more marked, and she will lose her sight completely. What is Jessica supposed to do with her then?

'Put her in a home, of course,' said Rudi. 'You could always find somewhere pleasant – Catholic, naturally – or she might prefer to be shipped back to Spain. Have you asked her? What about her family?'

So Jessica tried.

'You know we love having you with us, Rosita, so it's not for that reason I am asking, and you mustn't for one moment think that it is – but if you ever feel you would rather go back to your homeland, for a holiday, or longer, you know I would be happy to continue to support you financially.'

Rosita spat.

Jessica was so shocked by the obscenity of the gesture, let

alone its violence, that she never felt she could refer to the subject again.

Now she says: 'One of these days, Rosita, you must bring some friends back for a cup of tea. You could sit out in the garden – get some strawberries. There must be some nice people at your sugar class.'

'I spoke to the woman next door today.'

Jessica jumps and scatters the nuts; they slip like mercury all over the white laminated table. 'Damn!'

'Yes, she was on her way to the Post Office, and I was on my way back indoors. She bade me good afternoon most politely. She has never spoken before and I must have passed her a hundred times.'

Jessica, grabbing frantically for slippery nuts, glances quickly over her shoulder and smiles. 'Well, that's nice for you.'

'I thought I might ask her inside one day.'

'This is your home as well as ours, Rosita. You are free to invite whoever you like. Of course you are.'

'Some wine was delivered earlier. For Mr Rudi, from the wine club. I put the bill on the spike.'

Rudi might have told her! As if they haven't enough wine. There soon will be nowhere to store it. 'Oh, good. Thank you, Rosita.'

'And I did out your bedroom this morning. Changed the sheets. Boiled them up. I've hung them out.'

'I have asked you before, Rosita, time and time again, actually, to use the drier. It doesn't look nice to have sheets hanging around in the garden. What if we decided to go and sit out there with our drinks this evening? Please use the drier. After all, that is what it is for.'

'It steams up the kitchen.'

'Well, it shouldn't. If there is something wrong with the machine, please call in the man. The numbers are all there on the pad. There is nothing difficult about it.'

Does the woman do this deliberately? Does Rosita, her father's lover, derive some kind of perverted enjoyment from goading Jessica . . . every time? Is she resentful because James

Galbraith Holden, the Pyramid Man, failed to leave her a direct gift in his will, after she left her native shores and followed him round the world like a dog?

Not only did he fail to provide for her, but James Galbraith left his Rosita dependent, to a great extend, on the good will of his daughter.

But the greatest betrayal of all is to die before one's partner.

'Sheets need fresh air.'

Aha, so there is nothing wrong with the drier. The woman is just being perverse again. But the last time Jessica suggested that Rosita might like to take things more easily, asking how would it be if she employed a girl to do the heavy work upstairs during the day, leaving Rosita completely free? – Rosita swore a terrible oath in Spanish, crossed her chest, and wouldn't say a word to Jessica or Rudi for a week.

It is often very hard to get through to, or to understand, the Rodriguez woman.

Rosita, with her secret angers, watches her exit.

Jessica's skirt is of such a length that she has difficulty getting upstairs if she is carrying something, and this evening she is carrying a bowl of olives in one hand and a tonic refill in the other. So she splays her feet like a duck to avoid treading on the expensive fabric . . . the only time in her whole life when Jessica moves in an uncoordinated fashion.

Even on the loo, and therefore completely safe and alone, she remains decently upright.

She wants to prepare the ground for Rudi, who is due home by seven-thirty after a game of squash at the club – and no doubt several drinks afterwards. He is twenty-eight years old, and yet Rudi, a free spirit, lives the protected life of a child, playing with his friends. Tonight Jessica does not have to collect him. He has, thoughtfully and unusually for him, arranged for a lift. So she's got the time for a bath and a soak and a gin, and she has popped the casserole into the oven. It is Egyptian lemon chicken – a favourite dish of her father's, according to Rosita. The meat has been marinating beautifully all day.

A whole evening in together has become a rare event; one to savour and one of which to make the most.

He smells of foreign nights. He moves like an animal, wild and free, with slightly flaring nostrils.

Jessica's mouth parts naturally. Her tongue comes out to cool her lips, like a whore posed in a window.

She always feels the same rush of passion when first she sees his face, his knowing grin, his lusty eyes, the glint of that gold earring. She marvels at the way he wears his clothes, silks and scarves and chains, jacket slung across his back any old how, but somehow settling there, just right.

And nothing cheap, of course. Certainly not those black leather trousers. His thighs might be lean and narrow but when it comes to the front, Linford Christie has nothing on Rudi.

She is wet already. Her nipples are hardening under her dress and she wants him. He greets her invasively by pushing his tongue in her mouth and a finger between her legs, claiming her inside and out. 'Guess who it is? Wow, lady, I shouldn't have left you.'

Jessica's voice is already dreamy as Rudi's finger probes on. She lets her long loose legs fall wide apart, despising this passionate obsession that turns the man into her lord and master, that makes her crave for the darkness, and bed, in order to come alive. 'Then why did you?'

'Never again. I swear. I swear.'

Does Jessica – intelligent, successful, sophisticated Jessica – ever wonder what would become of her stud if he really were the free spirit he insists he is . . . left to his own devices in a hard and lonely city?

Penniless and beholden to no one?

No, the possibility of a down-and-out Rudi, his wares dependent on market forces at stage doors and hotel foyers, does not occur to Jessica. He would be snapped up by one of her friends the moment he appeared at a party without her.

And he would be just as happy without her.

He is exotic like a hummingbird, and too divine to be trusted.

As he sits down with his drink beside her he tells her proudly about an audition that went well today. It was at a small alternative theatre, and 'not a waiter this time, but a gondolier.'

'Maybe your rowing will come in handy.'

And Rudi stares at her for a minute, without blinking.

Rudi lights the candles and draws the curtains.

Jessica presses the bell on the floor beside her dining-room chair.

The dumbwaiter rises with a grinding reluctance, as Rosita winds the Egyptian lemon chicken, steaming hot, with the salad beside it, up from the basement.

Can she smell garlic? Jessica is sure she did not use any. Can it be that Rosita has tampered with the dish – or has some of her strong, natural smell wafted up on the wind with the dinner?

Now is the time to tell him, as they sit either side of their table of glass. Jessica is good at adding embellishment to plain facts. It is her job . . . she does it every time she designs a new catalogue, and there is no Honesty Clause here which holds her responsible for describing the goods, i.e. Brenda, as *badly distressed*.

'To you,' says Rudi, as he always does, viewing her sexily over his crystal glass.

'To us,' replies Jessica, as she always does, moving her lips in a silky, slippery, sensuous smile.

She broaches the subject mildly as she picks up her gleaming silver knife. 'Rudi, I was thinking about exactly that today – about us. About turning the two of us into the three of us . . . about the reproductive process which has so far failed to produce the results.'

Rudi eats on, ravenous and cheerful to the very last mouthful.

Rudi is smiling. The object of Jessica's worship smiles a mischievous smile and his black pupils glitter. Is Jessica serious?

'But why her? Why this particular girl? And how did the subject come up?'

Jessica proceeds to lie through her teeth. 'Because I feel sorry for Brenda. Because I like her. Because she is bright enough to see a chance and to grab it. And the subject came up perfectly naturally, when Brenda asked me if I knew anywhere she could advertise her services.'

'Sounds like a pretty mercenary type of character to me.'

'Not mercenary at all. Practical. The girl has nothing else to sell, only her body. I talked to her for a long time, pointing out all the problems that are bound to occur when sailing in these kinds of murky waters. And then she came straight out and asked me if I knew anyone . . .'

'She was taking a bit of a chance, wasn't she? After all, it is illegal.'

Jessica's fork twitches in her hand, but Rudi does not notice. *Kith and kin*. By offering Rudi fatherhood she is giving him the chance to defy his own mortality; at £15,000, it is cheap at the price. 'Brenda trusts me, Rudi – and I trust her, that's the important factor. Anyway, I just thought I'd mention it. I told her I'd have a word with you, but that I doubted you would be interested.'

'And what's to stop a girl like that deciding to keep the baby?'

'Nothing. Absolutely nothing. Except that Brenda is in no financial position to bring up a baby *and* keep her job, and the girl is very ambitious . . .'

'She must be. She must be as hard as nails. And what does this say about us, callously using a person as if she was a machine?'

'It is not Brenda I am recommending, Rudi,' says Jessica shortly. 'It is her womb. And with a little money of her own, Brenda would no longer need to be anyone's machine. That is precisely the point.'

But Jessica is exceedingly satisfied with Rudi's mild reaction. It is a huge step in the right direction.

'Pudding!' calls Rosita as the chains being to rattle.

Rudi pours his lover a second glass of wine and, by the look in his eyes, she might well feel a twinge of cystitis after tonight.

But Jessica's thoughts are not on that now; they are already directed towards the future and all the horrors of the first meeting.

What has she let herself in for?

OH MY GOD.

Chapter eleven

Soon it will be possible only to see the brightest stars. Because of pollution, only the most brilliant will be visible from the city, and the rest of the pale night sky will appear to be empty. For Brenda, sleeping there down among the skyscrapers and chimneys, there is only one star – Jessica. The pollution of misery has obscured everything else from sight. It is Monday night and there she lies, curled up and engulfed in her soft pink candlewick with her thumb in her mouth. Like a babe in a womb she sleeps.

With only the lav between the two bedrooms, next door to their pregnant daughter Derek and Rita lie with their two bums touching, brushed nylon cheeks against polyester, curled and facing outwards towards the edge of the bed. The mattress dips heavily on Rita's side, creating quite a dangerous slope.

Rita sleeps easy. She thought Brenda seemed a bit brighter tonight. It didn't seem worth making a fuss about, and anyway, when it came to the crunch she was far too tired.

From his elevated position under the window Derek snores heavily on, and his jaw hangs slackly open. It does not seem to matter to him that he slept for two hours this afternoon, in the break between athletics and darts. Derek would dearly love to buy a satellite dish so he could tune to the sports channel from after breakfast until supper-time, eating cheddar slices between thickly buttered cream crackers, and maybe Shane would turn up with a six-pack. But he wouldn't be allowed to get away with that. As soon as Rita gets home there is *Neighbours*, and after that a steady stream . . . *Eldorado, Coronation Street, Brookside, This Is Your Life.*

He rubbed Rita's feet for her tonight before she got into bed, with some new cream she had discovered in Boots – a quarter of the price of the massage lotion which Jessica gets from the Body Shop.

'Oooh, God, Derek. Don't stop, don't bloody stop, this is heavenly bliss.'

And a vague memory of distant days when he could inspire Rita to these euphoric utterances by stroking her breasts, or her inner thighs, gives him a faint erection.

It never mattered to Derek that Rita was large. He enjoyed the feeling of being diminished in bed, overwhelmed by wobbling female flesh. Well, you got the best of everything in those days . . . everything, and at least twenty per cent more.

Rita spied the stirring of the male member within his pyjama bottoms. 'That's enough now, Derek,' she said, withdrawing her hefty bunioned foot. 'I am tired if you're not and I want to go to sleep. It is Monday, not Saturday. Some people have to get up in the morning, even if you don't.'

The voluptuous Doreen, in her ivory chiffon across the corridor, wishes she had stayed at her fiancé Nigel's place. Her face glistens with cream and the flesh of her shoulders shines pink in the bedside light, as she props herself up on her pillows and lights an insomniac cigarette.

They are allowed to sleep together at Nigel's. His mum accepts as natural the fact that an engaged couple might want to share a bed, whereas Rita would go purple in the face with fury. Even if they hold hands in the sitting room, Rita is likely to nudge her daughter and say. 'There's a time and a place, Doreen, and Shane is trying to eat his tea.'

'I'm sorry! I'm so very, very sorry if me and Nigel holding hands is making people around here feel sick.'

'And there's no need to take that cheeky sodding attitude. There's such a thing as making yourself too bloody available, you know. In my day we managed to keep our feelings to ourselves.'

'In your day, hah! Don't make me laugh! We all know what went on in your day – all those parties and love-ins and mucky little affairs in bedsitters with the ironing board always up and trains shunting by outside. Free love . . . that's what went on in your day, Mum, and you can't deny it.'

'What sort of talk is that?' Rita retaliated promptly. 'I can and I will deny it, Doreen. Your father and I managed not to fart-arse about so sloppy, so I don't see why it has to be any different for you!'

Derek lit a cigarette and turned away.

'Holding hands is a long way from screwing, Mum! And how come Shane was born only two months after you and Dad got married?'

'You dirty little sod! The wedding was postponed because your father was ill, as you very well know . . .'

'Well then, so don't come preaching to me then.'

'Shut your mouth and get up off your arse and sort out those ashtrays and those dirty cups. Don't think you can go out there and stand for hours snogging on the step with Nigel and leave all this mess to me, like you did last night.'

Doreen, sulking, stared at the varicose veins behind Mum's massive legs. She hated herself for feeling distaste for her own mother. Doreen was afraid of what she saw. Tiredness and exhaustion were printed all over Mum's legs and on her feet, while her face remained virtually unlined, like a blank piece of paper, and her hair showed little grey.

Mum is angry about lots of things, not the boring shit she goes on and on about. That's just her way of letting off steam. No, Mum is angry about the way she did everything she thought she should, but nobody else played by the rules and so Mum found herself running on but with nobody else beside her.

Like a fool, carrying the old egg and spoon.

Mum never cries like other women.

She is too big to cry.

But Mum cannot bear to see the pebble-dash house in which she has always taken such pride, being submerged by the slums into which her neighbours have turned their own houses. Dogs crapping all over. Snotty-nosed kids. Broken chrome and rusty old bits of galvanised. Johnnies on the grass where the flowers used to be. She cannot stand to see Dad out of work, and Shane, Eddie and Roy hanging around the place with no future. She sent them to school, didn't she? She scrimped and scraped so they went on all the outings and enjoyed all the extras on offer. She sees it all as chaos, over which she has no control. Mum hates the fact that she has to get up every morning, knot her scarf under her chin and set off on her bike for Woolworths . . .

And then there's Gran. 'It's time you went over to see her, Doreen. She always asks about you. When's the last time you went round there? I don't think you've ever taken Nigel.'

'Mum, when do I have the time?'

'Nonsense! You've the time to sit on that sofa making moon eyes at him all evening.'

Gran is so embarrassing. Bloody hell, how could Doreen take Nigel there?

But Mum is proud of Brenda. Maybe Doreen should take some exams and try to get into nursing . . . Sod it. Doreen shuts her eyes.

Doreen thinks about Nigel and lets her legs fall open. She slides her hands down over her breasts, over her belly and down, down under the covers where it is warm and wet. She parts the lips of her fanny with her sticky little fingers. She wishes Nigel could give her the feelings that she can give to herself, but even so, she still wishes that she had gone back to his place.

At last Doreen sleeps.

A pinbeam of torchlight. The flip-flap of bedroom slippers shuffling across bare wooden boards. The short gasps of an elderly woman catching her breath on the stairs, and the brief little sentences of someone who is used to living completely alone, and who knows when and how to break the silence.

'Always the same time . . . more or less.' A few more stairs, then: 'By, it takes some doing getting up here.'

A pause, while Vera leans frailly on the banister and peers all the way down to the bottom towards the little pool of light in the vast vacuum of black.

'And that rug could do with a bit of a clean. I'll ask Rita to take it in next time Roy's got his van.'

It is a shame that Rita didn't move in when she married. She was given the chance – but there, every woman needs a home of her own. Vera could do with her daughter here now, though.

She feels like a mole snuffling around in the dark.

Vera might live in one room but it is important for Mullins Holdings to know that she is still able to patrol this house, day and night if necessary, and that she is quite prepared to call the police if she hears a strange sound or suspects something untoward is going on.

She creeps into every single room and shines the torch into every cobwebbed corner, making sure that the beam can be seen from the window by anyone prowling around with dubious intentions outside.

The Mullins' men have been known to sit and watch in their vans.

Before she started her regular patrols, nights used to take so long to pass. Sleep became impossible. By dawn she was a wreck, feeling every year of her age. She used to lie there in her chair with her eyes screwed tight, imagining she could hear whispers and footsteps, patterings that never stopped and even demonic laughter, just as she used to do as a child when left in the dark by herself. Nightmares. The dread ramblings of terrible fear.

Eventually, unable to stand the tension any longer, she started to phone the police.

'It is the Mullins' men again.'

'What's that, missus?'

'Mullins sodding Holdings.' Vera was almost too weary to explain. Already she imagined she saw four policemen, not two, wavering in front of her tired eyes. 'The company which owns this house, and which used to own most of the houses around here. They're all sold off but this one, and the buggers are after hounding me out.'

'Well, lady, Bert's been round the whole house, peered into every nook and cranny, haven't you, Bert – and there's no sign of anyone been breaking in here.'

Sod Bert. He looked like a Muppet, one of those old men who watches from the balcony.

'But I heard them, officer. The buggers woke me up.'

'Listen to me, my darling. I doubt that Mr Mullins would risk sending his bully boys into an old woman's house at night, no matter how eager he was to get rid of her.'

'You don't know them like I do.'

And she told the enormous officer all about the drains and the electric and the dog's mess through the letterbox and the water down the chimney and the broken front window. He thought she was senile; he thought she had that – what d'you call it? – Altzimers or something. She could tell that's what he thought by the way he spoke to her, by the way he casually pulled open her drawers and generally wandered around the room picking up private things and examining them. He ignored the teeth in the glass by the basin. He read the notes she wrote to herself that were stacked behind the Scottie dog on the mantelpiece. He sniffed and pretended to search for the source of the smell.

'Kids, probably, my love.'

She spoke to him too clearly, trying too hard to be believed, like a piss-head pretending to be sober. Humiliations like this happen when you're old. If you're over sixty they think you are batty. 'Officer, if I was living on the Pennystone Estate, where my daughter Rita lives, yes, I would agree with you, it would probably be kids. But here in Lippington Road there are no children who go round behaving like that . . .'

'Kids from outside the area then.'

Vera adjusted the hair-grip that had escaped the net and fallen over her face. She pushed it back under the weary nylon. 'Kids my arse. No, officer, not with the Neighbourhood Watch scheme, and all the houses full of valuables being fitted up with alarms. It's never worth them coming here.'

They thought she was wasting police time. 'Is this where you sleep, Mrs . . . er . . .'

'Evans. Yes, officer, the whole floor has become too much for me now. Cleaning and heating and such.'

'It could well be, you know, Mrs . . .'

'Evans.'

'It could well be, darling, that you'd be a damn sight better off moving out of these draughty premises and into somewhere more suitable for a body your age.'

'There is nothing wrong with these sodding houses. They were built to last. The insides might be crumbling but the walls and foundations are steady as rocks, and even the roof is still sound – not like the houses they build these days, flimsy as a pissing pack of cards. Surely, officer, to remain in my own home or not is my choice.'

'Not if you're going to spend every blooming night wide awake and listening to every sound, it isn't. Getting yourself all worked up at your age.'

'What about squatters? My daughter says there's always a danger from squatters, people who'd think nothing of slitting an old woman's throat.' Vera was very aware that her eyes looked hollow and staring.

The officer sniffed again, and registered distaste. She could have told him it wasn't her, it was the cats. 'There is no sign of anyone else's presence, recent or past, in this house, my darling, save for your own.'

Vera called the police out several times after that but their response was always disappointingly the same. 'You imagined it, darling. There is nobody here.' And they talked above her head and said it was a shame.

Rita says the Chief Inspector is probably a member of the same Masonic Lodge as Mullins. 'You tell 'em, Ma. You tell 'em where to shove their bloody police force.'

Anger gave Vera purpose and strength. Next time, she wouldn't bother with the police who so obviously did not believe her. She would get up, face her fear, and check the house for herself.

She is still frightened sometimes, but nothing like she used to be. She struggles on through the darkened house, her nerves quivering so much you'd think you could see them there, pulsating beneath the surface of her skin.

It is the act of searching; it is this ritual which wards off the fear much better than that old, helpless battle with the shadows. And over the years she gradually came to realise how much she now looks forward to the various excitements of the night – fear and all. Waiting for the night is almost like waiting for death.

SLAM! BANG! THUMP! THUMP!

Knock knock knock.

'Oh shut up, you silly old cow!' shrieks Rudi, thrusting near to bursting.

Rudi struggles on, and comes, and slides out all over the crisp clean sheets, and it is Jessica who is left cursing in her silent, burning frustration.

'We are going to *have* to move rooms. Rudi, don't shout at her like that. She and Rosita are making friends.'

'So – is that my responsibility? That dotty old pair of crones chum up and I'm supposed to put up with this sort of crass behaviour! SHUT UP, YOU SILLY OLD BITCH. DO YOU NEVER SLEEP?'

'Rudi, you are wasting your breath. She can't possibly hear you.'

'How do you know?'

'Because the walls are too thick.'

'So how does she hear the bed?'

'Because that makes quite a different sound. It's not worth worrying about. She will be gone soon.'

'We have been saying that for two years.'

'She is worse than she was.'

'How do you know?'

'Because I see her, sometimes. Doddering by.' And as Rudi clicks on the light and pads in his advertising manner towards the bathroom, Jessica catches sight of her own reflection in the mirror, young and beautiful with her overheated naked body stretched across the pure white counterpane. She, who has never feigned pleasure in her life in order to please a man, lies and thinks how her present happiness is conditioned by Rudi and how, without him, she too would grow wrinkled and wraith-like and shuffle backwards and forwards to the Post Office, unloved, frightened, and ugly.

Perhaps Vera Evans was once in love, and lay on white sheets in the house next door waiting to be made beautiful by the coalman.

A thousand years and seven children ago.

And finally, everyone sleeps. Including the black-haired Rosita, who in her young days made men's eyes pop out of their heads as she belly-danced for James Galbraith under the fabulous awnings and among the sumptuous cushions of a bell-shaped desert tent.

Rosita Rodriguez, the sultry woman in the basement, who knows all there is to know about fantasies and dreams.

Chapter twelve

In some ways, while Jessica's efficiency is admirable, it is also frightening. She never makes mistakes, never hits out at a wasp and spills her cup of tea doing it, never waves at anyone she does not know, never puts the wrong date on her cheques and never tunes in to the wrong station on the radio and listens for half an hour to the wrong programme before realising what she has done.

Jessica single-mindedly concentrates on what she is doing, and that is how she developed her expertise and was given the powerful job she loves in the respectable firm of Jackson Willow & Sons.

She is also beautiful, charming, and has a persuasive way about her – which is how she manages to get Brenda in at Bryan's at ten-thirty on the following Tuesday morning, 'for the whole treatment. Everything. No expense spared please, Bryan. And I leave the decisions entirely in your hands. Don't take any notice of anything Brenda says. Darling, she hasn't a clue.'

To the bewildered Brenda she says, 'You are ill – you are anaemic. Take the day off, go straight to Bryan's and I'll meet you for lunch at Marti's.'

'It is tonight, isn't it?'

'Yes, Brenda, I have arranged that you meet Rudi for the first time tonight.'

'What did he say?'

'Not a lot. If anything, he was rather amused. Now, you are absolutely certain that you are not going to change your mind about this, aren't you? I have stuck my neck out on your account and I don't expect to be let down.'

She might have said she had a great deal riding on Brenda, but that would have been too loaded and literal, given the unusual circumstances.

Brenda would not dream of letting Jessica down. Apart from anything else, she is in no position to let Jessica down.

Brenda would rather have a dog than a baby, not one like Jessica's Hiame but a wonderful black Alsatian which would sleep on a beanbag in her bedroom. Mum won't hear of it, though. Rita's got a thing about dogs, as a result of living on the Pennystone Estate where dogs have started running in packs. She throws stones at them when they crawl under the wire and come snuffling into the garden.

'Somewhere we are unlikely to be seen by anyone we know,' Jessica said to Rudi easily over breakfast, laid out by Rosita who is used to rising early. 'One of those grotesque pubs with a red carpet and a jukebox, or how about a motel?'

The smell of burnt toast rises with the dumbwaiter, overwhelming the freshly perked coffee. This morning, despite her night of enjoyable dreaming, Rosita will not be in a happy mood.

Rudi breakfasts in a silk Chinese dressing gown Jessica brought back from Shanghai last time she visited. This morning it is warm enough for the French windows to be opened and the birds peck for crumbs on the patio outside. A general rising of spirits greets this pleasant sign of spring which lightens the way for Jessica's campaign. Rudi is remarkably forthcoming, with only the one grudging comment, 'I am not taking part in any clandestine meeting in any dingy motel. Discretion might well be the watchword, but there has to be a limit.'

They decided on The Painted Lady, a Victorian pub on a corner, a rep's pub, which is near enough so that Rudi can walk there and Jessica will run Brenda round there in the car after work. None of their friends would be seen dead inside The Painted Lady.

They mulled over the matter in bed last night, after Rudi was flaccid and spent and while Jessica was still uncomfortably excited. Normally, at this point in time Jessica would demand release but, single-minded as usual, last night she directed that erotic energy towards a higher purpose.

Rudi nuzzled her breasts and made himself appealing. 'But how would you feel, Jessica, about a baby, that wasn't yours, that was nothing to do with you? A child conceived between me and a stranger?'

You could tell he was excited. Excited to be granted permission to screw with somebody else, by Jessica. One of the thousands of fantasies he never thought would turn into reality. Perhaps she will watch . . .

But wait till he sees Brenda.

Jessica, knowing full well what lay behind his initial interest, stretched out on her back with her arms behind her head, sleepy and warm. 'Rudi, if you remember, I was the one keen to adopt. I would have been happy with a child conceived by two strangers. At least, this way the child will be yours. It will look like you. It will think like you.' And Jessica almost convinces herself that Rudi's genes will be there to overpower the pale, weedy genes of Brenda.

Jessica knows full well that Rudi will only have to see his child, to be forever besotted. Sometimes she finds his fascination with children embarrassing. *The family*. He will stop in the street to admire a baby, he will coo into a stranger's pram. She has to drag him away. Whereas other people's children and dogs leave Jessica cold.

Jessica would rather forget the brief visit they paid to the dry woods and brilliantly russet hillsides of Rudi's peasant home. Sitting in the crumbling kitchen with his brothers and his mother – Mama Shapiro with her voice rich and husky and her foul-smelling cheroots – drinking purple wine, Rudi looked like any other Italian peasant with dark eyes and a flashing white smile. Grandmother, Grandfather – toothless. Aunts, cousins, nieces and nephews. And the children crawled over him. Whose children? Anyone's, or so it seemed. Barefooted children. Ragged children. They gathered in horrifying clusters like burrs to watch Jessica get into her convertible Saab, their fingers in their mouths and apprehension on their faces, as if they were waiting for her to throw them some money. Crucifixes were everywhere, and little grottoes, and swarms of biting flies. And the hot-blooded men in the towns grabbed at Jessica's breasts and her buttocks and muttered, 'Fuckee fuckee.' Ugh!

A smitten lady, in those days, in that first flush of joy, she overlooked it – the sagging double bed, the dirt floor, and the chickens in the kitchen.

'I thought your family were aristocrats?'

'We were, years ago,' said Rudi cheerfully. 'I told you to pack something simple.'

But it was good to get him back home to London.

Does he send his family money? Money which Jessica gives him? Poor Jessica. Under the circumstances, how can she ask him?

Today Rudi has another audition at the makeshift theatre in Hackney, after which he will play squash, lunch with some friends, then spend the afternoon having some new photographs taken for his portfolio.

This morning, annoyingly, on her way to work Jessica snapped the heel off her shoe and wondered, briefly, if this was an omen. She dismissed her own silliness and hobbled upstairs, relieved to see Brenda in her seat and already typing.

Thank heavens that Jessica's office is certainly not open-plan. Jackson Willow & Sons will have none of that; they operate as they have always operated, with their offices resembling suites of rooms in an hotel. There is Jessica's large and impressive office, and there is the anteroom outside where Brenda sits. The pair are completely cut off from the rest of the world when that door is closed behind them, and no one need have much to do with anyone else in the building – which is how it should be.

Thus the whole business can remain conveniently private.

Brenda had obviously been waiting for her arrival, because as soon as she saw Jessica she got up and trailed miserably into the office after her. She still had that wretched stain on her blouse.

'Anything happen last night?' asked Jessica immediately.

'No,' said Brenda sadly, her pale eyes fixed hopefully upon

Jessica. 'Nothing. The pregnancy test must have been right. It's six weeks now since my last period.'

'But we forget that fact, Brenda, don't we? From now on we put that insignificant matter out of our thoughts, and we say, instead, that you had your last period just two weeks ago. You are now at your most fertile and therefore not a minute must be wasted.'

And what we now have to achieve is the small matter of making you enticing.

First things first.

Jessica might not be able to perform miracles herself, but she knows a man who can.

So Jessica telephoned Bryan.

The sallow Brenda Hodges, dazed by the suddenness of events, lies on a table with a towel covering her private parts and submits to such an intensely personal massage that it is more sensual than anything she has ever done with Ginge.

She screams out loud when her legs are waxed, never having endured anything so painful in all her life. 'Don't do any more! Please! Please stop!'

'Soon be over,' say the stuckup women in their white overalls.

But when they move under her arms she sits there sobbing like a child. She wants to run away but dare not. To endure the pain is better than to face Jessica's wrath, and Jessica has already pointed out that this treatment is costing her an arm and a leg.

This is like nothing what Doreen ever does with her lotions and her gells and her tubes of hair-remover that stink out the house with the smell of burning.

Brenda's hair has been treated, coloured and permed in a 'spiral style', so it will hang like an electrified mop when it is dry – like an old English sheepdog. 'The whole area needs enlarging,' said Bryan, standing back like an artist at a canvas and ruthlessly ruffling Brenda's limp, dejected, shoulder-length bob. 'The head itself is too small. It carries no drama,' he said, with a pained expression.

Rita would say it was small and therefore 'beautifully

proportioned', but Rita is not here to see what they are doing to her daughter and Rita is not being asked for her views. This time the professional will have his way. But for the present, the effects cannot be judged because they are pushed up under a towel.

The steam is painful and so is the squeezing of Brenda's blackheads; her heart is thumping, but the facial massage is wonderful, and almost puts Brenda to sleep. She gives herself up to it completely and begins to think that this is better than another boring morning at the office.

Brenda is given a reviving cup of tea. She slips in a fag, although the sign says No Smoking, and Jessica goes on and on about the fact that now that she's pregnant, Brenda really ought to give up.

Then there's the manicure and the pedicure and all around her the beautiful ladies, like magazine people, are coming and going – and why do they bother to spend the morning suffering in here, when they already look like that? Beautiful people, not like Brenda.

'Ready for the make-up now, dear? It's time to put your clothes back on again. Are these things really yours?'

With her heart in her mouth Brenda knows that Jessica is going to be badly disappointed.

By one o'clock, they have done all they can. In glorious isolation Brenda sits in the pink boudoir chair in the foyer hardly daring to move, waiting, like a parcel with a rumbling stomach, to be picked up by Jessica.

Brenda rehearses her excuses. 'Mum, I had to go to a meeting with Jessica, so I had to get myself smartened up. The company paid for me to have my hair done, and for the new clothes . . .'

Normally Mum can see through her lies.

She peers out from under her fringe and she's never had a fringe before. It is the colour of the burnished warming pan that hangs in the chimney at The Bull. What *is* Mum going to say about this? What would Ginge do? If he noticed at all, Ginge would probably laugh. Even her eyebrows have been plucked. She thinks she looks like a little doll. Brenda's hands are clasped together in misery.

But, 'That's much better,' says Jessica, writing out an enormous cheque. 'You are quite an eligible young woman now! The different tones in the make-up have even brought out some kind of bone structure in your face – clever. At least you've got decent teeth. I hope you watched how they did it. Now it's just the clothes. Perhaps we'd better avoid the support bras and go for the boyish look instead.'

'We want a sweater that's going to bring out the colour of your eyes.' Jessica bends and peers at Brenda. 'What colour are they, dear?'

'Grey.'

'Grey eyes? Ah, that is interesting. Then we ought to settle for blue, something terribly striking – a shirt and leggings and boots. You are much too short to look good in a skirt. And let's have a look at that little jacket in the window.'

That jacket in the window costs more than Brenda earns in a month.

So it's a grey shirt, a denim-blue sweater, black leggings, pink boots . . . almost Doc Martins but not quite. And the jacket's kind of soft leather with silver buckles.

Brenda looks like a pop star.

She swallows and stares at herself in the mirror. Gone is the sallow skin. Gone is the grease from her lanky hair. Gone is the shine on the nose and gone are the dark shadows round her eyes. She stands up straight to look at herself – gone is the hump.

The last time she believed herself to be beautiful, like this, was when she was given her First Communion dress. She wanted to wear it all the time and cried when they made her take it off – and that was a castoff of Doreen's.

'Jessica, will I be able to keep these?'

'Well, they're certainly no good to me!'

Gaining confidence with every minute, Brenda says, 'You must be awfully rich.'

'Not really.'

Brenda gives a happy sigh. *Oh thank you, Baby, thank you.*

'And a bag – oh God, put that evil black thing down. We'll have a rucksack,' says Jessica, money no object. 'I think I prefer the tartan.' God only knows what Brenda will put inside it – apart from her fags and her matches, of course. The girl must be made to stop that habit.

The underwear and the night-things can be sorted out tomorrow, if Brenda passes the test and raises Rudi's expectations. No point in splashing out unnecessarily.

The final result is gratifying, bearing in mind the poor quality of the basic material, ignoring the fidgeting hands. The girl looks pretty, alluring in a naïve sort of way, frailly elegant.

Although Brenda lacks style. Rudi will discover, too late, that his little princess is a toad.

Is Jessica jealous of her own creation? Can she still bear to think of Brenda with Rudi, bed companions?

Well, it isn't too bad because the girl is merely a child, size 10, young and bony as a barrow boy and therefore no contest for the rounded, size 16, big-breasted Jessica.

Unless, of course, Rudi has kinky leanings about which Jessica does not know.

Chapter thirteen

Four o'clock.

Tea-time for some.

Tea-time for ladies in country houses as the trolley is wheeled in bearing cakes and sandwiches.

Tea-time for the factory-workers, called to the canteen by whistle.

Tea-time for the roadmen, brewing up in their little red huts and opening tins of delicious condensed milk.

Doesn't it get up your nose the way some people brag about their kids? I mean, you ask them how they are and they reply with rolling eyes and a sigh of disparagement, 'Oh, fine. Mark is travelling somewhere in Turkey, Suzie's gone skiing again with the school and Frances is loving it at Essex.'

Bloody hell. They sound so fed up with it all but nobody's fooled. Their attitude is their defence against jealousy because they believe that your kids are nothing but hopeless failures.

Rita's sister-in-law Jane writes like that from Stevenage. And she talks like that when they meet . . . which is rarely, if Rita gets her way. When she talks about her children she has that special malignant gleam in her eye. You wouldn't think Jane and Tim have any life of their own. They never say so. It's just the kids, the kids, the pissing kids.

'My kids are of the boomerang generation,' Rita tells Dil, in the afternoon tea break, in the storeroom out the back, after easing off her shoes and taking the weight off her grumbling feet. She spreads her toes and rests them on the cool linoleum. Already she is dreading the painful journey home.

'What's that then, Rite?' Dilys leans forward to see through the boxes, catching her ash in her hand.

'You know, first there was the boom, and now there's the

boomerang – those kids who have come back home because there aren't any jobs and they can't get houses. Boomerang, see. That's what they're calling them now.'

'Well, maybe they'll boomerang out again once the upturn comes.'

'Upturn my arse.'

'Your girls are working, Rite. Those girls of yours do you proud, not like some I could mention.'

'You ought to see some of them round about us – hard-faced little tarts. And no older than thirteen, some of 'em.'

'You must see life in the raw down your way.'

'It didn't used to be like that, Dil, not when Derek and I first moved. It was lovely in those days – brand-new, clean. There were shops. A health clinic. There's nothing there now, though. All been boarded up. Now you've got to walk two miles to get to the doctor's.'

'It's got one hell of a bad name.'

'And I think the fact that they live there goes against the boys when they apply for work.'

'Very probably.'

'Brenda's done well for herself, though.' Rita rubs her bunion and clenches her teeth round the pain. 'That was her earlier on, ringing from some posh hairdresser's. She's working late tonight, some meeting with her boss, and they've given her the day off to go and get herself all dolled up. I'm longing to see what they've done to her.'

'You ought to do something about those feet, Rite. They've never been right, not since I've known you. They must think very well of her, to go and spend money on her like that.'

'Oh they do, Dil, they do. She's a personal secretary already, you know. And of course, they're a good firm to work for. Safe. Respectable. Well thought of. I only wish Doreen would take a leaf out of Brenda's book and go and get some exams herself, as an insurance against the future. I'm always telling her. Although she's got herself a very nice boy, Nigel.'

'They go their own ways these days.'

'I hope you feel strong,' says Rita.

'Why's that?'

'Because old Baldy over there wants us to spend the rest of the afternoon stacking these sodding boxes.'

And Dilys pours Rita a second cup of tea and gets out the biscuits.

Six o'clock . . .

Tea-time for some.

Tea-time for the kids getting home from school.

Tea-time and the last watery meal of the day for the patients in Princess Alexandra's.

Tea-time, and it's burgers and chips and bread and butter for the long-distance drivers passing the Bluebird Café.

Exhausted, and in some pain as usual, Rita pedals her way home with the shopping in the basket on the handlebars making the steering heavy. She has to watch out for her flapping trousers in the bicycle chain. She could really do with a pair of clips.

Worry worry worry. If she had time she would go and see Ma – but she hasn't. Never mind, she looked well enough last Thursday, sounded a little less confused. Perhaps Rita should be encouraging Vera to move. It would make life much easier if she knew that Ma was safely tucked away in Hooper's Tower, unable to escape. It is nice inside, apparently. Maybe she ought to take Ma and go and have a look.

Doreen will be upstairs getting herself dolled up for Nigel, although why she uses so much make-up and stiffens her hair like that Rita will never know. The girl looks far more appealing left natural, fresh from the bath and smelling of roses with her hair hanging loose. But when she thinks about what she used to do with her own hair, backcombed so high and lacquered so stiff she couldn't even force the end of a comb in, Rita smiles. A bird's nest. And those mini-skirts! And those flares!

All that effort, and it didn't make Rita look much better; it didn't improve Rita's chances, did it?

A bad girl – that is what Big Rita was, and Ma never knew.

Nobody knows the half of it, not even Derek.

Has Rita passed those genes down to any of her children?

And can behaviour be caused by genes . . . or was it more to do with the struggle to find a man?
Any man.

Rita pedals grimly on, pondering disagreeable matters.
Rita had truly believed that a husband and children meant a lifetime of perfect happiness. That is what the stories said in all the magazines. And the songs. And the films. And the fairy tales. And Ma. And isn't it reasonable to risk life and soul, to do everything in your power to achieve perfect happiness, to find the gold at the end of the rainbow?
Rita's was a fight against nature. The cards were stacked against her. Oh, to have been born a dainty, feminine woman.
Rita was wanton. Rita was anyone's and it paid off in the end.
At least when she caught her man – a small man, and kind – it meant she could stop trying. And Derek had never expected to marry a virgin.

Turning wobblily into the estate, as always, the first sight hurts her. Nobody knows how much it hurts her, so bleak in its desolation. The council have not even bothered to fill the potholes in the road, and no one collects the litter any more. It is left to lie and be blown in ever-growing piles against the chainlink fences and the walls. When it is windy, walking through the Pennystone Estate is like walking through Epping Forest in the autumn, with gentle leaves of newspaper and empty, battered cans. Despair comes swirling beneath your feet, along with the discarded bogrolls.
The evil dogs come sniffing. 'Sod off, you wicked buggers!' shouts Rita, kicking dangerously and wobbling badly.
As Rita turns down her own road she sees a group of kiddies, none of them older than twelve, forcing the shutters of a boarded-up house. This time she cannot look away. Something in her rebels so strongly that nausea rises in her throat.
She gets off her bike and props it up against the gate, ready to defend whatever it is she believes in.
Does she still believe in anything?

Big bad Rita.
But her hands are shaking.
To stop them, she places them firmly on her hips and she moves towards the vandals, determined.
'You pissing little bleeders, why the fuck d'you have to shit on your own doorsteps? Get off! Get off, you little bastards, and find something better to do with yourselves!' And Rita raises her fist and shakes it.
Two men stand watching on the corner.
The ragged group of round about ten kiddies stop dead, still clutching their bricks and their stones.
'Get off out of here, you little buggers. Haven't you got any homes to go to?'
Two of them, both girls though you'd be hard put to prove it, start giggling.
'You great fat slug, why don't you mind your own fucking business?'
Gobsmacked, Rita stands facing them, gawping.
'This your house then? This got something to do with you?'
And Rita says, 'No, it is not my house but—'
'Piss off then, dog breath.' And the boy with the baby face and the crewcut, the one in the red anorak, throws down his brick defiantly.
They stare on, unashamed. Fearless. And Rita tastes the corrosive hatred directed straight towards her and it's like sucking on a nail.
She tries to reason, as she would with her own. 'I have lived here nearly all my life—'
'Well good on you, arsehole.' The boy's eyes shine with a deadly look, a deadly kind of monotonous contempt.
'You little sods.'
Out of the corner of her eye Rita senses the first brick being thrown and stands back quick as lightning, only to avoid it by an inch.
She rounds on the angel-faced kid who looks stupefied, only just roused from his bed. Is he on glue? 'Don't you bloody well try that sort of trick again with me!'
And another brick comes from the opposite direction and lands with a thump in the dust at Rita's feet.

'Just let one of these bricks touch me and I'll fetch the law here so bloody fast—'

'Don't make me laugh, lady.'

Rita's fury boils and heaves, a stew of accumulated bitterness that has bubbled inside her for so many years. 'I shall find out where every one of you lot live, so help me, and I'll be over to see your Mum and Dad and see what they'll say when they know what you have been up to!'

Most of the kids are smiling – vicious smiles, quiet smiles. Their eyes meet hers and she feels her heart thumping, no longer able to speak or to move away. She shouldn't have interfered. Look, she is trembling from the strain. She should have ridden on home and turned a blind eye like everyone else. For the very first time she senses the danger.

The one who is smoking does not move, but blows smoke rings into the air – the aggressive, simmering air – while he watches her out of loaded, half-closed eyes.

There's a smash behind her as a brick slams into her bike. Her precious machine slides down the wall like a man dying with a rattling sound, and her shopping tips out of the basket. Another brick lands as she watches.

This is intolerable! 'I swear I'll bloody well kill you!' she bawls, and she lumbers towards them, blind with fury, sweat pouring from her armpits, shocked by the ferocity of their attack. They side-step, however, like matadors in a bullring, and now they are scattered and in a better position than ever to concentrate on the wounded bike.

They goad her. 'C'mon, lady! C'mon, you old cow! I thought you were coming to get us?'

Rita glares, throwing a look of bridled ferocity that would terrify anyone else, and moves cautiously back towards her bike and her shopping, but you can see their sweet little faces thinking . . .

Why do they despise her like this?

One boy, he looks no older than eight, moves in fast and jumps on the spokes of the bicycle wheel with his great thick clumping boots. There's the crack of breaking metal.

'Stop that, you buggers! Just let me get hold of you little bleeders an' I'll bang your heads—' But the words die on her lips and she has to duck as another brick whistles towards her. She watches helplessly as two of the little bastards scoop the shopping back in its carrier and tear away with the bloody lot. The rest are on the bike now, leaping about as if the damn thing is a trampoline while Rita struggles to move towards it, warding off the bricks.

Shocked and numb, distressed to the point of panic, Rita shrieks, 'But why? But why?'

Throwing down his cigarette, the angel-faced boy lowers his voice. 'We'll get you for this, cunt. See if we don't.'

Rita whirls round. 'Did you see that? Did you hear that? Can you bloody believe this? I ask you!'

But the men on the corner, strangers both, shrug their shoulders and wander off in different directions.

Rita, Big Rita, who was once the Queen of Lippington Road with permanently bleeding knees, stares after them for a while before she inspects her mangled bicycle and sets off for home.

Derek looks worried and scared.

Shane stands up and peers out the window, half-hiding behind the nets. 'You shouldn't have done that, Mum. Why did you have to get involved? They could have hurt you.'

Rita is in a hell of a state. 'Get out there, Shane, and sort them out! Get my shopping back! And you, Derek, get off your arse and give them a damn good hiding!'

'Mum, it's no use. There's no point in going out there. They'll be gone by now.'

'What? Are you telling me that we're just going to let them get away with it? Well bugger me, I am going to the phone box if nobody else will. I am going to call the sodding law!' Three hulking boys in the family and yet no one is willing to protect her?

Shane tries to explain. 'The phone box is still not fixed. And the law won't come. They know those kids will have scarpered long before they get here.'

'Well, what about identification? I'd know every one of them again, I certainly would!'

'Leave it alone, Mum.'

'Have a brandy,' says Derek.

Some humiliations we survive, others we don't. For this is Rita's loved one. Her dearest beloved. Her next of kin. The male protector with the club. He, whom she describes as totally reliable, is he not angry on Rita's behalf? Does he not mind about what has happened to his wife? Does he not rage? Is she too big to warrant protection from her husband, from her sons?

Doreen pops her curlered head round the door. 'What's up? What's all the shouting about?'

'Mum's had a set-to with the kids up the road.'

Doreen swoops to enfold her. 'Oh, poor Mum! Are you all right? You look awful.'

'Doreen, they threw bricks at me and they ruined my bike. They nicked the shopping – beef and onion pasties. God knows what we'll have for tea.'

'Oh Mum, how awful. How many were there?'

Exhaustion is setting in. Rita feels weepy. 'About ten. But only about five of them actually smashed up the bike. Who are they, Doreen? And why are they doing this? Look at the state of me now. Fit for the loony bin.' Rita holds out one large hand. 'Look at that. I am still shaking all over.'

'They are animals, Mum, that's why, and they haven't been taught any better. Now you sit down, take off your shoes, and I'll make you a fresh pot of tea.'

'Nothing but trouble,' mutters Derek.

'Thank God it was me and not you or Brenda. Thank God Brenda's got a lift home. But they were kids, Doreen, just ordinary-looking little kids.'

'Just kids, Mum,' says Shane, still standing there like a wally and staring out down the street. 'Kids who you have gone and upset. Kids who are angry!'

'And I made them angry? Shane, is that what you're getting at?'

'Mum, don't you see, it isn't as simple as that! Sooner or later they'll be back.'

'But Shane, they can't get us in here. This is our home!'

Rita, the fool, is still running, the only one taking part, and she's still trying to balance that silly old egg and spoon.

While all around her, standards are slipping.

Chapter fourteen

Standards have never been high in The Painted Lady.

'We'll sit here,' says Jessica, thinking, Where it is dark.

'What time is he coming?' asks the nervous Brenda, picking her lip. Jessica has instructed her not to smoke after Rudi arrives; he can't stand it.

'He will be here in a minute. Don't worry, Brenda. Everything is going to be fine.'

But is it? Has Jessica given Rudi sufficient warning?

'But what shall I say?'

'Don't say anything if you don't want to. If you want to join in, then join in. It is all perfectly simple.'

It might be perfectly simple for Jessica, who is used to chatting with strangers on a level which Brenda does not understand; it is nowhere between her one and her five. You chat to strangers as if they are friends, gasping when you are introduced and calling them darling and dear. If they are useful people you kiss them when you say goodbye, otherwise you just smile.

The nearest Brenda got to this was at her interview at Jackson Willow & Sons, but then she was led by the kindly Company Director, who knew how cheaply she came.

This is a bit like an interview, but Brenda is not applying for a job. She is applying for a bonk with the glamorous Rudi, the son of Mama Shapiro, who sharpened his skills on the raven-haired wenches who lifted their skirts on the mountainsides around and about his family home.

What does Brenda know of Rudi?

Nothing comfortable. Nothing familiar. Only that he is an actor, he rows, he plays squash, he likes parties and he beds the superior Jessica. And he wants a child. He does not play pool. He has probably never heard of The Bull and it is doubtful if he enjoys chips with vinegar on his way home of a Saturday night.

'And you live,' says Jessica, to make conversation, 'on the Pennystone Estate. Is that nice?'

Nice?

'It's okay, I suppose.'

'How long have you lived there, Brenda?'

'All my life. Mum's getting a bit fed up, though.'

'Oh, and why is that?'

'Because it has gone downhill. The new people have dragged it down.'

'Dragged it down? Oh yes, that's easily done. That hasn't happened where we are, so far, but it so easily could. Your mother should start a Residents' Association. That might help.'

'She might have done once,' says Brenda, nervous, and staring now and then at the door, 'but now she doesn't know anyone.'

'You don't have to know people to start a Residents' Association,' says Jessica, bored already and cursing Rudi's lateness. She can't go on making inane conversation for very much longer. 'That's the whole point of the thing. If you knew people you wouldn't need one, Brenda, would you?'

But the girl is not paying attention. They are not in the office now but Jessica is still the boss.

'I should suggest the idea, if I were you,' says Jessica, picking up the badly stained menu. Chips. Chips and more chips.

'Oh, that's my favourite!' exclaims Brenda.

'What is?' Jessica tries to follow her glance but the girl is staring into space.

'Listen! *The Wind Beneath My Wings*.'

'Oh, the music.'

Jessica had not noticed. Now she does, it becomes intrusive and irritates her beyond endurance. Why, oh why, must there always be music! Do people hate silence that much? Is silence *so* disturbing?

'Well, you look very nice, Brenda, so there is no reason why you should not feel utterly confident in this situation.'

'I wish my mates could see me.'

'You like your new hairstyle, don't you?'

Brenda grins, and it is not unappealing. 'I think it's wicked. And my clothes.'

'Well then. Whatever happens next, you have gained a new wardrobe out of the experience.'

Brenda gasps, 'He's here! He's coming towards us!'

How did Brenda recognise Rudi? Well, it really is not difficult. Rudi is like no other customer of The Painted Lady. Rudi stands out in this pub that smells of Dettol, like a sleek Saluki in a pack of motley mongrels. He oozes towards the table and holds out a friendly hand.

'Brenda?'

Brenda bows her head and turns in her chair, uncertain whether she ought to get up. She mumbles clumsily through clenched teeth, 'Hello.'

Then he kisses Jessica. 'Drinks?' he asks. 'Brenda?'

Brenda looks towards Jessica for guidance.

She does not know she is required to advise. 'What would you like to drink, Brenda?'

'Rum and black?'

Rudi does not bat an eyelid. 'One rum and black, two gins and tonics,' and he moves off towards the bar.

'Was I all right? Did he like me?'

'Brenda, you really mustn't worry like this. It is far too soon to say.'

'God, I could do with a fag.'

'It would be better if you tried not to, just for an hour or so. Anyway, it's a foul habit, and time you stopped completely.'

'Is that how long this is going to take?'

'Brenda, do stop asking silly questions. I honestly have no idea. And anyway, what did *you* think of *him*?' Is there nothing on this menu that Jessica can eat?

Brenda sighs and clasps her hands. 'Wonderful. He looks just like Agassi, but darker. He's got the same twinkling eyes, and his smile.'

Jessica snaps, 'Well, that's all right then. Now, you had better decide what you want to eat. Are you hungry?'

'Famished,' says Brenda.

Dad used to bring them in here sometimes for birthday treats, when he was working, and Mum used to give them 10p each to put in the jukebox. The last time they came here, Shane nicked four place-mats with deer on, and badgers, and gave them to Mum for her birthday. She never found out. She never knew.

Brenda knows what she's going to choose without having to look – scampi and chips if they still do it. But she has to remember her manners this time; not to stretch, to wait until everyone's ready before she starts, to hand the sauces around, and the salt, before she takes her own.

In spite of her understandable qualms, now that she has seen Rudi, Brenda is quite excited. Part of that excitement is caused by the relief of sorting her problem out.

If only she can get Rudi to like her.

What sort of woman might Rudi prefer?

Quite obviously, women like Jessica, but he is making eyes at the girl behind the bar and she is nothing like Jessica so he must find other varieties appealing, too. Brenda, with her new hairstyle and modish clothes, watches him warily and tells herself she is still in with a chance.

What would they say about Rudi down at The Bull?

What would Jessica do if Rudi decided he fancied her – that he *preferred* her to Jessica?

Brenda is young with hope in her heart. She is pleased – no, *amazed* – by her own transformation. She imagines Rudi's experienced hands, hard from rowing, and his dreamy eyes, moving over her quivering body. What is more natural than that Brenda should dream these dreams while she sits in the corner of The Painted Lady, waiting for the return of her lover-to-be?

It is so hard to keep faith.

What have I done? thinks Jessica, scanning the awful menu to take her mind off her wounded pride. She will have to have the salmon salad, without the chips if they'll let her.

And although this is her idea and she is the one who made all the arrangements, Jessica can hardly believe it is actually happening.

Up until now, Jessica had imagined that Brenda was the victim – underprivileged, shattered, pregnant Brenda, trapped in her predicament and depending on her for survival – but now she sees the girl eyeing Rudi under her shaggy fringe, speculating, thinking Jessica does not notice, and Jessica is forced to review the whole precarious venture.

If this is going to work at all it is essential that Jessica maintains control, complete control, over the whole operation. Emotions must not come into it. The head must rule the heart. They have to stick to the physical and not involve the mental.

Jessica has no idea of Rudi's initial reaction. He would never be so cruel as to allow Brenda to think she had failed. Rudi is rarely cruel to anyone to their faces, especially women, and among women the only one he is content to see suffer is Jessica.

The whole experience is distressing. Rudi might try to make it so, but this really should not be turned into fun, at the expense of . . . who? Jessica!

And Brenda must not be allowed to get cocky in this novel and fecund situation.

'And so that's how I came to work at Jackson Willow & Sons, and that's how I came to meet Jessica.'

Brenda hiccups. Her eyes fail to focus. Brenda is drunk but she does not know it. She is unused to drinking wine with her meals, on top of two drinks beforehand. She tips it down as if it is water.

'How long have you been with me now, Brenda?' Jessica genuinely hasn't a clue. She hardly notices when one girl goes and another comes to replace her.

'Nine months,' says Brenda, suddenly glancing guiltily down.

'That long?' murmurs Jessica.

Rudi smiles. 'And what gave you the idea to offer your womb to the highest bidder?'

Brenda giggles and says, 'Oh, that sounds awful.'

'It is fairly awful,' says Rudi, 'when you think about it. It is not the kind of thing you would expect a modest young lady to do.'

'But I am no modest young lady,' quips Brenda, with a silly grin.

This is getting too close for comfort. 'You are always doing yourself down,' says Jessica. 'You really must be more positive about yourself, Brenda.'

'Why should I be? What have I got to be positive about?'

'Well, there is your answer,' Jessica puts in quickly. 'That is why you are doing what you are doing. You want to break out of the trap.'

'The poverty trap?' asks Rudi.

'The boredom trap,' says Brenda.

Rudi keeps a serious face. It is a face designed to keep secrets. His voice is sexy soft when he asks, 'And having a baby for somebody else isn't boring?'

Brenda simpers horribly. 'Not when it means going with someone like you.'

Rudi laughs and raises amused eyebrows to Jessica. His lover just sits there and shakes her aristocratic head. 'Brenda has had far too much to drink.'

'You have to drink here,' says Rudi, 'in order to camouflage the taste of the food. Look at the state of this mixed grill. And what is this piece of peach doing on my ham? I think Brenda is being very sensible.'

'Oh, I wish you'd had the scampi,' gushes Brenda. 'The scampi was really lovely!'

'Then I'm glad for you,' says Jessica sweetly, tossing the last of her salmon aside and glaring at the lacklustre English salad. 'Although I really think the tartar sauce would have gone better with it than the Daddies.'

'But I always have Daddies.'

'She always has Daddies,' mocks Rudi, 'and you ought to know that!'

'Jessica,' starts Brenda, timidly. 'D'you think it'd be all right if I put a record on?'

'Why not? Go ahead. Nothing could be worse than the last selection.'

This is it. Quickly, while Brenda's gone.

'Well?'

'I think she is rather a sweetie,' says Rudi, 'in an obvious sort of way.'

Jessica ought to feel pleased. All her good work has paid off.

'And you feel we can trust her?'

'You know her better than I do. I suppose we can trust her as much as we could trust any other woman in this peculiar situation and, as she says, she is not prepared to stay a typist forever. Although I'm not quite sure where she thinks fifteen thousand is going to take her.'

'She certainly approves of you,' says Jessica, hiding the bitterness.

'There aren't many women immune to my charms,' Rudi jokes, but it isn't so funny.

'We must remember why we are doing this.' Jessica fiddles with a piece of limp lettuce, and shakes it by the scruff of its neck. 'This is a business relationship and nothing more than that. If anything further develops – and that is up to you, Rudi, you can see what an impressionable kind of child Brenda is – then we are bound to run into trouble. There is absolutely no need for you to go over the top. Remember, this is not easy for me.'

'It is not easy for me either, Jessica. You are asking me to screw a rubber doll, and that I am not prepared to do. You are too vulgar. I have my pride and my standards. The girl has to be treated like a human being.'

'You managed to come in a test tube . . .'

'Brenda is not a test tube.'

'She *looks* like a test tube.'

'Jessica! Let's be adult about this. Brenda does not look like a test tube and it is your behaviour, not mine, that is likely to damage this enterprise.'

'You are right. You are quite right, Rudi, and I am sorry.'

Rudi reaches out and takes her hand. 'Trust me,' he whispers. They stare at each other across the plastic peonies, two beautiful people so very much in love.

'Dear God,' says Rudi, suddenly aware of the sad and meaningful music chosen by Brenda. 'Do you think that this is a message?'

'Good Lord, I sincerely hope not, not already,' says Jessica briskly.

Chapter fifteen

By night, the Pennystone Estate goes dark. Completely dark.

'It's rather difficult to see where we're going,' says Jessica peering forward, her soft hair swinging. 'All the roads look exactly the same to me.'

Brenda, sitting nervously in the back with Hiame, is leaning towards the driver, giving directions. 'Turn right at the next lamp-post.'

'But why aren't any of these damn lights working?'

'Dunno. They never work now.'

'Not very nice for anyone walking home,' says Jessica, trying to see out and marvelling, yet again, at the simple obedience of people who are prepared to come and live in such places.

Why don't they march?

Or revolt?

She would.

'Nobody does walk home any more,' says Brenda. 'No one'd be so silly.'

'If you lived here you would need a dog,' says Rudi, pulling his coat around him. His gypsy earring flashes like a touched nerve. 'A pit-bull or a Rottweiler at the very least.'

'Or an Alsatian,' exclaims Brenda, excited. 'Preferably black. But Mum doesn't like dogs. She's never let me have one. Once I was allowed to bring the stick insects home from school for the holidays, but Mum made me leave them outside on the porch and they all died, or escaped to find some privet. Anyway, we couldn't find them. The teacher was okay about it, though.'

'I don't think poor little Hiame would last here very long,' shudders Jessica. 'Without getting torn to pieces. Is this it?'

'This is it. And thank you very much for bringing me home. And for the drinks. And for the meal. I enjoyed it very much.'

'Aren't we going to be invited in?' Jessica and Rudi have discussed this and decided that, however unpleasant, it would be prudent to inspect the members of the surrogate's family, to examine the stock, as it were. I mean, people used to be very careful about their wet nurses . . .

'I would ask you in,' says Brenda in a panic, thinking that Dad would be snoring in his chair and Mum would have her curlers in and her sore feet cooling on the tiles round the fireplace, 'but it would be fatal to leave your car out here.' And Doreen might be snogging on the sofa with Nigel.

'Just for a moment?'

'Yes. Even for a moment. Thirty seconds and the kids would be stripping it. Or taking it off for a ride.'

'At this time of night? Aren't the wretched children in by now?'

'Some are, but the older ones are always skulking around.'

Jessica surveys the dereliction that stretches ahead of her, picked out by the beams of the headlights – potholes, litter, broken glass, pieces of torn tyre like black tongues licking the kerbs. Animals. You can see what they do to an area if they are left to themselves. 'Brenda, I don't know how any of you can sleep peacefully in your beds, with all this mayhem out here.'

'That's exactly what Mum says, but Dad tells her that no one is interested in our house. And we are lucky, I suppose, as we've never been burgled. Mum knows an old woman who's been broken into twenty-four times, but at our house there is always someone in.'

'We would have liked to have met your family,' says Rudi reasonably.

'Yes, but not now.' And Brenda climbs out and closes the heavy car door with an expensive, determined click. 'What will you do?' she asks through the window, carefully avoiding Rudi's eyes. 'When will you decide?'

'We will let you know for certain tomorrow,' says Jessica. 'Don't worry, we won't keep you waiting. That would be very unfair.'

*

'Well? What do you think?'

The house smells of Shane's trainers, and the noodles and chicken chop suey which Roy went to fetch from the Chinky to replace the stolen beef and onion pasties.

'Brenda! Stand back a bit, let me have a look. Hasn't Miss Holden come in? I cleared up in here specially, and your Dad has kept his teeth in all evening just in case . . .'

'She didn't have time, Mum,' says the curly-headed Brenda. 'She said she was sorry.'

'Well, I dunno.'

'What d'you think of my hair?'

'It's smashing,' says Doreen brightly, moving forward to touch it. Poor Doreen, with her hair so often bleached it has gone the texture of candy floss, has been refused a perm at the hairdressers in case it falls out. They dare not take the risk; they cannot afford that sort of insurance, so she is forced to do it herself, at home, and often blocks the plughole with handfuls of sticky blonde matting. Whereas Brenda has strong hair, untouched until now. 'Shake it, go on. God, look at that, Mum. It just falls straight back into place.'

'If you can call that a place,' says Rita. 'It's all over everywhere.'

'Oh get on, Mum, it's fabulous.'

'It does suit you, Brenda, in an odd sort of way. And look at that jacket! What colour would you call it – beige, fawn? What the hell did they pay for that?'

Brenda, flushing, made almost beautiful by her new-found desire, says, 'Nearly five hundred quid.'

'What?' Rita's mouth drops open and forms a wide O, like the hole in her outsize tights which are slung, discarded, over the back of her chair.

'Yep,' says Brenda proudly. 'That's what it cost.'

'You can tell,' says Doreen, fingering it lovingly. 'God, what I'd give . . . you lucky cow.'

Raising her heavy eyebrows Rita stares at her daughter sharply. 'But they didn't need to pay that sort of money, surely, for one meeting? For one night out, working? Why would they spend that on a secretary, somebody taking notes?

Firms aren't made of money these days and it just doesn't make any sense.'

Brenda turns round, showing her clothes off like a model. She swings, almost knocking the ashtray off the bark-shaped coffee table. She is not facing Rita when she says, 'It wasn't just an ordinary meeting, Mum. It was more of a social occasion really, meeting the clients, chatting them up, making sure they had drinks. It was a kind of office party, you see, and important that everyone made the right impression.'

'Still . . .' Rita's head is going like a calculator. She thinks of her own annual staff party at Woollies, in the back room amongst the boxes. Rita is far from convinced.

'And Jessica did say that they tended to do this sort of thing, rather than giving out a bonus which would only be taxed. This way they can claim back expenses. I've been with them for nearly a year now, Mum, and the wages aren't all that high.'

'Probably some kind of tax dodge,' mumbles Derek knowledgeably from his chair, as comfortable there as a cushion, string vest adding an extra pattern to the colourful floral Plumbs stretch covers. One gloomy arm dangles over the edge, picking nail clippings off the nylon carpet. Brenda is glad that Jessica did not come in. She wishes her father would do up his collar. Derek has a scrawny neck, and looks old with the buttons undone and white hairs poking out through the triangles of his vest. How can Mum bear to go to bed with Dad? How can Dad bear . . . I mean, Mum's feet are so ugly. 'They're all bloody at it nowadays,' adds Derek. 'Bastards.'

'That sounds more likely, Derek, I suppose. Nice for Brenda, though. Doesn't she look different?'

'I wouldn't have known her,' says Shane, his face pale and nervous beneath the stubble. 'She looks like a pop star's moll, you see them at the airport.'

'Looking baffled,' says Doreen.

'I didn't know I was looking baffled,' says Brenda, pained. 'I thought I was looking beautiful.'

'I'll get you a cup of tea,' says Doreen, 'and you can tell us all about it.'

'Give us a fag, for God's sake. I haven't had one all night.

They don't approve of smoking. Nobody smokes any more, only us.' Suddenly the smell in the house disgusts her, and the vague pall of yellow which hangs on the pictures, the curtains, the walls. The constant, flickering light of the telly in this over-warm, over-cosy room is like a pressure on her head.

It is on, but nobody's watching.

And this is what Mum and Dad have slogged and fought to create.

She wants to tell them what's happening to her. She wants to burst.

Brenda puts down her rucksack and displays her new jars and tubes of make-up. Overcoming her jealousy, Doreen sniffs them, and tries out the colours on the back of her hand.

Brenda has got to start telling lies, detailed lies, to her mother. Is she bright enough? Can she do it?

She did fine.

Rita was most impressed.

Brenda hangs up her new clothes with love and a great deal of care.

So much has happened in such a short time.

She cannot wait to get into bed, to turn out the light and to think upon Rudi. Rudi the beautiful. Rudi the stud. Brenda feels ashamed when she thinks about Ginge. She has been defiled by him, but soon she is going to discover what it is like to be properly loved.

She lies in bed and plays with her little pink nipples, closes her eyes and remembers Rudi's competent, long-fingered hands. Not stubby and square with dirty nails like Ginge's.

With the lights out the house is dark, completely dark. No street-lights shine through the thin nylon curtains disturbing the dreams of the sleepers or the fantasies of the wakeful. There is only the barking and howling of dogs, like wolves in the woods, and the occasional car revving home through the loose grit of the roads on the Pennystone Estate, carrying bursts of loud and unidentifiable music.

Rudi is just about to move his hand between Brenda's legs, in a four-poster bed onto which she has just been carelessly flung, when the shout, followed by the crashing of glass takes the rest of her breath away.

'Hey, what's that?'

She is out of bed in a flash, meeting everyone else on the landing, in shock, confused, racing, calling . . .

The revs sound like racing cars. They roar towards the house . . .

'Christ, Derek . . .'

'Get downstairs, everyone!'

'What the fuck?'

'It's the kids!'

'Bastards . . .'

'It's rubber burning. And petrol!'

'What's going on?'

'They've smashed through to the garden . . .'

'What are they doing?'

'Oh dear God, the carpet. It's ruined.'

'Mind out, Doreen, it's a firework—'

'Stamp on it!'

'Get some water!'

'Come away from the window!'

'They've broken the fence, they're revving out there, backwards and forwards.'

'My washing's still out there, bugger it!'

'The lawn—'

'Is the tree still standing?'

'Get out there, somebody! We can't just hide!'

'Nobody move! Stay indoors. We don't know how many there are.'

'Where's Roy?'

'But they're only kids, for God's sake!'

'A whole bloody gang of them. Shut your face, Rita.'

'But there's six of us in here. Three grown men and three strong women! What are we going to do? Just bleeding well stand here and let it happen?'

They've gone.

It's all quiet.

Too quiet?

*

'This is what happens, Mum. This is what happened to the Jordans, don't you remember, when they reported those buggers who were nicking slates from the next door's roof.'

There is no need for Eddie to sound so self-satisfied when he adds, 'They had to leave in the end. Never got a decent night's sleep afterwards. It was a kind of vendetta . . . the law couldn't touch 'em. Too young, they said – nothing they could do. And the Jordans were buying theirs.'

'But we are not like the Jordans,' says Rita, still shaking. 'There are six of us, seven when Roy's home. And we've been here the longest.'

As if that should count for anything.

'It doesn't make any difference to them, Mum.' Shane is trying to be gentle, but underneath he feels angry. Mum should have known not to go interfering. 'It's probably more fun, them with their twisted minds. That's what they want. They'd like nothing better than for us to run out there, floundering about in the dark. But there's too many, don't you see?'

'They're just little kiddies.' Rita seems to be stuck in a groove, willing to believe anything rather than face the reality of this new and intolerable situation. 'We played out,' she says, 'in my day. We played out till it got dark, but we never got up to anything like this. I shouldn't have gone for them, should I? I should have just passed by, on the other side of the road, like the Pharisee.' As usual Rita brings up the good old days.

Does she really consider them the good old days? What is it about those good old days, that she has to erase them and rewrite the past?

'Just 'cos you're bigger than anyone else, you think you can sort anything out.'

'What's my sodding size got to do with this, Doreen?'

'You take on too much, Mum. You always feel responsible.'

She eyes her daughter angrily. 'Somebody has to be responsible.'

'No they don't, Mum. It isn't like that any more. You aren't responsible for anyone else.'

Rita follows on with well-justified fury. 'That's just it, Doreen, isn't it? That explains everything. No one's responsible any more – and see what happens when everyone takes that lethargic attitude. *This* is what happens.' And Rita throws out her mighty arms as if to encompass, not just her house, or the Pennystone Estate, but the whole of life and more. The life she knows is out there somewhere but impossible to imagine, let alone reach.

'It's what I've always said,' mutters Derek, foolishly attempting to enter the fray. 'And that's what's wrong with the kids. You've always taken responsibility. They all come to you. It's your attitude, Rita, which has stopped them taking responsibility for themselves. You've made it far too easy . . . You can't make everything right. You might believe that you can, you might want to, but you can't. You can't fight the world on their account.'

'Well bugger you, Derek, that's all I can say. So it's my fault, is it? Everything that goes wrong around here is my fault? I see. Why don't you all go into the attack . . . what are you waiting for, standing there with your mouths dropped open, looking gormless? Come on! Come on! I'm big enough to take it, aren't I?'

Big Rita looks pathetic and she sounds pathetic, standing there like a baited bear, and already Doreen regrets that she ever mentioned Mum's size. Or her attitude. Everyone is upset enough as it is.

'I've told you before, Rite, and I'll say it again,' says Derek, picking up shards of splintered glass and laying them between the doubled-up sheets of the *Sun*, 'you can't change anything around here. It's been going from bad to worse for years. You say so yourself, only you don't really believe it. We should put in for a council exchange and get out.'

'Retreat?' shouts Rita contemptuously. 'We'll be joining the sodding New Age travellers next.'

'And what's wrong with retreat?' Derek, small and red-faced, defends himself. He rubs his slippered foot over the burn mark on the carpet. 'I don't fancy spending the rest of my life living behind barricades.'

'And nor do I,' says Shane.

'An exchange where?'

'Anywhere. Anywhere but here.'

'Oh?' sniffs Rita. 'And who is going to want to exchange houses with us? Who is going to be daft enough?'

'We can ask, can't we?' says Derek. 'We can't lose anything by asking.'

'You don't think we should give it a few days . . .'

'No, Rita, I don't. I think we should make enquiries tomorrow.'

'So who is going to do that? Are you prepared to get off your arse and go down there, or are you expecting me to go in my lunch-hour, although how I'm going to get to work now without my bike I don't know.' But Rita feels she has to go. A fighter by instinct and from painful experience, she needs to deal with important matters herself.

Derek looks worried. 'I dunno about leaving the house . . .'

'I'll do it if you like, Mum.'

But Rita feels tired, and shaken, and frightened. 'No, Brenda, love. You do your fair share, and you're not forceful enough. Your Dad will do it, won't you, Derek? Shane can stay and guard the house and Eddie can keep you company.'

Poor Mum.

But it's true what they say.

All her kids are too weak, Shane and Eddie and Roy and Doreen and Brenda. They run back to Mum when life is too cruel; they depend on her to pick up the pieces.

And if Mum isn't there to listen, abandoned, they turn to somebody else. Someone powerful. Someone determined. Someone who will battle on their behalf.

Someone like Jessica.

Chapter sixteen

If asked to compare herself to a sweet, Brenda would probably choose an Opal Fruit. Doreen is a marshmallow, and Mum is a slab of home-made treacle toffee, hard to get in your mouth and fatal for fillings.

The birds weave the morning into their tapestry of song. The sky is so purely blue you wouldn't believe this is England, the little white puffs of clouds mere islands in the far far distance.

Jessica, Bournville Plain, bittersweet and sophisticated, calls to Rosita, the stick of liquorice, on this blissful Wednesday in spring. On these kinds of days she wishes she did not have to go to work. 'There'll be a guest tonight, probably for a few days. I shall meet her at the station and bring her home with me after work.'

'Do I give the flat a clear out?'

'No, Rosita, she will sleep in the spare room.'

'Oh. Did you say it was a *her*?'

'I did. So what are you getting at?'

Rosita retreats like a dark spider to its web. 'Nothing at all, Miss Jessica. Nothing at all.'

One hour later, Rosita can be seen carrying a ladder-back chair up the basement steps and placing it carefully bang in the middle of the pavement. She wears her slippers of silver brocade and her glittering snood muffles her normally wild black hair. She brings the grey knitting out of its patchwork bag and proceeds to get on with it, clicking the needles just like Brenda taps the keys on her keyboard. She nods politely at passers-by, the postman, the milkman. Those she does not know she treats to a menacing stare.

*

Vera looks out of one of the front bedroom windows, absorbed in the first of her morning rounds like a surgeon checking his patients.

She knows that Rosita is not part of Mullins' plot, because she has seen her going peacefully about her business for the last two years or so. Rosita is a person who knows how to mind her own business. In fact, Vera was quite surprised by their short conversation on Monday.

Vera would dearly like to pop round the corner for a replacement packet of ginger nuts to dunk in her eleven o'clock cup of tea, but dare she? She went out about this time yesterday, and she has to vary her morning programme so the Mullins' men cannot establish a routine and take advantage of it.

Vera hobbles downstairs. She tips the cats off the coalman's ebony chair and carts it to the door. Rarely used, because she is better hidden at the back, the front door creaks open, and she forces herself and her cumbersome chair under the heavy deckchair material and out onto the porch. She puts down the chair and sits on it, glancing down every now and again at her industrious neighbour.

Vera would knit, but she cannot afford the wool.

'Nice morning,' offers Vera.

Rosita merely looks up, and squeezes her eyes against the sun.

Rosita knits on.

Vera remembers how her own mother used to sit on the step, all those years ago, and chat to the women, after they had blackened their steps and polished their knockers until they were gleaming. Funny. Up until now she had completely forgotten about that.

The kiddies would play round their feet.

Women used to talk to each other in those days, not pass by with their noses in the air as if they were in competition.

Rosita remembers how her own mother used to sit on the step, all those years ago, and chat to the women as they went by, leading their goats and lugging their baskets of washing to the river. Funny. Up until now she had completely forgotten about that.

The kiddies would play round their feet.

Women used to talk to each other in those days, not pass by with their noses in the air as if they were in competition.

By God, Vera could do with a ginger nut. Perhaps she should take this frightening initiative. She calls, 'I don't suppose you have any ginger nut biscuits which I could borrow until I go out tomorrow?'

'Only shortbread, I am afraid.'

'No, shortbread won't do. It won't dunk. It falls apart in the tea.'

'Why don't you pop round the corner? It wouldn't take you a minute.'

'I cannot leave my house.'

Rosita looks up again, puzzled this time, staring at the woman perched on the step at Number 6. 'Why not?'

'In case they get in while I'm gone.'

'Who?' shouts Rosita. 'Who would get in?'

'Hang on a minute.' Vera, excited, festooned in her many cardigans, bends and picks up her heavy chair. 'I'm coming down.'

'Leave that chair where it is,' says Rosita crossly. 'It is far too heavy for you to manhandle all this way. I'll go inside and fetch one out of my kitchen.'

'They have hounded me for years,' finishes Vera, staring unhappily about her, 'and the police just turn a blind eye.'

Rosita, nodding gravely, changes her curtain of wool from under one arm to the other.

'Have you any proof?'

'Proof? I don't need to bother with proof. Nobody's going to prosecute. Nobody's got the money to take companies like Mullins Holdings to court. They would walk all over you and take you to the cleaners. And you don't know who is in the Masons these days, that's what my daughter says. How would you know that your expensive solicitor wasn't in the same

Lodge as Edward Mullins? That is what Rita says and she knows about things like that.'

'Noises in the night? That's odd,' says Rosita, shifting slightly but still knitting away.

Vera studies the ground thoughtfully before she goes on. Naturally she is awed by Rosita, this exotic foreigner in her heavily embroidered dress with the dull gems on her bony fingers. As is her habit in these situations, Vera mimics her betters. She copies the Spanish woman's stilted, formal English, the kind of speaking you sometimes used to hear at the pictures. Vera slips into it from the cockney like you'd slip into a warmer coat if the circumstances warranted it, for comfort. 'But just lately I have been thinking. I have had an idea. Would you like to hear it?'

'But of course,' and Rosita changes arms.

Vera sits forward on the edge of her seat. 'I have been watching these programmes on the telly . . . about homelessness and schizophrenics, where the reporters go underground . . .'

'Oh yes?'

'Yes, most fascinating, and I wondered whether anyone might be interested in me.'

'Interested in what way?'

You can see Vera feels awkward, and fears that Miss Rodriguez might sneer at the very idea. Her voice is troubled as she continues, 'I wondered if someone might take on my case.'

Rosita stops knitting and stares at her neighbour. 'Investigate the noises, you mean?'

'Yes, but not just the noises. Derek says the state of my house is a scandal, bearing in mind I'm a tenant and supposed to be protected and all that. And there's the dripping chimney, and the broken glass . . .'

'I think you should give this matter a great deal more thought, Mrs Evans. I realise your great need, but to go to the television! Anyway, they would probably not be interested.'

'No, probably not. But I have jotted down some notes already – times, dates and the like,' she confides. 'They're in an envelope indoors, waiting till I have a chance to put them down in a letter.'

Miss Rodriguez stares at her neighbour with hard bright eyes. Her response is careful. 'You might find that you upset Mr Mullins and precipitate a dangerous reaction.'

'I am prepared to take that chance, Miss Rodriguez, although I know that my daughter would take the same attitude as yours – cautious, wary, saying that going to the telly would be an enormous step.'

'I have to tell you that your daughter sounds like a most sensible person to me. Why don't you wait, Mrs Evans? Wait a while. Who knows, when Mr Mullins realises you are not reacting, he might well stop.'

Vera answers her sharply. 'But I can't wait, you see. I hoped you might understand. I can't wait, Miss Rodriguez, because it's not getting better it's getting worse, and I have to do something before things get completely out of hand. Even my cats are in danger. I reckon there's people like me all over this city – afraid to go out, afraid to sleep in their beds at night. This is exactly the sort of thing these programmes take up . . . public scandals!'

'A public scandal?'

'Of course it is a public scandal,' nods Vera.

'Yes, yes, I suppose it is,' concedes Rosita, at last resting her knitting for good on her draped black knee. 'Now you pop along to the shop for your ginger nuts and I will sit here and guard your house.'

'They might not look suspicious. They have been known to use disguises.'

'Don't worry. I will guard your house like the fiercest dog, and nobody, not even the fire brigade, will get one foot inside it.'

'I would be terribly grateful,' says Vera, standing at the ready, picking up her purse. Her new friend might well prove to be a godsend.

'I would be delighted to do it,' says Rosita. 'After all, we are next-door neighbours. If you can't help a neighbour out it's a pretty poor show.'

Vera offers a ginger nut to Rosita, who takes one politely.

'I'm a keen knitter.' Vera leaves the biscuits out. 'What are you making?'

'I just knit, unravel it, and then knit it up again,' confesses Rosita, 'because I can no longer see to read the patterns.'

'I have patterns and I can read. I have a whole boxful of patterns inside my house somewhere, if they haven't been moved by the home help, or Rita. If you hang on here for a minute I will go inside and have a look. I could tell you what to do for the next ten rows or so. You could even ring me up. I am on the phone. My daughter thought that was essential, bearing my situation in mind, and I don't make many calls out so of course I get the discount.'

Later: 'I am sure that my daughter Rita would not approve of my going to the television people but it's nothing to do with her, don't you see? It is *me* who is living under a state of siege. It is *me* who is suffering with my nerves. And anyway, she only visits me once a week so I don't see why I'd have to tell her.'

'No.' But Miss Rodriguez sounds uncertain.

'The trouble is, and I'll be honest with you here, the trouble is that I wouldn't dare do it on my own. I would rather have someone at my side when they come – you know what I mean. I find it hard to deal with people, sometimes. Important people.'

Miss Rodriguez' response is hesitant but Vera is obviously determined, with or without her help. If she agrees to support her, perhaps the old lady will calm down and take the difficult matter no further. It is all to do with being tactful. 'I would be prepared to be at your side,' she offers. 'I am only out on a Monday and a Wednesday, at my sugar decoration classes. The rest of the week is my own to do with as I like. I am often bored, as with my poor eyesight I can't do an awful lot. Yes, yes, I would welcome that sort of diversion.'

'This is extremely kind of you. People are generally so uninterested in other folks these days, the buggers. Particularly the elderly. I cannot tell you how grateful I am for your interest, Miss—'

'Please call me Rosita.'

'How do you do? And I am Vera. It's this feeling of powerlessness that gets me down so much, you see.'

And the two old ladies formally shake hands, and share the packet of ginger nuts.

'What I must do is write a convincing letter. I will fetch some paper and do it at once, while you're with me. I do hate talking about things and not getting down to do them immediately. I won't be a moment, Miss Rodriguez.'

Taken aback by the suddenness of events, Rosita stalls. 'While you are gone I will make another pot of tea, if you like.'

'That would be most kind.' And satisfaction rings in Vera's shaky old voice.

The two empty chairs, with their bright red cushions, stand alone on the pavement for no longer than five minutes. Both women hurry to get back to the brand-new sunshine.

'If I dared to go further from my house, I would suggest that we both go to Boots where you try on those cheap, ready-made spectacles. Who knows, Miss Rodriguez, you might well find something that suits, and then your life would be changed beyond all belief. How on earth do you see to do such delicate work with your sugar?'

'That is quite different, funnily enough, Mrs Evans. That is one of those things you develop a *feel* for . . .'

'I know exactly what you mean.'

'And you are saying I could go to this . . . *Boots* . . . and pick up a pair of glasses over the counter tomorrow?'

'Oh yes, certainly you could. You don't have to make any complicated appointments, or pay out the earth any more. Oh no. My daughter Rita picked up a pair for reading for round about fifteen pounds, and that was two years ago and they are still going strong.'

'Do you know, this is just the sort of ordinary problem, as a stranger in this country, that I find so difficult to deal with. It is hard, sometimes, to communicate with Miss Jessica, and Mr Rudi, from Italy himself, is most unlikely to know.'

'So many busy people,' sighs Vera. 'And always in such a hurry.'

'Ah yes. That is so.'

And so it is between these interesting and informative bursts of conversation that the two new friends complete their letter and address it to:

The Director of Current Affairs,
BBC Television,
Broadcasting House,
London.

The letter is signed twice – R. Rodriguez and V. Evans. *Yours faithfully.*

Goodness knows what Rita is going to say.

Chapter seventeen

When all is said and done, it is only a matter of instinct on the most basic animal level, thinks Jessica to herself as she drives home with Brenda in her car. This is nothing more, and nothing less, than a pair of dogs coupling, than deer in the park, or a couple of cats out on the prowl amongst the night-time chimneys.

It is human beings who have made the sexual act into the fuss that it is today. Walked round it, sniffed it, poked it, rolled up their eyes at it, revered it, banned it, sanctified it, and raised it to a level above the act of defecation, or feeding, or giving birth. Is dying the only human process not directly connected with the genitals? In law it is called 'sexual intercourse', in the Bible 'having knowledge of', and in books 'making love'.

What crap.

How many times is a good old bonk a declaration of love, and not merely a mutual release from some physical craving?

And this is what this is going to be . . . a good old bonk. There is no need for any kind of extra-sexual bonding.

So why on earth should Jessica worry?

She worried about the nightdress when Brenda chose it – from Dorothy Perkins. Jessica decided it wasn't worth splashing out a fortune for something extra special. After all, it should only take a couple of nights. A hospital gown would have done, clinical rather than sensual. It would have been more appropriate, actually, than the prissy little white job with the ruffles at the neck which Brenda pounced on the moment she saw it.

It makes her look like a virgin.

A virginal sacrifice. Something of a Druid.

A style which might well appeal to Rudi's unfortunate sense of humour.

*

She worried about the perfume and talc and bubble bath which Brenda insisted upon.

'You can use mine, Brenda. You don't need anything of your own.'

'Oh, I do. I'd be all wrong smelling like you. I would not feel myself at all. I am not sophisticated or elegant, Jessica, nothing like you.' She sounded like a little lamb, particularly when she picked the apple. Everything apple, from the Body Shop. Fresh. And green. And young. And fertile.

She worried about the sheets which Rosita had put on the bed –the white cotton sheets with their sprigs of blue forget-me-nots. Little-girl sheets, which smelled of fresh air. Innocent sheets, which were soon to be desecrated by Rudi's spunk and Brenda's bodily juices.

Funny she had not noticed Brenda's youthfulness before, Brenda's excessive youthfulness compared with Jessica's thirty years. At thirty you are mature and into the timespan of trees and houses, and antiques can be thirty years old – things like sixties paraphernalia, or punk memorabilia.

Rudi is four years younger than Jessica and he makes sure that she knows it, the devil. It is one of his favourite put-downs when they are out and he wants a quick laugh. He rubs it in. He seems to consider it funny.

Jessica would feel far happier dealing with a whore.

'We will have a pleasant, relaxed evening all together, with lots of wine, lots of lovely grub, and then you will have a bath and get into bed,' she explains to the eager Brenda as they pull up in front of the house.

'Oh!' says Brenda, peering all around her. 'You live here!'

'Don't take any notice of the house next door,' puts in Jessica quickly, more out of habit than anything else. 'That's our peculiar next-door neighbour, an eccentric old body and not terribly pleasant, I am afraid. Mad as a hatter. But we tend to ignore her, as does everyone else around here. We are all hoping they will move her soon, for her own good, naturally.'

Brenda closes her mouth quickly and makes no further

comment, but she stares at the house next door rather worriedly and goes slightly pale as she jumps from Jessica's car and hurries inside Number 8.

'You're very keen,' laughs Jessica from the road, making sure that she locks the expensive blue machine. 'There's no need to hide!' The girl is probably nervous. Jessica laughs, but she does not feel like laughing at all.

'Like it?'

Brenda turns round and round in the hall, staring up at the chandelier and the way the tiers of the staircase go up and up, so unlike the house next door, the house where Gran lives.

Nobody likes Gran . . . this is a possibility which has never occurred to Brenda before, and why should it? She believed that everyone was probably concerned for her, and loved her, and worried for her, like Mum does. Like she does. Brenda has always been very fond of her gran. It is a shock to know that Gran is despised by everyone in the road, and that they want to be rid of her. And also rather hurtful.

It is hardly possible that the inside of a house can be changed so much. She would love to go over and invite Gran round to have a look. She would probably scream with laughter and wouldn't Jessica be surprised?

She has obviously never noticed Brenda visiting. But then, Jessica is not the sort of person to watch out of windows. She's not lonely. She's not bored. She's not interested in her neighbours. So why would Jessica do that?

But Brenda is going to have to be careful not to be seen, although she has been perfectly truthful, and told Mum she was staying with Jessica. 'To help arrange the next exhibition.'

'This is rather sudden, surely. And why do you have to stay there? Why can't Miss Holden come and fetch you every morning?'

'Because we are going to be working late. It involves all sorts of odd hours, fetching and carrying and arranging. It is very exciting to see how it's done, and I'm lucky that the girl who was going to do it dropped out with a stomach bug at the last minute.'

'I hope they are paying you overtime for all this, Brenda.'

'Oh yes. And I'm learning, Mum. I am learning all sorts of things which are bound to be useful in the future.'

'But how many nights will you be away? When should we expect you?'

'I'll be home by the weekend, probably.'

'Well, so long as you're all right.'

'Miss Holden will make sure of that,' said Brenda brightly.

'She sounds like a very nice person,' Mum declared. 'And to be honest, I'm not sorry to see you safely out of the house, what with all this going on. No one's going to get a wink of sleep.'

'But you'll be okay, Mum, won't you?'

'Don't you worry about me now, Brenda. You concentrate on yourself, and your prospects. They must like you. They must be pleased with you to want your help on such an important occasion.'

'You grate this Parmesan cheese for me, Brenda, there's a good girl.'

'What are you going to make?'

'Spaghetti with pesto sauce.'

Brenda dips her finger in the half-finished sauce and sucks it. 'My mum would wonder where you got your energy from. She never feels like cooking when she gets home from work.'

'I expect she is on her feet all day.'

'Yes, she is. And she's got seven to cook for.'

Catholics, probably. 'And you could spread some butter on that bread.'

'We have marge at home. Not because it's cheap, but because it is better for your heart.'

'That is a debatable point,' says Jessica, knowing full well that these stories are put about because of the bad eating habits of the lower classes, and that sensible people choose their own diets with an inbuilt, natural knowledge of what is good and bad. Brenda probably never eats fruit or brown bread, for example, or drinks fresh orange juice. That must be why her skin is so sallow – that, and the smoking.

'Now you are going to have to take it slowly with the wine tonight,' she reminds Brenda. 'You know how quickly it goes to your head. And we are drinking red this evening, which is worse. You don't want to be ill, in the circumstances.'

No, not ill, just pleasantly tipsy.

The thought of Brenda, pissed as a fart, is not encouraging. Rudi would not consent to go near her; he loathes drunken women.

'Ah, here is Rosita, looking very pleased with herself. How did the sugar class go this afternoon?'

'Very well, thank you, Miss Jessica. Most enjoyable.'

'Rosita, this is Brenda.'

'How do you do?'

'Very well, thank you,' says Brenda, taken aback by the Spanish woman's penetrating stare.

'I used the blue sprigged linen . . .'

'Yes, yes, that's fine, Rosita, thank you. The room looks very nice.'

'You are eating in, Miss Jessica?'

'Yes. We thought we would have a night at home.'

'It is becoming a habit . . .'

'Pardon, Rosita?'

'Oh, nothing.'

'I will be finished in the kitchen in half an hour.'

'Please do not hurry on my account.'

Jessica pointedly and noisily gets rid of her bits using the waste disposal unit. Rosita staunchily refuses to touch it, silly woman, just like the drier, just like the microwave: 'It gives you cancer,' she mutters behind Jessica's back, but loud enough so that Jessica can hear her.

'We'll have a drink while we wait for Rudi,' says Jessica, settling down, lighting the lamps and then straightening her perfect hair before the enormous mirror. 'Why don't you try something slightly different this time? Something a little less strong perhaps, Brenda. How about a Dubonnet, with some bitter lemon to make it last?'

'That would be very nice, thank you.'

Brenda is ill at ease in this sumptuous drawing room with the thick green carpet swirling with Chinese patterns. She almost disappears into her chair, it's so soft and saggy and satiny. The chairs are distant from one another, positioned like strangers on a train – not like at home where the fat arms touch – but it didn't feel right to share the sofa with Jessica.

'I love your house, Jessica, and I love my room,' whispers Brenda. 'I've never been in a house like this before.'

Jessica is almost touched by Brenda's obvious sincerity. 'We like it,' she says. 'It suits us, a house with a history. And it's nicely central.'

'My mum likes new houses best.'

'Well, some people do. What a good thing that everyone's different. What about you, Brenda, which sort of house do you prefer?'

'Oh, this one,' sighs Brenda, with wonder in her eyes. 'One day I would like a house exactly like this one.'

But you wouldn't keep it like this, would you, dear? thinks Jessica unkindly. No taste, that's the trouble. They demand what we have and they get it, cheap, with gilt handles, and they honestly don't know the difference. It's just the same with music and art . . . they demand it and they get it. They go to the Costa Brava and imagine they've been to Spain. They go to watch Jim Davidson and imagine they've been to the theatre. They buy a poster print from Athena and imagine they've bought a piece of art.

Jessica is going to have Brenda's baby and imagine that she is a mother.

Brenda looks up, startled. 'This soup is freezing. It's cold!'

'It is supposed to be cold, Brenda. It is called *gazpacho*.'

'And do all these little bits really go in it?'

Rudi laughs easily while Jessica clears her throat.

Spaghetti is always tricky. Rosita grinds it up in the dumb-waiter, *rattle rattle rattle*, steaming in a pottery bowl – a peasant bowl, like the ones they use at Rudi's house but fifty times more expensive – along with chunks of hot bread in a basket.

Brenda chops hers up with a trembling spoon and fork,

timidly. 'I would live in a house like this, and I would cook food like this.'

'You like it?' asks Rudi, looking extra virile tonight in his Chinos and pale blue silk shirt, with the sleeves rolled up over his dark and hairy arms.

Brenda blushes like a bride and her breath comes faster. The thought of what they are about to do, the two of them, so intimately, is almost too much to bear. She itches with desire. Four hours to go and nowhere to put her eyes; they keep pausing shamefully on Rudi's fingers. She will bend over if she can, to make her breasts look bigger. 'Oh yes, yes I do.'

'I think it's my favourite as well.'

'Oh, is it? Is it really?'

Brenda's hands, simple and ringless, give her a look of deliberately exposed nakedness. Under her clothes her body will have the same simple, natural appeal. A lustful appeal. Bold, for a girl of her age.

'It is quite simple to make. There's nothing difficult about it,' says Jessica curtly. 'Most Italian dishes are . . . colourful, mostly show.'

Music. What sort of music will appeal to them all?

Jessica tries a selection, although she feels out of place and unnatural. She is creating the atmosphere; even when she turns down the lamps she is pimping for her lover.

Rudi ought to be doing this.

But if he were, Jessica knows full well that she just could not stand it. No, distraught or not, it is better by far that she create the atmosphere, better that she maintain control for as long as she possibly can. Right up till the very last minute.

When the door closes behind them. She winces at the very thought.

Rudi with Brenda.

Jessica shivers.

Rudi doing things to Brenda. All that erotic energy directed towards that teenage body.

Perhaps it would have been easier if Jessica had gone out. She might have been spared some of the pain. She could have gone to the theatre with a friend and tried to forget all about it. Or put herself to bed with a handful of tranquillisers, a barren woman dead to the world.

But Jessica must steel herself and remember what this is all about. This is her idea, and Rudi is only doing her bidding. There is nothing unfaithful about it. She must remember her old school motto and walk in faith – because how can someone like Jessica possibly be jealous of a silly little snippet like Brenda?

The very idea is quite absurd. Surely.

Chapter eighteen

When there is no reason to get up in the morning, you tend to stay up late, watching the late-night films. You tend to leave your curtains drawn, the fire on, and sometimes you go to sleep on the sofa or in your chair.

There doesn't seem much point in getting undressed.

This happens to be one of those nights, and Shane, Eddie and Roy, who has materialised from somewhere, wish they had a satellite dish so that they could connect to Red Hot Dutch and put it on when Rita and Derek have gone upstairs. This Wednesday night they are having to put up with a western.

The first gunshot coincides with the stone through the window.

'Not again! Oh shit, no, not again!'

'Mum'll go out of her mind. She spent the whole of last night wide awake.'

'Come on,' says Roy. 'Bleeding heck, pick up a weapon and let's get out there.'

Brenda languishes in Jessica's sunken bath letting her fingers linger over her body, deeply pink and rubbery.

She ought to be bathing in asses' milk, like Cleopatra.

The different soaps, shellshaped, pastel and perfumed, are piled in a china water lily and Brenda has used far too many bubbles so when she raises her arms the froth eases over the edge and falls, like pieces of whipped-up topping, onto the thick green carpet.

In the narrow bath at home it is impossible to submerge every part of yourself at the same time. There is either a bent leg, or a resting foot, or you have to heave yourself up so your top half gets cold . . . ducking to avoid Doreen's dripping pants, her nylon bras, or her tights.

Doreen favours black. She considers anything black to be sexy. Black = wicked. Black = night. Black = erotic emotions.

But Brenda has chosen pure white underwear from Dorothy Perkins. Even the name, Dorothy Perkins, has an unsophisticated ring about it. Whoever Dorothy Perkins is, she is surely not a whore . . . whereas Janet Reger has different connotations and definitely smacks of the city. Cotton white underwear and a pure white, full-length nightie. White = innocence. White = submission. White = eggs waiting to be fertilised.

Snow White.

For the first time in her life Brenda has painted her toenails. Jessica allowed her to choose her colour from the drawerful of pinks and reds and beiges in her bedroom. Pretty Peach. She stretches one languid leg and lets it rest on the side of the bath. Pretty Polly. The whole of her leg is transformed. Brenda's feet look neat and shaped and elegant, like somebody else's.

Brenda lies back in the soft blue water and parts her legs as widely as the sides of the bath will allow.

A bread-knife. A cricket bat. A claw-headed hammer. These are the weapons which the Hodges boys wield as they venture out into the night, go out into the violent streets and the garbaged, stealthily whispering, dog-fouled grass of the Pennystone Estate.

No shops. No Health Clinic. No police house. No local garage. Nothing.

But the people.

They stand and they listen, three wiry young men in jeans and white T shirts, grown in their father's image – except for Shane, of course, of dubious paternity, who has a slightly different slant to his eyes and a sharper nose, hardly noticeable – and trying to be brave, a little larger than Derek but not sufficiently so to make them imposing enough to dominate whatever hides out there in the darkness.

Doreen in her ivory, upstairs where the lights are on, clings to her large and coarsely built mother, sobbing softly.

She wishes she had gone round to Nigel's.

'I don't know how long we can tolerate this,' says Rita, sitting on the edge of her sagging mattress with her dressing gown over her enormous shoulders, her daughter in her arms. 'Tell me again, Derek. Tell me what they told you at the council.'

Derek is getting dressed, slowly, with a view to going outside to support his gallant fighting sons. How many times have they gone over this? What he said, what they said . . . what sort of attitude they took towards him. 'They wrote down my name and address and said they would see what they could do, but they didn't hold out much hope, Rite. They said they were inundated with requests for transfers already. They suggested we advertised in local papers up north.'

'Oh, and how long do they expect this operation to take? Didn't you tell them what was happening?'

'A police matter – that's what they said. They asked if I had reported last night's attack, and that's when I went down the cop shop.'

'We are being singled out,' cries Rita. 'We are now the brunt of all the aggression. We are in physical danger! There is no longer any point in replacing the broken glass.'

'I told them that, Rita. That's exactly what I said to the inspector. And he said to phone if it happened again. What could he do, he said, if he wasn't given the opportunity to catch the buggers red-handed.'

'How can we bleeding well phone them when we haven't got a phone and the public one isn't working?'

Derek slowly pulls on his socks. 'I explained. Of course I explained. And they promised to patrol the area at given intervals throughout the night.'

'So where the pissing hell are they?'

Derek shakes his teeth free of liquid as he hoists them out of the bedside jar. 'It's not my fault, Rita. There's no point in taking it out on me.'

'I know, Derek, I know. But what is happening out there? Can you see anything from the window?'

'No,' says Derek. 'I don't want to get too close in case I throw a shadow for the little beggars to aim at. I can't see a thing. It's too dark.'

'There there, Doreen,' comforts Rita. 'There there, and look what you're doing to your pretty face. You should have stayed round at Nigel's. For the very first time I realise what Ma has been going through all these years. No wonder her nerves are in shreds. But at least her house is solidly built, and boarded up with thick pieces of planking. Sitting here feels no safer than sitting in a tent. All I can say is thank God, thank the Lord and all the saints that poor little Brenda, at least, is away from here tonight, safe and sound.'

Brenda lies in her fresh, forget-me-not-sprigged bed. The smell is of an orchardful of apples.

Little green apples. Bittersweet. They tingle the tongue like lemons.

This is a night she is bound to remember for the rest of her life.

Imagine spending the night with a dark-haired Agassi! The image, the spitting image of Agassi! Oh, if only she could tell Sandra.

Is Brenda not embarrassed? Does she not feel any maidenly shame, lying there so brazenly, prepared to be mounted by a virtual stranger?

No way. Twenty-five per cent of girls questioned in a recent survey said they would be prepared to have sex with a stranger for a million pounds. As Doreen rightly sneered at the time, 'What the hell's the matter with the others? Are they out of their minds?'

'No,' said Brenda, leaning over to take a look at the article. 'They were probably just lying. I mean, some people said they were not prepared to pick their nose for a hundred pounds and that's barmy.'

And a stranger means any old geezer . . . a dirty old man in a mac, a fat-fingered businessman with leering eyes, a gangly youth covered with acne . . . or someone with a stubby, prodding cock like Ginge. If the questionnaire had shown a stranger with the looks of Rudi, Brenda knows that the result would have been startlingly different.

The doorknob turns and in comes Rudi in a three-quarter-length silk dressing gown with Chinese dragons down the back. It does not look as if he is wearing anything underneath.

'Hi,' whispers Brenda shyly, aglow in the rays of the bedside light which she decided not to turn off. She is prouder of herself than she ever has been . . . with her new image, her burnished curly hair and her pure white nightie.

'You can say no,' says Rudi, coming to sit on the side of the bed and holding her eyes with his jet-black ones. 'Nobody is going to make you do anything you don't want to do.'

Brenda shivers all over. How gentle is his voice. How knowing is his smile. How different this is already. What a different approach from Ginge's.

'But I do want to,' she says, allowing Rudi to take her hand, and making the most of her eyelashes. Her hand feels small and soft inside his, a petal curled up in his hard one. 'I want to very much.'

'Not too much, I hope, Brenda. I don't want you to get hurt.'

'I know what I'm doing, Rudi,' she says. 'And I'm going to keep my eyes open.'

'They've gone,' says Shane, his slightly different eyes shining redly in the darkness. 'D'you think we have driven them off?'

'That's doubtful, but we might as well go back inside. We can't do anything but stand here and I don't think there's anyone around any more.'

'Come on, Mum, you can come down now,' Eddie assures her, laying down the hammer on the draining board where it is handy. 'It's all quiet on the western front and Shane's got the kettle on.'

'Are you sure?' calls down Big Rita. 'I've got Doreen here and she's terrified.'

'Yep. Whatever it was, it's all over.'

'For now at any rate,' mutters Derek, beginning to take off his clothes again.

'Cover yourself up, Doreen. You can't go downstairs like that. And your nose is running.'

So Doreen pulls a jumper over the chiffon, which just about covers her cleavage.

'What's that smell?'

Rita treads heavily down the stairs and pauses before the letterbox. 'What the hell is that poisonous smell?'

'Oh Mum!' Doreen trails weakly behind her. 'Oh Mum! Oh Mum, it's shit!'

'Shit? Where?'

'On the mat, look! Great big lumps of—'

'By God and it's human.'

Doreen screams aloud and starts pushing and struggling and sobbing.

'It's human all right.' Shane bends over in order to inspect the three great turds, holding his nose against the stench which, by now, has pervaded the whole downstairs of the house. Gone is the smell of chip fat and old cigarettes.

'They must have pushed it through at the same time they put the brick through the window. The bastards! The filthy, vile, fucking bastards!'

'Get yourselves into the kitchen and shut the door while I sort it out,' says Shane, retching. 'Give us a hand here, Eddie.'

'What are you going to do with it? Don't touch it! Don't touch it!'

'Of course I'm not going to touch it – what the hell d'you take me for? Give us the newspaper, Dad, quick.'

The *Sun* has many uses, but for this any one of the serious papers would be better.

'I can't bear it,' says Rita, all hunched up in manly brown, but still she does not weep. She is not the kind of woman to weep, for weeping never did any good and Rita is every inch her father's daughter. 'I cannot take any more.'

As if poor Rita doesn't have enough problems in her life.

'We should wrap it up and take it to the cop shop in the morning!'

'Just get it out of the house. Just get it away . . . and fetch the spray from the downstairs bog, and the Dettol from under the sink and scrub. It is an invasion,' moans Rita. 'And intolerable. What they have done to my house feels just the same as if they did it to my body.'

Well, it would do.

Rita swapped her body for her house when she married

Derek back in the sixties. She hated her body, but adored the house with its more acceptable pebble-dash skin and its marvellous custard-coloured carpets.

Even back then she managed to get the two structures muddled up.

So much safer to view the world through a pair of nets, rather than eyes that can cry.

Rudi is an excellent dancer and everyone knows that good dancers make good lovers. You do not have to bed a man to find out if he is up to scratch. Just watch him dancing. It must be something to do with rhythm.

'No, let me do that,' murmurs Rudi, in organising mood, while Brenda's body moves ceaselessly beneath his caressing fingers. 'Turn over, Brenda.'

Brenda never dreamed she had so many titillating holes and openings, so many intimate places to be intriguingly explored to the muttering of all those shockingly exciting four-letter words.

He feels her he tastes her he licks her he sniffs her.
He kisses her he flicks her he bends her he sucks her.
He rubs her he probes her he teases her he parts her.

Okay. Okay. That's not fair. We have been waiting so long we deserve something more explicit than that.

He strips her nightdress over her head and falls like an eagle upon his innocent prey.

Brenda's body swells and glows as she flails and threshes beneath him; it seethes with excitement. She has been mounted by a devil rider, despoiling and unmerciful, who drives her onwards towards a quite unendurable excitement.

The force which is Rudi, boisterous and tremendous, batters her as if she's a reed in the wind, in violent gusts, rending, bending and breaking so that nothing could survive its violent rage. She will be torn by her roots right out of the ground, and the land itself will be broken and devastated by the storm which rages around her, heedless and exhaustless, across her violated body.

Hot, wet and steaming Brenda struggles with her little-girl fears. She claws him as he whirls her off into space once again, trying to thrust him from her, raking her nails down his back and leaving livid red welts behind her. She tries to fasten her teeth in his neck, looks up and catches the glint of an earring and the sight of his face, dark and tempestuous, with a strange, triumphal smile, the smile of the vanquisher.

And Brenda's gone. With her legs wide open and her small breasts bouncing and her eyes rolling as he pumps his energy into her. And his seed. Her body is slippery with sweat and come. Fallen right off the edge of the world, she is bouncing around in a pit of erotic seethings.

'Are you okay?' asks Rudi.

Brenda cannot answer. Her voice seems to have left her, and all she has left is the broken caw of a rook.

Cystitis tomorrow, I fear, for Brenda, pounded and beaten like that. But for the moment she cannot stop sobbing.

By the time her lover is locked in congress with her secretary in the bedroom across the landing, Jessica is stalking the floor in her own room, hollow-eyed, gaunt and staring, all shrivelled up with terrible thoughts.

Rudi assured her that he would use only the minimum of effort in order to scatter his seed.

'Clinically, please, Rudi,' she said.

'Well naturally, my angel.'

Perhaps a triple brandy will help her to sleep tonight.

Chapter nineteen

We have to skip three weeks now and move on in a hurry to the end of May, which is round about the time that Vera Evans has made an official appointment, on the phone, to meet Theo Rosenthall, a producer from the BBC.

'Shall I come to you?' asks Vera, in her new mode of getting about, because Miss Rodriguez is happy to mind the house for an hour or so, as long as it is not a Monday or a Wednesday.

'I would rather come to you, so long as that is convenient, Mrs Evans. I shall need to look over the house, and I am planning to bring several bits of old newsreel of Lippington Road, and some stills, which I am sure will be fascinating to look at.'

'But I haven't got a video. I have nothing here except for a rented TV.'

'We will bring our own equipment, Mrs Evans. Don't worry,' says Theo Rosenthall. 'Do not put yourself out on our account in any way at all.'

'He sounded so nice,' says Vera to Rosita, when they sit out together on the pavement. 'Not at all iffy, like you would imagine. Not pompous, you know.' And she raises a cup of tea to her mouth with her shrivelled, mittened hand.

Rosita is wearing her bright red lipstick today, along with an embroidered skirt and a flamenco-type Spanish waistcoat. Vera has noticed how she tends to dress up or down, with the weather. If it gets any hotter than this, and it will when the summer comes, Vera is going to have to bring an umbrella out here, for shade.

'A lot of these people are terribly left wing, with long hair,' Rosita informs her. 'Redbrick-University types. It's not all Establishment, like it used to be. You have probably got one of those.'

'And you will stay with me, Miss Rodriguez, when Mr Rosenthall arrives? I wouldn't feel happy to cope with it all on my own,' says Vera doubtfully.

'Of course I will,' Rosita assures her, changing arms with her old grey knitting which is now forming the hopeful shape of a knee-length sock. 'For the nuns,' she told Vera, when she picked out the pattern. 'All my sisters embraced the religious life.' Her newly acquired glasses sit perilously on the end of her pointed nose. 'I shall be most fascinated to see what he says. And you haven't informed your daughter?'

'My daughter has her own terrible problems at the moment, not so dissimilar to mine,' says Vera. 'And I would not like to burden her with an added worry. She is having an awful struggle to try and arrange a transfer of her council house . . . They tell her to advertise up north, but who wants to go and live in Birmingham, or Preston, or Berwick-on-Clyde? There's no jobs up there, and from all I hear it's just as rough as it is in London.'

'Maybe your daughter should move in with you? That is, of course, if you don't mind sharing a house with Rita and her family.'

'We did talk about that, but of course, as you know, the conditions inside my house are not particularly suitable for accommodating extra numbers. And unfortunately, according to my son-in-law, Derek, a great deal of money would be required to bring it up to the most basic standards.'

'Well, that is a great shame.' Rosita's small brown face crinkles into sympathetic wrinkles. She must have been pretty in her youth. She must have turned a few eyes in her direction. Vera wonders why she never married. 'All that room,' says Rosita. 'All that space. And your poor daughter suffering as cruelly as she does.'

'She's a fighter, is Rita, like her father. She has inherited her father's stubborn nature, and Jack, bless his heart, fought on to the bitter end. He died right there you know, next to that water meter just to the right of your foot, but the road was cobbled in those days. It's almost every night now. They daren't leave the house unguarded . . . and they haven't a trustworthy neighbour, as I have.'

'What a pity it is, Mrs Evans, that you do not see more of your sons.'

'They have their own lives,' says Vera shortly. 'But my daughter, Rita, is very special. It must be sad for you, Miss Rodriguez, never to have had children of your own.'

Rosita puts her knitting down. She stares at her knobbly, wrinkled hands. She removes her glasses and rubs the lenses with the hem of her thick, black embroidered skirt. She goes on slowly, pausing, searching for the words. 'Sometimes, yes, it is true, I do think that. But then again when I see the burdens and the worries that the young people today seem to bring to their parents, I wonder about that. I really do. And our lives were so full, you see, there was never the time . . .'

'Your lives?' ventures Vera nosily.

'Yes, James Galbraith Holden. Maybe you have heard of him? The Pyramid Man?'

Vera has not. 'It does seem to ring a bell.'

'Such love,' hisses Rosita, her black eyes shining and shocking Vera. 'Such passion as you would never dream of.'

Vera looks at the ground, at the spot where her husband fell.

'All gone,' Rosita continues alarmingly, while the tiny gold rings in her ears dance. 'All gone, and lost for a million years to the winds and the desert sands.'

It's no good, thinks Vera. Friend or no friend, foreigners are different, have always been different and will continue to be different. She would never discuss her Jack like that. 'I will pop inside,' is all she can properly say, 'and brew up another pot of tea.'

Luckily, Theo Rosenthall suggested a Tuesday.

'So what sort of programme are you thinking about?' asks Rosita, drab in her mattest black on this cloudy morning.

'It is a series of programmes about interesting people who have spent their lives battling against the odds and are still battling.'

Rosita was wrong. Theo Rosenthall is neither an Establishment figure, nor a leftie. He is a comfortable man, wearing a Marks & Spencer's V-neck sweater, sky blue, and with a bald head. He is the sort of person you would imagine sitting on his couch watching the telly . . . not the type who actually *makes* the programmes.

'Oh!' Rosita lights up. 'Similar to that wonderful programme about the woman who farmed in Yorkshire? Such a lovely lady! I even watched the repeats. I watched her going round Europe, too, but to tell you the truth I was a little bit worried about that – thought she was being manipulated just a tiny bit. No criticism implied, of course, but you do understand? I would have bought the books, but in those days I did not have my glasses.'

'Exactly, Miss Rodriguez,' says Theo Rosenthall, pleased, moving a pile of old *Woman's Realms* and finding a small space for himself. 'I am so glad you understand which angle we intend to take. And my first dealings with Mrs Evans tell me that she will make the most splendid subject. She has a most appealing personality, the same wisdom in her voice as Hannah Hauxwell's, as well as that same air of being slightly mystified.'

It takes hours to show Mr Rosenthall round.

Rosita makes the tea and hands round the ginger nuts while Vera spends the morning answering Mr Rosenthall's many and varied questions and adding little memories of her own. He is fascinated to hear that she was married to the local coalman, that she lived here as a child, when the houses were more like tenements, and that she was here all throughout the war. She is, in fact, the last survivor of the many families who have lived, died, and passed through this proud but decaying building.

'The last house,' he muses. 'And it hasn't been touched for a hundred years. How wonderful to see it just as it was.'

'Oh, Mr Rosenthall, it was never as bad as this . . .'

'Structurally, I mean,' he reassures her, dunking his third biscuit. 'To see it like this is to be made aware of a great tragedy unfolding. I wonder . . . I wonder if it would be possible to get a Restraining Order on the inside of this house, to make it impossible for the owner to "bijou" it.'

'I don't think Edward Mullins would be too keen to be ordered to do anything. This is his house, and in his opinion he can do with it what he likes. And that is my experience,' says Vera.

'We shall see,' says Mr Rosenthall, a man who does not search the house for smell, unlike the police inspector. Indeed, Mr Rosenthall does not seem to notice any untoward odour. 'Now then,' he leans forward and rubs his hands, 'I would like to show you some old newsreels of this road way back in the forties. And after that we must discuss getting on with this project as quickly as possible. These programmes are scheduled for the summer . . . I have three slots to fill, and I would very much like to make Number 6, Lippington Road, and you, Mrs Evans, the subject of them.'

Vera feels as if she has been chosen to star in a film – which she has. Her life is going to be glorified and she will wear her favourite hat. She is overwhelmed with excitement and smiles happily and expectantly, but Rosita, sharp as a knife as ever, is saying: 'I hope this will not cause any serious repercussions for Mrs Evans. She is already under a good deal of pressure, and already worried about her future.'

'On the contrary,' says Mr Rosenthall, while setting up his equipment on the cleared orange box. 'I understand your reservations but the effects will be quite the reverse. There is bound to be a strong public reaction to this outrage. I am not promising anything, but an outraged public can be exceedingly generous. I assure you, Miss Rodriguez, that the showing of this programme will do Mrs Evans' cause nothing but good.'

'I don't want pity,' snaps Vera, picking up the badly torn tomcat, Dixen, tattily furred, and stroking him anxiously on her knee. 'It was pity that got me that flat at Hooper's Tower. It is pity that forces old women out of their houses and into these terrible homes. It is pity that reduces them to playing Bingo and clapping their hands to Olde Time music and having their bottoms wiped by school-leavers. I don't want pity. I am not having any of that.'

How suddenly lives can change. Lives that have been pottering along exactly the same for twenty, thirty, or even forty years, and then suddenly, for good or for bad, these lives are turned on their heads.

Which is why suicide is generally such a bad idea.

A few days after that preliminary discussion, the film-maker comes round with his cameras and his men.

Suddenly, what with her new friend and all this excitement, nights for Vera no longer spill into day.

'What shall I wear? I have other clothes, you know, put away in the trunk on the second floor where Dora Baker used to live, with Amy and Linda.'

'I want you exactly as you are,' Theo Rosenthall reassures her.

'I must ask,' Vera quavers. 'I have to ask you this: have you contacted Edward Mullins yet? Does he know you are filming, and can I expect more trouble from him?'

Theo Rosenthall is focusing on Vera's face, trying to catch it at its most effective angle. It is a beautiful face, a marble carving with life's experiences picked out in furrows of old gold. Her gnarled hands are winter leaves, veined and dry from a lifetime of drying tears, washing clothes and scrubbing floors. Her clothes, stained and darned, hang off her shrunken bones as drapes do over a statue and her smile is sweet, her blue eyes twinkle with life. Yes, Vera Evans will make good television.

'Not yet, Mrs Evans,' he says gently. 'We will be contacting Mr Mullins when these initial takes have been done. That bit of drama will make for excellent viewing, without any doubt.'

They are positioning bright electric lights round Vera's over-lived-in living room, lights which pick up all the dust and fluff, unlike the kindly paraffin. She prefers the softer paraffin. Vera hurries about with a dustpan and brush, breathing heavily, moving slowly. 'What on earth will people think of me?' she frets, trying to sweep up dried scraps of cat food, biscuit crumbs, split sugar and that old split tea bag.

'What if they cut the electric off again?' she worries. 'We don't get any warning, you know. One minute it's on and the next . . . everything goes silent and dark.'

'Then we would use our own generator. No problem.'

Although the electric is now reconnected, Vera prefers the paraffin, apart from the fridge, but that is extra, not an essential. 'Once you get used to a system it is better to stick to it, and I can ring up and order the paraffin and pay them out of my purse, unlike the electricity people. And of course,' as she confided darkly to Rosita the other week, 'who knows if the electricity branch manager is not in Mullins' pocket, or a member of the same Lodge, for that matter!'

But maybe, to be fair, she ought to tell Rita. After all, Rita is going to get one hell of a shock one of these days when she turns on her telly to find her mother chatting breezily into her sitting room.

But what if Rita disapproves and makes her stop? What if she sends Theo Rosenthall and his nice men away? Rita does tend to get aggressive and rush into the fray without thinking. She always did. Even as a child she was fiercer and stronger than any of her brothers.

Vera had always secretly hoped that Rita would not get married. Not unkindly, you understand, but if only her last and favourite child, a girl, would stay at home to keep her company and maybe even look after her in her old age, how happy she would be.

For those, thinks Vera, were the happiest years of her life, after Jack died and the boys were gone and there was just herself and Rita. Oh, she missed Jack, of course. He was a good and upright man and she won't pretend she didn't. She grieved. She mourned like any good wife would. It was such a shock, with him being so young. The bed was cold although she certainly did not miss the sex. It was *bang bang* and not even a *thank you, Mam* with the coalman. But the first few months were lonely.

But there wasn't the cooking to get done on time . . . Jack worked hard whenever he could, when his back would let him, and he expected to find his tea on the table at the end of it, with a packet of shag and his matches beside it. And he was a fussy eater – meat and two veg, nothing else would do. Suddenly there wasn't the washing, all that black, grimy coaldust which got into everything, down between the cushions of the sofa, under the pictures on the walls, even in the folded ironing no matter how clean she tried to keep the house. Scrubbing, cleaning, dusting. After Jack died she and

Rita pushed up their sleeves and gave the whole house a good going over, and it lasted, it shone, and it stayed that way for months.

The lavatory stayed clean and the two of them could watch what they wanted on the telly, and Vera so enjoyed those evenings when she and Rita would settle down after Rita got home from work, and have their tea on their laps, everything they needed on the tray.

Rita took over all the heavy jobs in the house and, to start with, she didn't seem interested in blokes – not like the other little scrubbers in the street with their skirts halfway up to their arses.

'Men are disgusting and cannot even aim properly,' Rita used to say, and no wonder, as the only girl and the house always full of her noisy, demanding brothers.

They teased her.

Sometimes, with their tricks, they went too far.

But Rita was a big girl and gave as good as she got.

Rita preferred to go out with her friends . . . to the pictures . . . to the café down the road, or she was happy alone in her room listening to her records. And Rita's spots *were* a problem.

Vera cannot remember exactly when things started to change.

Rita began to dress up and do her hair in those extraordinary styles.

'Where are you getting all this money from, Rita?'

'I do overtime and they pay me double. Why, where d'you think I'm getting it from? Nicking it?'

But one day Rita came home with Derek in tow, half her size. She had never even mentioned his name before and that was that.

Vera lost her.

Rita was a good girl.

Vera expected Rita and Derek to move in with her. Well, there was so much room and the cost of living was so expensive. But she didn't. She said goodbye to her mum with an ease which surprised and pained Vera.

When Shane was born two months after the wedding, Vera was so shaken she didn't even know what to say. But as Rita didn't have boyfriends, there was no doubt and everyone assumed the baby was Derek's.

Rita is still a good girl and a dutiful daughter, but she does have this tendency to take over.

No, Vera decides she will not tell Rita about Mr Rosenthall. Not yet. Not till the filming is done with.

Chapter twenty

There is much going on, around the end of May, about which Rita does not know.

Brenda, of course, is officially two months pregnant. She went out for a meal with Jessica and Rudi in order to celebrate. Champagne, caviar – the whole works.

She is also, unfortunately, in love, a painful fact of which both Jessica and Rudi are perfectly aware, although their reactions are somewhat dissimilar.

'You were cruel and callous to allow it to develop,' says Jessica. 'It makes the whole thing so much more sensitive, particularly as we have to work together. Surely you were not moved to utter any protestations of love?'

'No, I was not. But how could I help her response?' asks the mutinous Rudi. 'A girl like that would have fallen in love with a duck if it had given her pleasure. The poor little sod had never reached orgasm before.'

'Oh! And did she tell you that?'

'Yes, when I asked her.'

'So did you feel you needed to ask her? Were you perfectly happy to converse with the girl on that intimate level?'

'It is hard not to converse on an intimate level in that particular situation,' Rudi replies snappily. 'And anyway, why should you be worried? Surely you cannot imagine that I am going to go off with a little bit of fluff like that?'

Rudi is especially buoyant these days because he has landed a part in *EastEnders* . . . this happened on the day the pregnancy was confirmed, and he links the two joyful events together in his head. 'A lucky baby! Fate is smiling upon us and this was all meant to be!'

He has written an excited letter to Mama in Italy.

Already, in ebullient form, he has dragged Jessica round The White House linen store in New Bond Street and ordered towels, baby clothes, sheets, pillowcases and a whole drawerful of tiny bootees. 'But this is supposed to be unlucky,' Jessica protested.

'No, only the pram is unlucky,' Rudi happily assured her.

The decorators came in last week to receive the proud father's instructions.

'The whole flat?' asked Jessica, laughing. 'Is that really necessary! Does a baby need so much space?'

'Bedroom, playroom, kitchen and nanny's room. And this is the wallpaper, this is the material. It is *perfetto* – absolutely right!'

'Oh honestly, Rudi!' exclaimed Jessica fondly, amused by so many blue bunny rabbits and pink teddy bears. 'I never realised you were such an old softie.'

'Sebastian for a boy. Lola for a girl.'

'Lola? That sounds vaguely naughty to me. Why not Jezebel?'

'Well yes, actually, I like the sound of Jezebel . . .'

'We will stick with Lola,' said Jessica quickly. 'But she'd better be pretty to suit a name like that.'

'Oh, she will be.' The conceited Rudi is also convinced that his own genes will swamp the colourless, vapid genes of young Brenda who, sweet as she is, is no oil painting. 'But I would have liked to have met the family.'

'Perhaps it is better that we did not.'

'A December baby. Perhaps Noël . . .'

'Sebastian has a more positive ring,' decides Jessica, 'and the baby may be born before Christmas.'

'Babies can be late,' says Rudi.

'And they have also been known to be early,' says Jessica.

It is as she predicted, already. It is marvellous the way Rudi has changed his ways in just a few short weeks.

Already he wears an expectant, paternal look.

Even when walking with him along a pavement he no longer turns around and ogles pretty women, or whistles in that common way that annoys her so much. He no longer makes jokes about the size of women's tits or legs on the television – jokes that are deliberately hurtful and intended to make her angry, while he remains impervious to her distress . . . or glad of it, possibly? It must be a kind of perverted punishment for something she cannot and never did understand. Perhaps he feels trapped – trapped by the intensity of their relationship, or by Jessica's money? However, instead of all that he is far more embarrassing in the vicinity of a pram, or when he sees an advertisement with a baby in it. He keeps a notepad next to his chair into which he enters lists of the products he intends to buy after his child is born: nappies, orange juice, baby food, talc, shampoo . . .

And apart from her intense infatuation which cannot be helped and which is surely a passing phase, Brenda is being remarkably sensible and grown-up about the whole thing.

'Now, you won't make a mistake and mix up the dates in a lax moment, will you, Brenda?'

'Don't worry!'

'And you won't forget your next appointment? Those vitamins are essential.'

'They don't do any good. They just make my shit go black.' But Brenda has gone all dreamy these days and rarely complains.

'Well, you must take them, all the same.'

'I expect my blood pressure is up, what with all the trouble going on at home. Last night was as bad as ever. Mum cried, and I have never seen her crying before.'

Brenda is always trying to inveigle her way into the flat at Lippington Road, and Jessica honestly wouldn't mind, if it wasn't for the infatuation. After all, she does not want to encourage it, but then again Brenda must be looked after. It is a tricky situation . . . fraught with problems. 'Well, Brenda, you know you can move into the flat if you feel you need a break from it all – a short break. Haven't you got any relatives who would have you, just while this dreadful problem is sorted out? Grandparents, for example?'

'Doreen has already gone to Nigel's – she lives there permanently now. And I've only got one gran, and she hasn't the room at the moment.'

'Well maybe, in a little while, your mother will be able to sort something out, or these attacks will stop. I must say, I cannot imagine what the police think they are doing. How are these little savages allowed to get away with their vicious behaviour, night after night?'

'The police don't want anything to do with it,' says Brenda morosely. 'They don't really like coming to the Pennystone Estate after dark. And the kids are slippery as eels. They know their way around in the dark, in and out of all the lanes and alleyways.'

My God. What lives some people are forced to endure.

It is almost unbelievable!

Thank God Jessica can afford to live in Lippington Road.

Rosita's friendship with the unpleasant old character at Number 6 is slightly worrying, though. Apparently, Jessica has been told, they sit outside on the pavement together, the whole morning and sometimes most of the afternoon as well. The other day Jessica found a fingerless mitten on the gleaming white laminate beside the toaster.

'Rosita, has that friend of yours been here?'

'Why, Miss Jessica?'

'Because I have just found this . . .' and she held up the disreputable accessory between finger and thumb.

Rosita smiled. 'Oh no, I found it. She left it beside her chair by accident so I brought it inside in case somebody pinched it.'

'And who on earth would want it? Look at it, Rosita. Look at it! It is absolutely filthy.'

'Mrs Evans is a very old lady . . .'

'I daresay she is. But there *are* limits.'

'Your father was never a snob, Miss Jessica,' says Rosita slyly.

'No, sadly, it is quite apparent that he was not!'

'And I thought you said I was free to invite my friends down here.'

'Well, of course you are, Rosita. I am not trying to argue with you, but one has to be careful, these days, to whom one gives one's friendship. There are people . . .'

'Yes, Miss Jessica?'

'Well, we'll just leave it there. I thought Mrs . . . Evans was moving out.'

'Not now,' says Rosita with unexpected confidence. 'Not for a little while, anyway.'

What on earth can Rosita see in her? 'Well, in future, Rosita, please endeavour to keep the kitchen surfaces free of such germ-ridden rubbish. Who knows where this has been! One only has to look at it, never mind touch it, and the mind boggles.'

And Jessica wonders whether, for the old woman's sake, she ought to get onto the council. After all, the council tax is enormous – surely some of that money could be well-spent clearing the unhygienic conditions next door.

She and Rudi were sitting out having a drink last Tuesday evening when there was a familiar crackling sound next door, of something heavy being dragged through the grass, and a soggy flump as it was forked on the bonfire.

Then it came again . . . all that black, belching sooty smoke.

Hiame's eyes started out of her head and the poor little thing began coughing. Jessica held a dainty handkerchief up over her nose. 'Go and have a word, Rudi, for goodness' sake! Tell her to put it out or to damp it down or something!'

'We went through all this last summer and it didn't do any good.'

'What the hell is she burning, anyway?'

'Probably all her winter rubbish, by the smell of it. Or dead cats.' But Rudi went over reluctantly and called through the fence: 'Mrs Evans? Mrs Evans! Do you have to start burning your rubbish on the first really pleasant summer evening, when some people are trying to sit out and enjoy the fresh air? It does smell very unpleasant, you know.'

'I can't help that,' the voice from next door came cawing back. 'It's not against any rules. It says in my lease I can burn my rubbish whenever I like, except on a Sunday.'

'Well, I just wish you would give a little more thought . . .'

'If you don't have a bleeding washing machine how else are you expected to get rid of all your old clothes?'

'Well, perhaps you shouldn't be so extravagant, Mrs Evans. If you have got clothes you can afford to burn . . .'

'I don't ask for them,' the old neighbour shouted raucously. 'They bring them. They bring them and they dump them and the cats sleep all over them and I haven't time to wear them and the dustbin men won't take them . . . and you can just go and tell Mr Mullins that.'

'Mr Mullins? What has he got to do with this?'

'Aha, I know what you are up to and don't think that I sodding don't.'

Rudi shrugged and gave up. Screwy. Bonkers. Completely gone in the head.

'Charity,' said Jessica sharply, forced to retreat indoors. 'These fools who go around distributing their largesse to anyone over seventy, vicars, and middle-aged woman about their good works, don't they realise that some folks are beyond all that? Whatever you do for some people it is never appreciated. They should take her off and put her in a home, for everyone's sake!'

But even that uncalled-for setback could not destroy the happiness that Rudi and Jessica now share.

Rudi is proud and thrilled that his seed worked so efficiently; always the stud at heart, now, remarkably speedily, he has managed to prove it.

And Jessica has managed to buy him that which was always so dear to his heart. That which will keep him faithful to her forever. No more worries. No more agonising pangs of jealousy at parties, at dinners, or even out for walks in the park. It is as if a stone has been rolled away from her heart at last and she walks with a lighter step, her head held even higher.

After all, in spite of her qualms, in spite of their five nights together, in spite of the fact that she is the 'mother' of his child and powerfully fertile, Brenda does not really count.

Jessica is the boss.

Brenda is the underling in mind and soul and body, and yet Brenda has gained ground. She is no longer ignored by Jessica.

Jessica has been known to sit at her desk and think about Brenda, as Brenda once did about her. Jessica has to force from her mind the terrible picture she has, of Brenda, naked, with all that hairy softness between her legs . . . Brenda's hard little tits in Rudi's mouth.

Whereas Brenda has often thought of Jessica in that way, to make her less intimidating, like some people enjoy imagining the Queen on the lavatory.

The Queen is probably the most thought-of person sitting, dignified, on the lavatory, in the whole of Her Dominions.

Standards are slipping.

Tap tap tap on her tinfoil feet goes Hiame.

Clack clack clack on her Gucci shoes goes Jessica.

'Good morning, Brenda!'

'Good morning, Jessica!'

'And how are we this morning?'

'Fine, thank you very much.'

'Give me five minutes, dear, and then you can bring in the coffee.'

Luckily, so far, there is no sign, nothing to give away the fact that skinny little Brenda is pregnant and three months gone. With a bit of luck she will reach the sixth month and still conceal her condition from the firm, and her mother, with some carefully chosen clothes. I mean, naturally Jessica does not want to have Brenda in the flat, in the newly decorated nanny's room, until she absolutely has to.

Chapter twenty-one

I hate to be the one to pass on such information, but our dearly beloved fairy tales are nothing but an orgy of erotica, and even the simple practice of spinning is a way of expressing female masturbation.

All hair signifies pubic hair, and those innocent little fairies are nothing but nubile vaginas on wings. The deviant story of Cinderella is to do with foot fetishes, and while *her* little foot represents virginity, the ugly sisters, with their huge and ugly vaginas, have definitely been about a bit.

There is no need to explain what part of the male anatomy Tom Thumb and Rumpelstiltskin represent.

Apparently it was the Victorians, ever on the lookout, who spotted all this nastiness, and edited the stories so that they were fit for the nursery.

If Rita, her mother, is the wicked queen or the witch, as all mothers are, and if Rudi is the toad-turned-prince, what can Jessica possibly be? Is she a rival?

It is not quite as straightforward as that, for it was Jessica who provided Brenda with her lover.

Could she be an ugly sister, a contestant representing experience and too much knowledge, trying to ease Brenda out?

That sounds much more like it.

But Brenda needs to cultivate Jessica, for without Jessica's blessing Brenda might never see Rudi again.

It is all so complicated, when really all Brenda is, is in love.

And can you honestly blame her?

'Where've you been? I waited for you all last Saturday and you never turned up.'

'I was busy, Ginge, and I never said I was going to be there.'

'Well, I won the match. You missed me winning the match. I won a hundred pounds. We could have done something.'

'What?'

'I dunno. But we could have done something.'

The thought that Ginge, not Rudi, is the father of the child she carries inside her is so unpleasant that Brenda has nearly come to disbelieve it herself. It is entirely possible, thinks Brenda with ignorance, that Rudi's sperm have by-passed Ginge's, have knocked them out of the way, thrown out the contaminated egg and fertilised another.

Brenda's little baby will look nothing like Ginge, with his coarse red skin, his freckles, his thickset features and his scowl. No, it will be blackhaired and finely modelled, like Rudi. And Brenda is going to give him the present that Jessica is unable to give, the most important and precious present he will ever have in his life.

'Well,' Ginge waits at the door with his beer belly bursting from his tight leather jacket. 'Are you coming out tonight then?'

'I can't. I don't want to leave Mum. The trouble might well start up again and she feels much safer if we are all here together. She worries about me being out. She worries about me getting back. And you haven't got any transport, have you, Ginge?'

'Since when have I had the money for a motor?'

'Well then,' sniffs Brenda, reluctant, sulking at the door.

'Are you giving me the push?' asks Ginge directly.

'If you like.'

'Well are you, or aren't you?'

'Okay then, if you want to know I am.'

'Some other bloke?'

Brenda simpers, 'Well, wouldn't you just like to know?'

So Ginge goes muttering off with his pool cue in its case under his arm.

Ginge could be the wicked dwarf, the one who has caught his beard in the roots of a tree. But Brenda, unlike Snow White or Rose Red, is not prepared to be nice to him. She knows that

Ginge will not turn into anything better and he certainly has no interesting sacks of gold buried in the undergrowth. And anyway, Mum doesn't like him.

'I heard you,' says Doreen, just visiting, as she does these days.

'Well, you shouldn't have been listening.'

'Couldn't help it. You've chucked him then? And about time too, miserable little sod. Mum'll be pleased, she never liked him. She thought you could do better than that.'

'I might have already,' says Brenda coyly. 'Wouldn't you like to know?'

'Tell me, tell me,' says greedy Doreen.

But Brenda is only dreaming, because Rudi is not hers to own. The only result of her brave decision is that she now has nowhere to go in the evenings, apart from round to Sandra's, and even then she has to be back before dark.

They all do.

All Rita's children.

'Maybe we ought to move to Vera's, just temporary-like, until we get something permanent sorted out,' says Derek at breakfast, up early for once in order to get a lift to the bookies with Roy.

'Oh no, not Gran's,' says Brenda, digging into a new jar of chocolate spread.

'What difference would it make to you? You're never sodding here. Always staying with that snooty boss of yours and never asking her in when she gives you a lift back . . .'

'That's not true, Dad. I sleep here far more often than I sleep there, and I like staying with Miss Holden. She talks, and does other interesting things. Last time she treated me to the theatre. You ought to be pleased.'

'But what's all this about not going to Ma's?' asks Mum, hurrying round searching for her handbag because she is already late for her lift. 'Surely you don't want to stay here?'

'But Gran's house is so dark, and big and cold. And where would we sleep? There aren't any beds.'

'We would take our own beds, of course. All our beds and all our curtains and carpets. And our chairs . . .'

'Maybe Gran wouldn't like it,' says Brenda.

'Of course she would. She has always been keen that we move over there. Right from the beginning she wanted us there, didn't she, Derek, and now, what with the Mullins' men, she'd be even more eager, I'm sure.'

'You're late, Mum. There's Dil blowing her horn outside.'

'I'm off,' roars Rita, stumbling out of the door with her coat all undone and her scarf all over the place.

'Well, I think we could make it quite homely,' says Dad, 'with a splash of paint here and there. That's what the Jordans did in the end – they had to move in with his mother.'

'We should wait,' says Brenda defiantly, 'and see what the council can do.'

'I thought you were fond of your gran.'

'I am, Shane, I am. I just don't fancy going to live in that house, that's all. The kids can't keep this up. They'll get fed up and leave us alone; it will soon be somebody else's turn. At least, here, we've got beds to sleep in. If we went to Gran's and she died or something we would all be evicted, and end up sleeping in cardboard boxes.'

'She's got a point, Shane,' says Dad. 'When you think about it.'

But you can tell he is disappointed.

Unfortunately, under the circumstances, going to Gran's does seem the most sensible option.

The Hodges cannot tolerate this sort of persecution much longer. Nobody could. Night after night they are hounded from their beds by the sounds of revving cars or smashing glass, and last week the little bastards smeared filth all over the remaining windows.

The house walls are covered in graffiti, mostly depicting the private parts of the human body.

You can see Mum's nerves are snapping.

Brenda has tried so hard to hide her family.

Guiltily, shamefully, bitterly, she has tried.

But if Brenda went to live at Gran's, there is no way Jessica would not find out. She despises Gran, and she would also despise the rest of Brenda's relations, viewing them with the same distaste that Mum felt for the newcomers, the problem families who now overrun the Pennystone Estate.

Lowering the tone of the area.

Just to think about it makes poor Brenda cringe.

And Rudi the discerning, Rudi the sensitive, who has had such run-ins with Gran over the banging of the bedstead and her habitual bonfires – all these incidents were related with cruel, unpleasant laughter – would view Brenda in a very different light if he knew she was related to Gran, if he knew from whence she came.

Jessica suggested just a couple of nights, but Rudi insisted that that might not be sufficient. It was he who persuaded Jessica to let him bed Brenda for five nights in a row in order to be certain. You could see how unhappy Jessica was, but she agreed in the end. She always agrees with Rudi in the end. So Brenda and Rudi had five blissful evenings, and once they didn't go to sleep until dawn. Making love with such raw desire. Making beautiful, wonderful love.

The memory of those nights torments her.

Oh Rudi! How Brenda yearns. Only to look at him gives her greater pleasure than anything she has ever experienced before.

The thought that she might never feel those marvellous sensations again . . . Rudi with his virile, powerful beauty, Rudi's body pressing against hers, Rudi kissing her all over, Rudi squeezing her breasts while he entered her from behind because with Rudi there was no shy modesty allowed . . . the thought of missing all this, forever, is so painful it brings tears to Brenda's pale grey eyes.

And still, even now, he treats her with all the respect you might give to a princess – kissing her hand, even when Jessica's there, pulling out chairs for her, and he bought her a rose that time they all went to the theatre. He bought one for Jessica, too, of course – but he didn't forget Brenda, did he?

In her heart of hearts Brenda believes that the spectacular Rudi secretly loves her, because how could you make love like that with someone you didn't care for? He could have just screwed her and left, couldn't he? He could have gone across the landing and spent the rest of the night in Jessica's bed, but he didn't. And when Brenda asked him about that he said, 'I'm not going to use you and walk away, Brenda. I'm not that sort of person. You are to be the mother of my child and for that reason, if for no other, you deserve a certain amount of respect.'

Respect?

But Brenda does not particularly want to be respected.

She did not choose that nightie in order to be respected. If she'd wanted respect she would have chosen something in grey silk. And he is still with Jessica. Perhaps Jessica knows how to please him? Or, more likely, he is still with Jessica because of her money.

Hopeless in her delicious anguish, Brenda wishes she was rich. Just in case.

She watched Rudi's face the day they went to get the pregnancy confirmed, the day they went to that posh Mount Hall Clinic, nothing like a hospital at all with its fitted carpets and bowls of flowers.

Even the receptionists were charming, and wore pretty polka-dot dresses of blue.

The tension would have been unendurable if Brenda had not already known she was pregnant; poor Rudi, he was so excited, he was so pathetically eager. But Jessica gave her a secretive smile while Rudi's attention was on something else, and in this way his two women could relax and enjoy their little deception.

Nothing but the best was good enough for Rudi's baby, and at Mount Hall the best was on display all around you.

Brenda would have her baby here, in a single room that was as comfortable and elegantly furnished as any hotel room. She would choose her meals, wine and spirits included, from a proper menu. She could even sit up in bed surrounded by flowers and watch the telly.

All this was a bit different from St Margaret's with it sterile rows of beds, hatchet-faced orderlies and its high Victorian windows.

But Brenda paled; she thought they could have done

something to make the delivery room look more inviting. Did they have to display that hard, raised bed, and the glaring lights, the chrome, and all the metal basins set out round the walls? No, Brenda did not approve of the delivery room, and even the hearty Jessica grimaced.

'You probably won't even have to come in here. Most women give birth in their rooms. You must remember you are down for an epidural, Brenda, so you will feel absolutely nothing at all. And we will be with you to encourage you on so you see, you really mustn't worry.'

Even the gynaecologist was polite and friendly, not like when she had to go in with her ear when she was six years old and Mum got shouted at for being over-protective and interfering. Mr Teddington-Jones was a comforting man with warm, squishy hands, and he put a towel over Brenda before he examined her, for modesty's sake.

'You will be pleased to know, Mrs—'

'Miss Hodges, actually.'

'Well, Miss Hodges, you will be pleased to know that you are most certainly pregnant.'

'How far on?' asked Brenda, wringing her conspiratorial hands.

'Well, how long ago did you say you had your last period? Let me check your chart. Ah yes, just six weeks ago, and I would say that that was just about right. You can expect your baby in the last week of December, give or take a week or two. First babies are renowned for their awkwardness.' And then Brenda and Mr Teddington-Jones went back into the reception lounge to announce the good news to Jessica and Rudi.

First he kissed Brenda – lifted her right up in his arms and did a kind of jig, and then he kissed Jessica. In the end they were standing in a circle, holding hands together and beaming, almost a happy little family already. How different this was! How different from the unhappy beginnings her baby would otherwise have had . . . Confessions, Dad shouting, Mum swearing . . . and lined up like milking cows with your tights round your ankles, which is what Brenda had heard still happened at St Margaret's.

Oh yes, Brenda has good reasons to be grateful to Jessica.

'And this is the proud father,' said Mr Teddington-Jones, shaking hands.

'I certainly am,' said Rudi.

'Well done! Well done, sir,' congratulated Mr Teddington-Jones as if he was handing a jockey a cup, regarding Jessica oddly and no doubt wondering who she was and what she was doing in the winners' enclosure.

By Rudi, out of Brenda.

And doesn't that say it all?

That was the night they went out for a meal, to celebrate.

How Brenda loves sitting next to Rudi and watching him all night.

Brenda sits at her word-processor and ponders. So much is happening it is hard to keep track. D'you think she should have mentioned the fact that Ginge has bright red hair?

Chapter twenty-two

Things are hotting up round at Number 6, Lippington Road.

Vera not only considers Rosita Rodriguez to be her dearest friend, but also the kindly, interested Theo Rosenthall and his cheery assistants Craig and Matt in their jeans so tight they make Vera laugh. She has spent two whole nights in their company, and you cannot spend a night with anyone without getting to know them well. Nights are quite different from days in that respect, possibly because they are dark and quiet, much deeper than days, and seem to last twice as long.

The camera followed Vera on her ten o'clock, one o'clock and four o'clock rounds.

'Have you ever found anything?' whispered Theo.

'Not yet.'

'But what exactly are you expecting to find?'

'As long as I do my rounds, varying the timetable every night, and making sure my torchbeam can be seen through the windows, I don't expect to find anything. The Mullins' men would rather not be seen, you see. Like rats under the floorboards. Like cockroaches that prefer dark places.'

The camera follows Vera to the dark and musty top storey. Here the floorboards creak and little winds blow in through the cracks around the wobbling windows, and cry like lost voices down the throats of the large, deserted fireplaces.

'How can you be certain, Vera, that the sounds you have heard in the past are in any way connected with Mr Mullins?'

Vera smiled gently. 'Everyone asks me that. The police asked me that – even Rita asks me that. I know it in my *bones*, Mr Rosenthall, and I can describe it no more rationally than that.'

'Well, the letters you have shown me certainly prove this

Mullins to be a hard-headed businessman, but is he really so ruthless? Would he send his men in here to block up the drains, and pour water down the chimneys . . . ?'

'Oh, he's done worse than that, Mr Rosenthall. He has drowned my darling kittens.'

'Oh?'

'Yes. One night I came up here in answer to the sound of crying and found six pathetic newly-born kittens awaiting their fate in the box-room. And when I explored further, I found little bits of fur, where the Mullins' men have obviously done their foul works before, floating about in the water tank! I didn't mention it to Rita, of course. It was far too awful, it would have upset her too much.'

'Is Rita fond of animals?' asked Theo, following her around the echoing house, pointing out the shots he wants to Craig, who carries the camera.

'No, not particularly. In fact she refuses to keep a pet, even though poor Brenda has always wanted an Alsatian. My little granddaughter would have been happy with a hamster, actually – but no, Rita won't have it. But anyone would be made upset by such a heartbreaking story. It was not necessary to tell her, and so I did not. I do not like worrying my daughter unnecessarily, Mr Rosenthall. She has far too much on her plate already.'

'I see.'

'And do you know, Mr Rosenthall, not one litter of kittens has been born in this house since.'

Bearing in mind the rank whiff of cats, Theo Rosenthall could have said, 'And a good thing, too!' but he is far too polite a man to make that sort of heartless comment. He does not even like to mention the fact that the unreliable electricity connection to Number 6, Lippington Road is the simple result of bills unpaid. By the look of Vera's dresser drawer, stuffed with unopened envelopes, such payment could be so easily overlooked.

But you cannot argue with broken windows, dog's mess through the letterbox and water down the chimneys. Something is going on here to make the old lady as frightened as this, and it isn't something very nice.

That night, Vera was having trouble with her indigestion: even bicarb in warm water failed to shift it. Theo Rosenthall was directly responsible for her pain. At ten o'clock the film crew had rung up and ordered pizzas. Over-excited and unused to eating so late at night, Vera ate one and a half all by herself . . . and suffered accordingly for the next twenty-four hours.

Rosita says: 'They are staying at home far more than they used to, and I shouldn't complain but it does make me uneasy. You see, I am not used to sharing, although James and I spent many months travelling about and sleeping in hotels. Travel was his business, you see. He was not a man to spend more than a few days in the same place. I am far happier with the whole house to myself although, of course, I rarely leave the basement.'

You can tell Rosita does not entirely approve of her benefactors next door although she never quite comes out and says so. 'And since that new friend of theirs, Brenda, has been around, Miss Jessica and Mr Rudi are like two quite different people. All lovey-dovey again. All sunshine and roses.'

'Brenda? That's the name of my favourite grandchild.'

'It's an odd relationship, really. They call her a friend, and yet they treat her more like a child. For example, they have never introduced any of their other friends to me by their Christian names. Funny little thing she is, quite unlike anyone else Miss Jessica has to stay. Down to earth, you know, no airs and graces. Sometimes she will come down and chat to me in the kitchen asking all sorts of personal questions about Mr Rudi. Sleeps in the spare room, too. There is something going on between her and Mr Rudi.'

'How do you know that, Miss Rodriguez?'

'I wouldn't like to tell you how. All I will tell you is that I do the washing in that house.'

'Perhaps Miss Jessica is not aware it is going on?'

'But that's just not possible, Mrs Evans. You don't know Miss Jessica as I do. She watches Mr Rudi like a hawk, even goes through his pockets from time to time. At one time, I believe, she even had him followed.'

'Goodness!'

'So she would certainly be aware of any hanky-panky taking place under her own roof. No, no, I cannot explain it. It is all most strange. I don't know where she comes from, this Brenda, but I have a feeling she has something to do with Miss Jessica's work.'

'Probably a colleague,' says Vera.

'Probably. We shall see.'

'I would like you to see the footage we have already got – the rushes, as it were, because of course we need your permission before we can put any of this on air.'

Vera and Rosita sit watching, excited, on the cat-littered sofa, while Theo Rosenthall runs the unedited film, sucking his barley sugars as usual.

'Oh, I sound like such a fool!' And Vera hides her head in her hands. 'I would have put my teeth in if I'd known. Oh no, you can't show me looking like that!'

'But that is how you do look, dear,' laughs Rosita.

'No! No, I don't. And my voice certainly isn't anything like it sounds on there. What will they think of me?'

'But it is like that, Mrs Evans. And there is nothing wrong with it,' urges Rosita.

'I have never seen myself on film before. I never knew I had crooked legs. We never had a ciné camera, of course, and nobody in our family can afford these newfangled videos. In my day it was just black and white snaps with one of those old box Brownies and they go yellow after a while, and fade to almost nothing. My daughter-in-laws send me lovely photographs though, always in glossy colour.'

'Well then,' says Rosita. 'So now you know what you really look like.'

'Look at the sodding state of me. I'll have to do something about myself . . .'

'Nonsense,' says the comforting Theo. 'There is nothing the matter with you. You look like a real old character, and appealing.'

'I look like a bag lady.'

Nobody needs to answer.

'I look like a homeless person. You have made me look like an old dead tree.'

There is silence, save for the whirring film.

'I look like a down-and-out.'

'You look like an old lady in trouble,' says Theo firmly, 'which is exactly what you are.'

'I don't want pity!'

'You won't get pity. You will get understanding.'

'Bugger it, I don't like pity!'

'Nobody is going to feel pity, Vera. Trust me, please.'

Rita sweeps in like a stormy wind. 'What the sodding hell's going on here?'

'Oh Rita! I didn't expect to see you today.'

'I can see that, Ma. What's all this, then? And who are these people?'

Vera jumps up, flustered all over and blushing with guilt. 'This is my friend from next door, Miss Rosita Rodriguez. And this is Mr Rosenthall, from a company which makes films for the BBC. This is Craig and this is Matt. They are all friends of mine, Rita, so watch your mouth.'

'What's going on?' Rita is not prepared to observe the niceties of introduction. Ma is being taken advantage of. Ma is being used to promote somebody else's sodding career. Here is just another example of the haves exploiting the have-nots. It is true, she has only to turn her back for a moment on any one member of her family and all sorts of calamities are likely to occur. How can she be everywhere at once, with her eyes, as she puts it, in her arse?

'Keep your hair on, Rita, please, and wait till I tell you what's happening.'

'It better be good, Ma. I don't like the look of any of this.'

'Mr Rosenthall's making a film about my state of affairs and the people who used to live here. He's on my side, Rita, and willing to tackle that bleeder Mullins.'

Rita stares rudely at the harmless, friendly producer. 'So why didn't you tell me, Ma? You must have known this was going to happen. Why were you keeping it dark?'

Vera sits weakly down, narrowly missing Dixen, her

favourite tom. 'Oh, Rita,' she passes a hand across her eyes. 'It's your silly sodding attitude. It's the way you sweep around ordering everyone about and putting everyone's backs up.'

Rita is embarrassed to be accused in this way, and in front of these four strangers. Worn and frayed, and just about at the end of her tether what with one thing and another, Rita shouts at her frail little mother: 'I only ever act like that for your own good, Ma, as you well know. You make it sound as if you don't bloody well trust me.'

'Well, Rita, to be honest, you never get the results you're after, with your heavy-handed ways and your blusterings, but Mr Rosenthall here has such a gentle, clever approach . . .'

'Oh yes? Exposing all your personal problems, parading you, warts and all, before the general public . . .'

'But only 'cos I asked him, Rita. It isn't at all like you are making it sound. And who knows? Because of Mr Rosenthall's programmes, old Mullins might back off. Some good might come of it. I can only try.'

Rita turns to the gentlemanly Mr Rosenthall, who is on his knees packing his carrying case and pretending not to listen to this private conversation. 'This old woman is almost eighty years old, and I hope you realise that!'

He answers the strident, angry, menacing woman who towers above him calmly and with dignity. 'Are you trying to insinuate that your mother is not responsible enough to make her own decisions?'

'Don't come your bloody clever high-handed talk with me, mister.'

'It was she who came to me with her problems, I would like to point out, having nowhere else to turn.'

Rita whirls round, deflating. 'Is this true, Ma? Is this right?'

'I'm afraid so, Rita.'

'And you didn't mention it to me, your own daughter?'

'Rita, why don't you shut your sodding gob and think for once in your life. Why should I tell you, anyway? I didn't need you, did I, not when I had my friend and neighbour here, Miss Rodriguez, from Spain, who kindly stepped in to support me.'

Rita feels alienated. Her powerful force has been questioned and found wanting. In her hour of need her own mother has turned to a stranger . . . as Doreen has turned to Nigel, as Brenda seems to be turning to that snooty boss of hers, Miss Holden. Rita is losing control of the lot of them. She has even lost control of her home, and her own husband is now suggesting that they should move out!

The nest that Rita built is not strong enough to support them and the very ground is moving under her gigantic, size 9 feet.

Big as she is, Rita is going to have to ask her mother for help, and that's why she came here this evening. Her little mother . . . from whom she escaped way back in the sixties by hardening her heart and offering her body to all comers, a poke for a ten-bob note, a bonk for a tight skirt, a screw for a pair of knee-length boots.

For even Derek would not have looked at her dressed in the clothes her mother would have chosen – elderly checked skirts, worn out twin-sets and clod-hopping lace-up shoes.

Compounding the crime.

Did Vera deliberately do this to Rita, force her to work down Moffat's yard and dress her like an imbecile so that Rita and the sixties were total strangers, not even on nodding terms? Did Vera deliberately do this to her enormous, acned daughter, or was she so ignorant she did not understand?

And has Rita, unknown even to herself, been punishing her mother ever since, with the unreasoned revenge of the sullen, unsightly, gargantuan daughter?

But there's worse to come. There are all sorts of dark thoughts lurking in Rita's deepest subconscious, thoughts so terrible she would never allow them to surface. *Did Vera have to submit completely and allow all the coalman's children to look like their colossal father?* At least Rita was not so cruel. At least she managed to give way, biologically so to speak, to avoid passing on that fatal legacy to any of her children, especially her tiny daughters.

Or is Rita completely wrong? Isn't it more likely that the genes of Jack the coalman, deceased, are merely lying in wait?

Chapter twenty-three

Dear Mr Mullins,

Vanishing London

I am writing as the producer of the above programme, which is scheduled to be shown on BBC Television at the end of June, to ask if it would be possible to arrange a meeting to talk about a tenant of yours, one Mrs Vera Evans, who lives at Number 6, Lippington Road.

I would be grateful for an early reply as time is already pressing.

Yours faithfully,

T. E. Rosenthall

* * *

Dear Mr Rosenthall,

Vanishing London

Thank you for your letter on Thursday last requesting an interview concerning my tenant, Mrs Vera Evans, of 6, Lippington Road.

Before consenting to an interview I would be grateful if you would give me some idea as to the purpose and content of the above programme.

Yours sincerely,

E. G. Mullins.

* * *

Dear Mr Mullins,

Vanishing London

Thank you for your letter of the 21 inst. My reasons for requesting an interview with you are because Mrs Vera Evans, of 6, Lippington Road, the subject of my programme, has made various accusations about your past treatment of her as your tenant, and these I should like to verify before I include her undefended version of her last few uncomfortable years, and her experiences with you as her landlord.

Hoping you will speedily grant my request.

Yours faithfully,

T. E. Rosenthall

* * *

Dear Mr Rosenthall,

Vanishing London

Thank you for your letter of Monday last.

In view of the proposed contents of the above programme, I should like to point out the obvious legal difficulties that you face in going ahead with same without giving substantial air-time to my point of view.

Mrs Evans has been a tenant of mine for the last fifty years, taking over the lease from her father, Mr R. N. Slater, on his demise. During that time, as far as I am aware, I have received no complaints from that quarter.

Before I grant you an interview, I think you will agree that I am within my rights in requiring you to be more specific, so that I can refer to my files and respond as clearly and responsibly as possible.

Yours faithfully,

E. G. Mullins

* * *

Dear Mr Mullins,

Vanishing London

Thank you for your reply of Tuesday inst.

I note that you require more specific information from me before you grant my request for an interview regarding the above programme, and your tenant, Mrs Vera Evans of 6, Lippington Road.

I have been filming with Mrs Evans for some weeks now, and have been genuinely impressed by her forebearance and patience, and indeed, her good humour while forced by circumstances to exist on a level that is generally unacceptable in this day and age.

The decoration of the house leaves much to be desired. Are there any plans afoot to deal with some of these superficial but nonetheless depressing problems of basic maintenance?

The house is riddled with damp, which has resulted in substantial growths of mould, and widespread wet rot. In my opinion there is not sufficient heating provided or in such a way that your tenant can afford.

Mrs Evans is frequently disturbed at night by noises in the empty rooms on the upper floors, and in spite of frequent requests to the police they have not been able to locate the source of these disturbances. In my view they are probably caused by infestations of vermin, namely rats, and before the programme goes out I intend to pay for a specialist firm to confirm or deny my speculation.

And lastly, Mrs Evans holds a strong belief that you or your company are eager that she relinquish her tenancy as soon as possible. She has suggested to me that on several occasions you have taken certain steps in order to speed up this process . . . namely: interfering with the main drainage and water supply to the said premises; intimidating her by causing damage to the downstairs windows of the property, and there is also a suggestion that certain unpleasant substances have been inserted through her letterbox. All these unfortunate occurrences combined suggest to me that someone, if not your goodself, is determined to hasten Mrs Evans' departure from the said property.

As an investigative journalist I prefer to keep an open mind, and it is for this reason that I would be grateful for your reaction to these distressing but, so far, quite unsubstantiated accusations.

Yours faithfully,

T. E. Rosenthall

* * *

Dear Mr Rosenthall,

Vanishing London

Thank you for your letter of 31st inst.

First of all, I must emphasise how shocked I am that my tenant, Mrs Vera Evans, the subject of the above programme, has made her concerns a matter for public debate. Perhaps it would have been more reasonable had she contacted me first, as the owner of Number 6, Lippington Road, regarding the matters to which you refer.

As I mentioned to you in one of my earlier letters, Mrs Evans has been a tenant of mine, and my father's before me, for the last fifty years. In all that time I have received no communication from that quarter, apart from the regular monthly payment of rent, and certainly have been given no cause to respond to the kind of complaints that you mention.

As you must know yourself, 6, Lippington Road is an old

house, and in need of extensive repair. Mrs Evans' tenancy in no way covers my costs as a landlord. As the lease is due to expire towards the end of this year, and while we are hoping Mrs Evans might decide to take up the alternative accommodation which has been offered, it is not in my best interests to undertake extensive repairs to this house. I intend, as I have always intended, to sell it as soon as it is convenient.

Much of the damp inside 6, Lippington Road is a natural reaction to the house being mainly empty and unheated. For me to install central heating on the kind of scale you imply would be a foolish and ridiculous investment for which there would be no return, as neither Mrs Evans nor I could possibly afford to pay the running costs.

If there are rats in the house, and I am quite willing to agree with you that this sort of infestation is entirely possible, please consider the fact that Mrs Evans' eccentric lifestyle does nothing to discourage such pests.

Since the last tenants moved out of the premises some fifteen years ago, Mrs Evans has been offered more suitable accommodation, firstly by my company, and then by the local council on the advice of the social services, and so you will understand that it is not in Mrs Evans' own interests to remain there. Had I been a less patient landlord I could have contacted the social services myself and brought pressure to bear. The house is large, old and draughty. It is not possible for me or my company to do renovations on such a small scale as would be appropriate to the comfort of a person of Mrs Evans' advancing years and I am sure, in the circumstances, that nobody would reasonably expect me to do so.

As far as your last offensive remarks go – i.e. – the intimidation of my tenant by myself or my company, I can only assure you that you have been gravely misled in this direction, and that either Mrs Evans' age is telling on her mentally, or she is being encouraged to make trouble by some other party, namely yourself.

And lastly I would ask you to consider extremely carefully the legal implications of taking any of these suggestions any further. I am referring our correspondence to my solicitor.

Yours faithfully,

E. G. Mullins

* * *

Dear Mr Mullins,

Vanishing London

Thank you for your letter of 4th inst. I am only sorry that you deem it necessary to refer these matters to your solicitors, and that you and I have not had the opportunity to sit down and discuss the situation reasonably together.

I have to inform you that the above programme is being shown on BBC1 on Tuesday 29 June after referral to our own legal department, and that several implications will be made regarding the substandard housing and various inconveniences endured over the past few years by your tenant, Mrs Vera Evans who, by the way, is perfectly sound in mind and body.

Might I also point out that last week, when I was paying a visit to 6, Lippington Road, your elderly tenant was made extremely uneasy by the sight of a van parked outside her house for some hours on the pavement opposite. Mrs Evans informs me that this is quite a frequent occurrence. When, with her permission, I approached the driver I received a mouthful of abuse, but before he drove away I managed to catch a glimpse of a piece of notepaper on the back seat. Needless to say, the letter-heading was one of your own.

Yours faithfully,

T. E. Rosenthall

* * *

'Cocky little bugger,' said Edward George Mullins to his buxom secretary, June.

Chapter twenty-four

She has never been inside a gymnasium before, and is unlikely to repeat the experience.

It is an unpleasant, echoing place and smells of hot rubber and cold sweat.

Jessica, all silks and bangles, sits on a stiff bench . . . something like the form on which she was forced to balance at school, with her long legs crossed and her back rammed against a painful network of rigging. She hardly likes to look at all the swollen stomachs set out on the floor before her on cushions, in rows. Like a pumpkin patch. At least Brenda, now in her fourth month, shows little sign of changing her shape save for the tiny lump she swears was not there before. Exasperatingly, Rudi tends to treat the baby as if it is a living thing already. He puts his ear to Brenda's lump, presses his hand against it and swears he can feel Sebastian or Lola's very first flutterings.

When a woman is pregnant, thinks Jessica, everyone can imagine – everyone *knows* what she has done . . . while the fathers keep their secrets.

'Come on, Jessica, have a feel! It is the most miraculous, wonderful thing in the world!'

Rudi wants the whole universe to know what he has done.

'It might well be, Rudi, but I really would rather not. You mustn't humiliate Brenda.'

'Oh, don't worry about me, Jessica. I don't mind, really I don't. I like Rudi to be able to feel his baby growing inside me. Come on, give me your hand.'

And now they are at the private gym to which Rudi belongs, at the exercise class for pregnant mothers and fathers which is run on a Friday evening. Some of these women, relaxing with their jaws hanging open, as instructed, just don't care what they look like. I mean, how could anyone think of wearing a leotard, at eight months gone? Well, some of these women are. And Jessica would rather Rudi involved himself slightly less demonstratively. Not every father is down there on the floor behind his wife, supporting her shoulders, doing the breathing.

Rudi's breathing is louder than anyone else's, to the point that the motherly Dorothea, who runs the class, calls out, 'That's it, Rudi, splendid! Everyone stop for a moment and listen to Rudi. Watch how his chest rises and falls. Watch the way he works with the rhythm!'

Aha. Obviously the fresh-faced Dorothea has made the connection between sex, rhythm and dancing.

When Rudi's child is born, Jessica and he will marry. Brenda has agreed to sign the adoption papers, giving the child's father and his wife all rights to the baby.

'Women have been known to change their minds at the last minute. After the baby is born. After they have bonded.' All three interested parties have held discussions about this long into the night. Brenda has to be counselled . . . she will be seen by a social worker who is bound to read her her rights and ask her to think again. It is essential she has thought the matter through; it is essential she understands completely.

'I don't want to bond with it,' Brenda insisted. 'I don't even want to hold it. After it's born you can take it away . . .'

'Now that is just the sort of silly remark that makes you sound hysterical and childish,' reproved Jessica. 'You really have to be able to work it through more positively, recognise the child as your own . . .'

'And Rudi's.'

'Yes, of course, and Rudi's.' Was Jessica forgetting?

'Rudi has equal rights to my baby,' Brenda said, patting her stomach possessively, gloating over the something of Rudi's that she holds so protectively inside her. 'And if I don't want it and he does, it is only fair that he should have it.'

'Some courts don't see it that way. They see the rights of the natural mother as paramount.'

Brenda said, 'In normal circumstances, yes.' She gave Jessica a knowing look. 'But these are not normal circumstances, are they? Don't worry, Jessica. It won't matter what I feel about the baby. I don't like babies, and I don't want to bring one up on my own. I would far rather have a dog.'

Rudi leaned forward and stroked Brenda's tummy lovingly. 'Brenda, we are only pointing out that women's feelings often change, once they have given birth to their baby.'

And Brenda sat back, let him stroke her, and gave him a slow, maternal smile.

'We've got to get this straight,' Jessica said to Brenda at work, which is the only place where she can be sure of getting her secretary on her own, in the privacy of her office. 'I know you are infatuated with Rudi. It is so obvious, you can't even hide it. And, as a consequence of that, I understand that this is all much harder for you than we expected, but you and I, who know the truth, have got to go through this together with absolute honesty.'

Brenda cast her pale eyes down, like a schoolgirl in front of a headmistress. As if she had been caught scribbling her name on the science lab bench.

'There is no need to be ashamed of the fact,' Jessica encouraged her. 'I suppose I ought to have realised something like this was bound to happen. But I just don't want you to start imagining all sorts of fantastic possibilities that are not likely to come true. Do you understand, Brenda? Do you know what I'm talking about?'

'Like what?'

'Well.' Jessica sat back and fondled her fat green Buddha. Her rings shone gold on her slender fingers. 'For example, Rudi desperately wants this child, the child he considers his own, but if, for emotional reasons of your own, you imagine for a moment that he would change his allegiance if you refused to give up the baby, then I'm afraid I have to disappoint you, Brenda.'

'I wasn't thinking of doing that.'

Jessica rubbed her cool hands together. 'Good. I'm glad we have that little matter out of the way. And now we come to the question of your involvement with the child after it is born. No doubt you will want to keep in touch . . .'

'I would like to.'

'And no doubt we can come to some arrangement whereby you can have yearly photographs and reports.'

'But I won't be able to see it?'

Jessica sounded soft and sensible, as if she was only considering Brenda. 'Well, I don't know how that would work. You see, a complete break is surely necessary, so that you can mourn your loss and get over—'

'I don't want to mourn. I have never mourned.'

Brenda is such a stupid creature! 'Well, no, you don't think you will now, of course. But after you've given your baby up, you must anticipate the possibility that you will feel *some* sense of loss, and keeping in touch with a child which can never be yours will only prolong the pain. D'you see?'

'I suppose so.'

'So,' said Jessica brightly, 'it would be far better if you made a clean break.'

'But what if you brought it to work? I can still work here, can't I, afterwards? You promised me I would not lose my job.'

'And I fully intend to keep that promise, Brenda, of course I do. But I have been wondering whether it might not be better, after it's all over, if I were to investigate the possibilities of your moving to Wetherby's. I have connections there, and as you know they are our main competitor in the business and only a few stops away from here. It would be a promotion, dear, with more money. But that would be entirely up to you at the time.'

'I dunno.' Brenda picked at her stubby nails.

'Well, just think it over, that's all. It might be more sensible.'

Brenda raised accusing eyes and stared at Jessica for a moment before she dropped them.

'And now we come to the difficult matter of your feelings for Rudi. Are you able to talk to me about them, Brenda? Or would you be too embarrassed? I can quite understand that, but it is often easier to share your problems.'

'I love him,' said Brenda simply.

'You *think* you love him,' corrected Jessica, tapping her pen on the Morocco-lined desk, a valuable antique.

'I *know* that I love him,' stated Brenda.

'But he does not love you.'

Brenda raised those accusing eyes once again. 'How do you know?'

Jessica allowed herself a small, tight laugh. 'Brenda, dear, he would have told me.'

'Told you? Why would he?'

'Well, of course he would tell me if he didn't love me any more.'

'Perhaps it's not like that. Maybe he loves us both.'

'I thought that we could discuss this together like two adult people. I am sorry to see that I was badly mistaken. You sound like a lovelorn teenager.'

'I am a teenager,' said Brenda. 'And I have never been in love before.'

'What about the father of your child?'

'Who?'

Damn it all. Jessica nearly snapped her pen in half. She threw it on the desk in front of her. 'Brenda, you really must not allow yourself to forget the truth of this, no matter how distasteful you might find it. I should not have to remind you that Rudi is *not* the father of your child. This child is not, and never has been, Rudi's.'

'I know that,' said Brenda sulkily.

'And after the child is born it is unlikely that you will ever see Rudi again.'

'I can't bear it! I can't bear it!' And to Jessica's absolute horror, Brenda broke into uncontrollable sobs. Her face fell apart like a clown removing his make-up, and her narrow shoulders shook as she sat in the swivel chair hugging her agony. 'You . . . don't . . . know,' she stuttered. 'How can . . . anyone like you . . . possibly understand?'

Damn Rudi! Damn and blast Rudi and his sexual games. How could he, the wanker? How could he do this . . . to Jessica? The fool! The fool!

'Perhaps I did not realise, Brenda, quite how besotted you were.'

'Well, I am. So there.'

Jessica passed a handkerchief over her desk. Brenda

grabbed it and started twisting it between her inky fingers.

'Oh dear, Brenda. Oh dear. Heavens above. Heck. What are we going to do with you? Do try and stop crying . . .'

'I think of him every moment of the day and night. First thing in the morning I think of him, and all through the day, and when I see him my heart jumps and I go hot all over and I just want to die for him—'

'Now, Brenda, stop this at once! This is doing you no good at all.'

'But I have to tell somebody. I can't stand it! I want him to love me so much . . . I want him to love me . . .'

Now is not the moment to tell Brenda that Rudi does not, and never will, love her. She is not the sort of person whom Rudi could ever love. She just hasn't got the style, or the money . . . oh, the list of reasons is too long to go through.

Jessica sat back in her chair and waited until the jerking and spluttering had subsided. 'Well, I can see how you feel, but what do you suggest we do, Brenda?' She hesitated. 'Might it be better if you stopped seeing him now?'

'Oh no! Don't do that! I couldn't stand that!'

'Well, is there anything you can think of that we might be able to do to help?'

'I dunno. I just dunno.'

'What if I had a word with Rudi?'

'And said what?'

'Explained how strongly you felt . . .'

'Yes. Yes. You could tell him how much I loved him.'

'I think you have probably given him a hint of that already.'

'How?'

'By the way you sit staring at him, for a start.'

'I can't help it.'

Of course the little fool can help it. She sits and makes eyes at him whenever he is around.

'Perhaps if I saw him more often,' hiccupped Brenda. 'Perhaps if I was around him more, the infatuation might wear off. I might see him more as an ordinary person and less of an idol.'

She's cunning – Jessica has to give her that. But might that be the answer?

Jessica reached for her papers in a gesture of dismissal. 'We will go on as we are for the moment, because I can't really think of anything else. But you and I must keep talking about this together, because there is only one person who is going to get hurt in the end, Brenda, and that's you, whether you decide to keep this baby as a way of attracting Rudi – and I've already warned you that won't work – or whether you go along with what we originally planned. One way or the other, this obsession has got to stop. For everyone's sake. For the baby's sake. But mostly for your own.'

'And it's up to you to put a stop to it,' Jessica said to Rudi angrily. 'Nobody else can, only you. If you want this to go smoothly I suggest you put a stop to it right away.'

'But how?'

'Don't ask me how, for God's sake. How should I know? I haven't got a clue.'

'I can't just turn my back on her! She isn't a one-night stand!'

'Well, I know that. But what I do not quite know is how she got to feel this way in the first place.'

'You think I led her on, don't you? That's what you're trying to say.'

'And did you?'

Rudi shook his handsome head. He poured himself another drink and settled down on the garden hammock beside his distressed lover. 'Fucking her might have had something to do with it.'

'There is no need to be flippant. We have a very serious situation on our hands. The very thing I dreaded . . .'

'It'll pass,' said Rudi easily. 'Brenda is a child. These things don't last. She'll be screaming over the latest pop star next.'

'I hope you are right.' They clinked glasses with a summery evening sound. 'But what do we do until then?'

'Carry on pretty much as we are,' he said, putting his free arm round Jessica's swan-like neck. 'I really do not do anything to encourage her. Hell, Jessica, I cannot turn away when the wench comes into the room, I cannot frown at her when she smiles, or pull away if she takes my hand. I have never been in this situation before . . .'

'Perhaps you ought to talk to her. Tell her that her feelings are unreciprocated and that you are only being kind as you would be to anyone else in these weird circumstances.'

'I'll do that if you think it might help.'

Jessica groaned. 'Oh hell, she would convince herself that I had put you up to it. She would tell herself that you didn't mean a word you said. That wretched girl is so far gone she would believe anything rather than that her love was a pathetic reaction to a few nights of bonking, a pure waste of time.'

So now here they all are at the gym on a Friday evening and Rudi is down there on the floor suggesting that this is the only place in the world he wants to be.

Brenda looks like a lovesick calf. She stares up at Rudi as if he is a Sheik and she the slave-girl at his feet. That curly hairstyle certainly suits her, and maternity seems to have given her colour; her skin is softer, too, like the petals of a tulip. Is it pregnancy that does this to Brenda, or is it being in love?

Is Rudi being provocative, making everyone laugh, leading them all on with his breathing and his glib and slick performances? Dorothea has clearly been won over by his not-so-subtle charms. She bats her eyelids when she speaks to him and swings her heavy hips. And Rudi, of course, is even more full of himself than usual now that he has landed his part in *EastEnders* and they say that the work will last for at least six months. He has even got a proper contract, and a precious Equity card.

How he loves being recognised, being stopped in the street for his autograph.

And now Brenda is coiled up into a ball and Rudi is kneeling behind her, rubbing her back, following Dorothea's instructions. Are these movements sensual? They are certainly not meant to be, but Jessica can see, as she sits there staring, that all Rudi's movements are erotic, just because he is as he is. The other fathers are not rubbing like that, don't knead like that, don't whisper encouragement quite like that . . . and no wonder Brenda is the only mother-to-be who is wearing such a look of perfect bliss on her face.

She is supposed to be in the process of giving birth, and in agony for God's sake!

Damn him.

Damn him.

Damn him.

Chapter twenty-five

Nowadays Brenda would rather be anywhere than at home.

It is rotten at home now that Doreen's gone, with the atmosphere of tension that seems to begin around six o'clock and builds up like the apprehension you feel when you're not quite sure if you've lit the firework properly. Is it going to go off, or not?

Mostly it does not go off; everything is quiet, but that doesn't mean you go to sleep once you're in bed because you lie there waiting for the racket to begin and when it does not you wonder why. Is something even worse going to happen? Is tonight the night the vicious little sods are planning to burn the house down?

Mum got in touch with her MP – she had to ask at the library to find out who it was – and Janine Tanner came round to the house to 'see if she could help'.

'Will my car be all right?' asked Mrs Tanner, a slight woman with bright red sticky lips, 'parked out there?'

Mum has never come to accept women MPs. She approves of them in principle, and argues loudly in their favour, but any woman who comes on telly is immediately torn apart and criticised for her dress, even the weather forecasters.

'It should be,' she says now, 'while Brenda is keeping an eye at the window.'

Mrs Tanner, a fighter in the way a Jack Russell is a fighter, was shocked when she heard how far things had gone, and when Mum showed her the mess, for nobody bothered to clean the walls of graffiti any longer.

'But you must have some idea who they are,' she said to Mum, accepting the cup of tea Mum gave her, and settling rather worriedly on the sofa, well away from the window.

She took notes while she listened. She opened her briefcase and sat with it on her lap.

'I've got a bloody good idea,' said Mum. 'They told me not to go, Derek told me not to interfere, hadn't I done enough already, but I went round anyway. Ended up with nothing but a sodding earful. Single woman, of course, living alone, trying to cope with foul-mouthed kids who are just beyond a joke since her bloke buggered off and left her. It's all the same, they're all in the same bloody boat round here,' and you could see that Janine Tanner, listening nervously, was taken aback by the passion of Mum's anger. She almost stirred her tea with her pen. 'Men know they don't have to hang around any more,' said Mum, working herself up into a right lather. 'And why should they stay, when they're no longer the providers? When they can just uproot and go off shagging somebody else. None of them work, not round here they don't.'

'And I believe you have put in for a council house transfer?' Mrs Tanner's nose was short and sharp.

'For what bloody good it'll do us. There's already a waiting list as long as your arm. Nobody wants to stay round here, and would you blame them? Can you pissing well blame them?'

'What has the police response been like, Mrs Hodges?'

'What response?'

'You mean they have been no help at all?' For a woman wearing a business suit she didn't know much about life.

'Well, they haven't caught the bleeders, have they, if that's what you mean? Or stopped their little games. Look at the state of my house, Mrs Tanner. Just look at it!

'I know. I know. It really must be most distressing.'

'It is that all right, and the rest. This estate was nothing like this when we first came here. You knew your neighbours then, and you all mucked in together. Everyone kept their gardens nice and the kids would stop and pass the time of day. You wouldn't recognise it today, Mrs Tanner, not compared to those days you wouldn't and you wouldn't believe how I battled to get here. The kids these days are worse than fucking animals.'

'I understand you have a relative who lives nearby, who

might be able to accommodate you on a temporary basis.' Mrs Tanner stared at the nets. They looked peculiar and rather pathetic, still hanging in front of the boarded-up windows, and still a defiant, snowy white.

'Have you seen my mother's house, Mrs Tanner?'

'Well, no . . .'

'I thought not. It's no better than a barn – only fit for the beasts. A scandal. Might as well throw straw on the floor but it looks as if that's where we're all of us going to end up. But my mother's a sitting tenant and we shall have no rights after she dies . . .'

'You really are going through a bad patch at the moment, Mrs Hodges, aren't you?'

Mum stared at Mrs Tanner as if she could hardly believe her eyes, as if she was another corn she had discovered festering between her toes. 'You could say that, Mrs Tanner. Yes, you certainly could.'

And that was another problem – Mum facing the fact that, if matters did not improve, they would have to move out, as much for their health as anything else because everyone was exhausted.

Mum had asked Gran and Gran had agreed, but, 'After the programme, Rita,' she said, 'because we don't want to bugger it all up.' What Gran meant was that she'd rather Mum wasn't around if she was going to be dealing with reporters and people from the television. Mum did tend to put her great foot in it, wading into the breach like she did, and Gran was quite pleased she had managed to achieve so much on her own already.

From Brenda's point of view, it was tricky with Rosita, of course, now she and Gran were such good friends. Brenda was worried that Rosita might give the game away – and then the shit would hit the fan, like hell it would. Rosita was more of a problem than arrivals and departures from Jessica's house, because Brenda's comings and goings were always quick and Jessica's car windows were shaded. It didn't take a second to reach Jessica's front door from the pavement, and Brenda was careful to look in the opposite direction to Gran's.

Luckily, so far, she has never even caught sight of Gran.

Mum worried. 'God knows what Ma thinks she's up to with all this television business. I'm not sure that I trust that woman from next door, Rosita Whatever-her-name-is. I think she could be a bad influence on Ma, although she was against the idea originally, I do know that.'

'Don't see the harm in it all myself,' said Derek.

'I think it's great that Gran's going to be on the telly,' said Shane.

'Well you both would, wouldn't you,' said Mum. 'It's never you who has to pick up the pieces afterwards!'

'What pieces are you talking about, Rite? I don't see why you have to be so dramatic. Vera knows what she's doing and what harm can it do?'

'Derek! Have you stopped and considered what Mullins' reaction to all this is likely to be? He's hardly going to sit there in his great block of offices and take it on the chin, is he?'

'I don't see what he can do once it's all out in the open,' said Derek, switching channels. 'Not without exposing himself.'

'Huh. And I should think Edward Mullins knows all about that,' retorted Mum.

But she wasn't happy about the programme and she wasn't happy about moving back to Gran's. She never explained this last bit very well, though, and Brenda thought it was something to do with going back to her childhood again. After all, this was Mum's home, not Lippington Road, and she had always been so proud of it, so houseproud, always buying bits and pieces, little knick-knacks, so that Dad had to tell her to stop because the house was beginning to look like a souvenir shop. 'We could open up once a week and still be in business by the end of the year,' he'd once protested. 'What a load of junk, Rite.'

But Mum, arranging whatever it was and standing back to admire it would only say, 'Well, I like it.'

It isn't like that now. All the surfaces of the house have been cleared, all the junk has been wrapped in newspaper and packed in cardboard boxes. It feels as if nobody lives there.

*

Brenda doesn't know what she will do if her family moves to Gran's.

At least, with all this going on, Brenda can feel relatively safe with her secret. She is careful enough to keep buying Tampax every month, just in case Mum goes into the bedroom and notices, or Doreen, on one of her visits, asks to borrow something.

Whenever she gets the opportunity, Brenda stays over at Jessica's. She is looking forward to her pregnancy showing so that she will be forced to move into the flat for the last few months. They've got it really lovely. It is like a dream nursery, something you see in an American film, with patchwork quilts and mobiles and wind-chimes and built-in nursery furniture. But the crib is best of all. It is magical, like the crib of the Princess in the Sleeping Beauty when she had her party and the fairies came. Brenda's baby won't need fairies to bring her offerings of beauty, happiness and good fortune, and no wicked fairy will be allowed anywhere near. The wand has already been waved. Brenda's baby is going to be born with a silver spoon in its mouth. It will start off in life with everything anybody could possibly want . . . the sort of start that Brenda, in her wildest dreams, could not possibly give it.

Brenda still doesn't feel maternal towards it, this little lump that has stopped making her nauseous but leaves her tired and fractious instead, this little lump that made it possible for her to make love with Rudi.

For her to know what real love feels like.

She only feels grateful towards it, and thrilled that in this special way she is going to be able to offer Rudi the most wonderful gift in the world . . . to lay the child at his feet . . . to suffer the birth for his sake. And to receive some measure of his pleasure in return.

But for how long?

This thought scares her, and keeps her awake at night long after the vandals have packed up their paint-sprays and gone.

*

So what had Brenda imagined would happen, before those frank discussions with Jessica took place?

Well, nothing definite. More of a feeling that, once she had given her baby away she would, in a way similar to the child itself, belong. For how could she, as its mother, be separated from the child so completely? She has created the child and how can you just abandon the artist if you fall in love with his painting?

Well, of course you can! Nobody wants a poverty-stricken artist with a beard and filthy hair hanging around the house, burdening people with his problems, no matter how talented the man might be. What a ludicrous idea. Good gracious.

How silly.

Brenda hadn't taken the idea very far, but she imagined she would be part of the family . . . around Rudi, important to Rudi, wanted by Rudi, in quite a different sort of way from Jessica.

A difficult concept for some people to understand.

Oh yes, deep in her heart Brenda knows that she can never take Jessica's place. She would rather be accepted by Jessica as well in a kind of *ménage à trois*, but where, in this fantasy world of Brenda's, is Brenda's baby?

In Brenda's besotted mind the baby doesn't really come into it.

He is unimportant.

He is merely a means to an end.

With a headscarf covering her burnished head Brenda goes round to see Gran. She hasn't been to see her for months. She goes today because she feels guilty, and because Mum keeps scolding her for her selfishness. 'You used to go. You used to love going. But now, just because there are more interesting things going on in your life, you cast off your gran like a worn-out old shoe. You're every bit as bad as Doreen, but worse, really, because Gran has always been so fond of you.'

Brenda is careful to pick a time of day when she thinks Rosita will be safely out of the way . . . early evening. She gets off the bus one stop sooner than usual so that she can approach the house without passing Jessica's. She cautiously takes the path that skirts the back gardens, and goes into Gran's the back way. There is nothing unusual about this. Gran very rarely uses her front door.

Gran's garden has always been one of Brenda's favourite places. It is full of feathery grasses that tickle your face in the summer, and flowers that have grown up out of themselves and are now rampant and wild, scattering their seeds indiscriminately and beckoning to the butterflies. There is always a round black patch in the centre where Gran likes to light her regular bonfires.

When you were little you could get lost in Gran's garden.

'Let's see what we've got for you today,' Gran would say, when Brenda reached the age of caring about what she wore. And Gran would delve into the bundles of jumble the charities had brought her. Out with the clothes came a certain mothbally, damp smell, and sometimes Brenda would find a shirt, or a scarf, or a cotton skirt she could cut short, and hem.

When she got older, Brenda refused all Gran's offerings because she believed there was a certain charity smell about the clothes which other people might recognise. The smell of Gran's house.

Anything left over would go on the bonfire, along with much of Gran's litter, newspapers and packaging, the cat mess in bags which Gran collected in a shovel from around the house, and various other burnable bits of rubbish.

'I don't know why you don't put it out for the dustmen, Ma, like everyone else. At your age bonfires are getting too much.'

'I am only allowed one dustbin, Rita,' said Gran. 'It says so on the lease. And I am not about to give Mullins any excuses to turn me out. And anyway, I've always enjoyed a good bonfire.'

'The neighbours worry, Ma. About fires getting out of control.'

'Well, it's a great pity they haven't more on their minds to think about, like I have,' said Gran.

Brenda and Gran exchange pecks on the cheek, not the hugs they used to share. You can tell Gran was dozing because of the imprint of the cushion on her cheek – a straight line among the creases – but for some reason she pretends that she wasn't. Is Gran ashamed of going to sleep in the day?

'Brenda! What have you done to your hair?'

'Don't you like it, Gran? It's the latest style.'

'I'm sure it is! I remember when your Mum started wearing the latest styles and her poor hair has never completely recovered. It looks like a pan-scrubber, one of those little balls of gold squiggly wire.'

'And the jacket?'

'Well, I wouldn't wear it – but I daresay it looks nice on you.'

'Mum tells me you're going to be a star.' Brenda clears a space free of *Horse and Hound* and, after moving the kettle over to the fire, she says, 'Still not on the electric then?'

'Oh I am, Brenda, I just choose not to use it. The paraffin is better, and you can't beat an open fire. So I hear you're all coming to live at my house, probably some time in July?'

Brenda worries about her coat. She shouldn't have worn it. It is far too warm in this weather but she daren't leave it at home these days. Nothing feels safe at home, and now she is afraid of it getting covered in cat hair. 'I dunno about that, Gran. I just dunno. A friend of mine from work has asked me to go and share her flat while her flatmate is abroad, until after Christmas, and I think that would be easier for me, apart from everything else.'

'Everything else?' Gran's nose and her chin move closer together. You can see she is disappointed.

'Yes, the hassle of getting the rooms straight. The hassle of everyone in a muddle. I mean, you're going to feel strange with Mum and Dad and the three boys descending on you all at once.'

'Oh, but I'll enjoy it,' says Gran.

'I know but . . . I would quite like to see what it's like being independent, living on my own.'

'And what does your Mum think about that?'

'I haven't told her.'

'You're still very young, Brenda, you know.'

'I'm nearly eighteen.'

'Exactly.'

'That's grown-up, Gran, not like in your day.'

'Let me tell you, Brenda Hodges, that I was married and a mother by the time I was eighteen.'

'Well then, there you are. Exactly. Why shouldn't I be allowed some freedom?'

'Freedom? You call that freedom? And although I was a mother and married I still lived in this house. I still had my own mother nearby for help and advice when I needed it.'

'Well, it's not like that these days, Gran.'

Brenda gets up and pours the tea, trying to find a cup that is not chipped or already full of bits of sugar, flour, or custard powder. What would Rudi or Jessica say if they came in here and saw the state of this room? The very thought is a betrayal of Gran and Brenda feels uneasy with it. Gran can't help it. Gran has worked hard all her life and should not be despised by anyone.

'No, no, I suppose it isn't,' the old lady concedes. 'But I do expect you all to come round and watch my programme with me, on the first night if not all the others. You and Doreen and the rest of you. A reunion. A celebration. It is a special night for me, and I'd like to be surrounded by my family.'

'That would mean us leaving our house empty.' Gran's teeth are sitting on the mantelpiece, grinning at the Scottie dog, not even in their jar.

'One night won't hurt. No one'll know you've all gone. You can leave the radio on, or the telly. But I'll need you all around when they show it. Who would have thought it, Brenda? Your silly old gran makes the big time at last.'

'I'll see what Mum says, but I know she's nervous about leaving the house unguarded.'

'Well, I tell you what, Brenda. Fair's fair. You persuade your mum to come over to watch my programme with me, and all the family – I haven't even been introduced to young Nigel yet –and I'll have a word with Rita about this here flat of yours.'

'Oh, would you, Gran?'

Gran smiles gummily. 'We two must stick together, my dear.'

'We always have, Gran,' Brenda says guiltily.

'We always have, my dear, and we always will,' nods Gran.

Chapter twenty-six

Gran looks so sweet! Doreen and Brenda are well away with the box of tissues all battered and rumpled, and even Mum has tears in her eyes before the programme ends.

Yes, even Rita has to agree that they couldn't have made the programme with any more sensitivity. And the mixture of past and present, flashes backwards and forwards, seems to add impetus to Ma's current dreadful predicament. You can see she's had a hard life just by watching the old newsreels, there is no need to say it, and so Ma keeps her pride. A very great pride, actually, and Rita has never quite viewed her mother like this before.

She is a real old character. She is, like the songs say, a Londoner and one of the best.

'What a pity none of the boys could come down on this important occasion.'

'They couldn't change their arrangements,' says Mum, 'but they'll be watching. They all told me they'd be watching.'

'I wonder if that bugger Mullins is watching, too,' says Derek.

'Him and his solicitors most probably,' says Gran with a pleased little smile on her pleated, pie-crust lips. 'The world and his wife will be watching tonight, and they'll all be seeing me!'

Rita came over to Gran's house yesterday in an effort to clear some space for this evening's proceedings. 'Nigel can't come tomorrow night, Ma,' she said, 'because he has to work late, and Doreen sends her apologies.'

'But Doreen is coming, Rita, isn't she?'

'Of course Doreen is coming, Ma. She wouldn't miss it for the world!'

'Only I haven't seen her for months.'

'Oh Ma, Doreen is in love. And you know how that takes them.'

'No, Rita, I don't. I never guessed you were in love. You kept that cunning secret, right up until the end.'

No, I didn't tell you, Rita thought to herself, because Derek was a last-minute catch and I was pregnant to God knows who. Quite apart from the fact that you didn't want me to have a boyfriend at all, and did your damnedest to make me even uglier than I was. If you'd had your way I would never have left home.

And now I am forced to come back.

Rita smiled at her mother. 'Perhaps I wanted to surprise you.'

Vera huffed and complained that Rita was turning her room into a cinema. 'All those seats pointed towards the screen!'

'Well, there's no point in everyone coming and not being able to see it. All I can say is that it's a bloody good thing the electric's on. Let's hope Mullins doesn't pull the plug on you just before the programme.'

'Oh no – I never thought of that!'

'Perhaps the neighbours . . .'

'You must be joking. Snooty, stuck-up lot. I get to hear quite a bit, of course, from Miss Rodriguez, about that fancypants Miss Jessica and her lover-boy Mr Rudi.'

'What's their surname?'

'Oh, I don't know. Miss Rodriguez always refers to them in that way. Peculiar, I call it, and of course they're not married.'

'You've developed quite a close friendship with that Spanish woman, haven't you, Ma?' Rita trod carefully, moving onto unknown ground, although what was this feeling of unease and where did it come from? Could she be jealous? Jealous of her mother? Or could she be feeling guilty because the Rodriguez woman seemed to have given her mother more pleasure, and more help, than Rita ever had.

'She's a very nice person, actually, Rita, and she has been a good friend to me. It is years since I had a friend. In fact, I sometimes sit here and wonder – did I ever have one?'

Rita continued to heave the broken furniture round. Vera

stood watching, clinging to the mantelpiece as if to steady herself against the room which shifted under Rita's great hands like a sea around her. 'You were too busy for friends, Ma, with us seven. And Dad's back.'

'She's had such an interesting life, you know. Been all round the world, met all sorts of interesting people.'

'So what the hell is she doing living in next door's basement, ending up as nothing but a general dogsbody and a cleaner?'

'Oh no, it isn't like that at all. Miss Rodriguez is there as their guest.'

'In the basement?'

'It is a strange business, hard to get to the bottom of it, but from what I can gather Miss Rodriguez had a long-standing relationship with that Miss Jessica's father. Then he died, and Miss Rodriguez was given a home for a certain number of years in his will.'

'But not a home of her own? Bit nasty of him, wasn't it?'

'She was his mistress, Rita, not his wife and to toffs like them that makes a difference.' Rita was always a strong woman; even as a girl she was strong, and could arm-wrestle with her older brothers without making a fool of herself. Look how she was carting those boxes about, as if they weren't full of heavy old newspapers at all but absolutely empty.

'Even so,' and Rita tried to put back the arm of the armchair which, being totally rotten with damp and misuse, had fallen off onto the floor. 'There, that's it then,' said Rita, hot and flustered. 'Quite an achievement. Sufficient seating for eight! And I have piled all your bundles of magazines on the floor behind the door.'

When the introductory music starts they are all too excited to speak. Doreen, sharing the sofa with Brenda, clutches her hard and tries to hide her head in her lap . . . a little too close for comfort. 'Move that bloody cat!'

'Shush! Shush! Shush! It's starting . . .' But nobody's speaking. Nobody's making any noise. All eyes are staring fearfully at the box and Derek and Shane are puffing hard on their fags. What on earth is Gran going to look like and what are people going to say?

When the camera focuses on the house in Lippington Road it is time to stop breathing. When the striped curtain is moved aside and Gran comes hobbling through the front door, draped in dirty old cardigans and bending to pick up her milk, it is time for clenched teeth.

'Oh Ma!' says Rita, biting her lip almost in half. 'Oh Ma!'

But she is not just a shabby old lady, crabbing along, bent and wrinkly. Gran opens her mouth to speak and her words light her up . . . she is telling them all about Grandfather Jack and pointing out where he died. She is taking them all round the house and remembering how it was when 6, Lippington Road was full of families, children, cursings and laughter. Things she never normally bothers to say – or does she? Has she? And has nobody bothered to listen before?

Vanishing London. With their mouths in various stages of opening the Hodges family listen in silence to their very own history, a history told with pride, nothing forgotten, all the endurance of that generation. It is hard to believe that all this has been inside Gran's head, just waiting for the moment to come out.

She looks so sweet! It suddenly does not matter that she is dirty or that she smells. It is looking at Gran through the eyes of another. Doreen feels a stab of remorse at not inviting Nigel. She was too ashamed of her Gran to invite Nigel.

And then there's all the suspense of watching in the dark for the Mullins' men . . .

'It's a bleeding shame,' says Eddie, as if he is watching the life of a stranger.

When it is over the phone rings.

'Answer that for me, Doreen, please.'

'It's for you, Gran. Mr Rosenthall.'

And Gran, holding the phone at arm's length and shouting raucously into it, says that yes, it was fine, yes, everyone is here, yes, she thoroughly approves of the way it was handled, yes, she would be glad to talk to the press tomorrow, if they don't mind taking her as they find her.

'So now we just have to wait for the reaction,' Gran turns

round and tells them. 'And Mr Rosenthall says we must go out and buy all the papers tomorrow.'

The phone goes again.

'See?' says Shane. 'This is what happens when you get to be a star. You answer it, Gran. It won't be for anyone else. And you've got to get used to this sort of media attention.'

So Gran walks proudly towards the phone. 'Yes?' she shouts. 'Yes! Who is it?'

She turns to her gathered, admiring family and frowns. 'The fire brigade?'

'Give it here,' says Rita, with fear like ice rising in her chest, ice in a glass, turning the water cloudy. 'Give it here!'

'I'm Mrs Hodges, yes,' says Rita, while everyone stares, in the same way they stared at the television screen in disbelief, only moments ago.

'Yes, that is my house, yes.' Rita listens, her huge hand gripped round the phone and dwarfing it. 'How bad did you say?'

There's a pause.

'Everything? Everything gone? Nothing left? How can that be?' She listens intently. 'It took so long for the fire brigade to get there. It wasn't reported. I see.'

Derek gets up and moves uselessly to stand beside her, a can of Extra Strong in his hand.

'What is it? What's happened?' asks Doreen stupidly, with hysteria rising, and everyone rounds on her and tells her to shush.

'You think we should—?' You can see that Rita is in shock and doesn't know quite what is happening.

'Somewhere to stay? Yes,' she says slowly, looking round, 'I suppose we have.'

And then, after another long pause, 'Insurance? Oh no, I don't think . . . I'm afraid . . .' and she turns and lifts her eyebrows to Derek who tries to take the phone but she shakes him off with a burst of angry irritation, more like her old self again.

There wasn't much point in hurrying over, but Roy had his van and they had to, really.

Apart from anything else the police wanted to talk to them. For their reports.

The house in the Pennystone Estate has gone. Rita's house, her pride and joy, it burned out . . . and most of the house next door. The neighbours have had to move out.

The Pennystone Estate is no longer dark. The whole area is aglow with the firemen's bright lights, like a furious shout at the sky, and the stench of smoke is acrid and goes right down to your lungs.

The last time it was lit up like this was at the Silver Jubilee in 1972, when the residents had a bonfire on the green and clubbed together to provide the fireworks.

Residents, strangers in dressing gowns, stand around in huddles looking bored. One man throws down a cigarette and makes a big issue of stamping it out. The fun is over. They say nothing. Not even to each other.

The Hodges family wait in the turd-weary grass, watching the last few firemen as they march around in the smouldering ruins. Not ruins you pay to visit, not interesting ruins which tell of important events, battle scenes, glimpses of a glorious past, but just the ruins of ordinary lives. Small ruins with little puffs coming out of them every so often, like Rita's choked breathing.

'Petrol,' states a fireman, wondering past. 'They covered it with petrol. It went up like a beacon. Not a lot anyone could do.'

'Oh Derek. Oh Derek.'

'I know,' he says. 'I know,' and he tries to put his small arm round her.

Chapter twenty-seven

Jessica and Rudi do not watch very much television. When they do, it is carefully chosen – highbrow stuff like arts programmes, operas, current affairs and Rudi, of course, now watches every episode of *EastEnders* whether he is in it or not. Jessica, for support, watches with him.

But she can't help thinking – all those terrible people with their little lives, circling round like the froth on the beer at the Queen Vic.

They do not watch much television because they have better things to do with their time – remember Jessica's busy Covent Garden diary? – and most nights they are out enjoying themselves, or they return home late from work and have an intimate supper in the drawing room, with candles.

They do not scan the *Radio Times* or the back pages of the newspapers to find out what has been provided by somebody else for their evening's entertainment.

Hence they missed *Vanishing London*.

And it was not until a neighbour further down the road – the people who bought Number 18 after Dominic Bassett moved from Pimlico to Putney – made it her business to telephone almost everyone in the street that same evening, that they first heard of Vera Evans' arrival at the top of the publicity ladder.

'You didn't see it? Good God,' fussed the neighbour, 'what does it make us sound like, that's what I'd like to know. There she is, this poor little old woman, hounded to Kingdom Come and having to put up with these appalling conditions. A victim of the times, living right here under our very noses.'

'Did you record it, by any chance?' asked Jessica, disturbed, as if she'd received some dire foreboding. They could have watched it. They were in this evening, but they'd been listening to Debussy together and fingering each other in the garden.

'Well no, because when I turned it on I didn't realise what it was going to be about, did I? And they didn't give the name of the actual road in the *Independent* preview. It merely recommended it as a programme worthy of watching. By the time I did realise I was utterly engrossed and it was far too late! But it didn't paint the rest of us in particularly glowing colours, I can assure you. It made it sound as if we shouldn't have moved here in the first place! Should have left the old slums to fall down, should have left the community to its pie and mash and jellied eels, and not come barging in so bloody insensitively . . .'

'You sound terribly upset,' said Jessica, inspecting her nails, a rare nervous habit of hers which goes with difficult conversations.

'So would you be if you'd seen it. And now, I suppose, we can expect our cars to be blocked by the cretinous tabloid ratpack first thing in the morning.'

'Really? Was it that contentious?'

'Yes, darling, I am afraid it was.'

And Jessica wonders if Rudi can cash in, in some way, on the media interest. After all, he is the old woman's neighbour.

And so it is, when Rosita sends up the mornings papers with the toast and orange juice and the coffee, rattles them up the shaft in the walls of Number 8, Lippington Road, that Rudi and Jessica get their first glimpse of the heart-tugging story which appears to be shocking the nation.

'It's the silly season. They are building it up out of all proportion,' says Rudi dismissively, studying the reviews and staring at the pictures of the old bag to whom he regularly shouts abuse over the fence and through the bedroom wall, for he is not in Italy now. 'God, Jessica, I hope the television people weren't there on one of the nights . . .'

Jessica's flesh crawls. 'Oh Rudi, don't! Surely not.' And her long-lashed eyes chase along the lines, missing many of the words in her hurry, relieved to see that most of the allegations of harassment are directed at Edward Mullins and his men. 'There are two more episodes to come,' she cries. 'Maybe the worst is not yet over.'

'Rosita!' shouts Rudi. 'I bet she would know! The two old crones spend every morning sitting out there together, casting their spells round their pots of tea. I wouldn't be surprised if that sly old bitch hasn't had a hand in this, and if she has it's a penny to a pound she has taken advantage of this opportunity to express her own little resentments.'

'Resentments? We have shown nothing but kindness to Rosita. Why would she do a thing like that? What could Rosita say?'

'That we make her live underground, in the basement!'

'Rudi, that is quite untrue. I offered her the top-floor flat after Daddy died, but she chose to live in the basement – so she could walk out into her own little garden, she said, barefooted in the mornings. So she could watch the people walk by through the basement windows. I think you are letting your imagination run away with you, Rudi. We, after all, have nothing to blame ourselves for. There was nothing we could do to help that woman next door.'

'We never popped in to see how she was, or took any notice of her at all, actually.'

Jessica's sharp little teeth nip through a corner of toast, and her eyes are sharp like the crumbs that fall on her white china plate. 'We are not, and never have been, part of that working-class culture, Rudi. And anyway, nobody behaves like that these days. Even Brenda says the people on the Pennystone Estate – and you can't get more working class than that – Brenda says they ignore each other.'

Rudi gets up to look out. He stands beside Jessica's heavily draped and very expensive dining-room curtain. He feels like a fugitive in his own house . . . afraid to be thought of as nosy and yet . . .

In every window in Lippington Road the residents are secretly looking out, just as if their doorbells have been pulled by a prankster, linked by a common thread of worry. This hasn't happened since the old King and the Queen Mother rode through in their open-topped Daimler back in the 1950s, and then, most who could walk or be carried had lined the actual road.

'There are cars outside already. And a ruddy great navy-blue van with so much rust hanging off it it looks as if it has just been winched up from the sea.'

'But how could one programme make this sort of impression?'

'Perhaps if we'd seen it we might understand,' says Rudi. 'I'm getting dressed and going out there.'

'Don't be so common! You are worse than they are!' snaps Jessica.

'But I am common, my darling – remember? In every way I am the very epitome of the world's most common man. And you love it.'

At work that day Brenda seems very nervous, much more timid than usual.

'Nothing wrong, I hope?' asks Jessica.

'What could be wrong?' replies Brenda with a trembling lip.

'You just look paler than usual, that's all. And your eyes are alarmed.'

'We were burned out of our house last night.'

Total collapse. And the wretched girl starts her sobbing again. Sticky, unpleasant, messy sobbing. Honestly, it's amazing how Jessica gets any work done at all these days, with her secretary so emotional and highly charged. In any other circumstances Jessica would have sent her packing long before now. I mean, she is forced to keep a packet of man-sized tissues in the top drawer of her antique desk expressly for Brenda's use. 'Other people also have problems, you know, Brenda,' she would like to say, 'but other people have learned how to exercise self-control.' You see people like Brenda on game shows, breaking down in floods of tears in front of millions of people when they meet some long-lost horrid-looking old relative, or when they win a TV, for God's sake! No self-control, that's the trouble. Which is why these people should all be shipped off to boarding schools at a certain age, or they should re-introduce the National Service, to make quite sure they are taught it.

*

I mean, it wasn't much of a house really, was it? When you think about it.

'You poor, poor thing,' says Jessica, getting up and preparing to pat Brenda's back, which is the nearest she feels she can bring herself when Brenda is messy like this. 'And your poor, poor mother. What on earth are you going to do now?'

'We're moving to Gran's. We've got to.' And this idea seems to trigger Brenda off into a fresh burst of hysterics.

'And where is Gran's?'

'Not very far. Not very far from where we live already.'

'Well then,' says Jessica. 'Come on, Brenda, buck up . . .'

'But I don't want to go to Gran's! It's horrible there, and cold, and dark. Why can't I come and stay in the flat with you? It's nearly time, anyway,' and she tries to push her stomach out, to make herself look bigger. She chokes through her tears. 'The other day Mum said that I was putting on weight and oh, Jessica, it is getting harder and harder.'

'Brenda, dear, there would be tremendous problems if you moved in with us at this early stage. Your family, for a start – what would they think? They would worry themselves to death!'

'No, Jessica, not if I told them I was going to share a flat with a friend.'

People like Brenda don't have friends with flats, and Jessica knows that very well. She says gently. 'And would they believe you?'

'I think they would, because Gran is on my side.'

'Your gran sounds a very nice, kind person to me, and I am surprised that you don't want to move in with her. I really do think that that would be the best place for you now, settled at last after all you've been through on that awful estate for the past few months. At least you will be able to sleep at night without all that worry.'

'It's not that which keeps me awake,' says Brenda. 'It's thinking about Rudi, and missing him.'

'Now, Brenda, that's quite enough. We have been through all this before, round and round, and it gets us nowhere.'

'I want to move in with you. I do, I really do!'

And Jessica actually has to disengage Brenda's sticky little fists from her jacket.

'Not yet, Brenda,' she hisses, 'not yet!'

So it is not until the evening that Rudi and Jessica receive the ghastly shock. Not until they are settled down having drinks at the end of their interesting days, showered and swapping gossip as they wait for their evening meal to cook.

Tonight it is veal with rosemary – a spicy, tasty casserole, accompanied by lots of lovely dry white wine. They eat well, Jessica and Rudi. Food is important to them both.

Rudi opens the *Standard* and the very first thing to hit him is Brenda's face.

'Good God good God good God!'

'Christ, Rudi, what has happened? A bomb?'

'Worse than a bomb, much worse. For God's sake look at this!'

Jessica stares at the picture with dazed incomprehension. 'It's Brenda! It's her, standing there with a crowd of dreadful people! She never said anything to me today. She never told me!'

'It is Brenda,' says Rudi, rolling his eyes towards heaven, 'moving in next door with her whole family as a result of her house on the Pennystone Estate being burned down. The paper is using the whole lot of them as an example of what is happening to the most vulnerable members of society in this country today.'

'What?'

'Read it, Jessica, go on. Don't just stare at the picture – read it!'

'But it says here that Vera Evans is Brenda's gran. How can that be possible? We live next door. Brenda has been here many times. Why on earth didn't she say?'

'Now look at the picture again, and you will understand,' says Rudi weakly. 'Look at them all. Look at the state of that whole family, Jessica.'

'We never met Brenda's family, did we?'

'No, Jessica,' says Rudi mildly, 'because she never let us.'

'The sly—'

'Frightened more likely.'

'Frightened – why?'

'You can see why. Brenda was frightened of precisely this reaction. She is ashamed of her own family and did not want us to know who they were. And when you think about Vera Evans next door, can you really blame her?'

The photograph on the front page of the *Evening Standard* tells the story without words. There is Vera Evans, sitting erectly on a chair, like the Queen at a christening, with her various offspring arranged around her. Rita's face alone seems to take up most of the picture, like a sad full moon gazing down through the darkness at the wreckage of disaster. Then there is Derek, with his hair plastered flat on his head save for the fifties' quiff from which he could never bear to be parted, and the very obvious St Christopher round his T-shirted neck. Shane and Eddie and Roy appear to merge together to form one dim block of the virtually unemployable, and Doreen . . . well, Doreen's cleavage is as wide and brassy as the smile on her heavily made-up face.

And then there is little Brenda. Forced to pose for a picture that she most definitely wants no part of . . . pouting, glaring – trying to hide her face with her hand but her hand is not quite big enough.

Terror Tactics. Last Crumbling Blow For Family In Ruins As Uncaring Society Outdoes Itself reads the caption.

One emotive programme, and how quickly things can change. The media arrived to interview the persecuted grandmother, only to find the whole damn family encamped on the floor, hounded from their home.

Outrage ran the various headlines. *Old Woman's Last Cry For Help.*

And a cartoon of a blue lamp hanging over a police station door, with *Is There Anybody There*? printed on it.

'They do exaggerate,' sniffs Jessica. 'I know Brenda, and from what she said it was her mother's own fault for interfering.'

'She was trying to prevent a gang of vandals from smashing up somebody's house,' says Rudi.

'An empty house, actually. Well, she should have been sensible and phoned the police.'

'But that is just the point, Jessica!' Rudi is exasperated. 'She did not phone the police because she knew they would not come. But where does this leave us now?'

'In a pretty tricky position, with Brenda and her appalling family living on our doorstep. How we are going to keep the situation under wraps now is quite a different question. Unless, of course, we rent a flat for Brenda on the other side of London, but she wouldn't want to live alone. Oh Lord, this is all becoming far too complicated. You don't think, with all this media attention, that the whole thing will come out, do you? Nobody would understand our motives. With the climate as it is now everyone would believe that we were exploiting Brenda, and the press would make a meal of that – and you on *EastEnders*. My God, I hope she keeps her mouth shut.'

'All we can hope is that Brenda is still infatuated enough to do nothing to upset me.'

'But that can work the other way as well,' Jessica points out with pain. 'She might try a bit of emotional blackmail.'

'What? "Marry me or I tell"?'

Jessica sighs. 'I don't know, Rudi. I just don't know any more. I live in dread that all this other business is going to blow the whole thing apart. Once these types of people get the scent of a little bit of power, who knows what they might do with it. We are too far in to pull out. It is essential that Brenda does not tell a soul. I think that, perhaps, we are going to have to have her here, just so we can keep an eye on her.'

'But we can't keep her here without everyone knowing. And she's going to get steadily larger and larger.'

'No, Rudi, we certainly can't. But we can turn the situation to our mutual advantage, if we are careful. We are the neighbours. What more natural than the neighbours offering house and home to one of the dispossessed next door? I am Brenda's boss. Of course I would offer her one of our spare bedrooms, in these unfortunate circumstances. I mean, what other action could I decently take?'

'Would she come?' asks the bewildered Rudi.

'You fool, of course she would come. You know Brenda better than I do.' Jessica presses her point home unkindly. 'You don't need me to tell you that when you are around it is not difficult to make Brenda come like a shot.'

Chapter twenty-eight

The Lord will provide.

Oh yes, oh yes, the Lord will provide – with a little help from the bloody taxpayer, Jessica supposes. You would think, wouldn't you, that these people who have so few possessions would at least make sure that those they do possess are properly protected, and covered by insurance. A little less of paying out to those club books every week, a little less of living for the day, and more of accepting responsibility for themselves, and the world would be a far better place for everyone to live in.

'But the money keeps flooding in,' says Brenda. 'It is incredible. Little old ladies from Jersey, gardeners from Devon, shepherds from Scotland, the banks, businesses . . . everyone who watched the programme about Gran was touched by it, and she's got some really lovely letters.'

'Well fancy,' says Jessica coolly, making sure Hiame is properly comfortable before she starts the morning's work.

'And so's Mum,' Brenda goes excitedly on, 'as a result of being burned out. Theo says the story, and Gran, have touched the nation's hearts and united everyone in anger against victimisation and violence.'

'I am quite sure it has,' says Jessica smoothly. 'And what do you think you and your gran are going to do with all that money? It is important that you handle it responsibly, you know.'

'Oh, we know that. Theo, that's Gran's producer, has put us in touch with a friend of his, a solicitor, who suggests that we start a trust fund, so that we have enough money to live on – and some money to spend. Imagine – Dad might be able to buy a car!'

*

Jessica's fifteen thousand pounds are beginning to look pretty puny compared with the enormous and spiralling sums coming through the post at the BBC.

'And are you thinking about giving some of this money to other homeless people?'

'Mum says charity begins at home.' And, to Jessica's surprise, Brenda looks rather ashamed.

'Well, that's hardly very fair, surely,' says Jessica, born with a silver spoon, who is a life member of the National Trust, English Heritage and the Country Landowners' Association, although she does not own any land. She just likes the waxed jackets and Hunter wellies that their magazine advertises.

'I know. It doesn't sound very nice, does it?' Brenda frowns, trying to get to grips with a puzzling situation. 'But Mum says she has never had any money in her life before and that you shouldn't turn your back on good fortune. She says nobody bothered to help her before, and if they didn't have the money or the publicity, nobody would be prepared to help them now. Dad and the boys have even been offered jobs!'

'Presumably they will take them?'

'They're thinking about it,' says Brenda complacently.

Would you credit it?

'We really are so very grateful to you and your . . . husband,' says Rita, on another day, when the whole ménage come over from next door to 'help Brenda move'.

'Brenda has always been very fond of you, Miss Holden, and she is very excited at being asked to stay in your lovely flat.'

'It's no trouble. Absolutely no bother at all,' says Jessica, trying to bar the way so that Brenda's belongings, just a few bits and pieces recently purchased and still in their carrier bags, are left in the hall. She endeavours to keep the huge Mrs Hodges as near to the doorstep as possible. There is no need for Brenda's family to traipse all the way upstairs, snooping into every room in the process. 'Brenda is welcome to stay with us for as long as she likes.'

'I feel much happier,' says Rita, 'knowing she is so close, so that I can keep an eye. There was some wild idea a while ago about her moving in with a friend, and I wouldn't have been too pleased about that. Brenda is still very much a child, Miss Holden.'

'I am sure she is, and you can leave those things just where they are, if you would, Mrs Hodges. That's fine.'

It is apparent that Rita Hodges has also been out on a buying spree. She has unfortunate tastes. For such a big person she should not have chosen those enormous red stripes; she looks like a brigand with that wild red scarf round her terrible hair, but probably imagines that she looks foreign. Some people just haven't a clue.

She has her tiny husband in tow – how do they fit together in bed? – and he has the job of carrying Brenda's linen.

'Linen?' asks Jessica, flummoxed.

'Her new duvet cover and pillowcase set,' says Derek, as Jessica tries not to stare at those winklepicker shoes he is wearing. He has obviously discovered a specialist shop which deals in Presley memorabilia. On the back of his fringed leather jacket is a picture of Elvis' favourite guitar.

Jessica peers into the box and sees a riot of rosebuds and nylon.

'We have our own sheets here so there is no need for Brenda to bring any more. Take them back, Mr Hodges, and they will probably come in useful for somebody else.'

'But Brenda chose them.'

'I am sure she did. But it really would be more convenient . . .'

'If you say so, Miss,' says Derek, looking hurt.

'How are you getting on next door?' Jessica asks politely. 'So much happening to you at once, all this stress, it really must be quite intolerable. And the press . . .'

'I enjoy it,' says Derek. 'All I did was sit around the house before, no reason for getting up, you understand. Now there's the various rooms to sort out, the decorators to organise . . .'

'Decorators?'

'Oh yes. Theo say it's not worth doing it ourselves. It would take too long, when what we need more than anything else is to get settled in. And the press are in and out all the time, chatting and laughing, having a drink or two,' and Derek winks at Jessica. 'You know how it is. Would you like to come over and have a look? Cup of tea or something stronger? Any time. You don't need an invitation to come over next door, Miss Holden. We don't stand on ceremony, Rite and I, never have.'

'Well thank you, I will bear that in mind. But at the moment I have rather a lot to be getting on with and I'm sure you are up to your eyes. Oh, by the way, before you go might I mention . . .'

'Yes?' Derek turns back with all his fringes flapping like the tail-feathers of a preening bird. His quiff is an insulting signal he carries on his head, and at his age he should not try to get away with that cheeky little-boy smile. It just doesn't work. In fact, it is quite nauseous.

'It is merely the motorbikes, Mr Hodges.'

'What about them?'

'Well, they do make rather a lot of noise and I just thought I would mention—'

'Turn it down, you mean?' Derek grins. 'Kids! I've tried telling them, Rita's tried telling them, but you know how it is when they've got anything new. It's a craze, Miss Holden. Just a craze. And boys will be boys.'

But they are not little boys, are they? They are fully grown men.

Brenda has quickly settled into the nanny's room, a gorgeous bedroom with an original brass bedstead, built-in radio, television, and intercom to the baby's bedroom. The room has a Victorian feel, with colourful rugs, blanket boxes prettily painted, window seats prettily cushioned, and spectacular wallpaper with a background of powder blue and flowers as large as saucers. Over the bed there is an original Victorian patchwork quilt, darned and invisibly repaired.

'Now, Brenda. Our plans have been turned on their heads,' says Jessica, coming to sit down in the rocking chair beside the window where one day a perfect nanny will sit rocking a perfect baby. She is exhausted after inspecting Brenda's new buyings. They are all quite unsuitable. Entirely the wrong colours and styles for her shape and size. 'So you and I are going to have to decide what to do now. You are four months pregnant, no, five actually, and it is beginning to show.'

'It's come on so sudden,' says Brenda proudly. 'A week ago it was just a tiny bump, now it is like a balloon and hardly any of my clothes fit properly. I think this baby is going to be really big!'

'We can't keep you hidden up here away from your family. We can't go away, either, as I am not free to do that because of my job. I can't very well send you away on your own – unless your sister, Doreen, could be trusted . . .'

'Doreen'd tell Mum. She'd promise you she wouldn't, but she would.'

'So I just don't see where we can go next. It would have been so much easier of course if you had been honest with Rudi and me in the first place, and explained that your grandmother lived next door. I understand why you did it, you have told us you were afraid we would think badly of you, but it was a very silly idea and one which has landed us in these present difficulties.'

'Rudi could go away with me. Look after me. Stay with me.'

'Brenda! That is not an option.'

Brenda looks down like a naughty child caught with her hand in the sweet jar. 'Well, I don't want to go anywhere without him.'

'Let's go through the realistic options together. Now Brenda, what would your family say if you told them you were in the family way and that Rudi and I had agreed to adopt the baby? What if we presented them with a *fait accompli*, so to speak, so that they were not threatened with responsibility, or shame, or loss of face . . . You are living with us, you are coming to work every morning with me, you happen to be pregnant but it doesn't need to be turned into a drama because you have sorted everything out precisely so that they *won't* be upset. Now – how would that be?'

'Tell Mum I'm pregnant?' Brenda pales.

'Or your gran?'

'Part of the reason I did this was so that they wouldn't know.'

'I realise that, Brenda, dear. But things have moved on and we must face the new situation in a totally different way, while still heading in the same direction of course.'

Brenda, sitting on the high edge of her bed and smoothing her hand over her new pink dress, thinks for a moment before she says, 'Mum might not want me to give the baby away to strangers.'

'Well then, what if we were quite frank and told her the baby was Rudi's?'

Brenda stares at Jessica bleakly. 'She would expect him to marry me, like Dad married her. You see, Mum is all for girls getting married. The whole point about us having careers was to meet the right man and get married. She thinks that is the high spot in any girl's life. You are okay if you are married . . . you are sunk if you are not.'

'You don't sound entirely sure about that, Brenda, do you?'

'It's strange.' Brenda's little face crinkles up, and for a moment she looks like her gran. 'That's certainly how she used to think, but I dunno now. Since the vandals and the fire, and since we've come here, Mum's changed – in all sorts of ways. It's hard to explain. Mum feels different.'

'That's understandable – your mother has had a series of terrible shocks. But why don't you try talking to your gran about this? Can you trust her, Brenda? If you told her you were pregnant and that Rudi was the father of your child, would she tell anyone else if you asked her not to?'

Brenda hesitates for only a few seconds. 'No. No, I really don't think she would.'

'Because you see, Brenda, I do feel that the time has probably come for your family to be told. Slowly. Sensibly. This new situation has made that virtually unavoidable. And just so long as you are absolutely certain that you still want to go through with the plans . . .'

Brenda clasps her hands tight together. 'Oh I do, more than ever. I would never let Rudi down.'

'Well,' says Jessica, rocking backwards and forwards slightly with a yellow rabbit in her hands – a yellow rabbit made in Italy, sent from Italy, and probably not meeting the British toy safety standards. Its eyes might come out and be swallowed by Rudi's baby. It might even automatically combust. But, as a present from his excited family, to whom he writes every week, Rudi would be terribly hurt if Jessica threw it away. 'Shall we think about this for a few days and then talk again? With Rudi next time?'

'Okay.'

But unfortunately, everything that Jessica suggests is okay with Brenda. She rarely argues, or puts forward any ideas of her own and although, in some ways, this makes it easier, it is also frustrating for Jessica because how can she possibly guess the kind of response which is likely to come from Brenda's terrible family? The wretched girl knows them better than Jessica does. Only Brenda can predict the outcome of any such discussions and yet she allows Jessica to lead her in any direction she likes.

Like a sheep.

They are all like sheep when spoken to in a certain way.

Buying what the advertisers tell them to buy.

Going on holiday where the travel agents tell them to go.

Reading what the bookshops tell them to read.

Watching what the television wants them to watch.

Except for *Eldorado*.

Eldorado! Was its demise a rallying call?

Perhaps the masses are turning!

Perhaps the meek have decided their time has come to inherit the earth.

What an absolutely appalling thought, thinks Jessica.

Chapter twenty-nine

Whatever they do to the house, and whatever money they spend, Number 6, Lippington Road is not going to look anything like Jessica's.

Basically, their aims are different. The Hodges want their part of the house to be comfortable and bright in a very modern way, with a built-in bar – a lifelong dream of Derek's.

It's completely mental in here. Brenda watches the decorators gloomily while picking at a bag of chips. Dad is in his element bossing them all around and getting himself in the way. Will the time ever be right, will there ever be a perfect moment when she can confide in Gran?

Gran is still in great demand because the second and third episodes of *Vanishing London* were, if anything, more moving than the first because they concentrated more on Gran's latest years, after Rita left home and she was alone in the house, gradually retreating from the little bit of space she rented like a snail withdrawing into its shell as life became too much.

'You painted Dad in glowing colours,' said Rita, having hesitated for two days before making an honest comment. The keeping it inside her for so long turned the criticism into an accusation, as if it had mixed with some juices like bile in her stomach. 'All that about him being solid and reliable. You never mentioned his bloody back, all those years when you had to go out and earn instead, wearing your eyes out on the sewing machines at Dormer's. Bringing all that fluff back in your hair, itching you all over, thick under your nails. I remember all that, Ma. Ugh, when I think about that it was worse than the coal –harder to see, and it clung more. You could never get it out, remember?'

Rita was cleaning the paintwork in the hall and Vera was

watching her through the opened door of her room. Rita, in her button-through floral overall was stretching and wiping and rinsing, cleaning the picture rails in a hall that hadn't been touched since the day Vera withdrew. She was getting it ready for the painters tomorrow.

Vera watched her daughter working; her headscarf covered her silver hairclips, her small fire glowed behind her although it was a hot summer's day.

Brenda dawdled in the background, listening. She liked to hear women talking.

Vera gave the fire a poke and it spluttered blue and feeble. 'We look back on people in certain ways, Rita, as you will discover as you grow older, and it doesn't really matter a toss what anyone else thinks. I have painted the sort of picture of your dad that I like to remember.'

'Huh, and everything else,' said Rita grimly. 'Talk about rose-coloured spectacles. Dear God, I can't remember those chummy times when everyone was nice to each other and shared things. Oh no. I remember the women screaming like sows at each other in the street, and the fights over the kids. The neighbours used to drive you sodding barmy, that's what you said, fit for nothing but the loony bin. Have you forgotten those days, Ma?'

'It depends how you want to look at it, Rita. I daresay there were bad times, too, and I didn't leave all of them out. There was the war, for example. And anyway, what are you moaning on about? You didn't have such a bad time when you lived in Lippington Road.'

'Only because I had six brothers and was stronger than anyone else. No one took me for a girl because of my clothes and I've still got the scars that came from having to prove it! Garry Rudge shoved a stick up me once.'

Vera came shuffling over to the door. She hung on the frame for support. She watched her daughter at work with a kind of secret admiration. 'At least the clothes I put you in lasted, and the sturdy boots. You were such a tomboy, Rita, so fond of the rough and tumble of the streets. So like Jack.'

'Yes, and never allowed a doll, never allowed to ask my little girlfriends home, never allowed to stay indoors because of the mess I might make. And now look at it!' And she threw a glance of disapproval at Ma's cluttered, airless room.

'If I ever tried to brush your hair or smarten you up, you used to kick and pull away. I bought you a dress once, and you refused to wear it. Said it was all wrong, too old-fashioned. But look at you now, my girl! You haven't done so badly. You moved away didn't you, found your own man, got your own home . . . everything you pretended you never wanted.'

'Perhaps I pretended, Ma, because I thought I'd never see the day when those miracles happened. Have you ever stopped to think about that?'

Rita wiped her sweaty hands on her thighs, and climbed off the stepladder. She wrung out the dirty cloth in the bucket.

She turned to Brenda and said, 'It's no bloody good trying to talk to Ma. She never could understand. We were never close, not like you and me and Doreen.'

And now Rita has lost her home and is back with her mother again in a house which is not her own, but is full of another woman's private smells. Almost back exactly where she started.

They are doing up the rest of the ground floor, which means that if Gran stays in the front room and leads an independent life, the Hodges will have a kitchen, downstairs bathroom, a huge sitting-cum-dining room, three bedrooms and a box-room – twice as much actual floor area than they had when crammed into the house on the Pennystone Estate. So you can see how large these houses are, and to what extent the owner-occupiers have changed them over the years.

Gran did ask Mr Rosenthall if it was worth it, 'as Mullins is still trying to force me out. All this money down the drain. It pains me to do it, it really does.'

But he said, somewhat mysteriously, 'Wait and see, wait and see. Trust me, Mrs Evans, and remember that I haven't let you down yet.'

Apparently there is some talk of prosecution, but Mr Rosenthall and his solicitors are dealing with Mr Mullins directly about that. A settlement out of court is what they say they are after.

Meanwhile, Rita finds it hard to believe how easy it suddenly is to make money . . . the kind of money she used only to dream about. The *Sunday Mirror* have commissioned her to go back to the Pennystone Estate and be photographed there for some articles they are writing. 'Hah, perhaps you'll make the centrefold at last, Mum,' sniggers Shane.

She confided to Brenda: 'Somehow, standing there like a lemon in front of my burned-out house is a terrible admission of failure. And all those people watching. People who have managed to make a success of their lives – unlike us. What went wrong, Brenda? What really went wrong?'

'It was nothing to do with you, Mum. There are some events which are out of your control, you know!' And Brenda sounded just like Doreen.

Rita couldn't believe it when they told her how much they would pay her, Rita, who has never worked for as much as three pounds an hour before. Sometimes she goes round the shops, forcing herself to press on even when her sodding feet are killing her. Rita doesn't buy very much, save for the most wonderful pair of hand-made shoes with a bar across, in a bright yellow leather (the shop even made a sketch of her feet) but, as she explains to Brenda, the joy is knowing that she could if she really wanted to, for the first time in her life, spend money on herself without feeling guilty and sick afterwards.

'Ever since I've been married I have dreaded the arrival of the post,' she confesses.

Derek, on the other hand, does not seem to have any such qualms – and maybe he is right. Maybe Rita is worrying about nothing, as usual. Live for the moment! After all, what good does scrimping and scraping do? But Rita feels she has lost control. Of Derek. Of everyone. He goes out and comes back with armloads of carriers . . . he would spend like water if she didn't stop him. But they both agreed on motorbikes for the boys. Something to cheer them up, they said to each other fondly.

It is a relief to think that Doreen is happy staying with Nigel, and now they are saying they are to get married in the spring but Rita, whose dream was once of wedding bells and white satin, is suddenly not so certain. She's not so certain of anything any more.

Is Doreen sure?

They'll breed like rabbits because Doreen is that type of woman, with swinging child-bearing hips, sexy eyes and a big bosom with nipples which beg to be sucked, and then the children will come along and gone will be her chances of nursing.

Might it be better if Doreen took her exams first, and then tied the knot? Or else, one of these days Doreen is going to end up in Woolworths with feet like her mother's.

Rita did her girls a favour by absorbing all the coalman's chromosomes, but she seems to have given them some other disadvantage – one she is only now beginning to recognise.

Yes, Rita is going to suggest that Doreen postpones the wedding next time she sees her.

'You haven't got some secret you're not letting me in on?' Rita asks Brenda, making the poor child jump with fright. 'Some man you've got hidden away?'

'Why would I have, Mum? And I've only just split up with Ginge.'

'Just as well,' says Rita tartly. 'There's plenty of time for that. You've the whole of your life in front on you, Brenda, and your career!'

Mum would go spare if she knew that Brenda was having a baby. But the child is growing so fast inside her that Rita is soon going to know. She will either have to be told, as Jessica says or, eyes in her arse or not, it will soon become obvious.

'Gran, are you busy?'

Is she asleep, or just nodding?

'No, dear. Come in and throw some salt on that dead fire. Move those bloody magazines and sit down.'

'I don't really know how to say this . . .'

Gran stares at Brenda with her blue, gimlet eyes. Brenda

opens and shuts her mouth but no words will come. The heat in this room makes her drowsy. She stares at the kettle and thinks, In a moment, when I look at that kettle, this will be over. I will have said it and Gran will know. I am doing this for Rudi, she tells herself again in her head. I am going through torture for the man I love.

Brenda clears her throat. 'Gran, the thing is, I am going to have a baby.' Brenda thinks that this is the bravest thing she has ever done in her life, and far more dangerous than sliding down the roof of the school kitchens for a dare, so why is Gran taking so long to respond? Doesn't she know how Brenda is feeling, trembling all over?

'Not that Ginge?' says Gran, sighing deeply.

'No,' says Brenda carefully. 'Not Ginge.'

'Who then?'

'The man next door.'

'Which way?'

'Number eight.'

'Not the randy Italian?' says Gran, taken aback. Because didn't Miss Rodriguez mention that something funny was going on? Ages ago? Didn't she tell her that something was going on right under that Miss Jessica's nose? Vera tries hard, but cannot quite remember.

'Yes, Gran. Rudi.'

Vera feels herself bend almost in half with the weight of it. 'And your mother always thought you were safe in the care of that Miss Jessica! And I suppose you have told me so I can be the one to face the music?'

'I hoped that you might. And I hoped that you might explain the rest of it.'

'The rest of it?' Vera pokes the fire again. She wishes she could bring the poker down hard on Brenda.

'Rudi and Jessica want to adopt it.' She might as well get it all off her chest.

Can this get any worse? Vera waits before she answers, in case there is more . . . in case she has to find the brandy. 'And what about you, Brenda? To give up a child is an extraordinarily painful thing to do.'

'Not for me, Gran, it isn't. You see, I don't want it. I'm

not ready for a baby of my own, and I don't even like children.'

How do you talk to such a child? 'It's different when they're your own, you know.'

'I do know, but that is what I have decided. And that is why it is really nothing to do with you, or Mum, or anyone else for that matter. I have sorted the whole thing out with Jessica . . .' and Brenda, speaking of her baby for the first time to somebody else, feels the first betrayal of a mother for the unborn child inside her, feels the first pang of grief.

'So you have quite decided?'

'I have quite decided.'

'It's going to be difficult living next door,' says Gran, unable to think of a more useful remark. 'I will tell Rita when the time is right, but now, if you would kindly help me with my chair and the Vicar's golfing umbrella, I am off to sit out on the pavement with my friend Miss Rodriguez.' Gran sets off and Brenda follows, and the old lady looks like a small, trailing plant that's been got at by slugs.

'Now then, Miss Rodriguez, what do you make of all this? You know the couple far better than we do. Don't try and argue, Brenda. You have to agree that Miss Rodriguez has been next door for almost three years while you have known Miss Jessica for a fairly short time.'

'Your baby would certainly not lack any material advantage,' says Rosita cautiously, tapping her fan against her scarlet lips.

'But . . .' prompts Gran.

'Well, all I can tell you is that I personally do not have much natural rapport with either Miss Jessica or Mr Rudi . . . but that could well be as much to do with the circumstances as anything else. After all, when they inherited the house they did not really expect an old woman to come with it . . . fitted, like the carpets.'

'But as decent, upstanding people?' asks Gran.

Rosita nods her dark head; her crow eyes stare through Brenda as if she knows a secret. This bright summer morning, she is decked in a brilliant emerald green. 'As people, as decent, upstanding people, I suppose one could not fault them.'

'It is my decision,' says Brenda, feeling silly, hunching her shoulders, standing there between the two old women, the subject of such intimate discussions. She'd hoped Gran would be more discreet. The last thing she had expected was that Gran would deliberately confide in the resident of next door's basement – much as Brenda likes her.

'But maybe you, dear girl, are too emotionally involved to make any decisions at the moment?'

'I am not emotionally involved at all!' Brenda feels trapped, hemmed in by the Spanish woman's involvement and it is all Gran's fault. She wants to leave. 'And I cannot see how this is any of your business.'

'Oh? I am so sorry. It is just that I have observed the way you react to Mr Rudi when you are in the house.'

'You have been spying!'

Gran pipes up. 'Don't be so sodding rude, Brenda!'

Rosita ignores the interruption which does not seem to have worried her at all. 'I assure you I have not, but you cannot help but notice. When one knows what love is, one cannot help but recognise it . . . and in this particular case I feel that there is little future in it for you, dear child.'

'But you don't know that!'

'No,' says Rosita gently, 'but I know the feeling to have loved and to have lost.'

'Don't we all,' says Gran, glancing pointedly at the water meter, the only marker to the spot where the coalman died, embarrassed at the intimate turn the conversation is taking.

But, going on Rosita's reticent recommendations, although she feels uneasily that her friend was keeping something back, Vera is as good as her word. She corners Rita in her brand-new kitchen. It is evening, and all the workmen have gone.

'Oh Ma, it's you, come and have a look. It's beginning to take shape at last.'

'Sit down a minute, Rita.'

'Sit down? Hell, I've only just started. I've got all this mess to sort out.'

'Please, Rita, sit down.'

'Is it bad news, Ma? Has something terrible happened? Where's Derek?'

'This has nothing to do with Derek. It has nothing to do with anyone, actually, apart from young Brenda.'

'Brenda? What's she done? So help me I'll knock her bloody brains out—'

'Listen to me, Rita. Just shut your mouth and listen for once in your bloody life.'

'And so you see, nothing disastrous has happened, and everyone is going to be happy in the end,' says Vera lightly.

'Oh my God no! Not my Brenda! And me, never guessing.'

'Well, you have had other things on your mind. Who are you feeling sorry for, Rita, Brenda or yourself?'

Rita glares angrily at Vera. 'What d'you mean, sorry for? I'm sorry for all of us in another bleeding mess. We could do without this.'

'What mess, Rita? What mess?'

'Well, bugger me, Ma, Brenda can't just give her baby away!'

'She can, and she is and there's an end to it!'

'To the couple next door? Like a parcel wrongly directed?'

'As I explained to you earlier, the man next door happens to be the father, not some stranger who just picked her up off the street for a screw.'

Big Rita jerks to attention, almost speechless. 'And just what are you getting at, Ma?'

'Nothing that need be talked about between you and me, if you see sense and calm yourself down and stop living your daughters' lives for them. Brenda doesn't want to get married, Rita. She doesn't want a house of her own, or a husband, or a garden, or a baby. And that is her right! So . . . the girl has made a mistake, but nothing that can't be sorted. And give her her due . . . she seems to have coped quite admirably without my help, or yours! She has got herself into a mess and is dealing with the consequences.'

'So what do you expect me to do? Laugh? Shrug it off? Pretend that nothing has happened and say, "Oh well, that's life"?'

'That's exactly what I did, Rita, all those years ago when you came home so suddenly out of the blue with Derek in tow and God knows how many months gone. So I know how you feel. You never loved Derek and I knew that but I let you go your own way. What alternative did I have? You don't have to get yourself hysterical as if you've been personally wounded, just give her some support, that's all. Young Brenda is in enough trouble as it is without you adding to her problems.'

'Where is Brenda now?'

'She's gone back to Jessica's for the night. I told her you would probably talk to her in the morning.'

'I always wanted the best for Brenda,' cries Rita weakly.

'We all want the best for our children,' says Vera. 'And Brenda, not ready to be a mother yet, is doing the very best she knows how for hers.'

'I just don't know what to do any more,' cries Rita distraughtly into her pillow that night, surveying the debris of her life, and frightened of so many changes. 'Everything's slipping. Everything is slipping through my fingers and soon all I'll have left is the memories.'

Chapter thirty

Now it is not just the two old ladies who sit on the pavement outside Jessica's house in the morning, but most of the Hodges family as well. They have a grotesque assortment of chairs, including one sizeable armchair – a foam-filled thing with wings from one of those discount warehouses – and a couple of deckchairs.

Haven't they heard of garden furniture? Don't they know there are many uses for a garden, apart from turning it into a wasteland or an allotment? For years the garden next door has been left to go to rot, blowing its poppy and dandelion seeds over the tall fence into Jessica's place and breaking old Mr Legg's heart – Mr Legg her gardener, who plants arsenic from dented old tins down in the very heart of his roses.

Glorious, sweet-smelling, black-hearted roses.

The people of Lippington Road drive uncomfortably past Number 6, but nobody dares say a word lest they are thought of as persecutors, abusers of the poor. They dare not huff and they dare not puff because to criticise the Hodges is to be the wolf who burns their house down all over again.

These days strangers drive past in order to sightsee. The nerve! They even get out of their cars sometimes, and snap the Hodges having breakfast on the pavement, or stand right back for a wider angle, trespassing in the Gordons' front garden opposite, to get a picture of Number 6.

And Rosita, the fool, is being dragged right into the hub of it. It's almost as if she enjoys it, sitting out there surveying the world with her curtains of grey knitting. She has given Vera Evans her sombrero with which to shelter her ancient face from the sun.

Vera burns easily.

Like a witch.

And what is worse, rumour has it that negotiations are under way to allow Vera Evans to buy her house when the lease runs out. Surely not – that cannot be true. The public are never *that* generous. Apparently, Theo Rosenthall is arranging some deal with that shady character, Mullins.

In other circumstances the residents of Lippington Road might have clubbed together to buy it, to protect themselves from ruin and lack of status. But they can't do that now, can they? How can they be seen to be undermining a poor old lady like that?

She has been taken to the heart of the nation.

The newspaper stories now refer to her simply as 'Gran' and her postbag is flooded with scrawled letters from children who want to adopt her.

Rumour has it that she replies to every single one, thanking them for their kindness but assuring them that she does not need or wish to be adopted.

And last week there was that really appalling, unspeakable meeting, when the Hodges family, as one, came surging into Jessica's house uninvited to 'talk it over'.

'Talk what over?' she asked, horrified, at the door, counting them. She prayed that none of her friends would arrive unexpectedly for drinks.

Derek Hodges lowered his eyes. 'I think you know what we want to talk about,' he said, touching the side of his nose like a spiv or the purveyor of time-share homes in Marbella.

Mrs Hodges thrust her way into the house, saying. 'We have Brenda's best interests at heart.'

'All of you?' asked Jessica, showing them into the drawing room. 'Is it really necessary to discuss this with all of you?'

'We have always been a close family,' said Rita, making herself at home and slipping off her shoes, 'especially where the kids are concerned. I am not one of those that shoves my kids out of the house when they run into trouble and tell them to get on with it.'

'Well no, of course not.'

Shane, Eddie and Roy took up the four-seater sofa. They sat there with their legs crossed, three monkeys in blue jeans and white T shirts, white socked and – Jessica swallowed – trainers.

'Here,' said Jessica, when Shane leaned forward, took out a tin and began to roll a cigarette. 'I have some proper cigarettes in the box. Would you like one of these?' Although she knew that Rudi would be annoyed.

'I prefer my own,' grunted Shane, passing his tin along the row so they all rolled their own, in turn, and sat there with the skewer-thin results jutting from the corners of their mouths.

Derek wore a brand-new white shell-suit. And Rita's was fairground pink. The yellow shoes were out of this world. Quite, quite extraordinary.

Jessica started nervously, 'Brenda has told me how supportive you have all been . . .'

'Of course. She knew we would be,' said Rita, as if stung, as if she'd been insulted. 'I am only surprised she did not tell us before. It feels to me as if you and she entered into a conspiracy together to keep the truth from us.'

'Oh, no!' lied Jessica smoothly. 'I must assure you it was never anything like that. Brenda and I were merely trying to protect you from any distress because you and your family were going through such a trauma at home. Mrs Hodges, Brenda was trying to spare you.'

'Well, that sounds all very nice,' said Derek. 'It sounds very thoughtful . . .'

'You yourself must be upset, Miss Holden, with your own boyfriend up to such tricks behind your back.'

'These things happen,' said Jessica wistfully, looking sad. 'I was trying to help Brenda out at the time, taking her mind off her other problems, giving her all sorts of new experiences at work . . .'

'Pity they didn't stop with the work. Pity the experiences turned out to be so bloody fatal,' said Derek, looking rudely round at Jessica's drawing room, inspecting the lights, the pictures, the ornaments with his darting eyes.

'You trusted her,' said Rita, 'and then she betrayed you. I must say, you are being most generous accepting your boyfriend's baby, even prepared to adopt it. In the circumstances most wouldn't, I know.'

'We cannot have children of our own, you see, Mrs Hodges.' Jessica appealed to her woman to woman, allowing a slight glaze to her eye.

'Ah, so that explains it. That explains it, doesn't it, Derek?'

'That explains it,' said Derek, and his three sons on the sofa nodded in unison.

'It is very odd that Gran didn't see our Brenda coming or going. I can't understand why Brenda didn't pop over to see her, as she was staying here, and so near. What was the matter with her?' Rita laughed coarsely. 'Ashamed of her gran, or something?'

'Oh no, good heavens, nothing like that. But when Brenda came here we were always so busy. Of course she told us that her grandmother lived next door. We knew that, oh yes. We have always been fond of old Mrs Evans, kept an eye open for her, you know.'

'She said she thought you were in with Mullins,' said Derek rather abruptly. 'Banging on her walls at night and the like.'

Jessica managed to blush. 'Neither Rudi or I would have anything to do with such an unsavoury character. Surely, Mrs Hodges, having met us you realise that? And the banging on the wall was just rather unfortunate . . .'

Rita made a knowing face, a horrible, leering, knowing face. 'Ah, say no more, dear. We know how it is when you're young and in love, don't we, Derek?'

Derek looked blank, and started examining the delicate, slender Wedgwood figure on the coffee table – a favourite ornament of Jessica's which she was given as a child.

'Leave it alone, Derek!' said Rita. 'Go on, put it down. You'll only break it and have to replace it.'

'It is quite irreplaceable, I'm afraid,' said Jessica weakly. 'The factory only made one of those, and that is it.'

'So where do we go from here, that's what I want to know?' asked Rita.

'Well, as long as you are in agreement, Mr and Mrs Hodges, Brenda can remain with us until after the baby is born and we will, naturally, take care of any expenses which will occur. And then, if your daughter is still of the same mind, we will start the adoption proceedings.'

'What if there's something the matter with the child? What if something goes wrong and it's not quite right?' Derek, meaning to point to his forehead, missed and pointed to his teddy-boy quiff.

'I think that is most unlikely, bearing in mind the top medical attention that Brenda has already been given, but in the face of such a tragedy, of course the plans would go through just the same.'

'You mean you wouldn't back out and leave us holding—?'

'Shut your big mouth, Derek. Miss Holden has made it quite plain that the adoption would go ahead whatever the condition of the baby. But what I really want to know is this – what happens if Brenda changes her mind?'

'If Brenda changes her mind then we have no rights in the matter at all,' said Jessica matter-of-factly. 'The proper agencies will all be involved, everything we are doing is above board.'

'She won't change her mind, she never does. She has always been stubborn, that one,' said Derek. 'Not like our Doreen.'

'She was a fool to get herself in trouble in the first place. And your man ought to have known better, Miss Holden. I'm sorry but I have to say it. Brenda is only a child . . . not that sort of girl . . . and she comes here to your house in all good faith and look what bloody well happens!'

'I know. I know. I, too, suffer very deeply, knowing that.'

'Where is the blighter?' asked Derek. 'I would have liked to have given him a piece of my mind.'

'You will be given every opportunity to do so,' said Jessica, trying to stay calm. 'Naturally. But unfortunately he is not here at the moment.'

'Well, when will he be in?'

Jessica consulted her neat little diamond watch. 'Not until later this afternoon, I'm afraid. Would you like me to ask him to call on you?'

'Nah, don't bother,' said Derek, not really wanting a confrontation, and reluctant to mess up the plans which seemed, to him, to be more than satisfactory. 'I'll see him around, probably.'

'If you are quite sure?'

'No need for any more bother,' said Rita. 'No need for more than we've already got.'

'I agree with you, Mrs Hodges.'

'It's always us women that suffer,' said Rita heavily. 'Never the men. They're laughing.'

Jessica hastened to assure them. 'Oh no, Rudi is terribly concerned about Brenda and her welfare.'

'Well, I'm glad to hear it. It makes a change,' said Rita. 'Well, it seems that we've said our piece, we've said what we came to say, don't you think so, Derek?'

'I reckon we have. For now.'

'So we'll say cheerio.'

'Thank you so much for coming,' said Jessica, heartily relieved that the unexpected meeting had not lasted longer.

As it was, after the Hodges had gone, she had to lie down.

Now, ever since that visit, the terrible Hodges seem to believe they have established all sorts of rights . . . the right to lean out of their window and wave Jessica off as she drives to work each morning . . . the right to borrow her garden tools . . . the right to come in the kitchen and drink tea with Rosita.

'Have you considered what their attitude might be once this baby is born?' asks Rudi, frowning.

'They'll move. Mullins will get the old woman out somehow and the rest of the family will have to go with her. No matter what the rumours suggest, they'll move. They will never be able to raise the sort of money to purchase the house. It will probably go for auction, and that man Mullins might be a crook but he's certainly not daft. Once they've gone we will be able to relax. And when the adoption papers are signed we are not under any obligations. We can tell them to piss off if we want to.'

'And if they do buy the house?'

'Well, we'll deal with that when it happens, but if the Hodges moved into Lippington Road we would have to go. Most of the road would go. It'd be like the gypsies moving in and prices would tumble.'

'I thought you couldn't move. You told me it was all part of the same codicil: you inherited the house, and all your father's estates, provided you lived in it for ten years and allowed Rosita to take up residence with you. The ten-year clause, they called it. And so far you have only done three!'

'We could get round that, surely, Rudi.' Jessica nervously jangles her bangles. 'In the circumstances any court would understand.'

'I don't know, these trustees can be difficult. And anyway, nothing is selling at the moment.'

'Well then, Rudi,' says Jessica, annoyed, and cursing her father's idiosyncratic ways. He was always odd. Even when he was young, James Galbraith Holden was odd. He never married Jessica's mother – the curator of an Egyptian museum and long since dead – and Jessica, who never knew her, was brought up perfectly happily by a succession of nannies. Now she grits her teeth and says with her old determination, 'We would rent out the house through an agency and go and live somewhere else in the meantime. There are always ways. We could not survive living next door to the Hodges. Good God, I would rather be homeless.'

'And Brenda?' Rudi is worried, he is not prepared to let go.

'What about her? What difference will she make to anything, once those papers are signed? Like us all, Brenda will just have to go off and find someone else to fuck. Come to bed, Rudi. Come to bed and stop being so gloomy.'

It is weeks since Jessica's last bout of cystitis.

Now that he has proved his manhood, could Rudi possibly be flagging?

Chapter thirty-one

If fortune favours fools, then why aren't more people lucky?

'Now, let me run over this with you again, just to make sure you understand exactly what I am saying. You must also realise, both of you, that mine is only one suggestion. There are others . . . and there are other advisers to whom you are perfectly free to go.'

'No, no, Mr Rosenthall,' says Rita. 'You've done a lot for us, and what you say makes perfect sense to me. How about you, Ma?'

'Keep this house for another two years . . . live in it all together?'

'Quite so,' says Mr Rosenthall, offering round his barley sugars. 'We have managed to knock Mullins down to such a realistic price that you could afford to buy it and cover your expenses for about two years, so long as you were careful. Then, when house prices rise, you would sell at one hell of a profit and buy somewhere smaller and more suitable.'

'I can't believe that Mullins, the bugger, has gone down without a fight.'

'Oh, he fought. Believe me he fought, but he knows he is now liable for all sorts of structural repairs and huge maintenance costs if he doesn't comply, quite apart from prosecution. The man was just trying to mark time and he nearly got away with it.'

'And what about menacing me?' grumbles Vera, her ill-fitting teeth clacking audibly round the bulky sweet in her mouth. 'All those years, creeping around, banging about at night, trying to frighten me out of my sodding wits. And then there's the electric.'

'We have a slight difficulty with that,' says Theo Rosenthall, sitting back and pushing a moth-eaten cat off his knee, but it's no good – his suit trousers are covered in white cat hairs. 'That is hard to prove, you see, Mrs Evans. We only have your word for it, and I have to tell you that I think most of those electricity cuts could have happened because you forgot to pay your bill.' He smiles at the bent old woman with understanding.

'Never!' says Vera, insulted. 'I always pay my bills, don't I, Rita, and I always have!'

'Well, let's leave that there for now. You have been disturbed by various noises over the years and maybe somebody was messing around upstairs, for what reason, no one knows. But we cannot say, with our hands on our hearts, that we know it was Mr Mullins or his men.'

'I can,' says Vera, 'and I will. Till the day I die. You wait and see – they haven't given up yet. You mark my words. I know Mullins' type.'

Mr Rosenthall slaps both knees with highly satisfied hands for it is rare that he can follow a problem through so personally, and solve it. At times like this his stressful job feels worthwhile and he can be something more than a parasite, preying on people's difficult lives. He looks around, his bald head shining in the constant firelight. 'And all this is shipshape and Bristol fashion, I see. They've done a jolly good job out there, haven't they just? But didn't you want any changes, Mrs Evans? I hear you refused to allow the decorators in this room of yours.'

'You're telling me,' says Vera. 'I've got my room exactly as I like it. It has taken me years to realise that a body doesn't really need all that space to make itself perfectly comfortable. And my old chairs might not look like anything much but they fit me to a T, thank you.'

'A new carpet wouldn't have gone amiss, Ma . . .'

'And what would I have done with a new carpet, Rita? I ask you! Tiptoed over it, gone off alarming if the cats pissed on it or somebody dropped a crumb on it. No, no. I like my stains. Every one is like a photograph or a fingerprint and reminds me of something. I've been through all that, Rita, and thank God I have now come out of the other end.'

Rita tells Mr Rosenthall, 'It would have been different if she'd let me have my way.'

'Never mind. Just so long as everyone's happy. And I must say you've got it looking very nice.'

Very nice?

It is a splendid hall!

Throughout the vast and colourful hall runs a dusky mauve carpet covered with vivid yellow spots. An old red GPO telephone booth, something for which Derek has always longed and one that he found going cheap in a mate's back yard, stands at the far end. It is connected up, but inside, the actual telephone itself is in the shape of a duck. Together they make quite a novelty.

Derek's bar is shaped like the prow of a ship, and the rigging above it is slung with lights that flash on and off. A mate of his, who's done the identical thing in his own house, which Derek had always admired, came and did the job. Tall bar-stools like bollards stand beside the prow, and you rest your elbows on the actual deck. Naturally, all the accessories have something to do with boating.

You can follow the mauve carpet through into the lounge, because if they bought a few more yards, the salesmen told them they would get it cheaper, so they did. And here is a black, mock-leather chesterfield which squidges nicely when you sit down on it – but also causes unpleasant sounds if you sink down too quickly – and three gigantic armchairs to match. There's a black wall-unit which takes books, ornaments and videos, and a television in a black stand with a shelf for the *TV Times* underneath. Rita bought a cover for the *TV Times* from Smiths.

But Rita misses her own bits and pieces from home, the accumulation of her thirty-year-old collection.

And although she loves all her new clothes, and chose them with joy, they are not worn-in and trustworthy like the ones in her old wardrobe. They don't make clothes of the same quality today. Nothing is designed to last in this throw-away society.

Standards are slipping.

*

Does Rita want to spend two years back at Lippington Road, so full of painful memories? Does she want to capitalise on this 'once-in-a-lifetime investment opportunity' which Theo raves on about?

Wouldn't she rather take the money and go?

What is the audience shouting? She can't hear. The key or the money? Which should it be?

But with the money they've got, all they could purchase would be a little square house on a jerry-built estate, or a pre-war bungalow, probably with only one bathroom. In spite of what Derek says, none of the new furniture would fit into a house like that. The bar and the telephone booth would have to go in the garden, or be sold off. And with Ma and all, the squeeze would be impossible. And what is more, there would be no money left over . . . nothing to fall back on.

Whereas, if they follow Theo's advice, within two years the price of 6, Lippington Road, ridiculously low because of all the structural defects and because of pressure from Theo, would certainly double.

And then there's Brenda.

Wouldn't it be easier for Brenda if they moved away? Wouldn't it be better if the girl was given a more reasonable opportunity to get over her loss? Funny, but even with the baby due in two months' time, Brenda does not see it that way.

Brenda is all for staying.

Anyway, thinks Rita, what are memories? You are what you are – you are nothing to do with the person you were more than thirty years ago, and everyone who knew her then has moved out of the area.

And what about Vera? She was born in this house and has never stayed a single night anywhere else, except for that time they went to the guesthouse in Llandudno.

Vera knows she has got to go; she expected to have to face the painful departure earlier, so any extension to her is a long, long time. In her childhood, the words 'happy ever after' used to sound a lifetime away, but happy ever after at her age could well be two years. It would be nice to think that because she has held out, battled on here for so long in the face of terrible adversity, that her family would benefit in the end. Already she has money of her own to leave them – money she has earned, when only a few months ago she had nothing.

And neither had they.

Whatever happens now, it looks as if she's avoided her terrible fate, of staring out at the aeroplanes and pressing for a lift which never comes, in Hooper's Tower.

It is nice to hear laughter and singing in the dead old house again.

Yes, Vera is very eager to stay here for at least another two years.

And on the pavement in the morning she shares her happy news with her best and dearest friend, Miss Rodriguez.

'So it's game, set and match to us, and that sod Mullins has lost his coat and I don't know what else,' says Vera joyfully. 'It was worth the battle, and I never imagined there would be such a happy outcome. You see, I was right to go to the telly. You were against it, weren't you? You didn't believe it would do any good to throw myself on the nation's mercy.'

'Well, I'm glad,' says Rosita. 'And I'm glad you're going to be my neighbour for at least another two years. I would be very lonely if you left, you know. I do so enjoy our mornings together.'

Vera's wizened little frame tautens with satisfaction. She worries about Miss Rodriguez, living in that house with people she does not like, not one of the family and yet not a servant either. Already Miss Rodriguez is fond of Brenda, who spends most of her time sitting down in the basement in Miss Rodriguez's room talking about Rudi.

'Your poor granddaughter has got it . . . how'd you say . . . in a very bad way for that man. And I have to tell you he's not worth it, Mrs Evans.'

'Few men are,' says Vera, thinking of the coalman, who was a good and upright man, but not much else.

'Oh no, I disagree,' says Rosita. 'I have been so lucky in my life. I have been in love, and I choose that phrase most carefully, my dear. I have been *in love* for the last fifty years.'

'In love, as opposed to just loving?' Vera tries to understand.

'Precisely. In the most romantic way,' says Rosita, her black eyes flashing and her earrings trembling. Every time she refers to James Galbraith she vibrates with emotion, and it's terrible to see.

Vera tries to be kind, although she feels she has to point out, 'But he wasn't awfully fair with you, some might say. I mean, with you two so close and all. You can't enjoy living here, Miss Rodriguez, after all those sunny climes and exotic places.'

'Ah well,' sighs Rosita, staring straight at the sun and making her eyes water. 'Perhaps he did not know that he would die so soon. Without the proper preparations.'

Vera really doesn't want to argue, but for her own sake the woman must be made to face the facts. 'From what you have told me, it sounds as if he was most precise in making his wishes clear. This ten-year business, for instance. He has trapped his daughter and he has trapped his mistress. To me, that does not sound very kind.'

'Kindness was not one of James' great attributes, I'm afraid. He was too exciting, too self-centred to be kind. A very egotistical man, you see.' She makes him sound more like the coalman every day.

'Well, my Jack left me nothing but debts,' says Vera shortly. 'And to be honest, I was sorry when he died but I soon got over it. I had Rita, of course, so that softened the blow. Men cause a lot of extra work. You don't know what the word relaxation means till they've gone.'

'A drinker, was he?' asks Rosita innocently, clicking away with her needles, pushing her spectacles back with a fierce silver end whenever they threaten to slip over the parrot-like beak of her nose.

'He liked his drink, if that's what you mean.'

'James died of the booze in the end – a sozzled liver, you know.'

'Oh, I am sorry.'

'Well, you've got to die of something. Even these health freaks, even people like mine next door with all their snooty likes and dislikes, with all their boat-rowings and their workings- out, they think they are staving it off but they don't necessarily last any longer. I personally think that all this body-worshipping, orange juice and fibre, is merely an unhealthy fear of death. James, of course, was never afraid of anything.'

'Anyway,' says Vera, changing the subject abruptly, because she is not so keen on the idea of death herself and doesn't like to talk about it, 'I am just terribly grateful that, thanks to you, I shall now be able to pass something on to my own family.'

Rosita puts down her needles. 'I would like to do that, Mrs Evans.'

'But I thought you didn't have a family. I imagined you all alone in the world.'

'I have a family and they live in Cordoba – such a beautiful place. My three sisters are in the Convent of Santa Catalina.'

Vera is surprised and slightly shocked. 'But what use have nuns with money?'

'None personally, but a gift to the Convent is always welcome. And to be received into that community one needs a dowry.'

'A dowry? Like for a bride?'

'You must know that when a woman enters a convent she becomes the bride of Christ.'

Vera is properly shocked. 'But Miss Rodriguez, you are not telling me that you yourself would welcome such a life?'

'It is my dearest wish,' says Rosita, dropping her knitting and pressing her two hands together, and they look just like those ones in the cards you can buy, of praying hands.

'But what about your colourful life? All the excitements you have described to me – the heat, the dangers, the characters, the travels . . .'

'Yes, oh yes,' the old Spanish women nods in the soft, gentle way of the Madonna. 'But now that James has departed from me, all I want is love and peace.'

Well, what a shock. Who would have credited it? And how sad. Here she is, living out her last years down in a basement in Pimlico. Miss Rodriguez, poor soul, is probably one of those types who would prefer to throw themselves on their husband's funeral pyre. Her lover is dead and her life is all but over.

Chapter thirty-two

'Good God, what's that?' and Jessica shoots up in bed, wide-eyed and staring at the dark. What is the matter with Jessica these days, sleeping so lightly? Her nerves are fraying, and certainly not what they were.

'I think I've started.' Brenda, small, like an abandoned ghost in her little white nightgown, stands at the bottom of the bed and says, 'I think the baby's coming.'

'Rudi! Rudi!' Frantically Jessica shakes him awake. 'Get dressed, quick! Has anything happened, Brenda? What makes you think it's started?'

But Brenda can no longer speak. She doubles over and wanders round the room, groaning horribly.

'The contractions!' shouts Jessica. 'Have you timed them? How long between them? Ten minutes? Eight?'

'Five,' shivers Brenda between clenched teeth.

'Rudi? What are you doing naked in front of—' How easy it is to forget that her secretary and her man have once been lovers. 'Can you hear me, Brenda?'

'It's all right. It's all right now. It's gone.'

'Well, the thing is, are you well enough to get dressed?'

'Oh, oh no! It's coming again . . .'

'Surely not!'

'It'll be premature,' shouts Rudi, dragging on his trousers. 'It cannot survive!'

'Of course it can,' says Jessica sharply. 'It is only – what? – three weeks early. Rudi, that's nothing. They keep babies alive who are born months before their time. You mustn't be so pessimistic. We have to give Brenda all the support we can. You go and find her case and her dressing gown while I get the car out. And hurry, Rudi, hurry! We do not want to have to deliver this baby on the bedroom carpet.'

*

Time goes slowly. There was really no need for all the Hodges to bundle into Roy's van and accompany them to the Mount Hall Clinic. Jessica called from her car, 'We will phone you, don't worry! Stay where you are and get some sleep.' But it made no difference. And none of them bothered to dress.

So here they all are in the comfortable waiting room with the coffee filter machine and a fridge bar, well stocked, and the television on . . . playing a scratchy video of England winning the World Cup. The air is fugged with smoke, although a polite notice on the wall asks you not to.

Brenda has asked for Rudi and Rita to stay and help her through her ordeal, and although Jessica felt quite hurt about that at the time, she thinks it is possibly for the best because she really does not enjoy that sort of thing and cannot watch when birth of any kind comes on the television.

Nature, after all, is so crude.

'It's a funny feeling, this,' said a tearful Rita, before she left. 'It's my grandchild and yet *not* my grandchild. It doesn't feel right. Not at all.'

'It is just a shame that you had to know about it, really, Mrs Hodges.'

'She is my daughter, Miss Holden, so of course I had to know! You wait – your feelings will be different once you wrap your arms round your own little one.' And Rita burst into inexplicable tears.

Rita, who never cries. Who is known as a woman who never cries. It was a disturbing sight and sound, and it quietened her expectant family, except for Derek, who watched the video solidly from the moment he arrived, and Shane, who cursed when he discovered there was no lager provided, only wine and spirits.

'How will she cope? The poor little thing. There is nothing of her except stomach.'

'She will need your strength to get through,' Jessica reminded Rita. 'If you feel like a rest, come out for a cup of tea and I will take your place. But she really shouldn't suffer, Mrs Hodges. She is being given an epidural.'

This is so strange, this waiting for a baby which isn't your baby. Jessica is neither pacing father nor struggling mother, but stands, alone, with fists clenched at her sides, watching the hands of the slowest clock in the world as they jerk out the seconds beside the Picasso on the beige Clinic wall.

Mr Teddington-Jones comes in with a brisk and rather obsequious smile. He seems surprised to see the Hodges family *en masse*, and the stale pall of smoke in his smart and flower-filled waiting area.

'Ah Doc,' says Derek, offering him a cigarette. 'How is my little girl getting on?'

The specialist's face, smooth and white like a baby's talcum-powdered bottom, wrinkles slightly. 'It might be a long job,' he says, finding it preferable to address Jessica directly, and seeking out her interested, more intelligent eyes. 'The baby is so large and the mother, as you know . . .'

'But there's no danger, Doc? You'd tell us if there was any danger.' Derek puts himself between Teddington-Jones and Jessica, establishing his prior claim for the latest information. As the father of the mother.

'Oh no, there is certainly no danger. But it is often a fairly difficult decision to make as to how long to allow the labour to proceed naturally without intervening.'

'Intervening?'

Must this man repeat the words he utters? There is nothing more irritating and this busy doctor is hardly prepared to stand here and discuss intervention with a man in a Mickey Mouse nightshirt and a broad cockney accent. And can't these people read? Must the Clinic really put up a stricter instruction about the hazards and unpleasantness of smoking?

'But so far she is being very brave,' says Teddington-Jones, fiddling with the stethoscope in the pocket of his bright white coat and eager to be gone.

'But how is Rita doing?' asks Derek.

'Rita?'

'My wife,' says Derek loudly. 'Brenda's mother.'

'Well, I have to inform you, Mr . . . ?'

'Hodges.'

'I'm sorry to inform you then, Mr Hodges, that I did not notice the progress of your Rita at all.'

'She'll come out if it's too much for her,' says Derek, half to himself, above the roar of the video crowd.

So the baby is large, worries Jessica, standing, arms folded, at the half-opened door where the corridor air is cleaner. The baby is large and Rudi and Brenda are both fairly small. And she wishes she had asked more questions about Brenda's young man, but she feared too much interest might upset the girl. After all, she must have thought something of him to allow him to screw her in the first place. It's funny, though, because in all their conversations Brenda has never volunteered anything about him. It is almost as though he never existed, as if Brenda herself has come to believe that Rudi is the father. A good idea in some ways, and perhaps the easiest way for Brenda to deal with it psychologically . . . but in others?

Too late, Jessica tries desperately to conjure up the image of Brenda's 'bloke'. I mean, he could even be black!

Black as the ace of spades.

And then what would they say to Rudi?

Everything has been decided, because Jessica likes to get organised, no loose ends. After the birth Brenda will return to 6, Lippington Road, and the baby will come to Number 8, and be installed in its nursery. They have interviewed a series of nannies, Norland-trained, provided by the Agency, and all Jessica has to do is ring up and somebody will arrive.

Apparently it is not necessary to install a nanny beforehand. 'You are only paying for nothing,' said the efficient woman in charge. 'All our girls have been taught to settle down quickly and sensibly. Don't worry.'

Of course, living next door to her baby is not an ideal situation for poor Brenda, although she seems determined to go through with the idea at all costs, thank God. She has never wavered, so keen is the girl to please Rudi. And give him his due, Jessica has watched him carefully and he really does not encourage Brenda at all . . . it is only that she thinks he does, which is one of Rudi's problems. He always looks at women like that, and speaks to them like that, and touches them like that. And, throbbing and burning, they all fall under his spell, like electrified ninepins.

But is he to blame? Does he know what he is doing?

Poor Brenda. She is just going to have to get over it. And there is every justification for her to do so, because when she is ready to return to work, Jessica has arranged that she will start at Wetherby's as a personal assistant to Angela Brook of the Fine Arts Department, at double her present salary and with the opportunity of going on block release courses to learn about the business herself.

And that took some doing. She hopes the girl is up to it and doesn't let her down. But it would have been inappropriate for Brenda to return to Jackson Willow and face Jessica every day, and not feel able to ask all the natural questions. Not only inappropriate, but unkind.

Jessica understands that she will have to put up with the terrible Hodges living next door for two years. The rumour flew down the road like wildfire, and reactions were mixed.

'Well, at least it's only for two years. They can't do much damage in that time.'

'It's not worth selling up with prices as they are. We are going to have to sit it out.'

'Thank goodness there are no small children who might come out and turn the road into a noisy playground.'

'Or dogs, or animals of any kind as far as I can see, apart from those blasted moggies,' said another, wisely.

'Already it's a nightmare with those damn motorbikes.'

'The police have had a word about that, apparently. And that's what we must do. If we see anything untoward going on, we must jump, before it gets out of hand. It is up to every single one of us to keep a strict eye.'

Another, different kind of Neighbourhood Watch as the good among us stake out the bad.

A Caesarean section! Oh no, poor little Brenda! Whatever next?

But at least now she can cease her terrible labours, and she does not know anything about it.

Rudi and Rita leave her pretty little bedroom as she is wheeled out to a whiter, steelier, more efficient place.

Rita drops into a chair. 'I feel as if I've been through a wringer, I really do, and I never want to go through anything like that again.'

'She was very brave,' says Rudi, pale and wan, his hand shaking as he receives the cup of black coffee poured for him by Jessica. 'And they say it won't take long now,' he reassures everybody.

There is an eight-hour-lived-in feel about the waiting area. It is stiflingly hot and airless, and full of witless remarks to pass the labouring time. When all this is over, Jessica never wants to see the Hodges family again. The only members not present at this harrowing time are Doreen, who knows nothing about it and has probably spent the night peacefully sleeping, or happily fucking, at Nigel's, and old Vera Evans who has probably spent her time with her torch in her hand, creeping around her beleaguered house.

All this extra treatment – anaesthetists' bills, the surgeon's fee and use of the delivery room – is going to cost an arm and a leg, thinks Jessica, unable to help it and yet thrilled that her ordeal is almost over.

It's like a miracle. In a few minutes from now, Rudi is going to be a father and Rudi will be hers for life! The fact that she is thinking of money at a time like this means there is no nobility in her, but she knows that already. She realised it when, as a small girl, she watched *The Railway Children* on television and felt scornful when the children received such pathetic little home-made presents for Christmas. She knew the family were poor, and enduring some hard times with their father in prison like that, and she knew she should be rejoicing with them, but she didn't. She couldn't.

'It's a little girl!' announces Mr Teddington-Jones. 'And mother and child are doing fine, back in their own little room again and cleaned up and presentable.'

There's an unholy rush to the door, a stampede of Hodges, led by the massive mother herself.

'No, no, please! Brenda has had an operation and is very

weak; she cannot stand too much excitement. Two at a time, please. I really must insist.'

'I am the father,' states Rudi, positively and proudly. 'She would want me there, and Jessica, who is the adoptive mother of the child, deserves to see the baby first.'

'I agree with that,' says Mr Teddington-Jones, relieved to find one sensible calm person in all this smoky mayhem. 'You go in for ten minutes, and then the next two – Brenda's father and mother, I should think.'

Rita mutters under her breath, but is too exhausted to do much more, and Derek is tired after a whole night without sleep and wants his bed.

So there's little Brenda looking washed-out and sleepy, propped up comfortably in white sheets, waiting to be kissed.

Rudi the Romeo does so.

And there, tucked up beside her in a Perspex cot, that dear little pink lump with a head sticking out is a virtual replica of Jack the coalman, down to his cauliflower ears and his fat, flat nose, down to his stubby fingernails and his non-existent neck, down to his tough, unruly black hair.

'Twelve pounds fourteen ounces . . . a record for the Clinic! Isn't she beautiful?' exclaims the nurse, programmed to say that and unable to say anything other.

'Lola?' whispers Rudi, and the name is a question on his lips.

Well, at least the hair isn't ginger.

Chapter thirty-three

Things have not worked out quite as Jessica had planned. Oh yes, don't worry, Rudi is besotted with Lola. From the very first moment he saw her he seemed to lay down his life and soul at her tiny feet. He took her into his arms, he sat on the side of Brenda's bed, and he wept like a child.

'Lola, Lola, my own little Lola,' he whispered.

'Not quite so little, though, as we expected. A hospital record, for instance,' Jessica reminded him with caution, the only person able to see the child through honest eyes because everyone else's reaction was the same as his.

'Oh, oh, oh!' they cried, in foolish reverence, as you do.

'Oh, bless her little heart.'

'Oh, the dear little soul.'

'Oh hello, Lola! Hello, Lola pet!'

Shit, thought Jessica. I can't stand much more of this. 'Gertrude' would have suited her better. Or 'Maud'.

And, as the Hodges family circled madly round Rudi and Lola, for a split second Jessica was reminded of that unnerving holiday in Italy when Rudi's family clustered, clicking and clucking like chickens around him in his rude peasant home, almost a hut. But Rudi, a fond papa at last, didn't seem even slightly perturbed by the size or the looks of this monstrous offspring, and he smiled happily back at them.

When, four days later, Brenda and Lola are brought home separately, Brenda in Roy's rattling navy-blue van and the child in Jessica's Saab, the Hodges family hurry over to Number 8 immediately to wet the baby's head. Almost worse than the idea itself comes the knowledge that they have brought their own booze, and it is obvious, by the size of the two large Victoria Wine boxes, that they are intent on staying for the whole evening.

Brenda, of course, the star of the exercise, comes hobbling with them, bent double because of her stitches.

'We were about to work out the plans for the christening,' says Rudi – foolishly, for surely this is nothing to do with the Hodges, as he sits next to Brenda who is holding the child in her arms.

Not a good idea, in the circumstances. Definitely not a good idea that Brenda should be out of her bed and over here at all.

'It's ugly,' says Brenda, the only one apart from Jessica who can see Lola for what she is. 'And far too big.'

'She is not ugly at all, Brenda. How could you say so, your very own little girl,' crackles Vera, gazing down at her great-grandchild with weak but adoring eyes. 'She looks exactly how my Rita looked soon after she was born.'

'Oh no,' says Rita, 'this pretty little girl is nothing like her poor old granny, are you, Lola?'

Jessica intervenes. 'Excuse me for a moment, but do you think it is a good idea for you all to be smoking in here, with such a young baby?'

'Oh, don't start worrying about all that now, Jessica,' Rudi says. 'My mother, a virtual saint, bless her heart, smoked around all of us, black cigars, and it never did us any harm.'

Jessica is taken completely aback. I mean, he is the one who always complains . . .

'She takes after Jack,' says Vera fondly. 'All Jack's characteristics are there, running on through the family. She's not a lot like you, Rudi, I'm afraid, or little Brenda, but then Jack was always a dominant man . . .'

'None of my children had Jack's characteristics,' boasts Rita. 'They took after Derek, every one of them, and every day I thanked God for it. Terrible, to think a child could suffer like I suffered.'

'You? Suffered my arse!' snaps Vera. 'You were a very spoiled little girl, adored by your brothers and much loved. And this little darling looks very like you did, don't you, my pet?'

Lola opens her mouth and howls, long and loud. Her pudgy

little fists pluck and box at the air. To everyone there it is unpleasantly apparent that she has just filled her nappy.

'I'll do it,' says the fastidious, proud Rudi, hurrying out with his squalling bundle.

'Well, Miss Holden, and how do you feel now, now you've got your baby, after all those unhappy, barren years?'

'I'm not quite sure, actually, Mrs Hodges. It is all rather a shock. Hard to take in, now the stress is all over. Of course I'm thrilled, that goes without saying.'

Rita nods, understandingly. 'And Brenda is quite happy, too, aren't you, dear? No second thoughts?'

'No,' says Brenda, smiling. 'I am just pleased that Rudi has his baby at last, and seems so thrilled with it. And I'm glad we live next door, because at least this way I can see her every so often.'

Jessica says, 'Not too often, I hope, Brenda,' then faced with the sharp critical glances of the family of Hodges, she adds quickly, 'for your own sake. You are the important one now. And you don't want to give the matter any more thought? You are sure you are quite ready to go ahead with the adoption procedure? You realise that you can pull out at any time before the official three months are over?'

'Oh no, no, I wouldn't do that to you, Jessica. I keep my promises.'

'That's my Brenda,' says Derek, drinking straight from the can although Jessica has placed a beer glass on a mat in front of him. 'I said she was the stubborn one of the family, didn't I? And while we are at it, we wanted to have a word with you, didn't we, Rita? We didn't want you to think we were interfering, but—'

'It's the question of the nanny,' says Rita, taking over. 'Derek and I have been thinking and I know it isn't our place but we are involved and with Brenda being the mother and all, we feel it would be far better if I volunteered to take care of little Lola, her own flesh and blood, rather than a perfect stranger . . .'

'Oh no, Mrs Hodges. I understand your good intentions but that is quite out of the question.'

Rita looks hurt. 'I don't see why it should be! Brenda and I are no threat to you as a mother, no more threat than a nanny from outside would be. To be honest with you, Miss Holden, I do not enjoy my job in Woolworths, mainly because of my painful feet –a lifelong problem which does not improve with the years. Now, I would far rather spend my time looking after my . . . sorry, your little daughter, for only a small remuneration, and if I am ill, or otherwise pressed, which I very rarely am, then there's always Brenda at hand in the evenings, and Miss Rodriguez, I know, would be only too pleased to lend a hand.'

'I can see you have discussed this together.' Jessica, her face tight, digs her long red fingernails into the flesh of her hands. Where is bloody Rudi? He should deal with this. Why does she have to cope with everything! Why is he never around when he's needed?

'I think, in the circumstances, that this would not be a good idea. In fact, it would be quite wrong. A bad mistake.'

Rita, resting her nylon feet on the coffee table, and sitting with a double gin in her hand, says, 'I don't see why. Don't you think Brenda has given up quite a lot to provide you with your own little family?'

'Brenda had her reasons,' says Jessica coldly.

'She wouldn't have had any reason if your man hadn't been casting his piece about,' says Derek.

'Casting his piece? Might I remind you, Mr Hodges, that we had no need to adopt this child. We still have no need to adopt. Brenda is quite within her rights to change her mind this minute if that's how she feels. And the same goes for all of you. If you want this baby you have only to say so, and upset though we would undoubtedly be, we are certainly not going to be blackmailed into any particular style of behaviour to suit you. Lola is our baby, or your baby. She does not, and she never will, belong to us both. Now, do you all understand?'

'I didn't know we were suggesting anything of the sort,' says Rita, in umbrage.

But when Rudi comes back, babe in arms – he might have left

her upstairs for a sleep – the Hodges harp on along the same old lines.

'It's just the thought of a stranger looking after her,' says Brenda. 'It upsets Mum, that's the trouble.'

'But a Norland nanny is not just any old stranger,' says Jessica hotly, wearying of the battle with this ignorant lot who have no right to be sitting in her drawing room in the first place, and were certainly not invited. On this, the first day home for Lola, she and Rudi should be together, getting used to their new family, forging the bonds. Anyone else but the insensitive, stupid Hodges would have realised this and not dreamed of intruding at a time like this.

'Maybe Mrs Hodges has a point,' says Rudi benignly.

'What?' Jessica whirls round. 'Are you out of your mind, Rudi?'

'Why – what would be so wrong with the idea of Mrs Hodges coming over here in the daytime? In the evenings you or I would be home and able to cope. I am sorry, Jessica, but it sounds quite sensible to me.'

'But Mrs Hodges is Lola's natural grandmother, and it's not a good idea when we are planning to adopt.'

'Who says it's a better idea to cut off all ties with somebody's natural family?' asks Rudi, pulling silly faces at Lola in his arms. 'That doesn't sound very much like love to me. I think a child has a right to know about her roots.'

'But we would *tell* her about her roots, Rudi,' grinds Jessica. 'We don't need her to *remain* among those same roots, do we? Snarled up in them, as it were! I mean, if we're thinking of doing this, then why are we adopting in the first place?'

'You make it sound as if we are handing Lola back to her original family.'

'Well we would be, you damn fool!'

'Of course we wouldn't be. Lola belongs to us, don't you, my angel, my little cherub? We are her mama and papa and she'll have our name, but it's nice to feel she has a larger family, an extended family, amongst whom she can grow up.'

Oh my God. Jessica just cannot believe what is happening here. She will have to talk to Rudi privately and seriously when the dreadful Hodges have gone. And what time are they planning to go, that is the question? When, at half-past ten, Rudi lays Lola gently in her arms and goes to find the old dartboard, Jessica's heart tumbles a further twenty notches. Darts now! Darts, beer and sandwiches with the neighbours.

While the darts fly around her ears and while Brenda selects a suitable CD and plays it far too loudly, Jessica sits back, tight with tension, and stares down at Brenda's child. It should have been a boy. It doesn't look even slightly like a girl . . . sugar and spice and all things nice . . . with its great big face and a screwed-up expression like a boxer's. The big question is, after all this, after everything they have been through, can Jessica love it? Will she ever be able to love Lola? And would it be fair to adopt a child about whom she feels so uncertain?

But it is the child, or Rudi – and Jessica knows it. If she backed out now, Rudi would be heartbroken and Jessica would lose him.

To Brenda?

No, Rudi knows which side his bread is buttered and Brenda's family might have newly acquired funds, but they can hardly be called real riches.

'Rosita should be here! Where is she? Shall I go and get her, while we drink a toast to Lola?'

'No, no.' Jessica shakes her head. 'Rosita hates to be disturbed after ten o'clock. She is quite hysterical about that, for whatever reason. Even if the country is suddenly at war, she told me, she did not want disturbing . . .'

'But this is different,' objects frail little old Vera. 'She is one of the family just as much as anyone here.'

'No, I know how Rosita feels about this, and I must make it quite clear. She would be furious if she was woken, whatever the reason. I think she finds it quite hard to get to sleep, and is very odd about the whole ritual.'

It's interesting how Rudi has to back up her words before the Hodges will believe her, as if she has ulterior motives for everything she says, as if she doesn't want Rosita because of some in-built reason to do with class. In normal circumstances this would be perfectly true, but if the Hodges can spend the evening in Jessica's drawing room, puffing like chimneys and kicking their shoes off, then what the hell. Let everyone come.

Let anyone come! Why on earth not? How about the dossers . . . don't they want to come in, too?

'What Jessica says is perfectly true,' Rudi confirms. 'Rosita is quite obsessed with being left alone in the evenings. She is an early riser, but she makes it a strict habit to retire before ten-thirty and then nothing on earth is allowed to disturb her. We will just have to drink to Lola without her, and she can do it over a cup of strong black coffee in the morning. So, ladies and gentlemen, why don't you raise your glasses and join me in the toast. To Lola! May her life be a long and happy one. May good fortune walk at her side and may all her dearest dreams come true.'

'To Lola!' shout the terrible Hodges, and Brenda, looking weak and tired on the sofa.

'Bless her heart,' calls Derek, throwing a bull's-eye and causing some extra good-hearted mirth. 'That's luck if ever I saw it! And now, if you will allow me, I would like to entertain you all with my famous and well-loved impression.'

'Put the music on, Shane!'

'Have they got it?'

'Have we got what?'

'Elvis, of course!'

'Oh, I think there's something there, at the bottom of the pile, if you feel you really must. But it is getting very late and poor Brenda looks weary . . .'

'I'm okay, Jessica, honestly. I love to see Dad do his party piece. You wait! You'll love it, too.'

And so Jessica is forced to sit through the most embarrassing rendition of *Blue Moon of Kentucky*, not knowing where to put her eyes as the puce-faced Derek Hodges grinds on in his tuneless voice, his chubby fifty-year-old little hips gyrating before the marble mantelpiece, threatening the antique carriage clock with his flailing arms, clapped and egged on by his drunken family.

Derek sings as if the rest of his life depends on it, great strands of saliva forming at the sides of his mouth like glistening silver hinges, like a madman.

It is quite incredible. And Brenda is almost moved to tears!

This, if nothing else that has happened this evening, should bring Rudi straight to his senses.

Jessica turns towards him, but Rudi is sitting, silly as the rest of them, with a boozy, sheepish smile on his face, and tapping his foot to the awful music.

He is even murmuring the words, and looks as though he might get up to join the ludicrous Mr Hodges at any minute.

Go. Go home, the lot of you. For God's sake, *go*!

She feels the spread of warmth on her lap as Lola's urine seeps right through the terry nappy – and urine does not mix well with silk. Rudi refuses to use plastic pants; he considers the elastic legs too rough for Lola's tender skin.

Jessica closes her eyes and suddenly feels terribly sick.

Chapter thirty-four

It is a dark and windy night in deep December. Rain beats on the windows and tortured voices howl down the chimneys. The feeble cherry trees that grow at strict intervals down Lippington Road tremble and bend on their little stems and are probably wondering if they will see another spring. Will they ever bloom again?

But at least they are still there with their plastic labels flapping, and have not been vandalised.

Across the mauve carpeted hall goes Vera, shrivelled like a moth in the gloom, muttering to herself, so stooped that the hem of her top cardigan almost brushes the ground where it hangs before her. She clutches the warmth around her with her two cold, scrawny hands.

'Rita!' she hisses, on arrival at the first double bedroom. And then again, slightly louder, but she is competing with the slashing rain. 'RITA!'

Comfortable and warm in her already-sagging new mattress, Rita dreams that a poisonous viper is slinking at the foot of the bed, coiled and ready to spring. She mutters in her disturbed sleep, and turns over.

Vera hobbles closer, and pokes her. 'Rita! Wake up! Wake!'

Bleary-eyed and half-unconscious, Rita fumbles with the sheets and mumbles, 'What is it, Ma?'

'They are here!' Vera's eyes are glittering sharp. Her voice is nothing but a husky whisper, full of fear, and excitement, too.

Oh God, don't say this sort of trouble is about to start. Ma hasn't shown any real signs of dementia up until now. 'Who is sodding here?'

'Mullins' men!'

'Go back to bed, Ma, you are mistaken.'

But Vera prods on painfully; she will bruise Rita's arm in a minute. 'Rita! Rita! Wake up!'

'Okay, okay, I'm awake.' Rita sits up and frowns at the sound of the crashing wind. She shivers when she feels the temperature in the room. 'So where are they, Ma? And what do you think they are doing?'

'They're up the top again.'

'You haven't been right up there, not in this weather! Not all on your own!'

'Don't be silly, Rita, I am quite used to it by now. I have to do it, and it is important that Mullins' men know that I do it. And this time, I *know* they are there!'

Even though Rita disbelieves her, even though this is the same old story told over and over again, investigated by the police, followed up by Mr Rosenthall, even so, the sight of Vera's nervous face and the thought that somebody might be upstairs, wandering around the house while everyone is asleep, is a chilling one. And a summons that cannot be ignored.

'Derek! Wake your bloody self up. Put on your dressing gown and call the others. We are all going upstairs to sort this out one way or another for the last sodding time.'

Derek moves blearily. 'Haven't we had enough disturbed nights just lately without this.'

'Shut up and get up while I fetch the boys.'

Vera is already at the bedroom door and is hanging onto it, bony finger to her lips, listening.

'Be careful, Derek, we don't want to wake Brenda. She needs her rest.'

'Huh, and you think I don't?'

'Get off your bleeding arse and get out here.'

They traipse up the darkened stairs following Vera with her torch because only the downstairs lights are working; the bulbs to the empty rooms went long ago.

Unfortunately, they couldn't prevent Brenda from following, and she still walks like a little old woman because of her stitches; she's almost as doubled-up as Vera. 'I'm not sodding staying here on my own with you all up there. What if they double back and come my way?'

Rita hissed, 'There's nobody there! We are doing this for Gran's sake. Don't you realise she has got to get this stupid idea out of her head, or she's going to go barmy.'

'Maybe she already is.'

'There's no need to talk about your gran like that.'

So Brenda follows the others, shivering, excited, trying not to giggle at the very ludicrousness of the whole affair. If anyone could see them, creeping round in a nervous line, tiptoeing around this vast house in the middle of a storm, and in pitch darkness!

But it's all good fun. As Mum says, of course there is nobody there. It is just Gran's wild imagination, or rats. Ugh!

'Good God, Mum, what if it's rats? Thousands of them!'

'Rats don't scare me, Brenda,' hisses Mum, a huge shape in front of her, breaking through the darkness. 'I've dealt with many a rat in my time, and that's why I'm bringing the frying pan. Knock 'em on the head, the buggers . . . it doesn't take much to kill a rat.'

Brenda giggles, but she wishes she'd put her boots on. She imagines a sharp, ratty nose up her nightie, its long yellow teeth and its whiskers. Plague. Infection. 'But what if we corner them by accident? Rats attack if they're cornered, don't they?'

'Shut up and stop that tittering, or go back down where it's warmer, for God's sake, Brenda. Do think of Gran, and take it seriously for her sake.'

'See, Ma,' says Rita, ten minutes later. 'We've stood here on this top landing, freezing our arses off and listening for a good ten minutes, and there's been nothing.'

Vera raises an alarmed finger. 'Wait! Wait, Rita, and shush!'

So they stand there like lemons, all the members of the Hodges family except Doreen, who will be furious to know she has missed out on this bit of fun. She is over at Nigel's as usual.

There's a scraping sound, like busy little nails, in the wall.

There's a pause, and then it comes again.

And a bang, as if a stone has been heaved out of position, and set on something solid.

A slight clank of a chain, like a ghost, dragging, but not so heavy as a ghost, more like a bracelet.

'Jesus!' and the mighty Rita huddles behind the ineffectual Derek. 'Bloody hell, there *is* something there!'

Vera's face is a picture of joy. 'I told you! I told you! I told everyone. I said so!'

'And you think it's Mullins' men?'

'I am damn sure it is Mullins' men.'

'Well, what the hell are they doing in the walls of the house?'

'Trying to weaken it, possibly, so that it will fall down and we won't be able to buy it. Presumably Mullins would get quite a bit of money for the site alone. I *told* you he wouldn't give up without a fight. Not a man like that, he wouldn't.'

'You can't weaken a pissing house like this one,' says Derek, on edge and wishing he wasn't here. 'Not without a mallet and a sledgehammer and a ruddy great ball and chain. We are not back in the Pennystone Estate now, where you could just ease the walls over with a bit of bloody pushing.'

'So what are we going to do?' asks Brenda, shivering as much with excitement as cold. 'We ought to call the police.'

'That's no good at all,' spits Vera. 'I should know. The police have been round here thousands of times and never found a thing. They just think I'm barmy. Whoever they are will be long gone before the cops even get here.'

'There it is again,' whispers Eddie, a look of pure terror on his face. 'It came from the wall next to me, right there, just there, as if there is something just behind it scratching away . . .'

'It's rats,' says Derek, deciding. 'And there's not a lot we can do about them if they are behind the wall. We'll just have to call in the pest-control people tomorrow.'

'It is not rats.' And Vera looks like a martyred saint, holding her cardiganed arms out like wings, a dark bat about to take off from the top landing. '*It is not rats*. I know it is not sodding rats and I won't have you saying that it is, Derek! You're scared, that's what this is all about. So how d'you think I've been feeling these last few years?'

'Okay, okay, it's not rats.' Anything to shut her up so Derek can go back to his cosy bed. The draughts up here are so strong, gusting through all the cobwebbed nooks and crannies, howling down the derelict chimneys, that it almost feels as if you are standing outside and at the mercy of the bleeding elements. A mere dressing gown, even a warm one, is no protection from the weather in this house and Brenda ought to be back in bed. 'Come on, Roy, help me chip away this plaster and we'll see what's underneath.'

'Christ!' Roy leaps backwards, tumbling over the shivering Shane. 'That was a real bang! That could never be a rat, or if it is I wouldn't like to face it in broad daylight, let alone at night.'

'Get on with it! Get on with it!' orders Vera, in her shaky old voice.

So Derek, Shane, Eddie and Roy start chipping away the plaster, using bits of broken floorboard and a steel bar which Eddie has thought to bring with him. The wallpaper is already all peeled off, curled away, and this piece of wall bulges outwards, crumbles, and feels wet beneath the first layer of dusty cement.

'Keep going! Don't stop!'

'Calm down, Ma, or you'll have a bloody heart attack,' cautions Rita, because Vera is all but dancing as she watches, frustrated and made furious by their slowness.

'It won't be anything, Gran,' Brenda assures her, afraid for the old woman's disappointment. 'I mean, who could be small enough to fit in the walls of a house?'

'You don't know these old houses like I do,' says Gran darkly. And it isn't worth saying anything else.

Already the men have made quite a hole in the wall, and it gapes, like a cut, or like a stomach with its dusty old guts hanging out, grey, porridge-coloured entrails strewn all over the gritty floor.

Eddie taps the remains with his steel bar, and the wall is soft, no stronger than putty. 'It's hollow behind this bit,' he turns and tells them, puzzled. 'It doesn't feel as if there's anything there.'

'We must be through to next door,' says Derek, astonished. 'Go on then, Eddie, poke a hole right through the middle and let's see what happens. Everything's gone quiet now, anyway.'

'We've missed them again. We've sodding well missed them,' caws Vera, jumping up and down in angry desperation. 'You'll never believe me now.'

'Shut up, Ma,' says Big Rita, watching intently.

Eddie's bar slides through the wall like a skewer through a mushroom. And it is hollow. It is a hole. Eddie bends to peer through it.

'My God!' He leaps back and clings to his dad. 'Jesus!' The boy licks his lips. 'I saw an eye. Just staring at me.'

Rita begins to moan, clutching Brenda to her, and putting her arm round her stooped little mother. 'God help us,' she cries, 'the place is haunted. There's chains rattling now, don't tell me I don't hear chains. Can anyone else hear chains?'

They all leap back at the sound of the malevolent squawk that emanates from the hole . . . the defensive cry of a jackdaw?

Derek, for it has to be he, as father of the assembled family, snatches the crowbar from the trembling Eddie and gives the hole a further poke, this time sending showers of plaster and pieces of old grit and stone through to whatever it is at the other side. Without meaning to do so, he has created a hole the size of a window pane, through which everyone can see if they bend to the right just slightly.

'Rosita!'

And Derek crosses himself for protection.

Rita bends to look, and there is a crouching, dusty Rosita, wearing a look of absolute terror, staring through the hole like a cornered crow, straight at her.

'Rosita?' calls Rita, horrified. 'Is that really you?'

'It is I,' replies the Spanish woman. 'Yes, I am afraid it is I.'

Vera pushes past and takes Rita's place. 'Miss Rodriguez! What are you doing there, in the walls of my house? You must be so cold and uncomfortable, bent in half like that. How did you get there? Are you trapped? Do you need help?'

Rosita shakes a sorry head, and her witchy hair is almost on end. Her spectacles dangle dangerously towards the very end of her nose. 'Mrs Evans, I am so very, very sorry to have disturbed you yet again, and I have tried to be so careful and quiet of late.'

'But what on earth are you doing all cramped up in there, dear? Would you like Derek to clear the hole, so that we can pull you safely through? It looks as though you are stuck in a cupboard. Was it an awful accident of some kind?'

'I have come up here in the dumbwaiter.'

'Ah,' says Vera, nodding understanding. 'You lost control of the machine?'

'No, this is where I come most nights. Searching. I have been searching for three years now, and tonight, at last, I have found what I have been searching for.'

'And what is that, Miss Rodriguez?'

The rest of the Hodges family stand back gawping. Vera seems to be coping well. She knows the poor woman, after all. She knows how to handle her.

'The legacy James left me. The legacy which means that I can follow my heart once more, the dowry he promised me on his deathbed when he whispered the one simple word to me . . . *shaft*. Of course I wondered what he meant at first, knowing dear James, knowing his strange and eccentric whims. What did he want me to do to him . . . as a last gesture of love, perhaps? Was *shaft* something to do with it? He was too weak, you see, to say anything further. He died in my arms only moments later. So that is all I had to work on, that one word, that mysterious word – shaft.'

Mysterious? Mucky old sod. Rita raises her manly eyebrows, and turns to Brenda who is staring through the hole, blinking hard as if Rosita is a ghost, as if this must be a dream.

Vera works it out first and calls, 'The shaft in the wall – that's what he meant. The shaft which takes the dumbwaiter!'

'Precisely, Mrs Evans. And it took me some time to work that out, until I came to view the house, invited by Miss Jessica as part of the ten-year plan, the codicil he had made in his will. She showed me the dumbwaiter and I had never seen such a thing before and so I asked her. She explained how it ran up a shaft in the wall between the two houses. Of course, then I knew. I knew where to look.'

'What for, dear? What have you found?' Vera's little tortoise head is almost rammed right through the wall as she tries to communicate properly with her dearest friend who seems to be in some kind of trouble.

'This,' says Rosita simply.

'I can't see, dear. Hold it up, if it isn't too heavy.'

Rosita, with difficulty, bent in half inside the dumbwaiter, puts down her chisel and holds up a solid spiral of gold, and the inlaid jewels wink in the dark gap between the two old houses.

'Whatever is it? I have never seen anything like it. It looks like an enormous snake, and far too big to be a lampstand.'

Rosita's arms tremble under the weight of her find. It is four foot high and it spirals thinly up from a base which is equally large, spitting a venom of fiery gemstones. 'This is no lampstand, Mrs Evans. I only know what it is because James once told me a story about the one-eyed cobra and its unearthly powers to free the dead from their tombs, and I wasn't sure whether or not to believe him. He was like that, dear James. You were never quite sure.' Rosita's voice shakes with excitement; there are tears in her eyes and it's as if she is speaking of the Pyramid Man himself. 'It is the only one ever to have been found and it comes from the burial chamber of the Pharaoh Tutratta III, of the Old Kingdom, a brutal man who sacrificed a hundred and thirteen thousand slaves to the temple during his reign, and who died more than two thousand years before Christ. It was found in Amarna hundreds of years ago, then buried again, and James Galbraith Holden, the Pyramid Man, unearthed it.'

Vera is struck dumb.

'This article was first discovered coiled beside the mightiest of all the Pharaohs, as he lay, decked in gold, in his massive tomb.'

They are *all* struck dumb, and stand there staring through the hole in the wall with their mouths gaping open.

'The Pharaoh Tutratta sired more than five hundred children in his lifetime.'

Through Rosita's awe-inspired whisper you can almost hear the old Pyramid Man himself lecturing from the grave.

Rosita, still holding up the heavy gold cobra like a long-strived-for prize, and her eyes sparkling fierce as the myriad jewels, continues as if they are sitting on chairs out on the pavement, as if this is merely another, ordinary day, and she, with her knitting, talking of her eternal love. 'Of course, it is quite priceless. But he wanted me to have it. He knew I would find it. He gave me ten years to do so. He reserved his most precious find, his most revered possession – *for me.*'

'He loved you, Miss Rodriguez,' says Vera simply. 'And perhaps he believed in it, too. Perhaps he believed, if he buried it here, that his spirit would be freed to join you on earth once again.'

And Rosita has tears in her eyes when she says, 'Yes, yes. He really did love me! Oh, you should have seen me dance. Oh, oh, I wish you had seen me dance. And I loved him too, Mrs Evans.'

'I know you did, dear. I know you did. And you always will.'

Chapter thirty-five

Ka the one-eyed cobra, through whom the spirits of the dead are enabled to rise.

It is a shady practice, and one which the highly respected auction house, Jackson Willow & Sons, Est. 1862, Valuers by Royal Appointment, finds difficult to defend. But everybody does it and it's a hard old world out there and the Pharaoh's golden cobra, mounted on satin and encased in glass, realises an absolute fortune when it is put on the block in the musty sales rooms of that prestigious company.

And really, Jessica was given no choice. Brenda said nothing to persuade her, but for very many reasons Jessica was in no position to argue.

And anyway, the Hodges could perfectly easily have taken the priceless artefact to their competitors, Wetherby's, in whose Fine Arts Department Brenda now works. They would doubtless – in spite of their professional reservations, for the piece of Egyptian history is obviously off the back of a lorry – have auctioned it just the same.

The cobra raises seventeen million pounds. It goes to America.

The sparkling-eyed Rosita has her precious dowry, and because James Galbraith Holden, Jessica's piratical father, did not leave the cobra as part of the estate, the find cannot be contested by Jessica.

That, and the heavy burden of tax, let alone the illegal smuggling venture itself, were the reasons the crafty old fox packed it away in the wall. Luckily, as an expert, he knew exactly what he was doing, and wrapped it with all the correct protection for its essential preservation.

*

'No, I do not know how it came to be in my family. It is mine. It has always been mine. I have had it since I was a small child,' swears Rosita, flapping her blacks like an indignant bird, 'and something in my bones tells me that now is the time to sell it.'

'When I think about it, Miss Rodriguez,' says Vera, over and over again, 'when I think about it I shiver and go cold all over. What if you had failed to find it? I mean, you weren't given much to go on.'

It is midwinter, and far too cold to be sitting outside. They are huddled beside Vera's fire, dunking ginger nuts.

Rosita rolls up her sleeves, clenches her fists and demonstrates to Vera her muscled arms. 'Look at that! That comes from all that hoisting and tugging to get myself up to the top and back. It took some doing, I can tell you. A few nasty cuts and broken nails in the process. But no, it wasn't so difficult once I had been over the shaft a few times, tapped the sides a bit, and could see the places where the rubble was loose. The main difficulty was keeping quiet. I did not realise that sounds can carry so easily in an empty house, whereas in Jessica's house, everything's muffled, because of the heavy curtains and carpets, I suppose. And of course young people do tend to sleep more deeply than the elderly, as you well know, Mrs Evans.'

'But if only you had confided in me, Miss Rodriguez. If only you had trusted me enough, maybe I could have helped you in your terrible task.'

'When I realised how I was disturbing you I was so upset, you cannot imagine, and by then I was already so close. But I felt, and I hope you will understand one day, that this was something intensely personal between James and myself, something final that had to be finished, and not shared with anyone else. But I did try, I assure you. I tried so hard to work more quietly but I was in such a rush, you see, as soon as I realised that Mullins was likely to go in there and knock the house about if he'd managed to force you out. I was terribly afraid he might knock through and find my treasure himself. In the end I realised that going to the television was my only chance, as well as yours. But I am so very sorry that I caused my dearest friend such grave distress.'

Vera is honest enough to admit, 'I enjoyed it. It kept me busy – kept the old brain alert. But that poor bastard Mullins. I called him every single sodding name under the sun.'

'He deserved it, making you live in such conditions, a greedy man like that,' says Rosita.

'And I can only repeat how grateful I am, how grateful we all are, for your quite unnecessary generosity. You had no need to split the proceeds of your find down the middle.'

'I did it because I wanted to. You have been a very dear friend to me, Mrs Evans, and given me comfort in my loneliest and darkest hours. I have the money for my dowry . . . as a general rule the Convent of Santa Catalina is reluctant to take on women of my age. They can't do much heavy work in the gardens or among the fruit trees, and they tend to get ill and die on them, you see. Not economically viable any more,' and Rosita's smile is a wry one. 'But now I am taking sufficient funds to guarantee that the sisters of Santa Catalina will greet me with open arms.'

Vera leans forward and holds her friend's horny hand. 'And I can't change your mind, whatever I say? You are determined to leave us in the spring?'

'I appreciate your kindness, and your love. It is something I will always cherish and never forget. But you are surrounded by your own loving family now, and safe, and I yearn to return to mine. And to the land that I dearly love. You understand, Mrs Evans. At the end of the day there is nothing so important as roots.'

Brenda's not too bright. She doesn't know much – some people would say she doesn't know anything, with her wrinkled skirts and her wretched stains – but she does know that fortune has smiled upon her and that she has managed to enjoy the best of both worlds as far as it's possible for a girl of her age.

She nearly comes to grief, though. Very nearly. When Jessica cracks, Brenda finds herself sailing dangerously close to the rocks.

*

In the end, the caterers only require two trestle tables and thirty-two chairs.

Just under a quarter of the residents of Lippington Road agree to attend the street party, and that is no mean achievement – a real tribute to Theo Rosenthall's charm and gentlemanly gift of the gab. He, in turn, was persuaded to hold this traditional form of celebration, against his better judgement, by Crispin Medley-Smythe, his paymaster and boss at the BBC.

'What better way to soothe an anxious public and to show them how this family have been assimilated into their new community,' says Crispin in his smooth, fat accountant's voice, knowing that 'soothing the public' is less to do with the idea than the huge viewing figures the programme is bound to generate. An enormous sympathy still surrounds the desperate plight of the Hodges and their terrible persecution.

'They have not been assimilated at all, Crispin. A street party would give a totally false picture,' grumbles Theo, rumpling at the bag of boiled sweets in his pocket and wishing that he could pop Medley-Smythe in his mouth and suck him until he, too, turns into a slither on his tongue and finally disappears. 'It is manipulation of the very worst kind – a performance for the cameras without one genuine sentiment behind it. Apart from that, I doubt if anyone will agree to come.'

'You under-estimate Joe Public's craving for media attention, Theo,' says Crispin smartly, swinging round in his chair. 'Put a camera in front of him and he will perform for hours no matter how ridiculous he looks.'

'This is Lippington Road,' Theo is forced to remind him, pondering on the way fools such as these have risen, of late, to their prominent positions – a combination of arse-licking and total lack of imagination. 'Not Harlow new town.' In a moment Medley-Smythe will suggest the residents of Lippington Road might be lured to attend by promises of free grub and beer.

Nevertheless, having received so few replies to his initial invitations, Theo, dependent on Medley-Smythe's goodwill for much of his livelihood, dons a pair of comfortable shoes, a sincere face, his most unthreatening sky-blue sweater, and sets off to do his canvassing.

'It is acutely embarrassing to be asked, Mr Rosenthall, let alone to attend,' is the most common, tart reply. 'Anyway, we'll be away that weekend. Sorry and all that.'

Some see him coming and do not even open their doors.

The twenty who do turn up are either the most socially secure, do-gooders or socialists. The rest come for the laugh, and to see what will happen.

Jessica sits goose-pimpled in the wind. She perches on a slatted wooden chair labelled number three. A red balloon bobs from the back of her chair and now and again a breeze blows it annoyingly against her face. She is placed between Shane and Eddie and, knowing the cameras might well be running, every so often she pushes her hair back and attempts a genuine smile.

But this is the end of the road for Jessica.

All day she and Rudi have been at each other's throats.

'Why do we have to go to this godawful party? Tell me again, Rudi. Tell me in words which I can understand.'

'I have told you,' Rudi snapped, his earring winking angrily. 'You do not have to come. You must make your own decision.'

'But you're going.'

'Naturally I'm going.'

'But why do you say "naturally"? Why do you use that word? It's not natural at all. There is nothing remotely natural about going to sit outside in the street talking to people you don't know and eating paste sandwiches and platefuls of old pork pies.'

'Jessica – leave it alone. You know very well why I'm going.'

'You are going because you feel an obligation to the Hodges. And that damn Brenda! You can't stay away from her, can you?'

'I do *not* feel an obligation. I am going because it might do my career some good to be seen there, and because it might be fun.'

'Fun?' Jessica glared at him with contempt. 'Fun! Hah! You

know, sometimes, just lately, Rudi, I feel I do not know you at all. You have changed.'

'And Lola will enjoy it.'

'Rubbish. Lola is too little to know anything about it. Whenever you get the chance to turn that child into the centre of attention you take it, don't you? And it's quite sick, d'you know that? Quite repulsively sick! She won't thank you for this later on, Rudi. When she is older she won't thank you for all this ridiculous idolisation.'

'Jealous again, Jessica? Is that what this is about? Your nose put out of joint by your own baby daughter . . .'

'She's not mine yet! Sod off you stupid bastard,' snapped Jessica, watching tearfully from her window as the caterers blew up, and hung, a hundred red, white and blue balloons.

So here poor Jessica sits, with Shane and Eddie talking across her about various parts of motorbikes. Such ugly, metallic conversation and Shane's breath already resembles the fumes from a burning exhaust. Rosita, in scarlet, sits opposite with her knitting under her arm, chatting intensely to the bedraggled Mrs Evans who looks ludicrous in that straw hat. The whole of the Hodges family are enjoying themselves immensely, pigging themselves on the free food, tipping down the beer provided.

At least it is not raining, although the clouds between the streamers look ominous and low.

An empty chair is set significantly between their party and the few residents of the street who sit apart further up the table, who seem not to be talking much, but watching, furtively watching; women with their legs tightly crossed and men with nervous smiles on their faces wishing they have not agreed to come. Theo Rosenthall, sitting guiltily among them, is gallantly attempting to liven up the proceedings – for this ought to be fun – warming them up for the interviews he intends to conduct later on.

Brenda sits next to Rudi as usual, and Rudi, of course, has Lola on his knee. Lola, the huge ungainly child in the white nylon fur coat with the matching hat, the child from whom he refuses to be parted.

Jessica watches in thundery mood. Lola dribbles and Rudi coos. Brenda giggles and Rudi smiles as he hands the baby over. The fool. The dim-witted, pea-brained fool, so at home with this obnoxious family.

Peasant.

My God, if only he could see what an arsehole he is making of himself.

Jessica, whom he has brought so low, would adore to see her lover brought lower. She surprises herself with her own new thinking. She loves him – she lives for him, doesn't she? And they are about to get married. The invitations have already gone out.

But Jessica, gaunt and horrified to find herself here and in this ghastly situation, sits uneasily on her slatted chair, terribly close to the edge, and knows she cannot take much more of this.

Derek Hodges rises unsteadily in order to make a speech. Rudi, Brenda and Rita bang coarse encouragement on the table – some awful old custom, probably. The residents, up the other end, eye their self-appointed host with ill-concealed humour, for surely the BBC are the official hosts at this party? Theo is nervous because the camera cannot lie and he knows he is going to have to spend all next week editing most of this horror out.

Damn Medley-Smythe and his daft ideas.

'I would just like to say . . .' Derek burps and his quiff falls over his forehead and down, down, onto his nose where it spirals lamely.

Is he about to break into *Blue Moon of Kentucky*, something with which he is more familiar? Is he going to complete a sentence or is this to be a series of utterances, like: '. . . fine day, generosity, gladden the heart, good old days, sing-along, the war, God bless 'er . . .'

And then comes the fatal announcement that finally blasts Jessica up out of her chair.

'Our dear little grandchild . . .'

What? What? In front of the whole world, or at least ten million people! Bad enough that she lives next door but now, through Lola, Jessica is directly connected.

By family!

Enough is enough.

First Jessica shudders. Then Jessica's voice rings out high and hysterical. There are flakes of sausage roll on her bottom lip which she is too upset to notice. 'Yes, yes, your little grandchild, Mr Hodges, and you can bloody well keep her, lock, stock and barrel!'

Thank God none of this is going out live.

Rudi shouts in a broken voice, 'Jessica! What are you saying? Stop it! The adoption papers are almost completed!'

Jessica's nose begins to run and she's come without a handkerchief. Drained of all colour, she picks up a paper napkin and shreds it between twisting fingers as she risks her love, her life, her all. 'Lola belongs to the Hodges, Rudi! The child is nothing to do with us.'

'But I —'

She has started, so she might as well finish. 'No! No! You never did! Brenda was already pregnant! Lola is not yours and was never anything to do with you in spite of your rabid screwing, so there so there so there you tosser!' And Jessica shrieks with maddened laughter and with all her lipstick askew.

The party breaks up in some chaos and Theo takes his cameras home.

Chapter thirty-six

The moment of enlightenment.

The cat is out of the bag now and somewhere among the pigeons, and isn't it distressing how many one-legged pigeons you see in London these days, especially around stations?

Nobody moves but Rosita, who lays her withered brown hand upon the arm of Vera, a kindly gesture, while raising her heavy eyebrows in shock. 'I knew something was up,' she whispers into the sudden cessation of time, 'but I never dreamed . . .'

'What are they saying?' Vera still cannot understand. 'Has there been some conspiracy?'

'A concealment of the most disgraceful kind, between your own granddaughter and Miss Holden, and I can see no happy way out.'

The two old women – Rosita's hair controlled by her snood and Vera's under a battered straw – stare at the trembling Jessica who dominates the moment, bristling in all her terrible disarray. Not daring to take her eyes off her, Vera whispers: 'So Lola is not Rudi's? Was never Rudi's, in spite of his belief?'

'Apparently not, my dear,' says Rosita.

'But how can this possibly be? And whose is she, then?'

Rosita casts a black eye at Brenda. 'Indeed? But that we may never know. And now can you understand why it is my wish to retreat from the world and join my dear sisters? It is precisely this sort of thing, my dear Mrs Evans, and at my age I find it has all become too much for me.'

Brenda, quiet and frightened, draws apart from Rudi, swallows and chews her bottom lip.

Finally Rudi speaks. There is a dangerous look on his face, the flaring nostrils and the stabbing eyes of a furious horse.

How easy it is, always, to compare poor Rudi to a horse.

The stunned company is silent, and those few residents who remain and are not involved eye each other, alight with excitement, concealing their smirks.

With hands trembling on the edge of the paper tablecloth he directs his first incensed remarks towards Jessica. 'You cow. You fucking cow.'

A shimmer of satisfaction flutters across her maddened features. Free from her secret knowledge she is through to him at last.

'What a fool you must take me for,' shouts Rudi, impassioned. 'Exploiting me like this. What an insult to my intelligence. You have never given me credit for a brain, never. You are always demeaning me, humiliating me in public. It's my prick you are after, you bitch, you fucking, whoring, stuck-up bitch, and it's never been anything more than that, has it? Has it? HAS IT?'

There is truth in what he says and Jessica shudders, the realisation that she has lost him spreading like a flush across her skin. Tormented, her hopes and dreams lie dead as the slice of asparagus quiche in front of her, flopped and drowning in old beer. But it is too late to turn back the clock and all she can do is bite at her hand.

Oh, what am I going to do now? How am I going to live? 'I did it to give you what you wanted,' she shrieks. 'I did it because I loved you, you tosser. But it didn't work out, did it? You made such a prat of yourself and that goddamn apology for a child! How could she be yours, Rudi?' she howls in her desperation. 'Look at her! Open your eyes, damn it! How could you create such a creature . . . how could you possibly?'

Stunned by her cruel remarks, Rudi gazes at Lola who rests fatly, a sticky-eyed lump sucking on a dirty dummy in Brenda's skinny arms. Despite his fury he looks puzzled. 'Lola? I do not know what you mean!'

'Look at her,' implores Jessica now, contorted by distress. 'She is disgusting! Open your fucking eyes and look at the state of her! She is a Hodges, how could she ever be a Shapiro?'

'I am looking, sod you,' Rudi screams back, his eyes hollow and staring. 'I am, I am, I am!'

Rita, warlike, wades into the fray. 'How can you say such terrible things? Lola is perfectly normal.' Her big face is burning and her sleeves are pushed up; she is only short of the rolling pin. 'And I do not know what the hell you are getting at!'

'If you love her so much, why don't you bloody well take her?' shouts Jessica, going to pieces, scarcely aware of what she is saying any more. 'You've got the money, you've got the house, you've got the love of the whole of the fucking British public . . . There's no excuses. Take her and sod off, you interfering old bag, and stop ruining other people's lives!'

'Oh. Right.' Rita draws herself up to her full height, and it's not unimposing. 'I never could understand why a creature like you would want a child. It was always hard to see how a hoity-toity bitch like you could love anything but that stinking dog of yours and yourself. Right. Right. Say no more. We all know exactly where we stand.' And Rita grabs Lola out of Brenda's arms and rounds on her daughter. 'As for you, Miss, you slut! Don't think you can sit there dozy as you like. You've got some sodding explaining to do to me and your poor dad. Get off your arse and get straight into the house before I wallop you here and now, cameras or no sodding cameras.'

But the cameras have long gone. This is no performance. And, babe in arms, Rita disappears into her house, dragging a puffy-faced Brenda behind her.

Brenda has done all she was asked to do. Brenda has trusted everyone and has been trustworthy herself. This is all so unfair. Has she no right to happiness? Can people like Brenda Hodges never win?

'And so you can just drop this daft adoption idea here and now, forget about that bloody Casanova next door and get on with your life,' says Rita, having listened, dumbfounded, while Brenda confessed the awful revelations, doubled up with her pain. 'I will look after Lola while you are out at work.'

'But Mum,' whines Brenda. 'You don't understand. I don't want that . . .'

'I am perfectly capable and there is no "but Mum" about it.

All these silly-buggers' goings-on have got to stop. That's what's going to happen and there's an end to it.'

'But I love him,' sobs Brenda, small and shrunk. 'And now he must really hate me.'

'I should think he does hate you. And why shouldn't he, Brenda? You haven't given him much cause to feel anything else, with your shocking behaviour. Even now I find it hard to believe that you and Miss Holden could be so brazen . . .

'I was pregnant, Mum! What else was I supposed to do? It seemed a good idea at the time, when Jessica suggested it.' It is just too cruel, and Mum can't even keep the pleasure from her face. She has always wanted Lola for herself.

'And that woman,' snaps Rita fiercely, pursing her lips, 'is nothing short of downright evil. Getting you into bed with that man for her own outrageous purposes. Bribing you with money like that. If anyone should find out the truth! Oh Brenda, how could you?'

But Brenda, of low moral fibre, is way past listening to this. Betrayed by Jessica, the person she most trusted, she is only aware that she is prepared to surrender everything she is and everything she has for Rudi to smile upon her again, for Rudi to forgive her for her crude deception, for Rudi to take her once more in his arms. The blue sky she found so briefly has clouded over with black storms. Life for Brenda has lost its point.

Is this all there is now? Is this the future? Mum nagging on, going to work every day, Dad and the telly and the boys with their motorbikes?

She cannot live without him.

Brenda, a tragic figure, just wants to lie down, exhausted, and die.

Jessica propels herself over to the bed, sadly and tiredly. A tear plops into her empty glass.

Jessica, a tragic figure, just wants to lie down, exhausted, and die.

She cannot live without him.

She wants to cut out her tongue.

Is this all there is now? Is this the future? Lying, lonely on her white cotton bed in utter misery, staring into the mirror, listening for the sounds of his footsteps upon the stairs?

Oh Rudi I'm sorry I'm sorry I'm sorry.

And it's all my fault.

She might as well empty her bedside drawer for all the use of the items inside it. In the future all she will need are her cotton buds.

Rudi, deceived, slighted and humiliated, walks. He hurries on, panting for breath and struggling to control himself, down the dark streets between the tall houses. To the right and left of him the street-lamps lead to other streets which break into piles of shadow where anything or anyone could lurk. He gives a single, shuddering sob. The lovely Rudi walks alone through the streets of London, feeling sweatily sick and thinking.

Rudi shivers. It is cold out here. The loneliness makes him cold.

Rudi has dreamed a dream or two in his life and those dreams have always been relatively simple.

All Rudi's dreams have come true – or he thought that they had.

His first dream, as a bright-eyed urchin at Mama's knee, was that he got enough to eat.

Then, when he went to Luigi's café – thick with flies, men and purple wine – to watch the football on telly, his dream was to go to England. He longed to go to England. England was where his destiny lay.

He had always been a pretty boy, and even amongst his young comrades he stood out, taller, stronger, manlier than the rest, bedding every girl who caught his eye amongst the pine needles, crickets and goat dung. And when the English started arriving in that poor, blazing district of Italy he gave up on his own kind because the English were so much easier. Pale-skinned girls with hairless armpits. No angry Mamas on the march. No courting required, just a smile. Him and his mates watched with bold eyes as they arrived in the square in their coaches, giggling. They'd make bets. Pick the prettiest. Merely a wink, and these girls opened their legs and bought him clothes and cigarettes and beer.

Like slot-machines, they were. You inserted what you had and they chinked out prizes.

He even picked up a few simple words. Like 'fuck'. And 'screw'. 'Bed' and 'beautiful'. Such easy, meaningless conquests.

Some even cried when they went home, desperate not to leave him, and Rudi would laugh in their sun-scorched faces.

Pretty much as he laughs at Jessica.

The Streets of London. And now Rudi murmurs the words as he turns towards the city. He listens to the words of the song, becoming aware of their meaning.

Rudi groans to himself. London is a sad, oppressive place. There are men in doorways, crying like children, belonging to no one, with nothing to do and nowhere to go. Rudi sees London through the eyes of a ghost. The world is sad. Rudi is sad.

Rudi is inconsolable and so very sorry for himself.

Isn't it true that in some deeply subconscious part of him, he has been tormented by the knowledge that, in spite of all his frantic fucking, he has never become a father?

Trying for a baby with Jessica merely brought his terror closer to the surface. But his superego told him it was probably all her fault. In *that* department surely Rudi reigns supreme?

Jesus. You can't have a cock his size with nothing alive inside it.

Lola's eventual arrival had meant a great deal to Rudi, more than anyone could ever know.

Even Mama had expressed surprise.

Brenda and Jessica, conspiring together, could not have chosen a more vulnerable part to attack.

The bitches. The sodding, shitting, fucking bitches. Jessica might be beautiful but inside she is nothing but a mass of impurities. Her mind is ugly. Her heart is vile. Her emotions are shoddy.

And Brenda's as bad.

They have twisted his beautiful balls in their fists. They have carried out a kind of castration and he ought never to forgive either of them . . .

*

But . . . hang on a minute. Don't let's be rash.

Luckily deceit comes naturally to Rudi, and with it the birth of a brand-new hope. He toys with the unthinkable. There *is* somewhere for him to go after all.

He cannot really blame Brenda, can he? She adores him and demands so little in return, unlike the stern and beautiful Jessica.

Surely the naïve little Brenda has been manipulated almost as cruelly as he has? And after all, Brenda is not the girl she was. Brenda has expectations of her own – large, carefully invested expectations – and Rudi has always been a survivor.

And then there is Lola, of course, and try as he might Rudi cannot change his feelings towards her. She is big and bouncing and beautiful, the kind of child to be presented proudly to Mama. Just because she is not naturally his, does not mean he cannot take the place of a father.

He might never have another chance.

Rudi ceases his urgent pacings and turns back with a tentative smile. After all, there is nothing guaranteed about his *EastEnders* part, and it pays to be prudent. Jessica will just have to learn.

With a lighter step, like that of a dancer, he takes the direction of Lippington Road, and Number 6.

Like Romeo, he will throw a stone at Brenda's window, even though she is on the ground floor.

Chapter thirty-seven

When your dreams come true is the time when you realise they were never your dreams at all.

Just one hour later, Rudi and Brenda sit quietly amid the celebration tatters at the top end of the hastily deserted tables.

It is moonlight and everyone else has long gone, the residents to the quiet comfort of their own homes and safety, the Hodges to chew the fat, replete, with their shoes off in front of the football results.

Jessica is still lying down in her bedroom and refusing to talk to anyone.

Brenda almost fell off her bed when she heard Rudi's call. She clambered hastily through the window into the arms of the love of her life, but recoiled when she heard his proposition. She scorched red with shame, for this was far and away more embarrassing than being fucked by a stranger.

'Leave Jessica? Ditch Jessica and marry me? You're crazy! Betray her? But how can we do that?' Rudi is far too thick to understand, or to grasp that Brenda's in-built loyalty is as much a part of her culture as whispering after women is to his.

To Brenda, betraying Jessica would be the same as betraying herself, because all her dreams and wishes are to do with being Jessica, copying Jessica, *becoming Jessica some day*. And of course this is not only Brenda's dream, but her dream for her daughter, Lola – for why else is she so content to give her baby away?

'But Rudi, you don't understand,' Brenda flaps. 'I do love you. I love you very much, but the whole point of all this is that I want Lola to have what I never had and what any amount of riches won't bring us. I want her to have style.'

The smile fades from Rudi's face. 'Style!' He is exasperated. 'What d'you mean by style?' Here he is, offering himself, body and soul, and it is impossible to believe that he is actually being rejected. Brenda's attitude is deeply shocking. 'What the hell has style got to do with it?'

'Everything – can't you see?' How can Brenda convince him? 'Jessica has style. Jessica has contacts and friends in high places. Jessica is worldly and sophisticated, with influence. She uses lavatories, not toilets, restaurants, not canteens. I doubt she has ever ridden in a bus in her life. Any child of Jessica's will be successful. You see, Rudi, it is all to do with expectations.'

'But damn it, Lola would be far happier with you and me as her parents, for Christ's sake – two people who really love her. Think about it, Brenda. You are being too rash.'

But Brenda shakes a sorry head, as bewildered in her own way as he is by the fact that she is turning him down. Rudi . . . her idol . . . Agassi with dark hair . . . Rudi the stud and the perfect lover with magic fingers. 'Love alone is not enough,' she tries to explain. 'There was love on the Pennystone Estate, once. This isn't Italy. In this country class matters – how you speak, who you know, your attitudes – and I only wish I could make you understand.'

'But what about you, Brenda? Think of yourself. What would you have if you didn't have me?'

'Well, I'd be near to you always, for a start, and I'd be close to Lola. I wouldn't have the bother of being responsible for a child, and that means I could concentrate on my own career, which is important to me, Rudi, believe it or not.'

'But Brenda!' Rudi's is a cry of anguish. 'You love me! You want me!'

'Yes I do, Rudi – but you do not love me.' She stares at him directly; her cool grey eyes never waver as she understands her own answer. Brenda might be a skinny little thing, and not know much, but she's always been a stubborn one, unlike Doreen. 'And you never would, precisely because I am not like Jessica.'

'But I do love Lola,' he cries, shattered.

'And that is exactly why we must carry out the original plan.'

Rudi, never renowned for his bravery, is at the point of weeping. After all, he is terribly hurt – and what about his pride? He has never been turned down in his life before. 'That means I am stuck with Jessica.'

'If you want Lola, yes, I'm afraid it does. But I don't think you really mind, Rudi, do you? Be honest.'

'But don't you see,' he argues, and wants to shake her. 'After this, Jessica is quite likely to refuse to go through with the adoption. She might well not even want me back.'

'I doubt that very much.'

'What if she finds out about this? You won't tell her?' Rudi, on his knees, is begging.

'I wouldn't dream of telling her. Anyway, she would never believe me, because of who I am. But life for Lola is going to be different. See? Do you understand?'

And Rudi draws a shuddering breath and thinks about Brenda; he sees her through Jessica's eyes, thin and dull and uninteresting. Quite truthfully, Jessica is far more exciting. She's bigger, juicier and a damn sight better in bed. And he, too, has Lola's best interests at heart.

'Now then, why don't you go and make it up,' says Brenda sensibly, drawing her clean white nightgown around her. Brenda has always preferred dogs to babies. 'Go and make it up with Jessica. Take her to bed. Take her to dinner. Tell her how much you love her, Rudi, and that you don't mind, that you forgive her for her deception. After all, she did it because she loved you, because she wanted to keep you.'

'It was a terrible thing to do. A wicked deception.'

'Well, I'm sorry but I liked it. Every single minute of it.'

'And so did I,' says Rudi, smiling his sexiest smile, and causing Brenda some uncomfortable throbbing and burning. 'Can I ask you something, Brenda, while we are having this little chat?'

'Yes, of course you can.'

'Who was Lola's father?' There is a note of admiration in Rudi's voice. 'He must have been a giant of a man.'

'Wouldn't you just like to know,' says Brenda, coyly joking. 'But that's my secret.'

*

A close shave for a moment there. A narrow squeak. But Brenda's not that daft. How would she cope with Rudi? How can you live with an idol, a dream, a fantasy?

So now Brenda's big, bouncing, noisy baby has not only got the kind of riches most people only dream about, but she also has two beautiful parents of whom no child could ever feel ashamed. She will have influence. Power when she needs it. And not only that . . . she has her extra, loving family living right next door like a second blessing, able to give her the love and security which Jessica, being the kind of woman she is, might find difficult.

Brenda may be ignorant but an innate kind of wisdom tells her that as Lola's mother, and therefore sacred in a cow-like, saintly sort of way in Rudi's peasant eyes, she will never be rejected or jilted or treated unkindly and with the kind of cruel mockery that Jessica sometimes has to endure from him. And Brenda is young. There is so much time for Brenda. She even realises, deep inside, that she might meet somebody else as the years go by, and forget Rudi, get over the pain that wracks her when she sees his hands and imagines them playing over her sensitive body . . . something she might never experience again, and it's a great sorrow she carries inside her. But how much more wonderful to be the one with the yearning and the longing . . . to be the one with the stars in her eyes.

But Brenda betray Jessica?

Never!

Not for anything on earth. *Brenda needs Jessica.*

And Brenda has her fantasies, better than any reality. Brenda spends a great deal of her time engrossed in her wonderful fantasies down in the depths of her bed.

This is the first time her younger daughter has fought her and won.

She positively insisted that the adoption go ahead, in spite of that terrible woman next door. 'But what sort of a mother will she make, I ask you?' argued Rita, beside herself with worry.

'Lola is my baby and I am making the decisions. Mum, it has nothing to do with you. Stop interfering or I will leave home. Right now!'

And things could be worse.

Rita is obsessed in quite another way now she no longer has to go and slog through her days at Woolworths. While Derek is deeply involved with the house – a complete renovation, he calls it – and he and the boys have started their own building firm in order to do the work, Hodges & Sons, Rita is perfectly happily obsessed by Brenda's child, to whom she is official nurse. She spends all her time with Lola, giving her the love and gentleness she feels she never had herself.

And making sure she has pretty dresses.

And dolls.

And foamy, little-girl bubbles to bathe in.

And frilly sheets.

And dainty, girly ways.

Lola might be big, but she needn't be treated as if she is big. She might look like Attila the Hun, but that's no reason to keep her in trousers or give her soldiers to play with, or leave the ribbons out of her straight black hair.

Rita has already started to curl it, and although she is only a baby, it is time she had those ears of hers pierced.

You can see that Jessica doesn't approve, and thinks that Lola is being treated as a sissy. She loathes the dresses Rita insists on buying – silky dresses with the layers of petticoats, 'common' she calls them – but what's wrong with being a sissy? What's wrong with a little prettification, Rita would blooming well like to know?

Damn it. The neighbours are in there for good, with more than enough money to buy Number 6 outright, convert it and live there forever without a day's honest work.

Really – would you credit it? Fortune and fools. Standards are slipping.

Rudi took the truth marvellously well. Jessica's silly little outburst . . . she thought she had lost him for a moment when she saw that flash of rage in his eyes . . .

He came back that very same night and laid his head on her knee.

But Jessica under-estimated his devotion to the dratted child. It was Rudi and Lola, or no one at all, so Jessica is stuck with the brat.

They had a quiet little wedding at Caxton Hall, and although the Hodges were not officially invited, they came. Like they came to the christening, like they came to the champagne breakfast which Jessica organised for her colleagues and friends, a select little gathering at Claridge's.

Like Jessica knows the Hodges will come – all of them, mind, never just one or two – to every function which involves Lola from now on right up to her twenty-first birthday, her wedding, her own child's christening, and beyond. Imagine: school plays, sports days, visiting days, birthday parties, surrounded by the loud and clueless family of Hodges. What sort of impression will they make at the kind of schools Lola will attend – small, private, select schools! And imagine if you can the reaction of the parents of Lola's friends – nice people, professional people, sophisticated people, rowing-club people, tennis-club people . . . people like herself and Rudi.

Oh dear God.

And, to be quite frank, she is not entirely happy with her new surname, Shapiro. She goes round it inside her head. 'I am going to keep my maiden name for work purposes,' she tells Rudi. 'And maybe we should consider a combination. How about Shapiro-Holden, or Holden-Shapiro? How do you think that sounds?'

'Pretty awful,' admits Rudi.

And yes. Yes, it does.

And then there is Lola herself, Jessica's longed-for child. Jessica's suffering was little short of Brenda's so she deserved more than she got. Lola, such an unfortunate name in the circumstances, is hardly the sort of little girl Jessica had imagined, with an oval face and huge brown eyes, petite and pretty and dainty. Great big clumsy Lola, with her great big clumsy voice, just like her grandmother's. Lola the coalman's great-granddaughter and my God, how it shows.

Lola is the kind of girl who picks her nose and flicks it, no matter how carefully she has been taught.

Lola is the one who wets her knickers in front of the whole class.

She is the person who cheats, and is caught stealing at her first birthday party and the little hostess' mother has to say, 'I don't know whether I ought to tell you this or not. I am so sorry, it is embarrassing for everyone, I know, but . . .'

She is the lolloping gangly girl who bleeds through her dress at her first grown-up dance.

She is the one who smells of old sanitary towels, and BO, in spite of any amount of washing and telling.

Lola is the ugly one who goes round with the pretty one, and who tells lies and manipulates other people.

How can Jessica foresee all this? How does she know? Surely you cannot make claims like that for an innocent little baby!

But Jessica knows. *Deep in her bones she knows.* There were always girls like that at school – clodhopping girls who played lacrosse and sat round the edge, hating the boys at parties. Jessica used to wonder where they came from, for they were a breed apart.

Now she jolly well knows.

Rudi, with his *EastEnders* contract already extended, is quite a star, and an extremely contented family man.

The wanker.

He is even turning into a family man with a bit of a gut . . . more like the ghastly Italian grocer who takes up residence on the ever-so-famous square itself, wearing a white overall, a silver bracelet, and placing apples on his stall.

Jessica is glad now that she kept the contents of the letter from him – that stark letter from the hospital naming him as the culprit, the infertile party. It would have been too cruel to do anything else . . . with Rudi so keen on family. She left the letter on her desk, on the top of her in-tray in its envelope before she changed secretaries, so that fate might take a hand and entice Brenda to peek. Jessica doesn't know to this day whether she did so or not, but it was only fair that she gave her the chance, in case Rudi started seriously slipping. At the moment Brenda prefers dogs to children, but every sensible woman keeps one eye on the future . . . doesn't she?

The frightful Hodges and all that comes with them, bags and baggage, do not seem to worry Rudi, apart from the occasional irritation, and he is alarmingly at home with them, all the more so as time goes by.

He frequently pops next door for a drink, and sits at Derek's boating bar sharing a six-pack of lager. His attitude to Brenda does not change; Jessica watches him carefully but there doesn't seem to be any untoward hanky-panky going on.

Anyway, thank the Lord that that sly fortune-hunter, Rosita, will be gone within a few days, and good riddance to bad rubbish. She never offered to share her wealth with the one to whom it really belonged – James Galbraith's only daughter.

The cobra in her family for years . . . my foot! Some people will believe anything.

Some people are so selfish.

Thank God Jessica has her work and can go there every morning and throw herself into it. Sometimes she gets home late, busy entertaining her clients.

She's got a new secretary now, of course, but she couldn't tell you what she looks like. She hardly remembers the wretched girl's name but she is not as efficient as Brenda, and her shorthand speeds are not nearly as fast.

Strangely, Vera Evans has stopped patrolling her house at night. Everyone feared the habit might continue, that the discovery of Rosita would make no difference, that the problem lay in her own head and she was just one of those women who are doomed to walk – you see them in shopping malls, on the verges of soulless roads, on the steps of multi-storey car parks, down country lanes, with their shopping bags over their arms . . . with blank eyes . . . seeing nothing, just walking.

Walking, Walking.

So it wasn't Mullins' men after all.

Vera does not walk, but neither does she sleep. She sits in her moth-eaten chair among her purring cats. She sits by the fire and smiles at life, at herself, at her kids and their kids, at the house that protects her and has always protected her.

She has no need to go on wandering, for Jack the coalman is sleeping at last. Vera's man is peacefully sleeping, and no longer rattling the locks, stamping on the floors, banging on the walls or pouring water down the chimneys.

For the sounds Rita heard were not the sounds made by Miss Rodriguez.

They were made by her Jack. Diddled by Rita and her brood of tiny children. Diddled out of his genetic inheritance and released by the powerful relic in the shaft.

She smiles and her shrunken face splits in half.

She should have known it was him, he was ever a rude and demanding bugger. Thinking of nobody but himself and his own satisfaction, meat and two veg, a quick bonk on a Saturday night and his packet of Sampson Shag.

There is no need for Jack to call her in the night any more, to disturb her elderly slumbers further. He is satisfied. He is at peace.

Dear little Lola. Born in his image.

Perhaps, in some spiritual way, Brenda heard her grandfather's footsteps.

Freed to roam by the one-eyed cobra, Jack the coalman came one last time, pressed his heavy print on the world and now has gone to his rest contented.

also available from
THE ORION PUBLISHING GROUP

☐ **Mothers and Other Lovers** £5.99
JOANNA BRISCOE
1 85799 248 2

☐ **Judicial Whispers** £5.99
CARO FRASER
1 85799 377 2

☐ **The Pupil** £5.99
CARO FRASER
1 85799 063 3

☐ **The Trustees** £5.99
CARO FRASER
1 85799 059 5

☐ **All my Friends are going to be Strangers** £5.99
LARRY MCMURTRY
1 85799 141 9

☐ **The Desert Rose** £5.99
LARRY MCMURTRY
1 85799 140 0

☐ **Streets of Laredo** £6.99
LARRY MCMURTRY
1 85799 139 7

☐ **Terms of Endearment** £5.99
LARRY MCMURTRY
1 85799 192 3

☐ **While the Music Lasts** £5.99
ALICE MCVEIGH
1 85799 342 X

☐ **House of Splendid Isolation** £5.99
EDNA O'BRIEN
1 85799 209 1

☐ **Astonishing the Gods** £5.99
BEN OKRI
1 85799 374 8

☐ **Absolution** £5.99
OLAF OLAFSSON
1 85799 227 X

☐ **Beastly Tales** £4.99
VIKRAM SETH
1 85799 305 5

☐ **A Suitable Boy** £9.99
VIKRAM SETH
1 85799 088 9

☐ **The Crow Biddy** £5.99
GILLIAN WHITE
1 85799 204 0

☐ **Mothertime** £5.99
GILLIAN WHITE
1 85799 208 3

☐ **Nasty Habits** £5.99
GILLIAN WHITE
1 85799 338 1

☐ **Rich Deceiver** £5.99
GILLIAN WHITE
1 85799 256 3